Please enjoy – Jean

Romance
STE

LG
Gift
12/11

Troup-Harris Regional Library
LAGRANGE MEMORIAL LIBRARY
115 Alford Street
LaGrange, GA 30240

# Druid Duet

Garland of Druids

JEAN HART STEWART

Cerridwen Press

# What the critics are saying...

ꟗ

### Song of a Druid Princess

**5 Lips** *"Song of a Druid Princess* is the third book in the ***Garland of Druids*** series and it may be my favorite. [...] Gabriel's fight to overcome his demons is heartbreaking. The passion is sweet and touching. This is a fantastic story that will bring hours of enjoyment." ~ *Two Lips Reviews*

**5 Hearts** "Ms. Stewart gives her reader not only a very hunky hero but a very tortured one at that. This story brought tears to this reviewer's eyes. It's full of emotion and heart-wrenching tenderness. The love scenes are also very sensual, romantic, and hot. An all around wonderful story." ~ *Love Romances and More*

**5 Hearts** "Set in post WWI France this excellent book has mystery, suspense, history and of course love and lust. Ms. Stewart manages to work them through to a happy ending even with Gabe kicking and screaming his fears to us, and ready to give up. I love it when an author can make a character give us what we need in a delightful way." ~ *The Romance Studio Reviews*

**5 Angels** "Ms. Stewart has written an interesting story about two rather public people who each have things they keep hidden from the world. Kate's family is in the public eye, but she is private person. Gabe, a widely acclaimed war hero and a concert pianist, keeps his own secrets. A story about trust [...] a book worth checking out." ~ *Five Angels Reviews*

## Kiss of a Druid Bard

**5 Hearts** "Another great story in this captivating series. A fascinating story full of adventure and emotion. Stephen is a wonderful hero who discovers his roots and his powers while on his journeys with the help of the heroine he is destined to love. Ms. Stewart throws lots of stones and rocks in his way. This reviewer has read every one of these marvelous stories and hopes Ms. Stewart has lots more stories up her sleeve."

~ *Love Romances and More*

**5 Hearts** "Ms. Stewart has again built the kind of characters I'd love to have as friends and family. The dialogues are excellent, filled with humor, compassion and friendship. Each scenario has all the little details that help us visualize the setting and keep the story flowing. This great story will make you want to know more about the Druid way of life." ~ *The Romance Studio Reviews*

**5 Artifacts** "Set in Brittany in 1920 Dr. Stephen Lavornios has left his practice to travel as a bard in search of his druidic heritage. This is a book with a rich and interesting background and a romantic and erotic love story. The characters must work together to solve the many problems. Stewart guides us through this complex story and interesting characters expertly. It is extremely enjoyable." ~ *Gotta Write Network Reviews*

**4 Cups** "This is a fabulous story of love and personal discovery. Stephen's character is wonderfully sensitive and masculine. I highly recommend this beautifully written love story to everyone. The adventurous and romantic spirit of Ms. Stewart shines through on every page." ~ *Coffee Time Romance Reviews*

A Cerridwen Press Publication

www.cerridwenpress.com

Druid Duet

ISBN 9781419958380
ALL RIGHTS RESERVED.
Song of a Druid Princess Copyright © 2007 Jean Hart Stewart
Kiss of a Druid Bard Copyright © 2007 Jean Hart Stewart
Edited by Helen Woodall.
Cover art by Syneca.

This book printed in the U.S.A. by Jasmine–Jade Enterprises, LLC.

Trade paperback Publication December 2008

With the exception of quotes used in reviews, this book may not be reproduced or used in whole or in part by any means existing without written permission from the publisher, Ellora's Cave Publishing Inc., 1056 Home Avenue, Akron, OH 44310-3502.

Warning: The unauthorized reproduction or distribution of this copyrighted work is illegal. Criminal copyright infringement, including infringement without monetary gain, is investigated by the FBI and is punishable by up to 5 years in federal prison and a fine of $250,000.
(http://www.fbi.gov/ipr/)

This book is a work of fiction and any resemblance to persons, living or dead, or places, events or locales is purely coincidental. The characters are productions of the author's imagination and used fictitiously.

Cerridwen Press is an imprint of Ellora's Cave Publishing, Inc.®

# Druid Duet

ꟸ

# Song of a Druid Princess

ജ

# Dedication

&

*To all the generous and supportive women of RWA.*

# Trademarks Acknowledgement

&

The author acknowledges the trademarked status and trademark owners of the following wordmarks mentioned in this work of fiction:

Renault: Société par actions simplifiée France

Rolls Royce: G & S: Automobiles

# Chapter One

## *Paris, 1919*

℘

Kate stopped at the doorway to Maestro Jourdain's class, her whole body thrumming with anticipation. She was here! Here in Paris, the citadel of her musical dreams. She was standing in the world-renowned Conservatoire de Paris. *Actually, really, physically here.* And best of all, she was about to attend her first session of Maestro Gabriel Jourdain's beginning class in composition.

She was so very lucky he'd allowed her to enroll. He took few students and worked extensively with those chosen.

She took a few steps and paused, looking for a seat as close as possible to the lectern. A handful of students were already gathered in the room.

"Ah," a deep, sarcastic voice boomed. "At last."

She stopped short. A beautifully modulated voice, appealing to any musician's soul. Making the skin on her arms crinkle for some weird reason.

She jerked her head up.

The voice resonated from the man at the lectern. She'd seen him pictured in the newspapers, but he was much more striking in person. *Stunning.*

"How fortunate we all are." Jourdain made no attempt to moderate his sarcasm. "The British princess has deigned to attend our class. Does she not know my students often gather early to be sure not to miss a word? I offer incomparable wisdom, as my students know. But a princess lives by her own rules, of course. She may come when she wants."

Too stunned to speak, Kate paused. What on earth had spawned such biting derision? She'd never even met the aristocratic man at the head of the classroom.

The Conservatoire de Paris had strict rules, as befitted the best musical academy in France. Of course she wouldn't be so rash as to be late, but she'd never even thought of being early.

She finally found her voice and said what first came into her reeling brain. About twelve students were in the room, most of them swiveling around to gape at her. A few seemed amused at her public condemnation. Certainly being named a princess would not endear her to any of them.

Probably being a British princess was even worse than a French one.

"Sir," she ventured. "I apologize for not knowing your rules. But I am not a princess in any manner whatsoever."

The tall man at the head of the room pounced. He was surprisingly handsome, although not in the common way. Perhaps a little lean for his tall frame and broad shoulders. A shock of striking steel-grey hair topped a stern ascetic face. A face classic and cold enough to inspire a sculptor who worked in granite., but a young face that contrasted sharply with his grey hair. His blue, blue eyes were piercing her with an anger that made her own begin to simmer. Dark eyebrows, contrasting starkly with his shining hair, now arching upward as she spoke. Surely it was his unjust anger causing the shivering up and down her spine.

"Ah, but I think you are indeed a princess, mademoiselle. At least in your own mind. You come from a noble and privileged background. Your wealthy grandparents have accompanied you to Paris to insure no common peasant has a chance to sully your pristine existence. Your French is pure and decidedly upper class. Doubtless taught in the most expensive schools. Surely these are attributes of a favored princess."

His incredibly beautiful eyes were filled with an emotion she could not begin to understand. What sensations seethed under his cold exterior? Anger, she knew well, intelligence, of course and what else?

Kate took a big gulp. Her first day and she must decide how to respond to an unprovoked attack from the most honored professor in the school. One of the most revered musicians in all of France.

Her sense of dignity saved her, surging to the forefront and lending her strength and the words she needed. A little anger at the unfairness of it all edged her tone.

"M. Jourdain, I make no apologies for my background. I had nothing to do with it, after all. It simply happened to me. I did not know my antecedents had any bearing on my ability as a musician. That I am wrong is obvious."

Kate knew well her voice crackled with resentment. Of all the pretentious egotists, to expose her to ridicule for no reason at all. Why had he turned on her without giving her a chance?

She wheeled to leave. She could learn little from a professor who for some reason seemed predetermined to dislike her.

Jourdain took several long strides to the door and blocked her departure.

Kate found herself looking up into blazing cobalt eyes and then he dropped his lids a little.

"We will forget what I said. I sometimes amuse myself by checking to see if a student has the *savoir faire* to handle inimical audiences. Come in, Mam'selle Dellafield. The class is about to start. You have earned a place in it, according to the admissions committee at the Conservatoire. Take any seat you wish."

His voice, no longer crackling with icicles, showed little interest in her decision. With a quirk of his black eyebrows he left the choice up to her.

The scents of the classroom surrounded her. Chalk, rosin, the leather of instrument cases, the various woods and metals of the instruments themselves. Too many for her disturbed Druid senses to analyze. She glossed over them all and focused on the hostility M. Jourdain exuded. What would his scent be without the anger streaming from him? It might be enticing, if she ever had the chance to know. He loomed before her, an extraordinary man.

Jourdain went back to the head of the classroom as quickly as he'd come to block her. Kate hesitated. She didn't believe him when he'd tried to pass his statement off as a kind of hazing test. For some unfathomable reason he thoroughly disliked her. However, she could put up with a lot in order to learn from the formidable Gabriel Jourdain.

She quietly took the nearest seat she could find at the back of the room. Before she gave herself over to complete concentration she sent a thought winging to her twin, Vivie.

"Just wait, Vivie, 'til I have time to tell you about this angry man who humiliated me in front of the whole classroom. Maybe you should teach me how to wish a big boil in the middle of his forehead. You're so much better at casting spells than I am."

She heard Vivie's laughing assurance she'd be waiting. Shutting off her twin's voice, Kate gave her complete concentration to M. Jourdain. The composition of music was as important to her as her violin playing.

An hour later a smile returned to her contented face.

Goddess of us all, but she'd been right to remain. With his first lesson he opened vistas she'd never imagined. He deserved his superior reputation. She took notes as fast as she could, her mind expanding as Gabriel Jourdain reviewed his fundamentals of composing.

The whole world knew of Gabriel Jourdain. He was the principle reason she'd come to Paris to pursue her musical studies. He'd been known as a musical virtuoso before he'd gone to war. His father, a well-known diplomat, was returning from an assignment in the United States when he and his wife were killed in the sinking of the *Lusitania*. Jourdain's tragic loss only made him more revered by the French.

She'd known all this, but not how devastatingly handsome he appeared in person. His newspaper photographs didn't do him justice. Nor had she in any way expected his animosity.

She sat and absorbed every word. At the end of the class she rushed home to try out some of his theories.

Her grandmother, Mama Viviane, met her as she swirled into their apartment and started up the stairs. Kate's face glowed and Mama Viviane laughed.

"Dear goddess, but you're in a hurry, child. I take it you had a good day at the Conservatoire?"

Kate chuckled. "After Maestro Jourdain vented his anger he gave a marvelous lecture. But his ridiculous resentment is not important. What I'm learning is. Wonderfully important. I've got an idea for a piece I'm in a hurry to put on paper, but I'll be down to dinner. Love you, Mama V."

Her twin called their grandmother Mama Viviane, but Kate had shortened it to Mama V. Much easier now they were living together. Even Vivie was coming round to using the shortened version.

She blew her grandmother a kiss and scurried up the stairs to her room to start putting notes on paper. She'd been teetering on the threshold of composing a theme expressing her wonderful childhood. Now she knew just how to compose the melody running in her head.

She needed to talk to her twin Vivie, just finishing her apprenticeship as a nurse at London Hospital. They hated being apart, but thank the goddess they possessed their Druid ability to converse with their minds.

Putting down her pen she opened her own mind to Vivie's. She'd soon told her twin the story and Vivie seemed baffled.

"It doesn't make sense to me, Kate. Did you check his aura?"

"Yes, but I couldn't tell much. Swirling clouds around him, mostly grey. A bluish grey that keeps deepening and churning. No true color I could pin down."

Vivie sighed. "Churning. Hmmm. Sounds to me as if he's an unhappy man. Why don't you proceed on this premise? It's hard to go wrong if you treat him gently."

Kate snorted. "I'll try. But you know mama told us once the things we remember most are our humiliations. I'll have to try hard to forget mine from today."

Vivie laughed. "You're too smart to let him upset you like this. Give my way a try. Somehow I know he's an injured soul."

"Okay, twin. I'm sure I can forget my resentment since he's such an exceptional teacher. I can do it, Vivie. I don't have quite as much temper as you do, anyway. I'll be as sweet as these wonderful French pastries. Maybe a gooey Napoleon."

"You've got plenty of temper when you need it, twin."

Both girls giggled, thinking of some of their childhood scraps and Kate went back to work. Difficult to think of M. Jourdain as requiring gentle treatment, but Vivie was usually right.

* * * * *

The days went by, each one bejeweled with one of Jourdain's lectures. Kate thrived on his teaching, although he pointedly never called on her in the classroom. She might as well not exist, which was of no importance. As long as she could listen to him she didn't care to be noticed.

She worked hard and rejoiced in her efforts. Her composition was going slowly, as she tried to use all she kept learning and still produce the effect she wanted.

She thanked her goddess she'd done her best when M. Jourdain singled her out later in the week. For the first time since that disastrous first day he spoke directly to her, his expression closed and his tone neutral.

"Let's see how well our princess is progressing in her first composition for me. Please come to the piano and play what you've written so far, Miss Dellafield."

Vivie gathered her papers, explaining as she rose to her feet.

"I'm writing a composition for violin, sir."

Jourdain humphed. "Oh well, I didn't specify in the assignment, so of course you wrote for your own instrument. Come to the front of the classroom please and bring your doubtless expensive and superior quality violin."

Kate knew he deliberately intended to rattle her. She could see the smirking dark-haired girl, a cellist, who'd sneered at her the first day of class. Probably she was infatuated with their handsome professor and felt perfectly content to follow his lead and embarrass a fellow student. Kate put everything else from her mind and concentrated completely on the scenes of happiness her piece meant to portray.

She started to the front of the room with the half-gliding walk she and Vivie learned from Mama V. Their grandmother had once trained to move softly in pursuit of her duties as a Druid priestess and Vivie and Kate always loved to watch her walk. They drilled themselves to copy her, although they never felt they quite achieved her rhythmic grace.

Kate held her head high as she walked, thinking of her composition. She tuned her violin to the notes in her mind, smiled at the class and lowered her face to the instrument.

Jourdain watched her, his expression carefully impassive. Did the British princess know she displayed not only the most graceful walk he'd ever seen, but the most evocative? Her hips swayed slightly, not quite erotically, but almost. Just enough to suggest her remarkable suppleness. A suppleness likely to invade any man's dreams.

He watched her closely, his own eyes shuttered, as she looked down and began to play. The strain, one of joy and gratitude, floated out over the room. Kate concentrated on her family as she played, thinking of her twin Vivie and her brothers and her parents, as well as both sets of wonderful grandparents. She might not be a princess but she knew she'd been blessed far beyond being born to royalty. She was more than a princess.

The last notes died away and she lowered her violin to her side.

"I've barely begun, but what little I've written is what I meant to write."

"What have you named it?" Jourdain spoke without emotion.

"*Ode to My Parents.*" She spoke simply and faced Jourdain with regal certitude.

The hushed room waited, with every student eager to hear the maestro's pronouncement on the work of this girl he'd made plain he disliked. She'd musically thrown her aristocratic background in his face.

Jourdain spoke slowly. "I cannot fault the melody or its execution. You've plainly shown in harmonious measures you had a fortunate childhood. You are not to blame for that. Well done, Princess. I will try to show you how to make it even better."

Kate's knees nearly buckled in relief. Strange praise indeed, but not the biting sarcasm she'd feared. As she returned to her seat she noticed the angry disappointment on the cellist's face. Dorie was not her friend, nor ever would be. Kate's successful performance might well have sealed that enmity.

She sat down, hugging to herself the words her maestro had spoken. Why she remained so far out of favor she still didn't know, but at least he'd been fair. He'd not wanted to acknowledge her talent, yet he'd done so. His praise was sweet indeed.

He baffled her. Handsome, charismatic, a musical genius revered by all, yet imbued with a bitterness she could almost touch.

Would she ever understand him? What could be the answer to his unhappiness? Vivie was right to caution gentle treatment. He was not a monster. He was a wounded soul.

He baffled her. He was the most complex person she'd ever met. Those cobalt eyes revealed an unexpected layer of pain, hidden deeply inside him. She'd love to solve the mystery of Gabriel Jourdain.

Not that she'd ever have the chance. He existed on a level of artistry far above her. Individual students doubtless meant little to such an internationally known musician.

She sighed involuntarily as she thought of him standing at the front of the class, his charismatic presence dominating the room.

At least he was a pleasure to look at.

A most definite pleasure.

* * * * *

Two sets of eyes were staring at Kate as she resumed her seat. The envious eyes of Dorie and those of a male student she'd noticed looking at her before. He gazed at her too intently and too many times during each class. She ignored them both and shook off a faint sense of uneasiness, concentrating again on the informative lecture of the brilliant M. Jourdain.

She wondered if it were coincidence, or if he knew the points he illustrated were the exact ones she needed in the next phase of her sonata. Fascinated, every other thought flew from her mind as she frantically took notes.

She sighed at the end of the class, unable to believe how time vanished so quickly. As she gathered up her papers, the young man who'd been observing her hurried and stood by her chair. Blond, nice-looking but not handsome, as eager to please as a puppy.

"Mademoiselle Dellafield, may I congratulate you on your work? Certainly the most praise I've ever heard from M. Jourdain."

"Thank you, monsieur." Kate looked fully in his face, trying to read his aura, but she couldn't locate the hazy colors that told her so much. Seeing auras was very useful, but she could never count on her ability.

"Oh, I'm sorry, my name is Adrien Castelet. Could I persuade you to have a cup of coffee with me?"

Kate shook her head. "Thank you so much but my head is filled with notes I want to get on paper. I'm sure you understand."

She was not sorry to have a legitimate excuse. She didn't want to even think of anything else but music. A new friend might or might not be nice, but she didn't have time to find out.

Adrien stepped back so he no longer blocked her leaving.

"Another time, Mam'selle?"

"Yes, of course," Kate answered, already lost in planning the next stanza to her composition.

She walked away, still absorbed. A faint part of her Druid mind registered the hate the girl Dorie projected. Much stronger than the initial dislike of M. Jourdain. Real hatred, but not important enough to keep her from attending class. Why? Just because M. Jourdain formed his response to her playing in a sort of commendation?

She decided to walk to her grandparents' apartment at the Grand Hotel. They'd rented an apartment in the luxurious hotel so Kate could be close to the school. She loved walking and watching the crowds on the sidewalks and the bustle on the street. The chestnut trees dotting Paris would turn color soon, but now they were still summer green. More and more motorcars were joining the carriages now the Great War had ended and petrol was once again available. The sound of their honking horns added to her joy of being alive and of being in this exact spot. It was fascinating watching the horses and carriages maneuver among the faster autos. Kate wondered how long the two could live in tandem. Were carriages on their way out of the lively scene? Probably, since the demand for the new autocars far exceeded the supply. It was well appreciated that Renault taxicabs had made a huge difference by ferrying troops to the front and was doubtless one of the reasons production of cars would increase.

So many young couples strolling hand in hand. Women's clothes this year fit more loosely with slightly shorter skirts and the general effect was surprisingly pleasing. Some of the girls were wearing shockingly cropped haircuts, with curled strands flipping over their cheeks.

The Rue de Rome seemed always busy as did the Boulevard Haussmann. She loved every day. Paris was wonderful and she intended to enjoy each minute.

She sent a message winging to Vivie and then stopped on the spot, right in front of the huge Gare St. Lazare. She stood motionless while people eddied and passed her. Vivie had blocked Kate out of her mind. She could not get through to her twin. An unthinkable occurrence and Kate panicked. What had gone wrong with Vivie to make her take such soul-shattering action? Thoroughly alarmed, she probed again and then again, but Vivie's mind remained blocked to her.

She might as well try to breach a ten foot brick wall.

Devastated, she was certain of only one thing. Vivie must have deliberately shut her off. Something she could not begin to endure without the advice of her Druid grandmother.

She hurried along, turning into the Boulevard Haussmann, intent on seeking her grandmother's advice.

But why would Vivie do such a thing?

Her grandmother, Viviane Randall, listened to Kate with the complete attention she always paid to her granddaughters. Viviane, although married to an eminent British politician, continued her healing Druid activities. Kate thought her the wisest woman in the world.

Viviane's face conveyed only a slight pity. "You know quite well what this means, Kate. If Vivie closed her mind to you she is too unhappy to communicate, even with you. You didn't need me to tell you this."

Kate sighed. "I know. But I did so hope there was another explanation, Mama V."

"Give Vivie time, my dear. She'll be back with you when she can. She loves you as dearly as any one can love another. In any case and whatever is wrong, you can do nothing until she opens her mind again."

Kate felt torn in two separate parts. Although besieged by fears for her twin, she still was lost in a state of almost exaltation with the composition now inundating her mind both night and day. She accepted her grandmother's reasoning. She could do nothing. Nothing. And if she couldn't reach Vivie she would concentrate even harder on her music. She must wait until Vivie opened communication. In her whole life she'd never imagined not being able to speak to her twin.

This was a new world and one she must learn to navigate on her own. A world without any way to discuss with Vivie the little wins and losses of each day. No private conversations to put her daily world in perspective. She was frightened beyond expression. She'd lost the balance wheel of her existence.

She raised her head from her hands and straightened her spine. She must live with this and she would. And turn it all into a positive experience.

Vivie transferred her passion into an even deeper remembrance of her growing up, privileged on many levels. She knew well her relationship with her twin was exceptional and she poured those intense feelings into her composition.

She went to the Conservatoire the next day, sure in her mind she'd written a work expressing exactly what she wanted. No one might ever hear it except for her classmates, but that didn't matter. She'd done what she set out to do and thanks to M. Jourdain's inspirational instruction, she felt at peace with her work.

Would her esteemed professor agree with her?

She had no idea of the reaction of her mercurial mentor, but she craved the opportunity to present her work for his criticism.

If he tore the piece apart and made fun of it, would she be able to bear criticism from such an eminent musician? A man who haunted her thoughts much more than she wished.

She was *so* sure her score was good.

She mentally braced herself. She must be prepared to bear whatever he said with stoicism.

Dear goddess of us all, she hoped he liked it. For some reason his approval had become incredibly important.

As important as seeing him every day was suddenly important.

# Chapter Two

Seated in the *salle d'etude*, Kate smiled as she put the last touches on her finished work.

Just as she prepared to put down her pen, a girl she didn't recognize approached her.

"Mam'selle, I've been sent to tell you to please go to Maestro Jourdain's office. Immediately."

Surprised, but pleased, Kate rose to go. Should she take her work with her? No, that would be presumptuous and might seem to be asking for his help. He would see her composition in due time in the classroom.

She carefully arranged her work in a neat pile and hurried to M. Jourdain's office. What on earth could he want with her? She sighed as she thought of his almost sinful good looks. His silvery hair seemed somehow like a badge of honor. She knew he was only thirty-three, so either he grayed unusually early, or the war turned his hair its beautiful shining color. The whole school knew he'd earned several medals for valor, although he never talked about his experiences. Was one of them responsible for his lovely hair?

She knocked on the door to his office and he bid her enter. She stopped as he raised his dark brows in a question, although he did not seem displeased.

"Ah," he said quietly. "My British princess. And to what do I owe the honor of your visit, Miss Dellafield?"

Kate tried to overcome her stupid lack of breath. For some reason she'd lost it the minute she saw him and his intense glance.

"But you sent for me, monsieur."

His black brows arched. Blue eyes, accented by his gorgeous steely hair, fastened on hers. His slight smile was somewhat reassuring, but she still felt like gasping for breath. This man produced the strangest reactions in her chest, along with other places in her body she couldn't even name.

He briefly flashed a smile.

"I would not be so foolish."

"But I was told—"

Feeling like an idiot, Kate turned to go. "I'm sorry to disturb you, Maestro."

Suddenly Jourdain stood. "I do not quite like this false message. Who delivered it?"

"A girl I do not know, Maestro. She came to the *salle d'etude*. I'm sorry for disturbing you."

Jourdain took her arm before she could leave.

"Let us go back together to where you were. Perhaps someone in the room will know something about this mysterious messenger."

Kate's eyes opened wide as his touch spurred a frisson running up her arm and then down through her body. All he'd done was politely put his hand under her elbow and she felt as if someone had built a raging fire in the room. Utterly insane, as well as inappropriate. Something she'd love to discuss with Vivie if she could.

He walked with her to the study room, now occupied by only one student. Dorie was just leaving the room, a self-satisfied smirk on her face. She quickly sobered when she saw Jourdain, who stopped her with an imperious gesture.

"Why don't you come back in, Mam'selle Danton? Miss Dellafield and I are researching a little problem. Perhaps you can help us."

Why did he sometimes call her Miss instead of Mam'selle? Did he sometimes wish to emphasize her foreign status, or did he now take her British background for granted? A man with many unexplained facets, to be sure.

Dorie hesitated, obviously eager to leave. Jourdain stared at her and she finally turned and re-entered the *salle d'etude*. She hurried across the room and sat down at one of the farthest desks.

As Kate entered the room the dark blue acrid smell of ink almost overpowered her. Wet ink, lots of it and wet, wet paper.

"Oh, no," Kate gave a keening cry, falling to her knees by the scattered stack of papers. "Oh, no."

Her manuscript pages were strewn around the floor, each page thoroughly drenched and mutilated with ink.

Jourdain dropped beside her. The ink was still spreading and his face blackened with anger.

"Despicable," he hissed. "Do not touch them yet, Miss Dellafield. When dry we will assess the damage. Disturbing them now might make it worse."

Kate stood stricken, as a tear escaped and started down her cheek. She hated the salty taste of the tears clogging her throat, hated the weakness they signified. She struggled to control herself. Jourdain stretched his hand toward her, but did not touch her. Instead he rose and stared at Dorie, now white and shaking.

"What a shame," Dorie stammered. "Who could have done such a thing?"

"Surely you know the answer, Mam'selle Danton. Your hands are splotched with ink, the inkwell and several others beside you are empty and I would guess you sent a friend to summon Miss Dellafield to my office."

His voice and cold eyes were those of the army captain he'd been. No wonder his men had followed him. His air of command was absolute.

Kate stiffened and set her Druid mind free to probe. She and Vivie long ago vowed not to infringe on anyone's mind unless it proved absolutely necessary. This seemed to her to be one of those rare times.

Dorie Danton's aura wavered with the yellow of cowardly fear, as easy for Kate to smell as to see. Her boiling mind contained guilt and apprehension, but no remorse. Only a kind of hidden glee, along with defiance and hatred. Kate reacted instinctively. Druids did not use their power to harm, but this girl needed to be jarred out of her complacency and pleasure with her disgraceful deed. Kate concentrated on projecting a boil on each cheek of the defiant girl. Not too difficult a trick, really, but in this case, devastating.

Kate watched with fascination as huge red eruptions appeared on Dorie's cheeks. Dorie flung her hands to her face and then ran to the window to try to catch her reflection. No need to look at the boils, they were inflamed and about as nasty as boils could get. Kate stared, amazed at her own success. The sores appeared so quickly, more quickly than she'd expected.

"She's a witch," Dorie shouted. "She's a Druid, you know. A Druid witch. I never would have done it if I'd known she could cast spells. She should be thrown out of the academy. She's a Druid demon."

Jourdain looked at both girls. Puzzled and incredulous, he turned to Kate.

"Do you claim to work spells, Miss Dellafield? Surely you're not responsible for what is doubtless the result of a guilty conscience?"

"But of course I'm responsible. I wished it on her, maestro and I'm not sorry. Perhaps I should be, but I'm not." She tossed her head, pride in her ability more powerful than her caution.

Jourdain shook his head. "Wishing something bad to happen to someone who wronged you so deeply is understandable. Surely it is a coincidence Mam'selle Danton's guilt manifested itself in such a dramatic fashion."

He put up an imperious hand. "No, we'll not mention this again."

He turned to the shaking Dorie, the scarlet boils on her face contrasting with her pallor as she realized she'd just confessed her guilt.

"You will leave the academy immediately, Mademoiselle. Your belongings will be collected and sent to your home. You will be fortunate if Miss Dellafield doesn't file suit for destruction of valuable property."

Dorie tugged at his sleeve in abject humiliation and regret, but Jourdain shook her off.

"Goodbye, mademoiselle."

Again the army commander took over. His tone slashed cold enough to freeze even the innocent, let alone one as guilty as Dorie.

Jourdain and Kate watched her leave. Kate heaved a sigh coming from the tips of her shoes and bent over to scrutinize her papers. Not much looked decipherable. She couldn't stop the tears running down her cheeks, as she realized very few legible stanzas remained from her beloved work.

Jourdain stood by for a moment and then bent to help her, lifting the pages gently to separate them. She caught his personal scent, a very appealing mixture of man, some spicy cologne, lemon soap and mixed in with more than a little anger. Anger no longer directed at her.

He straightened with some of the drier papers in his hand and suddenly, with no warning, took her in his arms and pressed her head to his shoulder.

"You are very bright, Kate. You will be able to reproduce this. I can help, you know. I have an excellent memory for music and can reproduce the beginning stanzas you played for the class. Can you do the same for the rest of the piece?"

She looked up at him, torn with so many emotions she could only swallow and say not a word. Distress at the lost work, of course, astonishment Jourdain could be so sweetly consoling and pride she'd been able to produce the spell she'd invoked. She might not be as powerful a Druid as Vivie, but she'd come through when necessary. Her smile wavered through her emotions, thanking the magnetic man who was holding her. How tempting to stay right where she was, enclosed by his strong arms and let the world go on for just one more minute.

She shook herself slightly.

"Yes, you're right. I'll get to work. The music is clear and forceful in my head. I can do it."

Her smile was a little strained, but M. Jourdain seemed to appreciate her attempt. He patted her shoulder, told her he'd begin immediately to reconstruct the first part of the ode and left.

Kate sat down on the nearest desk.

Life was amazing. If it needed destruction of her labor to bring out the softer side of Gabriel Jourdain, it might even be worth the setback. Together she had little doubt they could soon revive the stanzas. She smiled, inside and out, while she reached for fresh paper and began to draw once again the notes of the last part of her ode.

* * * * *

Word spread like a firestorm through the Conservatoire. Dorie Dutton had been dismissed in disgrace for destroying the Princess' score. The Princess was a powerful Druid and somehow raised disfiguring boils, instantly and with devastating effect, on her tormentor's cheeks. Mme. Dellafield acknowledged being a Druid, whatever that meant. Was she really a witch? Could she work spells on all of them?

Gabriel heard the rumors and let them swirl. They would soon die out and making an issue of the gossip would be the worst possible action.

He flexed his fingers and laid down his pen. He'd just finished his reconstruction of the beginning to Kate Dellafield's charming 'Ode'. The girl was undeniably talented. He'd reached the professional opinion she should concentrate on composing. While she was an excellent violinist, her tones true and compelling, she didn't have the tiny extra spark of genius and determination needed to be a top-notch artiste. The life of a soloist was so demanding that only the superlative, those who were so driven as to have no choice, made it through. Although god knew her beauty would carry her far if she chose performing.

May the same god help him overcome his compelling interest in her. He remembered with a fiery flash the soft curvature at the nape of her neck, as she'd bent over the desecrated manuscript. He'd forgotten completely how alluring and sensuous a woman's flesh could be. Full of mysterious curves and, in Kate's case, smelling like flowers in spring.

He folded his arms and lowered his head to rest on them. He'd known the instant he saw her coming into the Conservatoire for her admission's interview he must stay away from her. It sounded insane, even to him who experienced it, but he *knew* she could come to mean everything to him. He could never let such a disaster happen. A disaster he tried to avert.

Fervently, with every inch of his body, he wished he'd never even seen Kate Dellafield. Well, almost every inch. He couldn't quite obliterate the deepest element of his heart, constantly reminding him she was the most beautiful and intelligent girl he'd even imagined. Her sweet defiance fascinated him, when she'd accepted but did not accede to his bullying. The way she tossed her head of gorgeous auburn hair, which fell almost to her shoulders and curled around her lovely face. Not the current style, but eminently suited to her. Her green eyes seemed to speak in his own private language, calling to his distressed soul. Her scent, a delicious distillation of what he guessed was lilacs, invaded his every conscious moment.

He'd never seen a more likely candidate to break his heart. She was the embodiment of every fantasy, every image of his imagined heaven. He knew, knew only too well he could never please a woman. He thought of Amelie's callous rejection of him when he'd first returned from the war and her revulsion at his injuries. And she hadn't even seen them all. Disillusion with the girl he once thought he loved had caused him pain, although he'd soon recovered. Kate was a different matter. Being close to Kate and then losing her would be unbearable. Much better to keep his distance, by whatever means he had to use. She must never be permitted to know of his physical and mental scars. Of all the girls in the world, she could most devastate him.

He couldn't endure rejection from Kate.

He gathered his papers together and went to deliver them. She was attracted to him, he knew from the way she'd sighed and nestled in his arms. A terrible mistake when he'd reached for her, but one he couldn't regret. Still, her welfare demanded he let her know they had no future beyond teacher and pupil. He'd already allowed matters to go too far.

He winced as he remembered how he'd tried to steer her away from his class. She hadn't allowed him to win, had she? Her spirit amused him in spite of his knowing he should have never admitted her to the classroom.

With an inward sigh, his cobalt eyes smoky with unhappiness, he straightened his shoulders and to his feet.

Better to get it over with.

* * * * *

Kate worked furiously to reconstruct her ode. She thought she'd done fairly well, but would never really know if the new version exactly equaled the old. Still, she'd finished. Stretching and rotating her neck to get out the kinks, she stood by her desk. Whatever would be, she'd done her best.

Adrien Castelet stuck his head in the door and seeing her standing and stretching, grinned his attractive boyish smile.

"Time for coffee, Miss Dellafield? It's the one way you might agree we French outdo you British. Oh, and you mustn't forget our marvelous *brioche*."

Kate couldn't help but smile at him. Why not have a cup of coffee with the young man? She deserved some relaxation, after all. The Bistro de Deux Amis was quite close and would take little time.

"Yes, I'd enjoy some food," she said and walked to join him. "I have the most tremendous appetite when I work this hard."

"Then let us feed your formidable appetite."

With an exaggerated gesture he offered his arm and laughing, they strolled to the café.

Gabriel, seeing them go, felt a rush of relief. He didn't have to destroy his friendship with Kate quite yet. He'd need to summon all his willpower to be as cold to her as he must be. Still he must force himself to turn her away from him. Completely. No matter the cost to his yearning heart.

*She must not be allowed to get any closer.*

Although he'd find it desperately hard to endure if she became close to a coxcomb like Castelet.

* * * * *

In the café, Kate listened to Adrien's profuse compliments on her loveliness with a sinking heart. She and Vivie had long ago decided to disregard anyone whose interest focused on their spectacular appearance. Adrien kept mouthing the commonplace platitudes on her beauty she despised. She said nothing however, not answering him, just drinking her coffee.

As she finished, she knew she wanted nothing more than to return to the Conservatoire. Perhaps Gabriel had finished his promised reproduction of the first part of her ode. This effusive young man, although pleasant enough, offered her nothing at all. Nothing she hadn't heard too many times before.

She stood up to go, but Adrien rose also.

"Please, mam'selle, I cannot bear it if you leave me so soon."

Something frantic in his voice stopped Kate. She looked at him closely. The boyish look shifted, briefly replaced by an avid and alarming look of a fanatic. He gathered himself and smiled again, but Kate's Druid mind recognized he was not the innocent and polite young man she'd thought. A frisson of anxiety made her lower her lids. This was a situation she must handle carefully.

Fortunately another couple stopped, drawing another minute table close so they could talk. A dark-haired gamine and a tall young man with the features and coloring of a Scandinavian. They were both beaming with friendliness.

"It's good to see you relaxing, Princess. You work so hard you put the rest of us to shame."

Delighted that "princess" had become more of a nickname than a pejorative, Kate beamed back at the girl.

"I don't mean to be reclusive. Not at all. I would welcome new friends. It's just I've been forced to spend all of my time reconstructing some music I'd written. I fear I became much too absorbed."

The brunette girl pulled her chair closer. "We all heard about the shameful destruction of your work. I'm Chantal Le Claire. I'm a pianist, although I sometimes wonder why. Here I am, eighteen years old, and a nine-year-old admitted just this week to the Academy can play pieces I've yet to attempt."

She gave a mock sigh and grinned at Kate.

The tall stringy blond boy introduced himself as Sven. Adrien's pouting face made it plain he did not appreciate the company, but Kate rejoiced. She'd been lonely since Vivie shut herself off. These two young people were bright and happy and just what she needed.

"We all so admire you, Kate," Sven said. Kate stiffened. She'd likely walk out if this nice young man started spouting about her appearance.

"You were so calm when M. Jourdain singled you out the first day in class. Funny, I never heard him be so rough on anybody, at least not without reason. And then your lovely ode was destroyed and you worked so blasted hard to do it all again. But now you're finished, maybe you have time to be friends."

"I'd like to." Kate's lovely smile showed her sincerity. Adrien stopped sulking, obviously thinking he was included. The four began chattering about the school and their professors.

Sven played the cello and Adrien the drums. A comparison of the importance of their four instruments soon had Kate laughing. Suddenly it was wonderful to have friends. Kate realized she'd been lonely since Vivie shut her out. Her grandparents were wonderful and she dearly loved them, but it was nice to know others her own age. And even the formidable M. Jourdain might possibly turn out to be understanding.

Could he ever be a true friend? He was not that much older, after all. There was just the right difference in their years.

He was so sinfully handsome. She could sit quietly and look at him all day. Probably he despaired of female students who did so, but if she shut her eyes she could see him now, his beautiful pewter hair and black eyebrows, a severe face with its chiseled features as compelling as Casanova's must have been. Did he know how striking he was? If so, he held his appearance in low regard. And, like her, probably despised those who judged him by his gorgeous outer shell.

They had much in common. Somehow she didn't think he knew or appreciated how much.

What a pleasure it would be to have him acknowledge their similarity.

She'd gone off into thoughts of Jourdain, as she did far too often, until Sven called her back to the discussion.

She turned with a smile and forced herself back to the Café.

"What do you think is the most important instrument in a full orchestra? You haven't voted yet, although I'm sure you'll say the violin."

Sven's friendly grin was impossible to resist.

She smiled and joined the affable argument. She refused to vote, however, saying most of the instruments were essential for the fullest tone.

"Whatever I say will offend one of you. How can I upset new friends?"

Adrien glowered a little at her inclusion of the newcomers, but said nothing.

Kate listened and enjoyed the chatter.

Her unruly thoughts kept turning to Jourdain. Why couldn't she shut him out of her capricious mind? He showed little interest in her except as a student.

Why did she want to know him better, when he obviously had no such desire? Where on earth was her pride?

# Chapter Three

ꢭ

Gabriel sat bolt up right in bed, his own screams resounding in his ears, sweat pouring from his agonized body. He dimly realized he was awake and in his own bed, although the sound of the shells from Big Bertha still ricocheted around the room. He covered his ears and waited for the cacophony in his mind to die down.

Would he ever be able to erase the sounds and smells of the battle of the Somme? Once again he'd been buried under bodies hurled into the trenches by the shelling at Pozieres. Almost smothered by dead and dying men and, even worse, by bleeding parts of their anatomies. He'd fought free and tunneled himself out, but the feel and stench of mutilated limbs and dying men haunted him almost nightly. He could sometimes close his mind to the sight of the horrors as he fought free, but nothing would ever erase the reeking odors. At the time, he'd crawled out spattered with the blood and brains of other men and gone back to the battle, scarcely knowing what he was doing.

The remnants of a shell hit him soon after, lacerating his torso. He broke a bone in his right hand as he fell, just before his men carried him out of the trenches. He regained the use of his hand, but he'd never again be a world-class concert pianist. Thank God he could still play at all.

After every nightmare he told himself how lucky he was to be alive. The Somme was the graveyard of countless brave men. Some nights, like tonight, the terror loomed too close to convince him of his good fortune. Would being calmly dead be better than this painful agony? Or would these abominations follow him even in death?

He waited, sweating and shaking, his face buried in his trembling hands. Thank whatever gods might be the noise was finally dying down.

Raoul, his former sergeant, now his valet and best friend, came in bearing a glass of whiskey and some sweet wafers. Built like a grizzly bear, his battered features gave no clue that his heart purred like a pussy cat's. Only danger to his captain could change him into a tiger.

"Here you are, Captain Gabe. You go sit in the chair while I put dry sheets on the bed. Thank God you sleep in the raw so you don't ruin your nightclothes with sweat. Come along now."

He pulled Gabriel from the bed and recognizing his dazed state, led him to a nearby armchair and wrapped his fingers around the glass. Raoul tucked a fresh blanket around Gabe's shivering body.

Gabriel heaved a sigh and accepted his man's ministrations.

"Damn you, Raoul, call me just Gabe. I'm not a captain anymore and I'm sorry I ever was."

He sipped the whiskey slowly. He couldn't afford to gulp it down as his body urged him. He couldn't afford a few hours surcease, which was all drink brought him. He'd be better off to force himself to stay awake and work. The stench of death and blood still permeated the room. He shuddered and sniffed his whiskey to lose his memories in a present and pleasing scent.

Thank God for his work. He'd run mad without it. When his phantoms visited him his mind and his body were a crazy mix of feelings, all of them hammering at him. This time his nightmares displayed a new dimension. This time, through his dreadful recollections, the lovely face of Kate hovered smiling at him from one corner of even the most dreadful scene. Her beauty offered him consolation he could not accept. He could only cherish her in his every private thought.

She was beginning to like him, in spite of their meeting when he'd consciously tried to send her away. Duty demanded he somehow again convince the beautiful Druid he disliked her. He must force her away from him before she inched closer. His nightmares had made his obligation plain indeed.

He put down the glass and again buried his head in his hands. The thought of her brought him pain, but she also provided dreams of peace and love he'd not known for some time. He'd never be able to tell her, but she granted him vistas of heaven. Even though heaven was unattainable to him, still it provided solace to his beleaguered soul.

Raoul stood in the corner, watching him anxiously.

Gabriel put his glass aside and went to his desk. He'd be afraid to sleep again tonight, with the dreadful sounds of thundering cannon still pounding in mind. He could at least work on the sonata he'd started. A sonata for violin and piano.

"You're sure you should be working, Captain Gabe? Can't you try to sleep again?" Raoul's anxiety showed plainly in his voice.

"Don't worry so much, Raoul. I've started a sonata that's coming along beautifully. I like it already."

A sonata written undoubtedly for Kate's violin, although he'd never tell her she was his inspiration.

* * * * *

The next day Gabriel sought out Kate. He found her in the practice room. He stood in the shadows outside the door, listening as she played Brahms First Concerto for Violin. He'd give a part of his soul to accompany her on the soaring score. He'd never be a concert pianist again, but he'd find great pleasure playing with Kate. His hand might permit him, but not his conscience.

With a groan, he forced himself forward. Best to get his disagreeable errand completed. He must find the courage to alienate her. Just as he took his first step, she turned away from him and shrieked with seeming delight.

"Vivie! You're back. Don't ever, ever do that to me again."

She evidently heard something he could not, as tears began to roll down her cheeks.

She listened, saying nothing herself, nodding her head at times. She finally buried her face in her hands. Gabe could no more stop himself than he could a surging wave.

He went to her, his hands outstretched.

"Princess! What's wrong? Can I do anything to help you?"

Once again his stupid arms went around her and she accepted his hard body pressing against hers.

"Oh, I'm so glad it's you." She lifted her face and her spontaneous smile lit his heart. "Everything's wonderful. I was so startled I think I answered Vivie aloud, as well as in my mind. You must think I'm insane."

She threw her head back and her emerald eyes searched his own. Her long dark auburn lashes were matted with tears, although he could see her face was shining with joy. Her beautiful face, surely one deserving to be painted by a master artist or sculpted by the foremost craftsman of the ages, smiled with joy.

He thumbed some tears off her cheeks with a tenderness he did not try to conceal. He'd break with her later.

"My dear girl, you'd better explain. I have no idea what you mean."

Kate gave a shaky laugh, but made no attempt to move from his embrace. Suddenly realizing how his arms so sweetly enclosed her, he dropped them and stepped back. She fit against him as if she'd been made for just this one purpose.

She looked puzzled, but used her fingers to comb her auburn hair from her face.

"It's hard to explain to a non-Druid, but Vivie and I talk a lot in our minds. She's my twin and we've always done this. For the last few weeks Vivie has shut me out, for the first time in our lives. I felt so lost without her. I was overjoyed when I felt her mind opening to me just now I must have called out. Usually our communications are silent."

Her adorable face looked so anxious and yet so delighted he could say nothing for a long moment. Truth was he didn't know how to approach this ridiculous statement. She obviously believed in the nonsense she spouted.

"You're telling me you were having a conversation with your twin and it took place in your minds?

"Yes, that's exactly what I'm saying."

"And where is your twin right now?"

"At the clinic in London, of course."

Her face started to shadow as she saw the pity in his face.

"You don't believe me. Oh dear, I should have known. Wait. How can I explain. What's today, August nineteen, right?"

As Gabriel nodded his head she exclaimed. "I'll ask Vivie if anything happened today in London which would soon be in the papers here."

He watched, but although she closed her expressive eyes she made no motion of her lips. Very soon however, she opened her lids with a look of triumph.

"Vivie says our father just stopped by and told her Afghanistan was granted its independence today from the United Kingdom. Will newspaper confirmation convince you?"

Gabriel couldn't think of a thing to say. He knew Kate's' father, Lord Lance Dellafield, was a prominent British politician. He could certainly know the latest political news. That Kate believed what she was saying was obvious. Still the whole thing was too ridiculous to contemplate.

He couldn't treat her unkindly at such a time as this. He couldn't destroy all her shining confidence until he knew if she were ill or delusional. She needed support. Definitely not the time for the man who'd just held her in his arms to state he wanted nothing to do with her.

He hugged her to him again a brief moment and then set her aside.

"I don't believe in minds speaking directly to minds. Although I imagine there are some psychic connections I can't understand."

She flashed a smile which nearly sent him to his knees. But somehow he found the strength to turn away.

"At least a start," she murmured.

"I can't agree with what you say you can do, Kate. But I'll certainly check the papers tomorrow."

He walked out of the room without looking back. Every nerve in his body told him he was a fool for leaving her. Every bit of his brain told him to walk away as quickly as he could.

Whether sane or delusional, she was not for him. In spite of her fancies, she deserved the most marvelous husband this planet could offer. He'd help her in any way he could, help her with all his heart. Her delusions were somehow charming, in spite of their impossibility of being true. Might they be dangerous for her sanity if she carried them too far? He'd talk to her grandparents if she showed more symptoms. This should be something easily fixed, since she was so extraordinarily bright in every other way.

He'd help her. It was the least a gentleman could do. And then he'd leave her strictly alone.

He just didn't know what leaving her alone would do to his own mental health. He couldn't really imagine how bleak his life would be without her wondrous smile.

* * * * *

Kate let herself be persuaded to go for coffee with the trio of Adrien, Sven and Chantal. Chantal charmed her, she might turn into a delightful friend. She was a pert *Parisienne,* voluble, animated, easy to be around. Sven was a big blonde clown, at least on the surface. Kate suspected he hid solid depths beneath the gaiety. She treasured his ability to keep everybody laughing and gay.

Kate sat at the table with them wondering why French café tables were always so minute. She loved watching the interplay between Sven and Chantal. Obviously they were strongly attracted to each other and enjoyed the flirting. Not yet willing to go beyond the invisible line, but still loving the tension and sparking electricity.

Adrien was another matter. Although he quickly retreated when she showed disdain for his almost fawning compliments, he worried her. A little too much heat in his glance, a little too much boldness as he tried to take her hand or smooth her shawl. He used any excuse to touch her and his touch made her shiver with revulsion. He did nothing she could call incorrect, but still it made her edgy.

"Kate, let me walk home with you after we finish our coffee. I know you usually walk to the Grand Hotel. That's a rather long trek, but you seem to enjoy it."

Kate licked her lips as she swallowed the last of her delicious *brioche*. She lowered her lids. She didn't like his knowing her habits. Not one bit. She loved her walk home. The Gare St. Lazare dominated the distance when she started out and as she came closer and passed it she loved the hustle of cars, hansoms, buses and people. Her love for Paris grew whenever she walked the ever-interesting streets. Her walk meant a good deal to her, but she could savor it more without Adrien.

Still she strained to be polite.

"You're very kind, but I think not. I have so much on my mind and I use my walking home time to try to sort out my stupid head. I do appreciate your offer, Adrien."

His face seemed to freeze into a mask of the affable features she was used to seeing. He smiled at her, but somehow his smile conveyed a lurking anger. Something frightening lurked deep in his eyes. Kate shuddered slightly and started to rise.

"Are you sure, Princess? I think I could be a very good friend, if you'd let me."

She didn't want him for a good friend. Suddenly Kate could hardly wait to leave. She said good-bye to them all. Sven and Chantal were holding hands under the table, not really noticing the menacing air Adrien projected. Or was she being hyper-sensitive?

Kate decided she could legitimately let her Druid mind probe and swallowed a gasp as she knew how correct her intuition had been. Adrien's aura blazed a deep crimson, the red of anger and threatening violence. None of this raging menace showed on his controlled surface.

She and Vivie had vowed never to invade another's mind unless it was necessary, but this time she knew she'd been wise to look. She tried to control her disgust as she turned away from the vicious pits in his mind. Smiling brightly, she hurried off.

Adrien watched her leave him and glowered at her departing figure. He fought and held tight to his temper. Her independent spirit posed a challenge he relished. It would not serve her well in the long run, as he meant to break her to his desire. She would be forced to acknowledge his superiority in every way. In a way her resistance was pleasurable and offered a challenge he'd enjoy to the fullest. When he'd mastered her he'd remind her of this moment, when she'd been so stupid as to spurn his company.

She would pay, he would see she did. Just the thought of pinning her to the bed and mounting her stiffened his body until he could scarcely leave the table. Subduing a woman, by any of the methods he'd mastered, was the deepest pleasure he enjoyed. The more reluctant, the more profound the fulfillment. Kate could fight him all she wanted. It would prolong his ecstasy and do her no good at all.

His smile became a grimace as he thought about how often his boyish exterior led females right into his trap. Kate didn't seem to be fooled, but that only made her more interesting.

Adrien tried every day to get her to come to coffee with him. She refused each time, at first politely and then with determination. His smile grew more contorted each time, while the coldness of his eyes became more noticeable. Kate tried to avoid him as much as possible, but since they shared somewhat the same schedule she had little luck. Sven and Chantal now seemed to want to be alone, so she was not forced to decline coffee with them.

Adrien kept close track of where she went and what she did. If she stopped in the hall to speak to a male student his temper simmered. He didn't even like her talking to the females in the school. She was his. Only his. Kate felt his menacing thoughts, but tried to ignore them.

His perseverance paid off several days later when he spotted Kate alone in the practice room. She was again practicing Brahms First Concerto for Violin. Completely absorbed in the music, her lovely head bent in concentration, her eyes half closed. Adrien backed into a corner and watched her, blood pumping through his veins, strengthening his determination to have her. She was too lovely not to claim. He must have her and soon.

How the deep red of her lustrous hair would shine against the white pillow. Just the way she drew her bow was seductive and her body swaying slightly in time to her playing made him wild.

The lovely phrases of Brahms floated out into the air. The practice room was almost soundproof, but not quite. Gabriel heard her, recognizing at once the sound of her violin, a Nicholas Lupot instrument, beautiful in both tone and appearance. Her violin possessed a sound of haunting beauty and one needing an excellent player.

In his office, he put aside his work. Kate's touch appealed directly to the soul of the listener. Gabriel loved to hear her play. Somehow she reached the inner depths of a listener and compelled him to acknowledge life as a marvelous force. Even he was content when he heard her play. She possessed a marvelous gift. Her technique. although not superior, grabbed her audience by the heart.

He'd read what he could find on Druids. There were still large groupings in France and many more throughout Great Britain, mostly on the western coasts. In fact they were scattered throughout Europe. Brittany was their main stronghold on the Continent. Their affirmative view of life intrigued him. Their tolerant beliefs doomed them when Julius Caesar invaded Britain. Druids accepted all gods as equal to their own goddess. Caesar, bent on spreading Christianity, could not allow such pagan reassurance. Everyone who did not worship Caesar's god was a barbarian. He'd pretty well wiped out the Druids and still some of his prejudiced accounts of them tainted modern thought. Their forbearance deeply impressed Gabriel. Even when they performed magic, as many accounts attested they could do, they never did harm. Magic was only allowed if it helped.

He grinned as he thought of the boils on Dorie's face. If, in fact, Kate put them there, she must have determined boils now were better than damnation later if Dorie did not change her ways.

And without question the information Kate's twin gave her on recent events turned out to be accurate. He could hardly believe it, but it was so.

Thoroughly intriguing thoughts. By god, he was starting to think spells were possible!

He shook his head, an amused smile on his lips and went back to his never-ending paper work.

He raised his head abruptly, as he realized Kate had broken off the final crashing crescendo and her violin was silent when it should be soaring.

Probably a string had broken. He listened, but after a pause, the music did not recommence.

Silly of him to worry. This was the girl he wanted to stay away from.

With a sigh, he knew he could not. He felt a driving need to know what caused the abrupt stop to her music and the forbidding silence now attacking his senses.

He put down his papers and started to his feet. Blazing fires, but this one girl had ruined his concentration, his sleep and now his work. He shoved off from his chair, his face glowering and strode toward the practice hall.

* * * * *

He opened the door on a scene even worse than he'd envisioned. He'd thought of Kate suddenly not feeling well, or perhaps distressed by an accident to her beloved instrument. He'd not imagined her in danger.

Adrien stood holding Kate's instrument high above his head and laughing at her futile attempts to rescue her treasure. He held her right arm twisted behind her back, so she had no leverage or chance of moving without injuring herself. Gabriel stood still, fear for her making him hesitate. He well understood her dilemma. If she injured her arm it would do her no good to rescue the instrument. A serious injury would mean she might never play professionally.

Adrien saw Gabriel, but did not lessen his grip.

"Stand back, Jourdain. I'll settle this with Kate myself. Or perhaps you'd like me to smash her violin?" His sneering tone and words astonished both Kate and Gabriel. This was a student, talking to a maestro. Completely unforgivable. To speak like this meant he'd decided to no longer be a student. It also meant he'd lost control of himself and could very well carry out his threat.

For a moment Gabriel didn't move and then Kate moaned. Adrien grinned, evidently not realizing the extent of Gabe's fury. He certainly hadn't known how fast he could move. Gabriel caught the violin with one hand as he plowed his other fist into Adrien's stomach. He pushed the violin toward Kate and then concentrated on finishing off Adrien. A powerful right to the jaw plus another blow to his gut put Adrien on his knees.

Keeping one eye on him, Gabriel half-turned to Kate.

"Are you all right?' He didn't even seem out of breath.

"I'm fine, now you're here," she said. She cast a contemptuous glance at Adrien. "I could have handled him if it were not for my violin. My three brothers taught me long ago how to take care of worms like this."

Adrien straightened, massaging his jaw. "I think you broke my jaw," he muttered. The wild look left his eyes and now bitter anger took over.

"I won't repine if I did." Gabriel's face blazed his still-active rage and Adrien shrunk back. "I'd like to work you over but I won't. You're despicable. Get out of here. Take your things with you. You'll not be allowed in any part of the Conservatoire again."

Adrien glared at Kate, then at Gabe, opened his mouth to say something and turned and walked away. Kate felt the fury and menace emanating from him and moved instinctively to Gabriel. He took her hand but his dark-blue gaze remained fixed on Adrien.

Adrien stomped out of the room, slamming the door behind him.

Gabe didn't doubt he'd seek revenge. Whether on him or Kate, he couldn't predict. Maybe both.

Gabriel opened his arms to Kate once again, holding her closely, much more closely than he'd done before. She sighed a little puff of pleasure and looked up at him, letting her candid emerald eyes speak for her. She put her arms around his neck, her gaze showing her delightful anticipation of his kiss.

She nestled in his arms, her lovely lips close to his.

Gabriel was undone. She was irresistible, her beautiful eyes shining, her mouth inching closer with every scented and enticing breath.

She smelled like a luscious fruit. What had she eaten for lunch? Raspberries? Strawberries? As he inhaled he decided she was the essence of raspberries and cream, mixed with the lilac scent peculiarly her own. Nothing, not even his rigid conscience, could stop him from tasting her.

It was so long since he'd clasped a woman in his arms. So very long. He'd forgotten the wonderful feel of a supple body melting against his. She felt smaller and more fragile than he'd imagined. She was still trembling from Adrien's assault, but she suddenly stilled in his arms and lifted her face even closer to his.

He lowered his head that last inch, slowly, prolonging the almost unbearably sweet suspense and then finally captured her lips. He'd meant it to be a restrained tribute to her beauty and courage, but her eager response sent all his resolutions flying. He felt his body harden like a stone, as all the blood supposed to be feeding his brain flowed in exactly the wrong direction. He kissed her almost frantically, realizing she was responding as enthusiastically as he could ever dare hope.

Blazing hell, but he'd like to hold her in his arms forever. How could something so wonderful be so wrong? She was compliant and responsive. He knew he could easily take her further into passion and the temptation beat in his body. They were alone in a room where few would interrupt the maestro and a student. The hardest act he'd ever performed was to unlock her clinging hands from around his neck and step back from her alluring body.

As Gabriel looked into her puzzled eyes, he knew he must tell her a little of the truth. She could not be allowed to develop a love for him. It was too late for him to avoid heartbreak, far too late. But hopefully not too late for her.

He took her hands and held them.

"You are the most lovely and tempting girl I've ever imagined, Kate. I'm honored you let me kiss you and I'll remember this moment forever. But I will never marry, indeed cannot, and so we'll act as if this never happened. I hope we can be good friends for a long time. Do you understand me, Kate?"

She shook her head, tears beginning to pool in her puzzled eyes, dampening those impossibly long lashes.

"No, of course I don't. All I know is you don't want me."

Gabriel's face froze. "There is little I can say except I want you to be happy. The man you marry will be the luckiest man under god's heaven. But god give me strength never to touch you again, Kate Dellafield."

The green of her eyes seemed even greener now they were awash with tears. "But I want you to touch me, Gabriel. I want that very much."

He looked at her in complete dismay. He turned to leave her and then came back.

"I'll send you home in a cab. I'll see you safe, at least."

She threw back her head proudly. "You may talk to your god in his heaven, if it pleases you. My goddess will hear prayers from me too, you know."

Carrying her violin, she walked to the door.

"Thank you for your concern, maestro. A cab is a good idea, but I'll call one myself."

He watched her go, loving her erect carriage and the nearly arrogant posture. His Kate was one in a million. No, much more. There was *nobody* like her.

What a damned hellish shame he couldn't follow her and make her his. He waited in the shadows until he saw her enter a cab and then he went back to his desolate office. Without Kate, his life would be forever forlorn.

But there was nothing he could do to change facts. He could never explain to her. Maybe it was for the best. This way she could more easily forget a man who trifled with her and then discarded her.

Not the truth, not at all, but certainly what Kate would think. What he was determined to make her think.

He slowly sat down at his desk in his lonely office.

Elation over one fact filled his heart and soul. One of his doctors worried his potency might be affected by the terrible wounds from the shelling. He'd felt little desire for a woman since then, but then he hadn't met Kate. Kate certainly proved his ability to make love. He had only to be in the same room and his body reacted with stunning immediacy. At least he was not handicapped in this one vital area. He was still a virile man. He could thank Kate for that reassurance, even though the concomitant longing for her would haunt him all his days.

He sat thinking at his desk for a long, miserable time.

He knew what Raoul would say if he could. He'd call him a damn stupid idiot and tell him to take what happiness he could get.

But he couldn't agree.

Not when it meant ruining Kate's life.

# Chapter Four

ജ

Kate found for the first time in her life she didn't truly want to share her most secret feelings. She and Vivie were communicating again, but Kate knew they were both sharing only their surface lives. Her twin loved a doctor who was engaged to another woman and was valiantly trying to put her life together again after a soul-shaking ending to her hopes. Vivie said little, but Kate knew she was working herself to exhaustion and she worried about her twin.

She and Vivie were no longer discussing their deepest feelings. Something she'd never considered happening. She knew it was as wrenching for Vivie as for her. Their relationship might be changed, although their love for each other had not. Vivie's heart was desolate and Kate could well sympathize but could not help. She missed seeing Gabriel the man, although still enjoying him as the lofty professor leading the class down enchanting pathways of music. She longed to see him outside the classroom, but his detachment from her was unshakeable.

He was always polite. Too blasted polite for Kate. Excessively courteous to her in class, but never calling on her. Mostly he acted as a distant and god-like creature temporarily come to earth. Detached in a cold way she couldn't fathom how to pierce.

Life at the Conservatoire was a crushing disappointment if she could not sometimes talk to Gabriel. She did the only thing she could think to do. Studied hard, composed constantly and played her violin. And thought incessantly of the man who didn't want her.

She gathered her papers to leave his classroom after an hour of concentrating on what he was saying and recording his suggestions as fast as she could.

She felt a familiar strong touch on her arm and looked up to see Gabriel standing beside her, a half-smile on his perfect lips. A look in his eyes she could not interpret.

Her heart did some kind of crazy loop-the-loop and then settled down in her chest with a plop. She was surprised he didn't hear it. He was as devastatingly handsome as ever. His steel-grey hair contrasting with the brilliant blue of his eyes would forever be her ideal of masculine beauty. Were his eyes even more haunted than the last time she'd looked deeply into them? She longed to touch him, but stayed her reaching hand.

She said the first thing springing to her mind.

"Did you check the newspaper the day after I tried to convince you I possessed some Druid power?"

Suddenly she needed the answer badly. Almost as badly as she needed to see him again as a friend and not a frosty instructor of music.

His appealing grin broke through his reserve. "Not the first thing I expected you to say to me. I wouldn't have dreaded so much stopping you if I'd known. I feared you'd give one look and dart away. Yes, your information was correct, Kate, and although I don't understand many things about you, it doesn't really matter. You are your inimitable self."

She grinned back at him. "A step in the right direction, surely."

They started to leave the classroom together, when Kate noticed the surprised looks of some of her classmates. He'd ignored her for too long for them not to notice.

Speaking in a louder than normal tone, she turned slightly to him.

"But I just can't understand why Berlioz is considered controversial. Surely no one has ever grasped balance, register and color as he did. His startling effects should make others revere him, not question his ability."

Gabriel smothered his grin and answered solemnly. "I have some scores showing how he managed to inject dramatic elements into his music more than most. Would you like to see them?"

After her loud, "Thank you, maestro", they said no more but walked to his office.

Once inside, with the door shut, Kate turned to him, her face uplifted and her eyes showing plainly she hoped to be kissed.

"Kate," he whispered. He kissed her forehead and then went to sit behind his desk.

"You must be the angel sent from heaven to chastise me for my sins. We will not talk about me, however. Today we will talk of nothing but a professional proposal I wish to discuss with you."

Kate heard his words with a sinking heart. He was determined, in spite of the sparks flashing almost like lightning between them, to ignore their attraction to each other. How could he? The very air sizzled. She wished she could search his mind and find out what was blocking him from taking her in his arms. Every minute gesture revealed his repressed desire. The forced rigidity of his countenance was a dead give-away.

She would *not* invade his privacy. She was in no danger that would make it acceptable. She'd be forced to probe to a deep level to uncover his secrets. If he ever turned to her, she wanted it to be of his own volition. Not because she'd forced him in any way at all.

She sometimes had visions giving her a glimpse of the future. She'd hoped and prayed for one since meeting Gabriel, but none came to her. But then, she knew she was not as powerful a Druid as her twin. She seldom experienced the visions Vivie seemed to have with regularity.

She would do her best to attract him without her Druid powers. Surely that would be best in the long run.

Gabriel's gaze was intent. Deep in his eyes she could see desire sparking, but he'd masked it well with his best professional manner.

"I have a request I hope is of interest to you as a musician. Surely you know I was once a recognized concert pianist. Before the war, of course. I was injured at the Battle of the Somme. So far I've told you nothing not common knowledge. But my right hand was also injured—broken, in fact—and while I still play fairly well, I've lost the ability to do the very fast crescendos."

Kate started toward him, hoping her pity didn't show too plainly. All the world knew Gabriel Jourdain was once destined for the highest circles of pianist adulation.

"No, Kate, don't come closer and don't look like that. I want no pity from you or anyone."

Kate rallied quickly and tossed her head with a flip of her hair. "And why would anyone pity you? You're recognized as a musical genius and that surely is enough."

Gabriel almost grinned at her brave words.

"I'm not sure I ever had the dedication to pursue the life of a star pianist for very long. Perhaps this is best. I was always torn between composing and playing and now it's been decided for me. I find I play almost as well as ever, but only almost."

His face seemed blank, so blank Kate had no idea how much he truly minded the loss of the little edge that makes a luminary.

And why did he tell her this? He, who'd never before confided the slightest personal detail.

He spoke again, in the melodious, deep voice she loved.

"In spite of this I have many requests to play and have decided to give a concert as a benefit to the veterans. I want to make this a dual concert, with you on the violin. I think I can pick pieces which give me the time I need to flex my hands in between some of the passages and scores not demanding the very fast crescendos. Are you interested in helping me?"

Kate floundered in stunned silence.

"Why me?" she stammered. "You do not need a student. Any number of violinists would be honored to play with you. You have only to ask."

Gabriel's grin twisted.

"But I can explain to you what we are doing. I don't like to confide in many people. My repertoire will be my choice, since I can count on you wanting to help me. You will not argue with your professor, but will cooperate with the works I choose. And one more important point. Although I can never pursue you as a lover, I find I need us to be friends. I find I need your friendship more than I expected."

"Dear goddess of us all," Kate murmured. *Why on earth couldn't he pursue her? Did he have a wife stashed away someplace? Had he contracted a disease of some kind? Was he fatally ill?*

She decided she really must know. They'd be together a great deal if she agreed to this proposal. A proposal any student in her right mind would never be brash enough to question. But she wasn't quite sane when it came to Gabriel. Kate found she could not agree blindly.

"Gabriel, do you have some strange disease you caught in the war? Are you perhaps secretly married? I know I sound brash, but I have to know."

Gabriel looked so dumfounded she knew the answer before he opened his mouth. His short bark of laughter told her the rest.

"Blazing hell, Kate, I would not even be speaking to you if either of those disgusting things were true. I think I should be insulted you even asked."

Kate bristled in her turn.

"I think not. You are deliberately mysterious and tell me little of yourself, yet ask me to commit hours of time to you. All the while warning me to carefully keep my distance. I do not understand you in the slightest. But of course I accept. Any violinist in Paris would accept. I thank you for asking me, but for now I'll leave you."

She wheeled and left the room.

Gabriel looked after her, admiration and love plain on his face since no one could see. She was everything and more he'd ever dreamed about. Dear god, what a privilege to know a girl with her spirit, character and beauty?

He ran his fingers through his distinctive shock of hair and smiled to himself as he thought of the way she'd flounced from the room. Her skirts practically stirred up a breeze. She recognized quite well what an opportunity he'd offered her. Being Kate, she had to think it through in her own precious way.

For her sake he must do all in his power to further her musical ambitions. And in the meantime, even though it broke him apart, do all he could to discourage her incipient attraction to him. And not by even a glance betray his desperate yearning to hold her in his arms and kiss her into the submission he knew he could achieve. He didn't dare envision the heaven he was certain he'd find if he let his passion for her loose and she responded.

Which one of Dante's nine circles of hell did that put him in?

Maybe all of them, one after the other.

Or all of them at once.

# Chapter Five

ꟗ

Kate had never worked so hard in her life. She'd not even thought it possible. She might never know Gabriel as a lover, but when he drove her so hard she wondered if she cared to know him better at all. As a drill master he proved a repellent martinet. She found it easier than she'd expected to be with him even though he was such a demanding, sarcastic, absolutely untiring perfectionist. There were a lot of other adjectives she could use, some of them learned from her brothers. Some of them they didn't even know she'd learned. To use some of the milder words, damned if he wasn't a bloody tyrant.

She'd worried practicing with him would bring him so close she'd have trouble keeping her hands to herself. So it did, but mostly because she longed to hit him. Or throw a music stand at him. Not her violin, but almost anything else at hand would do.

She seemed to be constantly fuming.

She couldn't quarrel with his knowledge. He arranged for her daily violin classes to be cancelled and stated he alone would teach her for the next few weeks. He was very, very good. His encyclopedic musical knowledge evidently extended to more than his piano. She'd never tell the demonic slave driver, but he was a better teacher than her former instructor, even though the violin was not his own instrument.

She worked and she sweated and she swore. She'd never dreamed of the concentration and sheer physical strength it took to keep up with Gabriel Jourdain. She had little time to worry about Vivie, although Kate knew her twin was still unhappy. Somehow her world evolved into nothing but her violin and Gabriel. He seemed to read her mind at times. Several times she'd wanted to question if he had any feeling at all for her, but he always spoke first.

"Kate, concentrate. Now. You're letting your mind wander from the music."

She more than once struck back.

"I'm tired of concentrating, your majesty. I'd like to laugh at least once a day. Just once would do. With you there's no time for anything but work. Certainly no inclination to even smile."

The corners of his beautiful mouth started to curve at her way of hitting back for being called a princess. Then he turned away and rifled the papers of her score.

"Here. Let's do this passage again. We both need work on it."

He was still a superb pianist. Perhaps he could never again be an artist for concert stages throughout the world. That wasn't such a bad thing, was it? He'd said he couldn't marry, but she didn't intend to accept such nonsense until she knew why. He had so much to offer a woman. His extraordinary good looks would be a bonus, but counted as nothing beside the integrity and passion his music revealed. And then a wife might not always be happy if he were forever away on a tour.

Did he know how much depth of character his magnificent piano playing displayed? There were layers and layers to him, layers she longed to explore. He'd made it plain she'd never have the right to fully know him. He'd locked himself away from her and ordered her to never open the door.

She wanted to understand him. He'd decided by himself their relationship should remain completely impersonal. Did she have to obey his caveats that had nothing to do with music? The big "no trespassing" sign on his forehead challenged her more and more.

What if she disobeyed his warnings to keep her emotional distance? What would happen? A delicious frisson shivered down her spine at the thought of dragging his face down for the kind of kiss she craved. She didn't think he'd resist too long.

Kate heaved a deep sigh. Most of the time she felt like throwing anything within reach at him and now she wanted to throw herself?

She began to watch Gabriel. Sometimes his hand lingered over hers as he corrected the angle of her bow. Sometimes he turned away as if it hurt him to look at her. At other times she caught him staring at her, just before he shifted his eyes back to the music.

"Come. Let's play that passage again."

She could hear him say those words in her dreams. He'd said it over and over. It became a phrase she hated.

But no matter how much he chided her, he held her in some kind of esteem. He covered up much, but the sidewise glances she sometimes caught told her more.

She wouldn't allow him to hold her at a distance much longer. She was determined to crack the façade of Gabriel Jourdain.

She wasn't a Dellafield for nothing.

* * * * *

A soundproof room at the Conservatoire used only by him housed Gabe's piano. When he'd gone to war, he'd worried that his bachelor digs were not safe for such a valuable instrument. He'd made arrangements to have his precious Bechstein transported to this place where it would be cared for. No one was allowed to touch it while he was away, although the faculty head saw to its being kept ready to be tuned to concert pitch.

The solace of his disrupted life, he'd often shut his eyes in the trenches and try to bring the beautiful shape and dark glowing wood to mind. Often the shelling made it impossible. When he finally returned, his piano greeted him, gleaming ebony and shining ivory keys, smelling of strings and polish and the faintly fragrant spruce of the soundboards. He'd forgotten how good his piano smelled.

When he'd been in the trenches the thought of those ivory keys and all they implied kept him sane. That and Amelie. His piano seemed to welcome him when he finally limped through the door of his room at the Conservatoire and sat down to play once again. Though his hand still ached, he found solace in the resounding notes he could still produce.

He'd next gone to Amelie, his heart rejoicing, grateful his life had been spared for this propitious day. Amelie de Maitre, a society beauty who pursued Gabriel from the moment she met him at the home of a friend. She wore his ring, although she'd written to him seldom and they'd not officially announced their engagement. He would fret over her sparse, uncommunicative letters and then remind himself what beautiful butterfly she was. Butterflies obeyed their own rules. He could hardly wait to see her.

She greeted him with a peck on the cheek and turned away from his eager lips.

"Naturally I'm delighted to see you, Gabe. But you've been gone so long."

She pouted and walked across the room. Her nervous hands fluttering, she stood looking at him and then away, her expression showing her uneasiness. Not at all the reception he'd expected.

A worm of worry slithered into his mind.

"Only as long as I had to, my darling," he said lightly, going to her and reaching for her again.

She ducked and sat on a chair, motioning him to one near her. Not to the sofa nearby where they could both have easily been comfortable and perhaps much closer.

The worry worm wiggled and grew fatter.

"I'm so glad you escaped serious injury, Gabe. Although I think we should wait on a formal announcement of our engagement until we're sure you're recovered."

Gabriel stared at her. "I meant to suggest that, Amelie. A little later, after we greeted each other properly. Do you think you could kiss your fiancée, my love?"

Amelie rose and gracefully walked to the window.

"Oh, Gabe, it's been so long. I feel we have to get reacquainted. I can't kiss a stranger now, can I?"

Gabe stood still. "Not quite the welcome I hoped for, my dear."

"But everything is changed, Gabe. You look so different with grey hair. And your limp, is it likely to be permanent?"

The questioning note in her fluty voice fluttered on the air and Gabe suddenly realized he was not being welcomed, but examined. His face flushed with fury and disappointment, disappointment with her and with himself for ever caring for such a superficial girl. He found it hard to believe how blatantly she displayed her selfishness. He drew himself up in taut defiance.

"Why don't I tell you what you seem to want to know? I was seriously wounded, Amelie. That was why many of my letters came from the hospital. I'm badly scarred from my waist to my knees. Very badly. I'm a revolting sight. I would undoubtedly be repulsive to you. My hair will never turn black again. While men of my family gray early, the war hastened mine. I do not know how long I will limp, but it will be a long time."

He watched, his heart cramping, as her brown eyes grew large with horror.

"I can't bear it if you're scarred, Gabe," she whispered. "Scars are so ugly. Are you still able to be a concert pianist?"

He looked at her, wondering he'd not seen before her pouting self-interest. Had the horrors of the Great War changed her, or had he been too infatuated to see through her lovely facade?

He turned to go, not saying a word and then turned back and lifting her hand, stripped his ring from her finger. With pointed calm he dropped the beautiful diamond on the rug, wheeled and left. His last sight was of her scurrying to pick up the ring.

The ironic thing was he'd meant to tell her about his terrible scarring and offer to release her. He wanted to tell her of his injuries while he held her in his arms. He'd meant to hold her tightly and ask her to wait a while until he knew the extent of his disabilities. He'd never thought of her not even listening to him.

So much for trying to play fair.

He'd walked slowly as far as a park bench, then sat down and buried his face in his hands. He tried very hard to tell himself it was for the best. Gradually the smells of grass and the sight of the blue sky soaked into his consciousness while he sat and reflected. Once some small animal scurried across his feet and he looked down and realized the world was still around him. He would definitely survive.

An hour later he arose, a different, more cynical man. War had changed him physically, but not his essential spirit. Now Amelie made her own lasting mark, one it would hard for him to erase.

He tried to temper his bitterness by gratitude he'd discovered her selfish nature in time. She'd not loved him, just the glamour of having a noted pianist as fiancée. He knew in his heart he was well-rid of her, but that hardly soothed the pain.

Always wary, he now almost shunned the female sex, especially the beautiful ones who were put on earth chiefly to drive a man out of his wits.

Kate torched all his resolves into ashes. She didn't even suspect her power over him.

He'd do his best to keep her from knowing she could turn him into warm mush with just a glance from her emerald eyes.

He realized he'd recovered from the pain of Amelie's rejection, but not the fear of being humiliated again. He knew he was a coward, but it didn't help. Would Kate turn away in disgust if she knew the extent of his injuries? No, she'd not ever be as selfish as Amelie, or as scornful. She'd probably react with something far, far worse. Her pity.

Knowing Kate's sweet and honest nature, she would probably try to mask her instinctive revulsion. While she might be able to conceal her first aversion, she'd not be able to hide the pity a kind woman might feel.

Gabriel thought he preferred disgust. Pity from Kate he could not endure.

His expression hardened.

He was right to refuse to snare her in his horrors.

* * * * *

They practiced daily. Soon everyone in the Conservatoire knew M. Jourdain had definitely lost his animosity to Mam'selle Dellafield.

They practiced far into the afternoon. Sometimes Kate would phone her grandparents and tell them not to wait dinner for her. As their rehearsals grew later. Gabriel would insist on walking her down the Rue de Rome and then the Boulevard Haussmann and to the doorway of her hotel. However, he consistently refused to meet her grandparents.

He had no way of knowing Viviane Randall, Kate's Mama V, once observed him from the shadows of the lobby. She approved of his aura, but resisted probing his mind. A sadness hovered about him she didn't try to understand. She saw enough to discern he was a decent and honorable man and handsome as a fallen angel. She knew he possessed the soul of one chosen by the goddess. He seemed to be favored in so many respects that his hidden misery didn't make sense. Still, all would become clear in time. She kept good thoughts for him in her Druid's heart, knowing her granddaughter was falling helplessly in love with the charismatic maestro.

One late afternoon Gabriel and Kate practiced until dusk. The darkness of autumn nights was coming on sooner and the lights along Rue de Rome and Haussmann Boulevard were glowing as they left the Conservatoire.

"I'm a slave driver without a conscience," Gabriel said as he tucked Kate's hand on his bent arm. "My houseman Raoul scolds me so much you really don't have to. Please let me buy you some kind of food on the way home. Heaven knows there are enough cafés around any place in Paris."

Kate's weary face lit up with her warm smile. She pulled a little on her left ear in that endearing way of hers and turned to him.

"I'd love that, Gabriel. Just a café latte and some rolls would give me new life. I do adore those huge cups the French use for their lattes."

"Not enough nourishment, my girl. We'll do coffee another time. There's a good brasserie close by where we can get an excellent meal."

Holding her hand on his arm he guided her around the corner of the Boulevard and down several doors to a brasserie where he was evidently known. The proprietor immediately bustled over.

"Maestro! So kind of you to favor my poor establishment again. And with such a beautiful companion."

Blowing kisses at Kate, M. Benoit bowed deeply to her. A large round man who evidently enjoyed his own cooking, M. Benoit took charge.

"No menus for you, my illustrious friend. I will pick and cook your meal myself."

As he bustled off to the kitchen Gabriel shot an amused glance at Kate.

"I sincerely hope you like what M. Benoit brings us. It seems we have no choice."

Before Kate could answer the chef hurried back with a bottle of red wine.

"Some of my best, Maestro. A wine I keep in my own reserve."

He ceremoniously poured two glasses, although he kept a towel wrapped around the bottle concealing the label. Then he waited anxiously until Gabe's eyebrows rose in pleased surprise and he saluted the chef with his glass. Kate sipped it with an appreciative smile and M. Benoit beamed and then scurried away.

"If his food is as good as his wine I'll eat every scrap," Kate said with a satisfied sigh. "I hadn't realized how tired I was. This wine is heavenly."

Gabe looked at her through his lashes, keeping his eyes half-veiled. What on earth had he let himself in for and why? The why was easy. An extra hour with Kate, with no one around who knew them. An hour he could use to find out a little more about her secret dreams. If she'd let him and if he could manage to keep his yearning thoughts under cover. Her dreams were becoming important. He needed to know a few more of them.

Just gazing at her was heaven, her tired but always beautiful face flushed from the wine, her gorgeous hair a little disordered. She'd taken off the perky hat she wore and run her fingers through the strands. When she started to put her hat back on Gabriel reached over and took it from her, laying it on his lap.

"I like to see your hair," he said simply.

Just those few words were enough to charge the air between them. As if a strong current flowed in the room, swirling around the two of them. The slight remark made Kate breathless, as if she were fighting for the air his presence consumed.

Kate leaned toward him across the small table and stroked his cheek. "I'm so glad I came to Paris," she whispered.

Gabriel took her hand and held it against his face.

"And to the Conservatoire?" His teasing tone held an undercurrent she couldn't recognize.

"And to your class." She smiled her glorious smile and then laughed, thinking of her miserable introduction to this wonderful man.

Gabriel flushed, quite evidently remembering their meeting. "I was impossible. Perhaps someday I'll tell you why I acted such a churl."

"It's not important now, Gabriel. I love every minute I'm with you, even when you're scolding me for being so stupid."

His dark eyebrows flared. "Is this a statement to make me deny your stupidity? You know well you're nothing of the kind and I never implied any such thing. To me you're perfection itself."

He held her hand in both of his, as she stared in astonishment at the faultless planes of his handsome face.

She felt her lower lip quiver and told herself to behave. "I surely don't deserve such a compliment, but thank you, Gabriel. Coming from you the words are doubly special."

Looking at her shining eyes, Gabriel knew Kate was more than half in love with him. Damn himself for a selfish lout who couldn't keep his thoughts to himself. He'd never meant to betray even a particle of his adoration. The whole situation would be even worse if she knew he loved her.

"Now let's see if the food is as good as we hope," he said, seeing M. Benoit coming with a platter. He held her hand a moment longer and then remembered to release it. He sat back, shaking out his napkin.

The meal was a fricassee of the most tender veal Gabriel had ever tasted and watching Kate devour her portion assured him she felt the same. He suddenly decided this was the time to ask her a few questions. So much depended on her answers. He swallowed hard before he spoke.

"What do you want to do with your life, Kate?" he asked in a determinedly casual manner. "After you leave the Conservatoire."

Kate delayed a few minutes, putting pleats in her napkin and then undoing them.

"I don't really know. Certainly my composing is more and more important to me and I can compose wherever I am. I've learned here I don't possess the quality of a concert artist, even though you're generous enough to share your success with me. I think I play better than I normally do when I'm with you."

Gabriel was not surprised at her assessment of her own talent. She was the most honest person he'd ever met.

"But marriage? Don't you want to marry and have children? A lot of little musical Druids?"

He tried to speak lightly, but he stiffened in his chair. He kept his eyes rigidly on his plate. Her answer would determine his future.

"Oh, of course, I think most woman want children sometime. But I'm in no hurry."

Gabriel reached for more bread and stuck it in his mouth. She'd said what he expected and feared. The doctors who'd carefully explained his war injuries told him it was impossible for him to father a child. If only she'd said she didn't want children, he would have felt free to pursue her. But then she wouldn't have been the Kate he loved if she'd given him any other answer.

"M. Benoit makes wonderful desserts. Let's see what he offers tonight." He tried to speak lightly, but he wasn't sure he'd carried it off.

Kate looked at him for a long moment and then agreed. He knew he'd perplexed her with his flat tone. Nothing he could do but to enjoy her company and once again shut off his emotions. Or at least try.

During the dessert Kate changed the subject to Sven and Chantal Le Claire. It was obvious they were either lovers, or close to becoming so. She kept up a light chatter, while Gabe tried to content himself with admiring her.

"They are really a darling couple. Sven, of course, is from an easy-going Scandinavian society. Chantal seems a little more repressed, although I don't know why. She told me she lives with two maiden aunts and that probably explains her attitude. She's worried about losing her virginity, which is silly, don't you think?"

Gabe nearly choked on his last sip of wine. What on earth did the little minx mean by such a question?

"I guess the answer is strictly up to Chantal."

Kate shook her head. "You're dodging the question, Gabriel."

"Of course," he said and tried his best to smile at his tormentor. "What male wouldn't?"

Kate's gleaming auburn hair was shining in the light of the myriad candles blossoming like flowers on all the small tables. Her lovely head was bent as she examined her desert. He longed to reach out his hand and stroke her lustrous mane. He knew if he touched her sparks would illuminate the room and they would both be lost.

How in hell could he keep his sanity when she was so near? Smelling like a flower garden. And was so damned desirable. He'd have to be with her every day until the concert and he certainly couldn't walk away immediately afterward. Even though that would be the smart thing to do. Something he should reluctantly consider.

He knew he couldn't reject her just yet. He'd let himself in for this agony and he'd see it through with the least possible harm to her. Even when being with her was guaranteed to tear him apart.

Dear god, he must indeed be an imbecile. What normal person would let himself in for the torture being with Kate and not kissing her?

# Chapter Six

Gabriel finally pronounced both of them ready. It was to be an invitation-only affair and although the list was sizeable it would still be a private audience.

He sat at his desk double-checking the names when a student came in with an envelope.

"This is for you, maestro and it's marked urgent."

Gabriel turned the envelope over in his hand. A woman's handwriting, but not one he recognized. He opened it and read it, dismay spreading over his classic features.

Before he could even assimilate the request in the letter, a knock sounded on the door and at his summons to enter, Kate rushed in.

Her face was ashen, her emerald eyes huge with shock.

"Gabriel, I don't know how to tell you, but I have to leave for England. Immediately."

He raised his eyes slowly to hers, still tapping the letter in his hand.

"Can you tell me why, Kate? I know it has to be terribly important for you to leave now."

Tears were ready to flow from Kate's huge green eyes.

"I just received a message from my mother. She and I sometimes communicate, but not as often or as easily as my sister and I do. My twin is very ill, very ill indeed. With polio. My mother begs me to come immediately to help. I must leave for London at once."

Gabe's heart clenched as he looked at her. She was obviously torn to the point of distress at leaving, but both of them recognized she had no choice but to go. Her beloved twin was in mortal danger. He looked down at the message in his hand.

"Did your grandmother phone you with the news?"

"No, no," she said, her voice impatient at his density. My mother talked to me in my mind. I know you don't believe we can, but she's a much more powerful Druid than I am. I must leave."

He still sat tapping the letter against his hand.

"I find I'm forced to believe in your powers, at least somewhat. Your grandmother sent this by special messenger, saying you and your grandparents would leave immediately for London. She asked me to tell you. She said your sister was ill, but she never mentioned polio. That you can communicate with your family is evident, in spite of all my qualms. Although I still find it hard to accept."

She smiled, a distressed and very brief smile.

"Thank you, Gabriel. Your understanding means a great deal to me. I'm so *very* sorry about our concert. You know nothing but an emergency would drag me away when we are so close to performing. Please find it in your heart to forgive me. I'm not sure I could if I were you."

He looked at the girl he adored and could imagine nothing in the world she could do would cancel his love. Certainly not loyalty to her family. He didn't hesitate to rise to take her gently in his arms.

"Kate, my dear. Our concert can wait. We'll just postpone it. Do you think you can help your sister?"

She lowered her head to his shoulder with a relieved sigh. "I don't know. I'm not a very powerful Druid, but my mother and grandmother are exceptional. They are both known for their healing power. Pooling our strength is our best chance against an enemy like polio."

She swallowed a sob, clutched his lapels and lifted her face so she could kiss him.

He knew at once he was in trouble. But the pulse throbbing in her neck and her vulnerability was more than he could resist.

At the touch of her lips his control slipped its tight leash. He couldn't think, only feel. She was leaving him. He grabbed her to him, grinding his already aroused body against hers, instantly taking them both into the passion haunting his dreams. Kate responded with a gasp, her body moving against his as responsively as he'd dreamed. Gabe kissed her with all the love in his heart, opening his mouth and taking hers into his control. For moments they remained locked in each other's arms, his tongue mimicking the thrusting his eager body craved. At almost the same instant they both recognized this was not the time or place to continue what they'd started.

Gabriel fought for control and gentled his kiss, his arms holding her as they would a precious piece of porcelain. They both were breathing heavily as Gabriel lifted his head.

Kate raised her hands and gently pushed him away. Gabriel took a panting breath and buried his face again in her glorious hair.

"That was wrong of me, but I can't regret it. Take care, my dear and come back as soon as you can."

"I'll think of you constantly," Kate said. She gave him an agonized look and turned and left the room.

Gabe looked after her, following her graceful walk for as long as he could see her. A curtain of darkness descended on his spirit. She took all the light and joy of his world with her.

He settled back at his desk, his face grave as he thought of her last words. Had she meant them? Yes, of course she had. Kate didn't know how to be duplicitous.

But if her loving words were true, he'd failed miserably in keeping his distance. His actions were reprehensible. She did not understand they could never marry, even though he'd once told her so. Everything he'd just done would seem to her as commitment. He faced the knowledge he'd been most unfair to her.

Dear god, had any other man ever been confronted with such an unsolvable dilemma?

He sensed he could bring Kate to love him, as he certainly loved her, but he had no right to pursue her. He could never give her the fulfillment she wanted and deserved. Although his body hardened just at the thought of holding her in his arms, he could never dismiss his revolting injuries and what they meant. Even if she didn't turn away in disgust at his scars, he could never give her the children she wanted.

Just as simple as that.

He could not be the husband to her she deserved.

If he told her of his horrible disfigurements, as Raoul urged him to, she possibly would still want to marry him. A heaven he didn't dare envision. But as the years wore on and he saw her envying friends' children…he couldn't bear the thought.

When he'd broken with Amelie he'd despised her. Right now he despised himself.

Through all his muddled contemplations, he knew one thing for certain. His heart wouldn't smile again until she returned from England.

* * * * *

Gabriel spent more and more time at the fencing academy. He customarily went once a week, but now he increased his visits to three or four times. Fencing required him to use his physical stamina to the utmost and in a way not injurious to his pianist's hands. He'd grown to love the advance and riposte, always improving his skill. He found this a form of exercise requiring all his concentration. He couldn't think of anything else when fencing, a most decided plus.

Fencing was a slightly old-fashioned skill, a fact which also appealed to him. He'd never enjoyed the rough contact sports, but fencing with its rigid etiquette and graceful dexterity was his pleasure. He habitually carried a cane with a concealed sword, just like gentlemen of the last century. He'd discovered his cane-sword in an antique shop. An unusual weapon, the blade was eighteen inches long, resembled an over-long, sturdy stiletto and could be released from the cane with a hidden spring. Gabriel found carrying his cane particularly appealing now crime had increased in all of Paris. In all the world in fact, as the soldiers returned from the Great War, often to hungry children and no job. Many were forced to thievery to support their families.

Although he didn't dwell on it, fencing also allowed him to wear the traditional costume, full-sleeved shirt and the tight pants covering all his scars. With Kate gone and his once-doubted libido firmly thriving, fencing also helped him work off his re-emerging and considerable sexual energy.

Should he take a mistress? He really needed some outlet for the sexual desires swamping his body. Several of the students and even two on the faculty subtly signaled their availability. The idea of a liaison flitted into his head and just as quickly flitted out. The very thought offended him. His stupid body wanted no one but Kate. He was fixed in a hell where only Kate could provide his escape and yet he could not pursue her and secure the key.

Fencing was his semi-release.

Leaving the Conservatoire late one night, he decided to go to Benoit's brasserie. Benoit could be counted on to lavish compliments on Gabriel's former beautiful companion. He found he liked hearing Kate praised, no matter that she was not with him.

He walked down the boulevard swinging his cane. As usual, his thoughts were lost in Kate. How was she coping with the dreadful illness of her beloved twin? If he went to the British Embassy, would they perhaps have information? After all, Kate's grandparents on her father's side were the Duke and Duchess of Lambden.

He'd check tomorrow. He himself was not a nobody to be pushed aside by some under clerk. If the British Embassy had any current information he could obtain it. He very much feared, however, Kate and her family paid little attention to anything but their own concerns and would not be inclined to share their problems. However, Lord Laniston, known to his friends and the press as Lord Lance, was Kate's father. Important enough to the government to ensure anxiety in anything pertaining to that illustrious member.

Yes, he'd check tomorrow.

He turned off the boulevard, onto one of the narrow streets leading to the Brasserie Benoit. Only a few steps away from the brilliantly lit Boulevard Haussmann, he stiffened as he sensed the atmosphere change into one of menace. Gabriel had come this way many times before. He didn't understand why he suddenly felt threatened, but his hand went to his cane. He heard a little voice in his head telling him to be alert and, startled at hearing a sound which did not exist, he drew his sword out of his cane.

An instant later two large ruffians appeared in front of him. One of them brandished chains linked around his right hand. Gabriel recognized immediately this was not a case of simple robbery. What it was, he didn't yet know, but he imagined he'd find out.

The light from a nearby café shone on his grey hair. It didn't illuminate the young face under his steely cap. Hopefully the two would underestimate him. Gabriel struck out immediately with his sword, slicing at the upper arm of the bully with the chains. His sword carved cleanly through the muscles and the ruffian let out a yell as his useless arm dropped to his side.

The second thug hesitated briefly but then came charging at Gabriel. Gabe held his sword out straight with the intent of skewering the ruffian. Both assailants, even though the first had use of only one arm, rushed him. Gabriel sliced his sword through the air, his fencing lessons giving him the strength he needed to cut down any assailant. His confidence and the sight of the carving sword proved too much for his attackers. Gabriel was left swinging his weapon at no one, as the assailants fled.

He stood, sword in hand, furiously thinking. One ruffian had plainly yelled, "*Merde,* nobody told us this pig carried a sword."

No random attack, then. Someone had sent hired scum to put him, Gabriel Jourdain, out of action. Perhaps to kill him, but the chains made him suspect plans were for a severe beating instead of death. He grimaced. He was not about to be frightened. Not even the bullies of the Paris slums could equal the hell he'd already endured. He sheathed his weapon, picked up his cane and walked slowly and steadily to the Brasserie Benoit.

One thought haunted him.

Who was behind this assault and what prompted it?

He definitely needed to figure this out. A bottle of M. Benoit's excellent wine should help. He strolled along, seemingly relaxed. Actually, every sense was alive until he came to the doorway he was seeking.

He'd been thinking of Kate before the attack. He'd definitely heard a command in his mind to be more alert. Almost as if she'd nudged him. Could his Druid have somehow sent him the warning he needed to force him to be aware and ready to repel the attack?

A very interesting thought.

One he did not dismiss. Kate would doubtless help him anyway she could.

She also possessed powers he could no longer reject. How this would figure in their future relationship he didn't know. She'd never been intrusive before and this time must have been because she needed to warn him.

A daunting thought, indeed.

He walked on, a little faster.

* * * * *

Gabriel put all of his considerable intelligence into trying to understand the attack. Who could hate him enough to hire professional toughs? Possibly either of the students he'd summarily dismissed from the Conservatoire. Dorie Duncan or Adrien Castelet. Gabriel had no feeling one of them was more likely than the other. Of the two, he leaned toward Dorie. She'd always seemed unstable, fixing him with the adoring eyes he was accustomed to but detested. He'd ignored her blatant interest—always a rebuff —even more so for an unbalanced female. Castelet wasn't as likely to hire someone to do the job for him. He was a nasty character. Behind that baby face, he was malicious enough to take care of an assault himself.

He walked on to the brasserie, concentrated but still vigilant.

"*Mon Dieu,*" exclaimed M. Benoit when he saw him. "You've been in quite a fight."

Until then Gabriel hadn't realized the thugs laid a hand on him, but now he felt the welt on his cheek and knew his left arm ached. The bastards landed a couple of blows, then. Nothing to what they'd have done to him without his sword.

"Two brutes who thought they could frighten me. A bowl of your best soup will fix me up. And your wine. Don't worry, M. Benoit, they were just the usual hooligans so prevalent in Paris today."

Benoit stood by, shaking his head. He didn't believe so for a minute. He'd not heard of hooligans so close to this busy and respected district. He bustled off for a carafe of his best wine. M. Jourdain was a man to be esteemed and treasured as a customer. A sad commentary on the times if a man of such stature as Maestro Jourdain was not safe on the streets of Paris.

Gabriel consumed the usual excellent dinner, all the while marveling at the small warning in his mind giving him the edge over the attacking thugs. His brain sizzled with excitement. Had his Druid Princess tried to warn him? Was Kate back in France?

He half expected her to appear in the café as he declined dessert, paid the bill and hurriedly left.

He debated whether to return to the Conservatoire or go to his flat. Raoul would be waiting at his flat and that at least would give him some companionship. A safe assumption, but not the companionship he wanted. He decided on the Conservatoire. A niggling feeling made him think something waited for him there. Perhaps Kate had left some word for him.

At the thought he went onto the street and waved his cane. A cabbie rounded the corner and stopped for him almost immediately and his heart flipped with joy. He was on a side street cabs didn't usually frequent. Definitely Kate was somewhere near. She was hurrying him to her.

He was almost running as he sped up the marble stairs to his office. Throwing open the door, he stopped short. Kate lay curled on the couch, one he used for napping during long stretches of work. Her glorious auburn hair had grown longer and curls now rioted a little past her shoulders. They clung to and surrounded her face, perfect and relaxed in sleep.

Gabriel went softly and knelt by the couch. His emotions were still high from fighting off his attackers, but now he felt a measure of peace. For the first time in weeks his world settled. He was content just to look at her, her impossibly long lashes curled on her soft cheeks. She was a little thinner, but that could be corrected now she was home. Home in Paris where she belonged. Her hair glowed in the light of a nearby lamp and he softly stroked the shining mass. He didn't want to wake her until he had time to get himself well in hand. Just the sight of her sent all his resolutions flying.

He felt his cheek and was pleased the welt had gone down. He didn't want to spoil their reunion by making her anxious.

She evidently sensed him even in her sleep, as her eyes slowly opened and she smiled. She reached up one hand and stroked his cheek.

"I knew you'd feel my presence and come to find me," she whispered.

Gabriel had no control left. His iron will had vanished in the weeks she'd been gone. He wanted only to hold her in his arms and so he reached for her and then nudged her over so he could lie beside her.

Then and only then, while his body surged hotly against hers, did he kiss her. His hips suddenly covered hers, as he lay half over her welcoming body.

The unrestrained passion of his kiss told Kate all she wanted to know. He might fight her and deny his love, but she knew it was a living force he'd someday have to admit. She felt his tongue urging her to part her lips and gladly opened her mouth to him.

He held her face firmly as his tongue searched every recess, dipping into her sweetness with devastating possession. He kept kissing her as his hands busied themselves with the buttons on her blouse. He soon was able to move his mouth onto the firm flesh of her breasts and then onto her nipples.

*How on earth had he managed to bare her breasts so quickly?*

His expert caresses left her so ecstatic she simply lay still and reveled. She wanted to return his knowing touches and give him the rapture he'd shown her, but she didn't know quite what she was supposed to do. Certainly she could duplicate his motions, at least as a place to start. She snatched at his shirt, but he laughed and getting to his feet, took off his coat and then unbuttoned his shirt. She held out her arms to him but he hesitated and then crossed to the wall switch to put out the lights.

"No, don't," Kate protested. "I want to see all of you, Gabriel."

He shook his head and left only a small light on his desk. The room hovered in shadows, barely illuminated as he walked back to her.

"As long as I can see your beautiful face, that's all that matters," he said in a low growl. "And I want to feel the rest of you. Will you let me undress you, Kate? Are you quite sure this is what you want?"

At her breathless assent his clever hands went to work.

The light was so dim she thought he must be undressing her by touch. She put her hands inside his shirt, loving the feel of his muscled chest and for a moment she simply glided her hands over his torso. His flesh was hot and his chest was covered with crisp hair she could trace to his belt line. It seemed to taper in a V and she longed to see where it went. She stroked his beautiful fencer's build, his lean waist and broad shoulders.

He was busily unbuttoning her drawers and he soon pulled them to the floor, but he left her skirt and petticoat on and simply flipped them to her waist. He unbuttoned his pants but left them on. When she started to ask him to finish undressing, he simply kissed her into silence.

When his hands reached a sensitive spot between her legs she'd never known she had, she gave a small shriek and tried to stop him. Kissing her feverishly, he held both her hands with one of his and kept caressing her. She'd never imagined she could feel so much so quickly, as she began to writhe and clutch at him. He was merciless in his caresses, expertly bringing her to passion's crest. Every touch seemed designed to arouse her with sensations she'd never imagined. No wonder she'd longed so often to have him reveal the wonders of the act of love.

With just his fingers he entered her, keeping up the continual stroking of her mound until she was wet and ready. He watched her carefully through hooded eyes. At the last moment before she climaxed, he flipped back the opening of his trousers and plunged partway into her hot, slick passage. Finding only a soft barrier, he thrust in with his entire stone-hard length. They both climaxed almost at once, after no more than three thrusts of his large shaft.

He quieted a little, then re-buttoned his trousers and took her in his arms again, holding her tightly while she floated back down to earth.

"Did you enjoy yourself at all, my dear one?" Gabriel's voice sounded soft in her ear and she caught the note of anxiety.

"Of course I did, Gabe. How wonderful! I never dreamed of such feelings. It was over too quickly, though. I'd like the last heavenly sensation to go on forever."

He kept his silence for a while, kissing her hair as he held her. She started playing with the hairs on his chest, but he stopped her roving hands.

"We'll not do it ever again, Kate. I could probably take you ten times in one night, but I won't. I should never have given in even once. You aren't experienced enough to know that while I reached ecstasy in having you, I did not do well by you. Nor will I, although you deserve much, much more than I gave you."

"I don't understand," she whispered. "I thought you liked it, but I did so want to see the rest of your beautiful body. You feel so different from me, so many sleek muscles. I love smelling your skin. It's so spicy and musky all at once."

She sniffed at his chest and he nearly came undone.

"Kate," he groaned. He rose and reaching for his handkerchief dried the dampness between her legs, then pulled her skirts down and began to button her blouse.

She stopped his hands. Her Druid senses saw a despair in his aura she'd not seen before. The beautiful blue that was his alone still had little red streaks of passion, but there was a deep, worrying band of gray around the edges.

"What is it, Gabe?" Kate asked, holding his beloved face in her hands.

"Can you read my mind?" he suddenly asked.

"No," she said, "Not exactly. If I tried I could probe your mind and find out what you're thinking at any one time. But I'd never do so unless you gave me permission, or unless you were in vital danger and needed me. I will never invade your privacy, Gabriel. Your thoughts about me are your own."

He kissed her quickly and then jumped to his feet. "I don't deserve to even be in the same room with you. I had no right to take you at all, let alone so quickly. I completely lost my vaunted control. It was not well done of me."

He stood perfectly still, his handsome face clouded with regret. He didn't even try to find her eyes with his. His head lowered and she couldn't begin to know what he was thinking behind his words.

"I'm so sorry I took your virginity, Kate. This is entirely my fault."

"Why worry?" she said, sitting up and grabbing his hand. "I had no use for it."

He didn't smile at her feeble joke, but just shook his head. He walked to his desk and sat behind it, steepling his hands and obviously fighting for composure.

There was a pause which Kate decided to fill. She started to straighten her clothes while she frantically wondered what could be so wrong. What they'd just done seemed right to her. Why was Gabriel distressed to this extent?

"My sister is well," Kate said. "It will take a long while for her to get her full strength back, but she's going to be healthy again. I'm sure you knew I wouldn't come back unless Vivie was better."

"I knew she must be," Gabriel said. "I never had a doubt. Did your Druid powers help her?"

At least he now talked calmly about her power, assuming she had a certain amount in her control and not denigrating the very notion as he once had.

"Yes, it did," she said simply. "But I was a minor part in her recovery. Sometime I'll tell you all about it. You'd like Alec Stratton, the doctor she's going to marry. Against all reason, he was the one who saved her. I grew to like him, although I never thought I would. He's a lot like you in many ways. Handsome and opinionated, among other things."

She grinned at him, but he didn't grin back.

"I have no right to meet your family, Kate."

She threw up her hands. "Gabriel, I hoped you'd learn to value our relationship while I was gone. You're as blind as ever. Don't you know we feel something special for each other? Something truly out of the ordinary?"

His face stony, he rose to his feet. "If by blind you mean I refuse to let you ruin your life, you're correct. Get your clothes in order, Kate. I'm taking you to your hotel."

She sat silently for a moment. He was not only being impossibly obtuse, but her body knew a lingering disappointment. The pleasure he'd given her had been so brief. She felt a little cheated. Why she didn't know, but she'd wanted to explore his body and learn every inch of it. He'd made it impossible to feel more than his chest and shoulders. Their striking strength thrilled her and she'd loved every bit of each caress. Still, she wanted to relish all of him. Next time she'd insist they both be naked so she could admire his powerful body.

She stopped and took a deep breath.

In her Druid heart she knew something was very wrong. She also was certain if she probed his mind she would quickly discover his secrets. The secrets keeping him locked in his mysterious prison. Right now they were close to the surface.

She beat the thought back. If he couldn't somehow, someway, come to confide in her himself, they truly had no future.

Her job was clear. She wanted him. She must make him *want* to confide in her.

She stretched out her hand, smiling her most brilliant smile.

"I'm ready," she said simply.

He stilled and gave her a lingering kiss on her forehead, holding her to him for all too brief a moment. And led her out the door.

Kate held his hand tightly. The tiny light on his desk was still burning and they walked through the shadows together.

Kate's busy mind planned how to make Gabriel acknowledge the love between them.

Gabriel's thoughts were thundering with regret he'd taken such advantage of the girl he loved.

He shut his eyes briefly. He couldn't bear to dwell on the pleasure he'd experienced. No matter how much he longed for her, Kate deserved the best. Not a scarred, defective specimen of a man.

Blazing hell, what had he done?

How could he have possibly been so weak?

The silent ride in the taxi seemed impossibly long to them both.

# Chapter Seven

Kate appeared at the Conservatoire the next morning, carrying her violin case and looking forward to practicing again with Gabriel. As she walked through the halls, she was pleasantly surprised. Everyone she passed welcomed her back, most of them calling out, "Great to see you, Princess." No longer did they think of her as an English princess, she belonged with everyone else at the Conservatoire and everyone made it plain they were glad to have her return. She was now *their* Princess.

She answered every salutation with delight.

Chantal Le Claire rushed up to her as soon as she entered the building.

"Kate, I'm so glad to see you. When can we talk?"

How completely like Chantal to not waste a minute.

"Chantal, it's wonderful to be back. But I just arrived from England. How about coffee late this afternoon? I think the maestro will demand all my time this morning."

"He's been a bear while you've been gone. I hope to heaven he'll be more reasonable now you're here. You've snared him, Kate. He just isn't smart enough to know it."

With a laugh and a flirt of her skirts, Chantal went rushing down the hall. Kate looked after her with a smile. Chantal was always in a hurry for one reason or another.

But how interesting at least one of her fellow students thought Gabriel was snared. She wished she could think so.

Gabriel himself greeted her coolly and suggested he and Miss Dellafield get to work immediately. Kate stared at him for a moment, her eyebrows raised. She'd expected him to withdraw somewhat after their tempestuous evening. But Miss Dellafield?

She stiffened her back and picked up her violin.

"Where would you like to begin, Maestro Jourdain?" she asked. Her tone was fully as icy as his. She stared at him, her emerald eyes flashing defiance and pride.

Gabe ran his hands through his shining shock of hair. Then he threw up his hands in mock surrender and strode toward her.

"Oh lord, Kate, I can't do it. Being cold and detached with you is just beyond me. Can you forgive me for a bumbling fool and go back to where we were before you went to London? I thought it might be easier if we were on an impersonal basis. I was wrong. I find I can't stand it if we aren't friends."

He took her free hand in both his large warm ones. As usual, his touch melted her. She probably should make him even sorrier for his stupidity, but his cobalt eyes burning under his beautiful head of pewter hair were just too appealing.

She'd missed him so much.

"Let's just forget everything else but our practicing," she said. She couldn't resist a tiny smile and his face cleared with gratitude.

"Thank you, Kate. Let's start on the third passage," he said. "The one we found just a little difficult before you left."

* * * * *

She met Chantal for coffee and plenty of rolls. She and Gabriel practiced through lunch and she was starved. While her playing sounded rusty, it wasn't as bad as she'd feared. Gabe carefully kept his distance, but she'd caught looks so smoldering she'd considered putting down her violin and rushing to kiss him.

She did not, of course. She planned to wear him down with sweet indifference. That plus an accidental touch or two should break him sooner or later. A touch in just the right place. A touch just happening to linger. A glance showing her interest and then shifting away. M. Jourdain had better prepare himself for a prolonged siege by a determined woman.

When she met her later, Chantal was quite interested in the Druid women in Kate's family.

"*Mon dieu*, four of you. How wonderful for you. You must all be very close."

Kate smiled with love. "We are. Vivie and I look identical to most eyes. Funny, her new fiancée recognized the difference the instant he met me. My mother and my grandmother, Mama V are only seventeen years apart and look amazingly alike. You'll see Mama V, I'm sure. She'll come to the concert M. Jourdain and I are giving. If Monsieur Slave-driver ever decides we're ready."

Kate laughed but Chantal did not. She began to play with her spoon, turning it end over end.

"I might not be here, Kate. That's what I wanted to tell you."

Her big brown eyes were direct. Whatever Chantal said, she was always forthright.

"I'm pregnant. I haven't told Sven, nor will I. He'd insist on an immediate marriage, which would ruin him. I'm going to leave. I wanted you to know the truth, although of course you can't tell Sven. Somehow I couldn't bear to have you think me a no-good flirt who ran out on a good man."

Kate thought she probably should have been shocked but she wasn't. If her brief encounter with Gabe had left her pregnant, she'd be ecstatic. Suddenly she needed to know everything about how Chantal felt.

"Your aunts," she asked. "Will they not support you?"

Chantal grimaced. "No, I'll be dead to them if I tell them the truth. They're very strict Catholics. I'll be on my own, but surely I can manage. I know I'm not concert material, the classes here have shown me clearly that while I'm talented, I'll never be a star. I thought I might go to southern France, become a mysterious widow and give piano lessons. I'm certainly qualified for that."

"You're going to keep the baby then?" Kate felt almost like an inquisitor, but she had to know. Certainly she would treasure any baby Gabe gave her, but did Chantal feel the same?

Chantal's glance was incredulous. "Of course."

Kate threw her arms around her. "I'm so glad. I think any child you and Sven produce will be exceptional. How can I help?"

Chantal flashed her gamin grin. "You help just by being you. When I disappear, I'll let you know where I am. I'd like to keep in touch. I trust you not to tell Sven."

Kate agreed. She didn't really want to talk to Sven. She wanted to talk to Gabriel.

* * * * *

Which she did, with surprising efficacy. Gabriel steepled his graceful hands, as he often did when he contemplated a problem.

"They're good together. I can't see the difficulty, Kate."

"Gabriel, she's going to run and have the baby alone rather than interrupt his career. I promised not to tell Sven, but I think she's wrong."

Gabriel looked at her as if she were an idiot.

"Of course it's wrong and not the way any decent man would want things to be. Sven's a fine musician. He'll have no trouble joining a first class orchestra. Chantal is a pleasant musician, but not a great one. However, there are many places she can fit in the musical world. She has great knowledge of what makes music come together, especially during a presentation. They could find work together, I'm sure."

Kate shrugged. "If he wants her to stay with him when he learns she's going to have a baby. He'd have to leave the Conservatoire to support her and the child. Perhaps nothing would reconcile him to that. I think the important thing right now is for her to tell him and see what he says."

"Is Chantal resolute to have the child no matter what he says?"

Kate arched her always expressive eyebrows. "Yes, of course. They'll make a beautiful baby. I can't imagine giving up a child. Can you? All children are infinitely precious, whether planned or not."

Gabe fiddled with the pens on his desk. "Then in her place you'd do anything to keep the child? Even if it wrecked your career?"

Kate drew her attention away from his beautiful and fidgety hands and explored his expression. His aura hovered around his head, a deep blue of anxiety. Why did he care so much? His intensity seemed out of proportion. She'd found out just this morning there'd be no repercussions from her sexual encounter with Gabe. At first she'd felt a brief flash of regret. But then, she planned to have other encounters. Would her getting pregnant be a problem to Gabe? Was this what worried him so? Was a hindrance to his career what he feared?

She spoke slowly, thinking as she talked. Once again she questioned her self-imposed restriction not to probe. Gabe's current thoughts were very much tied to the secret he hid from her.

"Children are the future of us all. Some sacrifices for them must be expected. I would delight in any child I might have, no matter the circumstances. Nor would I ever give her up."

Her words were slow and careful, her great eyes searching his face as she spoke. He reacted in the now familiar way, shuttering his gaze and closing his face to her.

Kate sighed. If only she could put all these little clues together.

So far she'd not been able to make any sense of the times when he completely shut her out. She wondered sometimes if something had given him a hatred of children. Or fear of them? Not likely for a man of Gabriel's sensitivity. She felt bewildered, completely at sea.

"I've assured Chantal I wouldn't speak to Sven. I wish I hadn't, but I did." Her right hand started to worry her left ear.

Gabriel came out of his retreat long enough to flash a little smile at her.

"Kate, leave your poor ear alone. I'll talk to Sven, which I'm sure is what you were hoping."

She flew to him and kissed his cheek. "Oh, thank you, Gabriel. I knew you'd help." She didn't comment on his slight recoil from her impulsive embrace.

Blessed goddess of us all, but he was a difficult man. Couldn't she have found an easier one to fall in love with?

Her one consolation was that her sister's romance had been just as difficult and everything finally worked out for Vivie.

Surely she was smart enough to figure out the blockage in Gabriel's stubborn mind. This task definitely belonged to her and her alone. For once she couldn't consult her twin. She must find her own way into luring Gabriel into opening his thoughts. Vivie might be fretting at her lack of communication, but maybe not. She thought Vivie was quite busy herself.

She put aside her thoughts of Vivie. Her twin was happy, she knew, and so she left her alone.

Gabriel was another matter.

Had any man ever been so blasted stubborn?

And why? Why?

* * * * *

One matter was resolved quickly. Gabriel had made no promise to Chantal and so he immediately asked Sven to come to his office. There he invited him to sit down. When he appeared comfortable Gabriel blandly told him he was soon to be a father.

At first Sven thought it a strange joke, but then Gabriel's sincere congratulations convinced him the maestro was serious.

Sven propped his arms on his knees and lowered his face to his hands.

"Are you sure? Why hasn't Chantal told me, instead of you, for God's sake? It's not as if I'm unapproachable."

Gabriel grinned a very masculine grin. "Definitely you're approachable, Sven. But she wanted to spare you. She didn't tell me, she told Kate. Chantal seems to be consumed with a desire to further your career and feels getting married will hold you back."

Sven snorted. A healthy masculine snort. "What does she plan to do then, the little idiot?"

"She simply plans to disappear and make her own way. Her aunts are obviously ultra-conservative and would completely reject her. She spoke of going to the south of France and teaching music."

Sven rose to his feet. "I think I'd better track down my future wife and knock some sense into her pretty head. What a to-do about nothing. I'm delighted to marry the little witch."

Gabriel sat grinning as Sven stalked out.

He seemed to be good at solving others' problems. But not his own. His Druid consumed his thoughts both night and day and he didn't know how to loosen his enthrallment. He wondered sometimes if she'd cast a spell on him, but decided not. She was too forthright to snare a man without his desire. God knows he burned with more than enough desire for twenty men.

* * * * *

The long days of practicing went on and on. Kate thought she would throw something at Gabriel if he fixed her one more time with his commanding stare and politely requested a repeat of what she'd just played.

Only once did she break into tears.

"You're a tyrant," she screamed. "I'm doing my best and it's not good enough. I'm not good enough. There are other, better violinists in the school. Go get one of them."

She started out the door, tears obscuring her vision so she fumbled her way around her practice stand.

Gabriel came immediately to her side.

"Kate, Kate, I'm sorry. I'm a difficult, demanding monster. You're wonderful in every respect and I want only you for this concert. Only you."

He rocked her in his arms and kissed first her eyes and then her lips. Not with the passion she wanted, but with a sweetness she couldn't resist. He took out a spotless handkerchief and dabbed her eyes dry with just the tenderness she needed. She nestled for a moment, then sighed, a sigh reaching from her toes. She straightened her back, moved away and picked up her violin.

"All right, maestro. Shall we try that last passage again?"

They both laughed and went back to work.

* * * * *

Their isolation was interrupted once again, when Sven burst into the practice room. Definitely not allowed, but one look at Sven's agonized face and Gabriel suppressed his anger.

"What is it, Sven?'

"Chantal's aunts have locked her in her room. Evidently she told them why she was leaving them. Not a wise move, although perhaps they forced it out of her. Maybe she tried to be fair. But you can't be fair to narrow-minded and repressed old maids who have no concept of tolerance. I begged to see her. They refused. They had the phenomenal nerve to tell me she'd get nothing but crackers and water until she repents and agrees to give the child to the church."

He clutched his head in his hands.

"Dear god. I don't care which one you pray to, Maestro Jourdain, but those aunts calling themselves Christians is surely a disgrace to any religion.

Gabriel looked at the distraught man, thinking how he would feel if it were Kate. Granted, a pregnant Kate was an impossibility, but perhaps his own anguish of the impossibility helped him to feel Sven's distress.

He steepled his hands on his desk.

"Obviously we have to rescue Chantal from the clutches of her narrow-minded aunts. Let me think for just a moment."

After a moment he lifted his head.

"I expect I'd better come off the heavy-handed maestro. I'm not sure of the law and how much indignity guardians can impose on their charge. I do know this situation is wrong. I have a certain amount of prestige I can call on. Let's see what I can do with it."

Sven snorted. "A certain amount of prestige, indeed. You're the darling of France, M. Jourdain. A famous concert pianist whose career had been stalled by war injuries. Whose parents were killed on a diplomatic mission during the Great War. My

God, maestro, you can ask anything you want in Paris and receive it."

Gabriel's lips twisted into a sardonic smile. "Let's hope these throwbacks to the Inquisition will agree. I feel as if we're dealing with someone in the middle ages. Crackers and water indeed! I'll go see them. I don't think you should go with me."

Sven snorted again. "I should guess not. You'd never get into the parlor if I were along, spawn of Satan that I am."

Sven was obviously worried to distraction about Chantal, but his cheerful disposition still was irrepressible. A charming man, Gabriel thought. He'd be happy to do whatever he could for the pair of young lovers, regardless of Kate's concern. Knowing Kate would approve just made everything easier.

# Chapter Eight

ᘓ

Gabriel set off to find the home where Chantal was imprisoned. It was a drab house not far from the business district encompassing the Boulevard Haussmann. The house appeared to be closed up tight. Not a sign anyone actually lived there. As he stood on the stoop wondering what to do he thought he saw a curtain flutter at an upstairs window, but could not be sure.

He rang the doorbell, not once, but three times and finally an older woman with a pinched face cracked open the front door.

Gabriel drew himself up to his full height. This left the woman with no alternative but to peer up at him, which was just what he wanted.

"I am Gabriel Jourdain," he stated in his most imposing voice. "I've come to see Mademoiselle Chantal."

The woman hesitated, her face a study in indecision.

"You may come in, M. Jourdain. But you can't see my niece. She's a wicked creature and not worthy of even speaking to a saint like you."

Gabriel eyed her as one might an insect as he strode into the narrow hall.

She'd stretched back her sparse white hair into a thin knot. She wore no makeup whatsoever, not even a dusting of powder. She was dressed in black, as if in deep mourning.

No flattery or cajolery would sway this woman. Still he needed to get into the house.

"Perhaps we can discuss the matter, madame? Your niece is a gifted musician and as such of interest to me. She's not been to her classes lately. Perhaps you can tell me if she's ill?"

Gabriel observed every expression on the woman's harsh face. He knew they'd given Chantal a home so she could pursue her studies. Her parents, what had happened to her parents? He'd have to find out before stepping into trouble with this shrew. If she possessed lawful custody the matter was grim indeed.

The woman snorted. "I'm Mme. St. Claire. Chantal is my brother's child. He entrusted her to me and I've failed him. I could not keep her from her wicked ways. Now we must all suffer. And no, you may not see her. She is not ill. She is being kept in seclusion until she confesses and then repents her sins."

The overly righteous note in her voice proclaimed a good deal of satisfaction. Surely she should be upset if she truly loved her niece. She showed no sympathy at all. At least he didn't have to worry about ruining a relationship between Chantal and her aunts.

"May I come in and sit down, madame? My leg does not like my standing so long."

Gabriel used his most conciliatory tone, although he felt far from generous toward this narrow minded specimen in front of him. He felt no compunction about over-emphasizing his war injuries. She seemed to suddenly remember a war hero stood here in her parlor and flushed an unattractive shade of red.

"Yes, of course, monsieur. "

She stood back and let him enter, although her reluctance almost screamed at him.

The parlor was drab and dark with shadows, as he'd expected. The blinds were drawn as if the home were in mourning. Gabriel repressed his shudder and sat on the nearest chair, although it barely held his large frame.

"I know little of Chantal except for her talent. Are you responsible for seeing she received such excellent training?'

Madame sniffed. "No, indeed. Women should not be indulged in such fancies. Her father left her with us when he went to war and paid her tuition before he left. We would never have so spoiled her. No good comes of over-educating women. She would have been forced to quit her ridiculous music quite soon, at any rate, as he left no more money for the school."

Gabriel sat thinking frantically. How had Chantal endured these months of living with such a sour and repressed personality? He'd always thought her one of the sunniest students in the school. How fortunate for her she'd been able to throw off the effects of her aunts at least part of the time. Looking at the sour face opposite him, his admiration for Chantal grew.

"And he was injured in the war, I take it."

"Killed, monsieur. Perhaps as well. He'd be desolate to find how his daughter's turned out. We will visit his grave and inform him as soon as we can report her repentance."

Gabriel felt as if he'd stepped into some drama on a shifting stage. Surely this woman couldn't be real. He noticed another white head sticking around the corner. The other aunt, no doubt. Not very vocal, but there.

"I am sorry for your loss, madame. I still insist on seeing Chantal, however."

Anger flushed Madame's face and the second gray head disappeared. Quite evidently this first one reigned as head hen of the household. A stringy, bad-tasting hen.

"I cannot allow you to do so, m'sieur Jourdain. I'll tell you the awful truth. She's sinned against God and is pregnant. A blonde young Swedish boy without a thought in his wicked body but corrupting girls. He came to see her once and we quickly threw him out. We knew he must be the one."

Gabriel suddenly remembered Kate's saying Chantal planned to quietly disappear. Why then did she tell her aunts? She must have known the reaction would be unbearable.

He studied his immaculate shoes for just a moment, crossing his long legs and trying to find a bit of comfort for a brief space. In this household any kind of solace was scarce.

"And Chantal? Has she indeed told you she was corrupted? Do you have her confession of such a thing?"

Madame's eyes blazed. "Indeed not. She is unrepentant, which is why she's being punished so severely. Some guardians would beat her, you know, but my sister and I are not so cruel."

Her fanatic face was one of the most unattractive sights Gabriel had ever seen. He'd seen religious extremists before and something about them always alarmed him.

"I did not accuse you of cruelty, madame, although I am still at sea as to why I can't speak to her. You tell me she has not repented. Are you then so sure she has sinned, as you call it? Perhaps it's all a misunderstanding."

Madame sprang to her feet.

"I'd not accuse her of fornication unless I was sure. My sister and I do all her laundry. We're not stupid, you know. We expected this to happen. Her whore of a mother died years ago, after tricking our poor brother into marriage. It's quite easy for us to tell she is pregnant and doubtless by that disgusting young man. "

Gabriel felt a frisson of cold as he watched the aunt's face twist and darken. He couldn't image the perverse mind who'd scrutinize a girl's personal laundry day after day and be delighted when no monthly blood was found.

One thing was mandated. He must get Chantal out of this house and as soon as possible.

Physical danger lurked in the shadows, just waiting for a chance to make its dangerous appearance.

* * * * *

Gabriel went back to his office at the Conservatoire, a worried man. Sven was waiting for him. Gabe would have preferred time to think things through, but perhaps it would help to talk matters over with Sven.

He definitely needed fortification to tell Sven how bad he'd found the situation.

"Let's go the Brasserie Baronne. I find I need a restorative drink."

Sven looked even more worried, but agreed.

The short walk to the Brasserie cleared Gabe's head a little. The brasserie was crowded as usual, but they found a table on the sidewalk. Gabe definitely appreciated the fresh air, after the stale and fusty atmosphere of that horrible house.

Gabriel refused to be drawn into comments until he'd sipped his first Kir. Finally he heaved a deep sigh as he put his glass down.

"It's worse than I expected, Sven. Chantal's aunts are throwbacks to the religion that burned witches. I couldn't manage to see Chantal, but I found out quite a bit. Her father left Chantal with the aunts when he went to war. He'd already paid for this year at the Conservatoire, so they let her attend. They're impossibly bigoted, Sven. Totally narrow-minded and determined to grind Chantal down to a level they can dominate."

He related the whole interview and Sven listened, his body tensing with every word. His anger visibly growing. He stiffened into a rigidity showing a man barely in control. The impression of a jovial young man with no serious interests dropped away. Sven's face mirrored his growing fury as Gabriel continued his tale of his encounter with the aunts. Or rather the one controlling and fanatical aunt. He imagined the other aunt was a kind of cipher, agreeing with whatever her sister had already determined. Surely there couldn't be two of them that appalling.

Sven finally exploded, springing to his feet.

"My god, sir. I find it hard to believe in this day and age such medieval beliefs still exist. Chantal never breathed a word of what she's been forced to undergo. We must get her out."

Gabriel was immensely reassured at Sven's indignation. Together they could certainly solve this problem.

"I agree completely. I think it's time I consult my personal lawyer. I'd guess these wicked women have no legal claim on Chantal. I certainly hope not. It sounds to me as if her father left her with them when he went to war because he had no other recourse. Probably he had no time to sign legal documents of guardianship even if he wished. I doubt if they have any lawful claim to her at all. But we must be sure. Give me twenty-four hours, Sven."

Gabe watched Sven flex his powerful fists.

"I can hardly stand doing nothing, M. Jourdain. But I'll give you twenty-four hours. If your legal experts don't come through I'm going to storm the ramparts and physically rescue Chantal. This whole situation is insupportable. Especially when I intend to marry the girl. I *want* to marry the girl."

Gabriel said nothing. He was amazed he felt so much empathy for Sven and Chantal. He'd closed his heart for so long to anything except his music. His music he could always rely on. Waiting for him, gorgeous chords and strains flooding his mind and making it possible for him to exist in a world otherwise gray with betrayal and misery.

Now the colors of the world were coming back to him. Another blessing from Kate?

Finally he spoke. "I think we're on solid ground, but I want to make sure. It seems unlikely to me Chantal's father meant to give the aunts legal guardianship. If that's the case, we can make aggressive moves. Give me time to check the legalities so we don't get Chantal in worse trouble."

Sven grumbled but agreed.

"I'll take the girl any way I can get her, maestro. I certainly can't let a child of mine have anything to do with those incredibly narrow-minded biddies. Can you believe they even still exist?"

* * * * *

Gabriel couldn't learn anything definite the next day. He also went to his friend, a high-ranking policeman, but found little help. Searching the records might take weeks and Chantal, shut up in a gloomy room with no knowledge of Sven's attempts to rescue her, was doubtless desperate. She was bound to be weakened by hunger. His lawyer commented it did not sound as if a formal guardianship had been conferred, but thought it a tricky situation.

Gabe consulted with Sven and together they decided to act aggressively on the assumption Chantal's father had neither thought nor time to make the guardianship formal. If they acted with a complete certitude, perhaps they could overwhelm the aunts.

Gabriel decided to call in Kate. Her indignation made the whole exercise worth while. Looking at her flushed face, her indignation blazing, Gabe scolded himself. He'd fretted at how long it was taking to solve this problem. Now he felt like a worm he'd ever resented the loss of time. Seeing Kate, her emerald eyes flashing like the jewels they resembled, made everything worthwhile. His Druid seemed about to march off and settle the whole matter herself when Gabe laid a restraining hand on her arm.

"Kate, my dear girl. You'll just make everything worse. I can't imagine the aunts doing anything but having a fit Chantal has a friend like you. A Brit, no less, let alone a gorgeous redhead who doubtless seduces men right and left."

Kate bristled and Gabe smothered a laugh.

"And what is so wrong with seducing men, pray tell?" she asked. "I can certainly tell those old crones what I think of their centuries old attitude. I can even shout loud enough Chantal will hear me and know help is on the way."

Gabe's rare laugh rang out.

"That's *not* why I wanted to talk to you. Can you persuade your grandmother to take care of Chantal for the time it will take Sven to arrange a civil ceremony? It will take at least ten days. The religious one will of course take longer, but I want her protected if the aunts track her down. Can you do this, Kate?"

She smiled her gorgeous smile, a little abashed now she realized what he really wanted from her.

"Of course, Gabe. Mama V will be delighted to help. She was into protecting women before I was born. No problem at all."

The next day found Gabriel ready to take on the Le Claire sisters. A thoroughly impressive and magnificent Gabriel. He'd rummaged through his dresser and found the medals he'd been awarded for bravery and outstanding performance. He'd never desired to even look at them before, but now he was glad he possessed them. He also wore the red rosette of the Legion of Honor in his buttonhole. He'd dressed as if he were making a formal call and his beauty made Kate's knees boneless. She breathed deeply and reminded Gabe she and Sven would wait around the corner. Kate was certain Chantal would welcome a friend as well as her lover.

Gabe shook his head. "No, come with me. I've decided you can help," he said. "I want you to go in with me to get Chantal."

He loved to be with Kate at any time, anywhere, but this time he knew she'd really help.

Kate's expressive face lit. "Wonderful. I'd love to do anything I can. What changed your mind?"

"I think I'm on more solid ground if I have the granddaughter of Chantal's new chaperone with me. It also should take care of any gossip these vicious two old ladies might start about Chantal running off with her music professor. I don't put anything at all past them. It wouldn't bother me, but there's no use giving them free ammunition."

They started out, dropping Sven at a corner two blocks away. Kate, nervous and excited at the same time, made only one remark.

"I can't imagine examining a girl's underwear to be sure it showed a virgin's blood. How despicable."

Gabe grunted. "I never should have told you. Certainly not the conversation a gentleman has with a lady. I never seem to behave properly with you."

Kate just shook her head, her nerves at meeting the two aunts now invading her attempts to be calm.

They simply must rescue Chantal.

* * * * *

The aunts admitted them to the house, although reluctance hovered like a buffer around them. Evidently they were afraid to antagonize one of France's most respected men. Kate doubted they'd have been permitted near the house without Gabriel's shining prestige.

Kate could hardly keep her eyes from him. As stern and unapproachable as she'd ever seen him. Power seemed to radiate from his dignified presence. He definitely awed the Le Claire sisters.

The second aunt, a mousey creature, said almost nothing. Madame Le Claire, although the "madame" had to be a courtesy title, recoiled when she saw Kate, her eyes flashing hatred. She spoke only to Gabe. Kate might not have existed except her presence seemed to stiffen Mme. Le Claire's antagonism.

"I do not know why you've returned, M. Jourdain. Certainly you can't think I'll change my mind? My sinful niece remains in seclusion until she confesses and repents. If you have a message to send her to hasten her repentance, I will deliver it. Otherwise you may leave."

Gabriel took his time about answering. He shot his cuffs and smoothed his hair. He examined his immaculate fingernails with absorbed care. He adjusted the rosette in his buttonhole. Finally he stood still and stared at the two women, his eyes glaring with accusation from under his dark brows.

Madame grew visibly more nervous. Kate's Druid senses picked up a sour smell, some of it fear, some of it sheer hatred. The second sister by now literally quivered with anxiety. Whether for herself or her sister or her niece, Kate couldn't tell. She only knew danger loomed in this bizarre household.

Gabriel drew himself and spoke with regal assurance. "You do not have legal custody of Mlle. Chantal. You have no paper from the courts proving guardianship. I therefore am taking her to Mlle. Dellafield's grandmother. She will stay at the Grand Hotel under the auspices of M. and Mme. Randall, the eminent British couple who have great power and reputation both here and in their own country. I give you ten minutes to pack Chantal's possessions and bring Chantal and her valise down to me. From now on you may visit her at the Grand Hotel."

Kate thought if it were possible for a person to explode with anger, she might just see one in Mme. Le Clair. Suddenly Kate's mind flashed her a remembrance of a vision of the night before. With a start, she recognized her vision took place in this room. She knew the large armoire and the dark drapes. The musty smell of the ancient furniture was familiar. The aunt had acted with violence, she remembered and she tried to concentrate on what she'd seen happening. At the time she'd not recognized the room or the people and thought it only a gruesome and unusual dream.

Mme. Le Claire turned a frightening shade of purple. Her voice and hands were shaking as she screamed at Gabe.

"You might be a hero to France but to me you're as bad as the man who seduced my niece. It never would have happened without the loose atmosphere in your Conservatoire. Decent people don't devote their lives to music when God's will is in danger on this earth."

"You now have nine minutes," Gabe said. His voice was as cool as ever and he showed not a smidgeon of anxiety. "Then I'll go fetch Chantal."

Her fury told Gabe he rested on solid ground. If there were a document of legal guardianship, the reaction would be quite different.

"I'll not do it," Madame declaimed.

Silence reigned as Gabriel pointedly took out his pocket watch and examined it.

"I can have all sorts of charges brought against you, madame. Abusive cruelty is one. Illegal detainment is another. Starving a minor in your care. I'm sure my lawyer will find more after we speak with Chantal."

Kate noticed the second aunt scurry off. Gabriel and Kate waited in silence, the furious Mme Chantal glaring at them with alarming intensity. In eight minutes they heard a sound of someone coming down the stairs and a pale, thin Chantal appeared. She carried a small valise in her hands. A relieved smile illuminated her face when she saw Gabriel and Kate. It was plain she'd not been told they were there.

She rushed toward Kate and Kate suddenly knew, knew with certainty, what was going to happen next. Her vision had been accurate up 'til now. Now she'd have to change the outcome. She tackled Chantal around the waist and they both rolled sideways and to the floor, as Mme. St. Claire heaved a heavy bronze vase at Chantal.

There was a moment of silence, broken by the clunk of the metal hitting the floor. Both girls took a deep breath and then threw their arms around each other. Gabriel was white with anger, as he helped them both up, all the time keeping his eyes on Madame, now quaking with fury and guilty reaction.

"You have doomed yourself, madame. If you ever attempt to see Chantal again I'll see you in jail for assault. Do not think I will hesitate to do so."

Not another word was said. Gabriel shepherded them ahead of him and out of the house. He stood guarding them with his body even as they climbed into the waiting taxi. Then he jumped in the front seat.

Kate wrapped her arms around Chantal, now sobbing with relief and Gabe only spoke to guide the taxi to the corner where Sven waited. Sven's first reaction was fury at his lover's state of exhaustion and hunger and he quickly climbed in the taxi and took her in his arms.

As they all rode to the Grand Hotel, Gabe filled Sven in on the latest assault. Then no one spoke, as a sense of relief gradually worked its way in all their minds.

Gabe asked only one question of Kate.

"How did you know to duck the vase?" His face showed a mixture of relief and awe, as if he expected he knew the answer.

"I'd seen that same vase flying through the air last night in my vision. Thank the goddess I remembered in time."

Seven and Chantal were too absorbed in each other to pay attention to her words. Sven held Chantal, tightly, her head pressed against his shoulder with one big hand.

Kate's voice was quiet and assured and Gabe half-shuttered his eyes. He was not really surprised. He was beginning to think his Druid capable of anything.

And he could in no way deny what he'd just witnessed.

# Chapter Nine

ℵ

Both Gabriel and Kate now concentrated completely on their coming concert. Practice hours were long and rigorous, as they worked into the evening and beyond.

Two days before the event Gabriel changed the pattern.

"I think we should cut the practice to just one run-through for the next two days. We're both perfectly prepared and I don't want you over-stressed."

On the night before the concert he asked her to play her *Ode to My Parents* for him.

"I find the melody restful," he said. "It somehow soothes me."

His thoughtfulness at reducing the practice time touched Kate deeply, especially when he took her to dinner each night and talked only of other matters. Political matters, Sven's search for a job, anything but the concert. The Versailles Peace Treaty had not yet been signed, although it was imminent. Much speculation swirled around Paris as to the effects it might have. Some newspapers lauded it as the end of war and others called it the beginning of the next war. It was only one of the topics they discussed, although they saw no true answer to it. Too much depended on future events for anyone to be sure.

The sad state of some of the veterans was a topic they agreed on. Kate and Gabe both were pleased their concert would be of help. At least they were doing what they could.

* * * * *

The night arrived, in spite of Kate's wishing she could postpone it forever. When she and the Randalls left the Grand Hotel she felt much more nervous than she'd expected.

"Don't worry, love." Mama V patted her restless hands. "You'll do very well. I'm quite, quite sure."

Kate smiled at Mama V's superb confidence. One thing she herself knew for certain. Once she saw Gabriel she'd feel better.

A large audience greeted them in the concert hall at the Conservatoire. The hall had never been planned for such a public occasion. Word that Gabriel Jourdain would play once again—and with his beautiful student—soon buzzed around the musical circles of Paris. Gabriel's invitations were planned to almost fill the hall, but he'd not counted on the interest his first appearance after the war would cause. Other students, his former fans, newspaper reporters, all simply crowded in.

"At least," Gabriel muttered to himself, "we're raising a nice sum for the veterans."

He worried about Kate. Her first prominent public appearance and she'd be faced with a throng exceeding either of their expectations. She might be frightened to death and there was nothing he could do to spare her. He should have been much more careful and closed the hall to all without a written invitation. The guards were being selective, but too many people made their way inside. Some were even standing against the walls.

He need not have worried. Kate saw Gabriel and the little frown between his eyes as he looked at her and instantly knew his concern was for her. She closed her eyes and called on her mother and grandmother to give her some Druid calm. Then she peered through the curtains at the large audience, turned back and smiled at Gabe. Her grandmother, Mama V sat in the front row with her husband, Devon Randall. Mama V was one of the most beautiful women she knew. Heads turned when she glided to her seat, her proud husband holding her arm. More than her beauty made her so special. She was the most powerful Druid in existence and renowned for her healing skills.

Kate turned to Gabe with a full-blown, glorious smile.

"Let's go, Gabriel. We're both ready. And you're the most handsome man in the hall. I've never seen you in evening dress before. You're beautiful."

He laughed. "Men aren't beautiful, my dear."

She only shook her head at him.

"*You* definitely are, dear teacher."

He took a moment to admire her appearance. She was dressed in an emerald green satin evening gown, hugging her perfect body and accenting the green of her beautiful eyes. Flowing chiffon sleeves were gathered to tight cuffs at her wrists and the square neckline sparkled with brilliants. She wore her hair loose, with diamond earrings hanging in small clusters at her ears.

"You're not only beautiful, my dear, you're gorgeous," he said. "And you'll play on a level equal to your loveliness."

He took both her hands and kissed her forehead. Then he walked on stage and to the piano, at first ignoring the applause creating a din in the small hall. He stood still for a moment, letting the applause build and finally acknowledged the tribute with a bow. He raised his hands for quiet and motioned to Kate to come join him on the stage.

"Miss Kate Dellafield and I will play for you tonight. This is not a formal concert, but rather an acknowledgement of my joyous return to music and my appreciation of my lovely associate's patience with a teacher turned tyrant. We'll play Beethoven's *Sonata in F-Major, Opus 24,* better known as the "Spring" sonata.

With no further ado he flipped up the tails of his evening coat and sat at the piano. His Bechstein had been transferred to the concert hall for the occasion and the beginning notes rang loud and true.

The strains of the beautiful sonata floated out, haunting in its melody and well known to musical aficionados. Its four movements were noted as a joyous expression of Beethoven's break to freedom from the restraints of his previous work. The second movement, the slowly paced adagio, perfectly suited Gabriel's hands and still allowed him scope for his impassioned playing.

Kate, listening to Gabriel, did not hear his words as much as she reveled in the delight his playing brought. Although she'd practiced these same pieces with him countless, literally countless, times, his playing tonight reached a level she'd not heard before.

She'd felt humbled as she held her violin to her shoulder and tried her best to match his rapturous notes.

When they finished the sonata, Gabriel stood and stilled the applause with uplifted hands. He spoke to the audience again. He was handsome and impressive in his formal wear and the audience clearly adored him.

"We will now play a sonata I wrote, one inspired by the beauty of the Spring Sonata and one I've written in gratitude for being able to play for you all again. Miss Dellafield knows my feelings and I accompany her with great pleasure."

A few chuckles sounded throughout the hall and then everyone quieted. Kate thought his composition brilliant, although she worried he'd concentrated too much on the violin, giving her star status she didn't deserve. She would have preferred to have his piano the focus of the music, but he'd not listened to her at all. He'd written a gorgeous piece, a dazzling composition deserving to be presented to the world. She had no doubt his publisher would have it on the market soon.

Her slight nervousness left her, as she strove to do justice to Gabriel's beautiful accompaniment. At the end of his sonata, she turned to him with pleasure and awe, as the audience exploded into wild approval and applause. He looked at Kate and smiled a slight smile, then walked to the front of the small stage and raised his hands again. He possessed enormous stage presence, which plainly showed this night. His beautiful hair gleamed in the lights of the stage and his assured bearing commanded respect and admiration from all.

"We have one encore for you," he said quietly.

There was more loud applause and Gabriel again smiled. A mischievous smile this time, doubtless melting every female heart in the audience.

"This particular encore will surprise everyone, including the talented Miss Dellafield. It's a small composition she wrote as a student in my class. She doesn't know I've written a piano accompaniment for it."

Kate stared at him. Her *Ode*? It had to be and she hadn't practiced it for weeks.

A look of understanding swept over her expressive face. So that was why he'd wanted to hear the *Ode* last night.

"I'll give Miss Dellafield a moment to recover from her surprise. But since she composed the piece, I'm sure she remembers it."

The audience cheered and laughed and Kate didn't know whether she wanted to kiss or shake him. She colored, glared at him and then adjusted her violin again on her shoulder. She played a few tentative notes. The blasted man was right, she knew her *Ode* too well to need extensive practice. She stood in the middle of the stage, smiling at Mama V and Devon. And began the piece she'd perfected under Gabriel's tutelage. Her graceful body swayed as she lost herself in the memories she'd written.

Before she'd finished the first few bars Gabriel's piano joined her, his brilliant accompaniment enhancing her simple melody with marvelous nuances she'd never envisioned.

*What wonderful harmony. I'm sure I'd cry at the beauty of his composition if I had the time.*

She laid down her bow, as she'd finished the last few bars alone. Doubtless exactly as Gabe planned it. Silence claimed the audience as her tribute to her parents resounded through the hall. Mama V evidently understood immediately what the music portrayed, as did Devon Randall and tears glistened in both their eyes.

When she lowered her bow, the audience again burst into riotous applause and Gabriel left the piano to join her. Holding her hand, he bowed with her, twice, three times and then led her off the stage.

Kate turned to him, wonder and love shining in her great eyes.

"You might have told me," she said.

"No," he said. His resonating voice was low and solemn. "You're now established as a composer, which is what I wanted. You're a good violinist, but going on the concert circuit would eventually prove distressful to you. I don't want your prime interest to be performing. This is my way of proving to you where your true talent lies. The one gift I dare give you."

Before she could reach for him he stepped slightly back and Mama V and her husband came up to them. As Kate introduced them, she saw Gabriel stiffen into his most reserved self.

Her grandmother hugged Kate tightly.

"You were magnificent, love. Your piece portrayed your growing up to be the wonderful girl you are, didn't it?"

Kate laughed, just a little. Her emotions were so close to the surface she was afraid she'd break in little pieces if she let her feelings loose.

"Really about my whole family, including you two." She paused and took Gabriel's hand. "Mama V and Devon, please may I present Gabriel Jourdain? Gabe, these are my grandparents, the ones I live with in Paris. Aren't they a gorgeous pair?"

Her light tone and outrageous words made it easy for Gabe to smile. The Randalls were indeed handsome, Devon Randall, a white-haired sturdy man in his sixties and Mama V, a truly astonishing beauty who seemed only a little older than Kate.

"It is indeed an honor," Gabe said as he kissed Mama V's hand and then shook Devon's. Kate looked at him sharply. His tone was flat, with no warmth and possibly a hint of caution. Had he deliberately made it so?

"Kate has come a long way under your guidance, M. Jourdain." Kate's grandmother's eyes were far too sharp for comfort, at least Gabe's comfort. A formidable lady, indeed. He shuttered his eyes, listening while both grandparents expressed their thanks for his interest in Kate and furthering her career.

Gabe said as little as possible. With a feeling of shock, he knew the time had come when he must take a stand. Far too soon. But her family was welcoming him with kind words and glances he did not deserve. He must make it plain to her and to her adoring relations he could not be considered up to their level, or as a possibility of anything more than an instructor. A music instructor.

He must save his Druid from future misery by causing her great unhappiness now. God give him strength. He simply couldn't stand being thought a hero by Kate and her family. The

Randalls were smiling at him, accepting him into their midst in a manner not fair to Kate.

He settled himself and let the talk flow a little. Kate chattered away, saying how she'd loved being at the Conservatoire and how she'd always cherish the friends she'd made. And how Gabriel's sponsoring of her in tonight's recital exceeded her dreams.

"He's the most wonderful teacher and inspiration any student could have." Her heart shone in her eyes and her smile and Gabe's own heart shrank to the nothing he knew it was.

Gabriel waited until she finished and then took her hand and kissed it.

"Always the gracious lady, our Princess Kate. I hope when she returns to England she remembers her days in Paris with fondness. We all treasure her and hope the husband she eventually finds in her homeland will cherish her as much as we do here."

He briefly flickered his eyes closed and then opened them and watched in pain as surprise and then resentment appeared on the faces of her grandparents. Kate herself looked completely stunned. No one moved or spoke and Gabriel felt himself tensing.

He didn't have long to wait. Tears appeared in Kate's beautiful eyes, but did not fall. Instead they blazed with anger as she took a few steps to Gabriel and, standing directly in front of him, slapped him in the face. Hard.

She turned and walked out of the room, leaving her grandparents to follow when they willed.

Devon Randall shook his head, then completely surprised Gabe by patting him on the back before he took his wife's arm to leave. Viviane Randall looked at him with sorrow.

"I hope you know what you're doing, Gabriel. You must think you do, but that was incredibly stupid and you're not a stupid man."

She did not speak in anger, in fact her tone was laced with kindness and regret. She patted the cheek gently that Kate had reddened and said softly, "Blessed be, Gabriel."

Then she left with her husband.

Gabe stood looking after them, rubbing his cheek. He'd never supposed Kate could smack him with so much force. But an even bigger surprise was the Randall's sympathy toward him.

After all, he'd just rejected Kate in a most humiliating manner. In front of her adoring family. He'd give a lot to know what Kate's Druid grandmother truly thought. She was intelligent to a frightening degree.

He wondered if Kate could in any way be as miserable as he.

Not likely. In fact, impossible. No one else could possibly be as miserable.

He had to be the world's most miserable man.

He dreaded going home and facing Raoul.

# Chapter Ten

ꙮ

Gabriel sat at his desk, his head buried in his hands.

He'd been too abrupt. In this anxiety to push Kate from him and from future sorrow. He'd been foolishly premature. Had he made a dreadful mistake? He'd broken with Kate so harshly she now had no use for him at all. Exactly what he'd set out to do, but he'd not dreamed how much he'd miss her. And how it would hurt. He'd known it would be torture being apart from her, but not that it would be *this* devastating. He should have tried harder to figure out a way to reject her and still keep her as his friend.

If such a thing were possible.

Kate was too proud to stop coming to his class but her set face never varied in its stony attention. Again gossip spread through the school, murmurs of puzzlement. Everyone knew the concert had been an outstanding success and he'd paid her great honor by playing her composition. Gossip swirled and amplified, with Kate and Gabe both unapproachable on the topic. What could have happened consumed everyone for days.

And he was doomed to see her beautiful face day after day, without the solace of even one word from her compressed lips.

He had only to glance at her to remember how she'd once melted in his arms and given him pleasure he would cherish the rest of his life.

Regret tore at him. Did he make the break too soon? Why hadn't he waited and been at least her friend for a while longer? Why had he been in such a damned rush?

Surely he could have allowed himself a few more weeks of the bliss of knowing she esteemed him. Then he would see her huge eyes, looking at him the night of the concert as if he were a god and know he'd been right not to allow her affection for him to continue. He must concentrate on her and her future happiness, not his present misery. At least he did not pretend to himself he was anything but miserable.

Sven and Chantal ranged themselves stolidly on Kate's side. They didn't understand what happened, they just knew their beloved Kate was devastated. They were not foolish enough to antagonize Gabriel, but their exaggerated politeness made their position clear. Gabriel was actually amused by them, but was careful not to betray his feeling. They were being nicer to him than he deserved. He turned aside their puzzled glances, knowing they were torn between esteem for him and fondness for Kate.

Most of the school, in one way or another, made their support of Kate evident. Gabriel not only accepted their barely concealed disdain, but reveled in it. His princess had proved herself in more ways than one. She might be suffering from his rejection, but she must know she was esteemed by the majority of the students in the Conservatoire. The name "Princess" now truly belonged to her.

He thought often of how he'd insisted on teaching a beginning class. He'd gotten in the impossible predicament of teaching Kate for an odd reason. A former talented Conservatoire student died beside him in the trenches, one who'd mourned he'd waited two years to be eligible for the Jourdain master class and would now never make it. He'd grieved at how much he'd always wanted to hear Gabriel teach. Holding the boy in his arms, Gabriel swore he'd always have one class to encourage beginners. His worthy resolution led him straight to Kate. He should be rejoicing his instructions led to Kate's advancement and stop thinking of his own pain.

Still he was miserable. Miserable as he'd never been before.

One other serious compunction worried him. The morning after the concert the guards at the Conservatoire came to speak with him. They'd been posted because Gabriel feared too many of his devotees might hear of the concert and try to attend. He'd only thought of possible overcrowding.

What the guards told him was more serious.

"There was this one dégénéré last night, maestro, who gave us a lot of trouble. Claimed he'd been your student and you'd want him to hear you. We didn't like him. His eyes were wild and shifty and when we questioned him he literally shook with anger. We kept him out. Another student who had an invitation said he'd been enrolled here once. I'm sure you wouldn't have wanted this one in."

"Did you take down his name?" Gabriel asked. He knew the answer before the guards gave it to him and he only nodded when they said it was Adrien Castelet.

He feared now, on top of his regret, he might have forced the break from Kate too soon. If Adrien were still incensed and possibly vindictive, he might go after Kate again. Damn the blasted bastard anyway. He should have beaten him up completely and put some fear into him instead of just expelling him from the school.

Gabriel went to Raoul for help. Raoul listened in barely controlled silence.

"Why don't you just go to Miss Kate and tell her your concerns?"

Gabriel flushed. "Because I've broken off with her, damn you. You know how I feel about tying her down to a wreck like me."

Raoul looked at him as one might a dead mouse found on the expensive parlor rug.

"I have no use for your self-sacrificing ideas, Captain Gabe. You're wrong, dead wrong and I've told you so time and again."

Gabriel looked at his long-time friend and felt his heart sink in his body. Could he be right if everyone else in the world thought him wrong?

"Will you help me, Raoul?" he asked quietly.

He looked at the one man in the world who knew just how scarred he was in mind and body. Raoul had helped drag him out of the trenches. How could this same man want him to expose his infirmities to a perfect angel like Kate? An angel without a single defect, at least in his eyes.

"Yes, I'll help you. Or rather I'll help Miss Kate. What do you want me to do?"

Gabe breathed an inward sigh of relief. "I know her schedule. I'll give it to you. I want you to follow her home when she leaves the school for the hotel. She always walks unless it's raining too hard."

Raoul snorted. "Easy enough. Although it would be much simpler if you just told her why you're trying to push her away and let her judge for herself. And then you could take care of her yourself."

Gabe shuddered. His perfect Kate staring at his welts and scars? The pity she'd not be able to hide. The desperate way she'd try to convince him his mutilation didn't matter. And there remained the one secret not even Raoul knew.

He was silent for a long time. His nightmares had come back since he'd forced Kate from him. Not as frequently as before he'd met her, but still enough to remind him of what he'd become. Knowing he'd been able to grasp salvation haunted him with almost every breath.

He finally answered Raoul.

"Thank you," he said. "She'll be safe with you watching after her."

As he turned back to his desk, he felt Raoul's eyes on him. His body agreed with Raoul. God knows he'd like nothing better than to go to Kate. He felt like a man starved of the sustenance of life.

He knew he'd be the worst kind of bastard if he gave in to the temptation to be with her.

Just one more time. Just once more.

* * * * *

Kate tried to walk off some of her desperate desires. She found it easier to subdue her longing for Gabe if she kept busy and active. Not that she ever really lost the desire to be with him, but exercise helped a little. Taxis, buses and the Metro were interesting, but she preferred to stride along.

Walking to the Grand Hotel from the Conservatoire, she felt a prickly feeling at the back of her neck. An unusual itchy awareness and yet she knew at once what it meant. Someone was following her. She was on the Rue de Rome. A street well known to the musicians in Paris. *Luthiers,* or shops of artisans repairing musical instruments, as well as shops selling instruments and musical scores were scattered along the street. A well-known and respected street in a colorful corner of musical Paris. A street she loved to walk upon.

Who could be following her ? And for what purpose? If it were Gabriel she'd be delighted. She'd been so miserable, but knew of no way to approach him in view of his complete and public rejection. She could barely endure the loss of their closeness, both in their music and in their unspoken communications.

Her grandparents said not a word, nor would she expect them to. She was blessed with a family who gave unconditional support.

She'd said nothing. She didn't want to admit to them that the man who'd rejected her was the one man in the world she wanted. Anyway, she imagined Mama V, if not Papa Devon knew. She'd buried her misery into her composing. She knew her latest piece was well-written and expressive, although not many would want to play a piece with such a sad theme running through it. Even though it expressed what she felt, this time she didn't want anyone to see her finished work. She'd worked some pain out of her system, writing down the sorrow in her heart on paper and in stanzas, but decided she'd best tear it up. She was ready to start another composition celebrating the way she thought love should be. Or at the beginning part. She didn't know how to write the ending for a true love. Although she knew in her heart love could be true and lasting. Surely love such as between her parents was worth any effort or risk.

If she knew what to do next to convince Gabriel.

Now she concentrated her senses, trying to pick out the step she'd heard before. When she'd stop, the other step would pause and then get faster. She'd turned on to the Boulevard Haussmann. The Boulevard was crowded, so she needed to focus all her Druid senses. She couldn't fathom who the follower could be. Too many impressions from too many people for her to sort them all out.

She did know the person following her was not Gabriel. Gabriel would march boldly up to her and demand her attention.

How Kate wished he would. Her life seemed to have little meaning without his enigmatic but encouraging presence. She walked on, not pausing again. She didn't want to betray her knowledge of being followed. She tried to determine the stalker's aura, but to isolate the aura of any one person behind her proved too difficult. Her probing told her only that the one following her was evil. She knew if she turned around and caught his aura it would be black.

Who was pursuing her?

Suddenly, coming from in front of her, were two laughing figures who grabbed her and caught her up between them. Sven gave her a bear hug and twirled her off her feet. Chantal kissed her as soon as he set her down.

"We had to come tell you. We were married today in a civil ceremony and are on our way to visit Sven's parents. They told us at the Conservatoire you were walking home."

Kate beamed with joy for them both, although her heart had yet to calm to a normal rhythm.

"How wonderful. I'm so glad you came to tell me. Will you be gone long?"

"Just a few days, at least for now." Chantal's face glowed with her happiness. She didn't yet show her pregnancy, but motherhood and joy were most becoming. Kate thought she'd never seen Chantal look lovelier. Her pert little face shone.

"What do you mean, 'for now'?"

Chantal and Sven's grins grew even wider.

"I want to introduce my lovely wife to my parents as soon as possible. And also Maestro Jourdain has arranged an interview for me with the Stockholm orchestra. If things go well we'll be moving to Stockholm. They also want to interview Chantal for the position of assistant to the mistress of scores."

Kate grasped a hand of each of them. "I'm so, so pleased for you. What about your aunts, Chantal?"

A little shadow flitted across Chantal's face. "I haven't heard a word from them, nor do I really want to. I'm going to write and tell them I'm married although I don't expect to hear from them ever again. Sven and I will make our own way. We'll have each other, after all."

Kate looked at the two glowing faces and wished with all her heart their dreams would come true. They were two wonderful young people.

She hugged them both, with all her strength, willing whatever Druid power she possessed into forging the happiness of these two precious people. In her mind she called on her goddess to hold them in her arms, blessing them throughout their lives.

She threw her arms around Chantal again and hugged her tightly.

"Blessed be, my good friend," she said, kissing Chantal's cheek.

Chantal's eyes widened. She seemed to somehow know that in spite of their different faiths, Kate's blessing was one of power and benefice.

"Thank you, dear Kate. We'll see you soon. Oh and if it's a girl, I'll want to name her Katherine."

Kate started to laugh. She threw her hands over her face, but couldn't seem to stop. Sven and Chantal both stared at her, until finally Chantal breathed softly.

"Kate?'

Kate mopped her eyes and grinned.

"And which of your three daughters gets my name? I don't think any of the three boys will want it."

Chantal and Sven both stared at her.

"Are you sure?" whispered Chantal.

"Oh yes. Six children. I saw them just now plain as day. They're all lovely and have a nice mix of your coloring."

Chantal hugged her again.

"Then your blessing will come true, Kate. Thank you for everything, my dear friend."

Sven kissed her on both cheeks, in the French manner, but with a huge grin on his face.

"You've blessed me too, you know. What fun we'll have making all those babies."

Chantal swatted at him and they went off laughing, while Kate murmured another and almost silent *blessed be.*

Kate breathed another prayer for their children, happy tears in her eyes and then started walking. She knew the evil following her had halted, afraid to go forward while she was surrounded by loving friends. She walked on, holding her breath. She desperately hoped the stalker had disappeared into the Parisian twilight. She was, after all, on one of the foremost streets in Paris. She should be completely safe.

She held her head high and walked on. Listening with her ears and her Druid heart. She took a quick gulp of air. The sense of danger no longer permeated her senses. Her fear began to calm, as she couldn't pick up the sense of anyone evil.

Why feel so much menace in such an open place? Surely no one could do her harm when she was surrounded by so many people.

She walked on, still with every sense alert. Her sensitivity felt enhanced beyond even her normal Druid abilities. Sounds were louder, much louder. The odors from a nearby bakery were pleasant but almost overwhelming. She could still taste the tinny trace of her leftover fear. Swallowing convulsively, she hurried on.

She felt exhausted from too many sensations, too much feeling.

She would be very glad to reach the Grand Hotel.

# Chapter Eleven

ꟗ

Gabriel listened gravely to Raoul's report.

"It was that damned Castelet, Captain Gabe. He'd almost caught up to her when two of your other students came running up from the opposite direction and grabbed Miss Kate and whirled her around. What they told her made her happy and they all laughed a lot. Even though they didn't stay with her long Castelet turned and went away fast."

Gabriel's face turned stony. The severity of his features reminded Raoul of the stern captain who demanded the best from his men. And from himself.

"I imagine the bastard was afraid they might have spotted him. What worries me is he'll no doubt be back. Fairly soon, I'd guess."

As he spoke Raoul blessed the fates he wasn't the object of the cold determination behind the icy blue eyes. Castelet might not know it yet, but he shouldn't have tangled with the Captain's woman.

"I think the only solution is for both of us to follow her when Kate walks home," mused Gabriel.

"Why don't you just make sure she takes a taxi every night?"

"I'm afraid it would only drive him to action at a place we might not know about. I hope this way we can catch and dispose of him. I don't want a menace like him lurking after any woman, let alone Kate. I hope to catch him and put him in jail. He shouldn't be out roaming the streets of Paris. If nothing else, I'll instill the fear of God in his wicked soul.

*Or the fear of Kate's goddess might be even more impressive, if I were pure enough to call on her.*

He closed his eyes for just a moment. He couldn't remember when he last slept for any restoring length of time. Certainly not since he'd driven Kate from him. He shook his shoulders and forced himself to be alert.

"I'm going to phone her hotel and make sure she's there. Then tomorrow you and I will both be waiting for Castelet."

Gabriel and Raoul stayed well in the shadows of the building, as they watched and waited. Gabe fingered the silver handle of his cane, his thumb resting near the secret catch. His sword would be ready if needed.

She seemed unusually thoughtful and a little smile played around her lovely lips. Gabriel imagined she looked just so when composing. Perhaps a new melody was racing in her head. His eyes feasted on the sight of her, the cold look she leavened at him in the classroom entirely absent. Gabriel suddenly realized the short walk from the school to the Rue de Rome might also be dangerous, when she'd not yet reached the open space of the Rue and its usual throng of people. He instantly calmed himself, this was too close to the main buildings of the Conservatoire to be a good spot for a kidnapper.

He expected an attempt at kidnapping. He'd spent a good many hours trying to think as Castelet might and he felt strongly Castelet would want to make her pay for her rejection of him. And pay dearly. He thought the man unbalanced and dangerously vindictive. Just striking her down in public wouldn't be enough. Getting Kate alone and in his power was almost mandatory. Gabe had read of beauty able to drive men mad. If that were possible, then surely Kate's beauty qualified to wreak havoc in any male mind.

Staying in the shadows, Gabriel and Raoul watched Kate's every step as she turned onto the Rue de Rome. Surely nobody but a madman would attempt an abduction in such a prominent place, but Gabriel had already established in his mind that Adrien was indeed insane.

She walked gracefully as always with a relaxed air about her as she headed toward the Boulevard Haussmann.

The huge Gare St. Lazare and the Terminus St. Lazare loomed closer, spewing dozens of people out on the boulevard and she eyed the busy scene with obvious satisfaction. Passing the two department stores, Le Printemps and Galeries Lafayette brought more crowds on the street. Gabriel was surprised she didn't take the shortcut of the Rue Auber, but she quite evidently enjoyed people-watching.

Gabriel and Raoul stayed a far distance back. Too close and Adrien would spot them and scurry away. Gabriel hoped to either catch him in the act and punish him on the spot or turn him over to the authorities. Preferably both. The cold anger he felt toward Adrien needed to be assuaged by personal action.

Their decision to keep far enough away to avoid being spotted turned out to be a mistake. Kate turned the corner, away from Haussmann, onto the Rue Scribe and to her hotel.

She'd gone halfway down the street when two figures jostled her, one on each side. Raoul and Gabe had barely turned the corner.

Kate's first reaction was astonishment. She'd been composing a lilting melody describing her love for Gabriel. She must have completely let down her Druid defenses. She'd felt no warning at all.

Now she found herself sandwiched between Adrien Castelet and Dorie Danton, each with a painful grip on the nearest arm. She couldn't help recoiling. The only two enemies she'd ever made and certainly few could be more threatening. She'd never faced such evil hostility as she felt coming from the two of them. She had no clear idea of how to deal with the menacing forces these two were projecting.

For just a moment the aura of wickedness about the two swamped her. Then she rallied. They were aberrations to mankind. She would not quail. She would not grant fear control of her mind in any manner whatsoever.

How could she best act to preserve the possibility of all the good she had yet to do in the world? And Gabriel? Could she let them conquer her and keep her from Gabriel? In one brief instant she realized anew how much Gabriel still ruled her heart and that she'd not given up hope of his acknowledging their love. Far from it. She'd fight with every asset at her command to conquer these two villains and save herself for the future and for Gabriel.

Suddenly she sensed her desired future could be there for them both. Eventually he would see reason and give in to the love she saw in his eyes. Now she must overcome whatever these evil two planned.

Jubilant at their victory, Dorie and Adrien never thought to scan the crowd three blocks back.

Dorie hissed her jubilation. "You'll pay now, you witch. Know that any spell you pass on me will come back to you doubled by my knife. A boil on my cheek gets paid with a gash on yours. If I'd had it with me before you wouldn't have gotten away scot-free."

Adrien gave Kate's arm a cruel twist. "She gets you after you pay your debt to me. I have a few little games in mind to play. You'll not enjoy them, *ma chere putain.*"

His demented laugh frightened Kate more than his words.

She couldn't imagine what their pitiless minds were planning, but malicious thoughts swarmed in both their auras. A deep purple black for them both. An unknown depth of pain would be inflicted on her unless she got her Druid brain working.

Two long blocks away, Gabriel and Raoul stopped and crouched for just a second as soon as they spotted Castelet and Dorie. The instant they saw the pair clutch Kate's arms they both started running at full pace. Adrien, unaware he'd been seen, shoved Kate toward the taxi waiting at the curb and opened the door and pushed her in. Dorie jumped in beside the driver, in spite of his spate of rapid French telling her she was not allowed to ride beside him.

The sight of the gleaming knife she held out along with a gutter-word silenced the cabbie and he drove off quickly when Adrien gave him directions.

Gabriel and Raoul stopped running. Gabriel began to quietly curse himself for his stupidity in not foreseeing what had just happened.

"Blazing fires of hell, I should be shot."

Raoul gathered his breath and let out a long whoosh. "You could not have foreseen this, Captain Gabe. It was neatly done. We expected him to accost her, but not with a planned way to escape safely. And not with a helper. The taxi driver obviously waited at the curb the whole time, paid to be there. We should have started running the second we saw Castelet."

Gabriel shook his head, deep in thought. "No," he answered, "we might not have reached her in time and this way he might not know we're on his trail. I think that gives us a slight advantage."

Raoul's features were heavy with chagrin, still locked in self-deprecating remorse.

"Your beautiful girl in the hands of a degenerate and a vindictive bitch."

Gabriel's stern features showed resolution as well as remorse.

"We did not anticipate their joining forces, although we should have. Together they are more than doubly dangerous. Each will egg the other on, I'm certain."

He turned and started to run toward the Boulevard Haussmann.

"We must get a taxi, Raoul. Immediately. I know Castelet's address. I think they'll head there. Dorie lives with her crippled mother and they'd not have the privacy they need at her place. We'll go to Castelet's lodgings. They need privacy to punish our girl."

They both headed off a run, but luck was not with them. Several trains had come in within a short space of time and the passengers were flooding the streets in front of the Gare St. Lazare. Someone grabbed every taxi as soon as it appeared and it took far too long for Gabriel and Raoul to secure a cab.

Gabriel jumped in, gave the address and then sat back to catch his breath.

"Pray god and Kate's goddess we're in time. I don't think either of those crazies is inclined to show mercy. We need all the help we can get."

Kate must have no idea they were coming. If she'd known she would have smoothed the way.

# Chapter Twelve

ꟾ

With one on each side of her, Dorie and Adrien bustled Kate to the door of Adrien's lodgings. Adrien rented a room from a widow who thought her good-looking lodger a gift from heaven. He'd spent time with her, sometimes even taking her to bed, often letting her cook for him. Knowing her enamored and vulnerable, he sometimes skipped paying the rent and chuckled when she never said a word.

As a game it amused him. Someday he'd let her know how repulsive he found her, but that day had not yet come. She still had her uses. He did not, however, want her to come home early from her job as a secretary. This so seldom happened he wasn't concerned. If she appeared early it would be too bad for her. The idea of another body left on the premises didn't particularly disturb him.

He'd never yet killed and the thought excited him. How fortunate those thugs he'd hired hadn't killed Jourdain after all. He wanted Jourdain to suffer when he found out Kate was dead. Then he'd personally stalk Jourdain. Stalk him until he found him alone and weaponless. Adrien had almost killed several times, but not quite. He'd reluctantly decided he couldn't let Kate live after raping and punishing her. Would watching Kate's last breath be as satisfactory as he thought? That would not happen for a long, slow while. Dorie had served her purpose. If she objected in any way she'd have to be disposed of also.

He didn't really expect her to object. Strange how cruelty spawned cruelty.

The delicious thought of actually killing pumped through his blood.

He fingered the gun in his pocket. Guns were easier to obtain than before the war, as soldiers often ran out of money and sold the deadly souvenirs they'd brought home. He didn't intend to shoot Kate though. Much too final a solution. The gun was strictly in case someone possessed the audacity to interrupt.

He could hardly wait to begin his little games.

Dorie could hardly wait either. She stood nearby, whispering to herself and holding her knife. Kate listened to the Druid voices in her head. Her mother and her grandmother were both giving her the same advice.

"You can make her drop the knife anytime you want, love. Just concentrate on the muscles in her hand. Make them weaken. Vivie had to do this once and she found it fairly simple."

Kate was willing to try. She wasn't a powerful Druid, but this didn't sound too hard. She didn't like to make Dorie even angrier though. Not at this point.

Just then they heard the door to the front hall open. They'd reached the top of the stairs and Adrien opened a door and shoved Dorie and Kate into his room.

"*Merde*! It must be my landlady," he hissed. "Don't do anything to make a noise, Dorie. I'll take care of her, but I don't want to kill her unless I have to. It would be an added complication right now. I'll get rid of her. Just don't make a sound. If you do I'll have to shoot her."

Kate thought furiously. If she shouted out, the only result would probably be the death of the innocent landlady. She stayed motionless through the long minutes, trying to pick up a word or two of the conversation. Dorie fingered her knife the whole time.

She also kept her ear pressed to the door, the desperation in her interest so pronounced it made Kate wonder. She'd followed Adrien's every move with adoring eyes. She must have transferred her extravagant affection from Gabriel to Adrien, which might complicate matters. She probably now hated Gabe as well as Kate.

Kate spent the blessed interlude in communication with her mother and grandmother. The three of them agreed on two principles. She should not let them hurt her physically and she could not allow them to frighten her unduly. Fright would diminish her Druid skills if she didn't control her reactions.

For Kate the delay proved a godsend. She held herself completely in control by the time Adrien came back, grinning like a demon from hell.

Adrien stalked into the room, his gaze fastened on Kate, but his words were for Dorie.

"She's gone to get ingredients for a particular supper I requested. The idiot thinks it to be a celebration of our engagement. I didn't want to take time to dispose of her body now. She'll be gone for quite a while. I asked for some special cheese from the Left Bank. We have nothing to worry about from her."

His depraved smirk frightened Kate more than his words.

"Now we can get down to business." His satisfaction was almost tangible, as he ran gloating eyes over Kate. Odors of desire and rank anticipation were streaming from him, his black aura streaking with red.

"I want her first," pleaded Dorie. "Then you can do what you want."

Kate could see no advantage to her whichever came after her first. They both meant only miserable and painful evil, unless she could stop them. The voices of her mother and grandmother were silent, waiting, as Kate was, to see what was needed.

Adrien's wicked side had taken over his unstable persona, obliterating any trace of decency he might have once shown. He backhanded Dorie across the side of her face.

"You'll get what I tell you you can get. I've waited a long time to have this bitch where I want her. You can wait a little longer."

His snarl and the blow effectively stopped Dorie, who withdrew a little.

"At least I can watch." It was half-question, half-protest and Adrien grinned his lop-sided, frightening grin.

"Of course. I enjoy an audience, especially with one as proud as this so-called princess. Having someone see me ravish her will make her humiliation truly enjoyable."

He shoved Kate on the bed and proceeded to unbutton his trousers.

"Make her undress first. I want her crushed with shame."

Dorie's gloating voice jarred Kate into the immediacy of averting the coming horror. She hadn't expected rape. For some reason that never occurred to her. How could Adrien, even though he now appeared to be deranged, have come to this? They'd all been fellow students at one time and the sadness of it almost overwhelmed her.

Adrien ignored Dorie's words and stepped out his trousers, revealing his swollen member, not long as much as thick and ready. As he started toward her, Kate suddenly knew what to do.

She giggled.

"Am I supposed to be impressed by that paltry tool? Gabriel's is much more exciting, believe me. You can't begin to satisfy me with such an inferior specimen. I've known the best, after all. Do what you want, it won't affect me in the slightest. I probably won't feel a thing."

She lay back pliantly on the bed, shrugging her shoulders and seemingly unconcerned.

Adrien hesitated and then loomed over her. Kate could discern the scent of rage as well as fear. She'd found his weak spot. His virility could not be disparaged.

"Go ahead. It won't matter."

She lay still on the bed and threw her head back against the pillow.

She'd never envisioned the raging hatred his florid face expressed. He reached out and almost knocked her off the bed with his fisted hand.

*"Putain! Imbecile putain!"*

His struggle to regain control contorted his face. Even as she watched his erection, which had temporarily receded, grew again into a thick and frightening stump. Mama V counseled her quietly.

"You can shrink his member easily, Kate. But be prepared. He'll be as furious as a man can get. Still, that's better than having him rape you. He'd be quite merciless, you know. Nothing at all like Gabriel."

Kate didn't have time to wonder how her grandmother knew about Gabriel. She began to concentrate her Druid mind. Even as Adrien climbed over her, his erection slowly vanished.

He shrieked in fury and hit her once again. Then he turned to Dorie.

"Do whatever you want with the witch. She's using her magic on me. Believe me, I've never shrunk before. She's a true daughter of Satan."

Dorie snickered even though she tried to control her mirth. His limp member flapping against his legs really was funny. At his words she forgot her amusement. Her own anger against her Druid opponent re-emerged, taking precedence in her gloating mind.

She advanced gleefully toward the bed, knife in hand.

"I think a big cross on each cheek, right where she placed the boils on me. Only she'll not be able to wish the scars away. I'll cut them deep enough to last forever."

Kate had immediately pushed herself to a sitting position when Adrian crawled off her. Now she eyed Dorie warily. With a prayer to the goddess of us all, she summoned the power of her mother and grandmother, channeled through her to the threatening hand holding the knife. She knew she was making both her tormentors angrier with every action she took, but she couldn't passively accept such torture. Her powers might not be as strong and developed as Vivie's, but she'd try.

To her surprise and delight, Dorie's fingers slowly pointed toward the floor and the knife dropped from her useless hand.

Kate watched and knew she'd ended up with an even worse situation, even though she'd taken the only path she could envision. She dreaded the next few minutes. She'd made both her foes furious. If they physically tackled her together she wasn't sure what she could do to beat them back. She didn't have the power to hold off two strong bodies.

Dorie shrieked as she looked with horror at her hands, her fingers hanging limply. Adrien, now struggling into his pants, looked up in surprise.

"What the hell? You're supposed to be carving her up by now. Lost your nerve?"

She shrieked again. "Look at my fingers, you idiot. I can't use them. The witch laid another spell on me."

Adrien's face grimaced into a mask, sending Kate's heart to her shoes. She didn't need her Druid powers to read his mind. There was no mistaking his wicked intent. He'd destroy her any way he could, with his bare hands if necessary and she couldn't stop him if he used his full physical strength. She could see the demonic desire to kill her in his frenzied eyes. Dorie, too, was mustering her mind in concentration of what torture she could commit.

Kate tried not to let her eyes focus on the knife Dorie had dropped. Even if she could pick it up in time, it would be little use against the brute strength of a half-crazed opponent. Still she had to try.

Adrien stalked slowly toward her. "I think I'll have a little sport the witch can't stop. A good thrashing with my cane, one until her bottom bleeds. I just wish I had a riding whip handy."

He dropped his gun and picked up a cane from the corner As he advanced toward her, glee and cruelty were written on every feature.

Kate stiffened. And prayed.

The door banged against the wall as Gabriel shoved his way in, his sword in his hand. Raoul was right behind him, unarmed, but massive and dangerous.

Kate did the only thing she could think to help as she took a giant step and kicked the knife against the wall. Raoul, saluting her with a grin, scooped it up and turned to secure Dorie. Gabe would want Adrien.

Kate's action had brought her closer to Adrien and he dropped the cane and grabbed her, holding her in front of him as a shield. She tried to wiggle free, but he grabbed her right arm behind her back and bent her thumb backward in a brutal grip. It was incredibly painful.

Kate moaned softly and Gabriel instantly stopped his advance.

Adrien chortled, knowing he had the upper hand of them all.

"I'm in charge now, maestro. If you make a move I'll sprain Kate's thumb. Probably break it. Have you ever wrestled? Probably not, since you wouldn't want to take a chance with your precious hands."

His mocking tone and hysterical chuckle froze Kate's heart, as well as those of the two men who'd come to rescue her.

"A thumb lock, if properly applied, can snap the bones of the thumb, maestro. While Kate's might mend well, it might not. She might never play again. Do you want to take the chance?"

Gabriel let his sword hand fall limply to his side.

"What do you want me to do? I'll do whatever you say if you'll let Kate go to my friend."

Adrien snorted. "I'm not stupid, maestro. Kate stays with me. Drop your sword and stand away from the door. Dorie goes first and then Kate and then me. I'll be applying the thumb lock the whole time, so don't try anything fancy."

As Gabriel hesitated Adrien tightened his hold and Kate made a small sound, part scream and part moan and Gabriel turned white. He dropped his weapon with a clatter, as Adrien laughed his insane laugh.

"Now you two stand to the side of the room while we leave."

Adrien looked around for his gun, just as Dorie made a dash for the door Raoul moved with a speed amazing for one of his size. He knocked Dorie into Kate, who was next in line, controlled by Adrien's thumb lock. The jar loosened his hold for just a few seconds and Kate jerked free and dropped to the floor. Raoul held Dorie easily with one hand and placed Dorie on top of Kate, then himself on top of Dorie, completely protecting Kate with both their bodies. He also reached out one long arm and scooped up the gun.

Adrien screeched with fury. He whirled around, trying to go back and pick up Gabriel's sword, but Gabe was there before him, wielding the weapon with a fencer's skill.

"Now. Stand still, Castelet. I haven't made up my mind what to do with you. Don't tempt me too much."

Adrien took a step forward and Gabriel quickly slashed his chest from top to bottom. As Adrien stood looking at his split shirt, with blood welling up from the slash, Gabriel flourished the deadly sword again. This time he deftly split Adrien's pants from the waistline to the crotch, laying his privates bare.

"If you don't want to be unmanned you'll do as I say."

Adrien, white as new snow, nodded his agreement.

"You're going to jail for a long term for kidnapping and assault, Castelet. It will be my pleasure to put you there."

Gabriel stood *en garde,* holding the sword ready to repulse any new move on Adrien's part.

Raoul hauled Dorie to her feet and reached out to help Kate to hers. As Dorie stood, cowed and with head hanging, Adrien looked wildly around the room. His one ally was helpless and Kate was safely in Raoul's hands. Adrien lunged at Gabriel, who instinctively extended his sword. Screaming with rage, his clearly crazed opponent ran at him and impaled himself on the steel blade. With a whimper, Adrien fell backwards on the floor beside the bed. Dorie ran to Adrien, kneeling beside him and keening in a shrill tone. Adrien appeared unconscious and certainly motionless.

Gabriel, now as white as Adrien, withdrew the weapon, wiping it clean with his handkerchief. Curiously the shocking wound was not bleeding much, although a thin red line kept trickling out.

"You've killed him," Dorie whispered, her eyes blank with shock.

Raoul came up, felt the pulse in Adrien's neck and shrugged.

"Perhaps," he said. He then went to Dorie and pulled her to her feet. "We'll call a doctor. In the meantime you're going to jail, mademoiselle. Same charges, I imagine, Captain?"

He took off his belt and bound her hands tightly, then turned to Gabriel.

"Now what, Captain?"

Gabe had folded Kate in his arms at the first possible second and she wept against his shoulder. Very quietly tears were flowing down her stricken face.

Gabe lifted his face from her hair. "I'm going to take Kate home with me. I'll get a police officer here immediately and also a doctor. Can you stay here and deal with the police? Tell them I'll come to the station house in the morning and will verify your report. I don't want them to talk to Kate tonight. The police chief knows me and I think probably knows of Miss Dellafield. The chief's son is a student of mine."

He cradled Kate in his arms for just a moment and then put her aside. Reaching into his inside coat pocket, he drew forth a wicked-looking knife, unlike anything Kate had ever seen. The intricately decorated handle curved in a beautiful arch and the long blade tapered to a slim point.

"What on earth is that?" she gasped.

"It's a jatagan," Gabe said. "I did a favor for a soldier from Montenegro once. It's one of their favorite weapons and he gifted me with this one. I've gotten fond of it."

Gabe took the jatagan and using an underhanded throw, tossed it to Raoul who neatly caught it by the curved hilt.

Raoul grinned. "Haven't seen this one for a while, Captain. I remember that particular incident, if you call saving the Montenegrin's life a favor. Guess you're still abiding by your rule a good soldier always carries a back-up weapon."

"Think you can manage?" asked Gabriel of his man.

Raoul, eyeing the now-thoroughly cowed Dorie and the prostrate Adrien, grinned.

"I'm pretty sure I can handle these two pitiful things. The police will step carefully when they know who these villains tried to kill. Take your lady home and see to her, Captain Gabe. She needs you more than I do."

Dorie was rocking herself and moaning, but Gabriel ignored her. Raoul would take charge.

Gabriel kept one arm tightly around Kate and they walked slowly out. Out of the room of killing. First he detoured to the kitchen and chipped some ice from the icebox, wrapping her thumb in the frozen chips, holding them in place with his handkerchief as a bandage and secured by his cravat. Even before Gabe phoned the police and a doctor he called for a cab and now it waited at the curb.

Gabe carefully handed Kate in and followed her. Putting his arms around her, he lowered his face to her shining hair and kept his silence as the cabbie threaded through the streets to his apartment. It was as if both were afraid to speak, or to make a move until the ride was over. Or was it they knew, knew in their hearts that once Gabriel kissed her they'd not be able to stop?

Then just as carefully, as if he were guarding a rare jewel, he walked her into his apartment.

Kate was conscious of nothing but the wonderful feeling of Gabe's arm around her, just for this moment secure and cherished by his love. She'd used up all her reserve strength in trying to save herself from rape and physical mutilation. She felt detached from her body, as if she were watching another Kate and another Gabe. This other Kate couldn't seem to stop shivering. She watched the other girl shaking like a bowl of gelatin and wondered why the silly thing didn't stop. She herself didn't feel any emotion other than pleasure in Gabe's loving concern.

Then Gibe kissed her forehead and suddenly she was alive again, knowing she was in Gabe's home. All her senses came to life as she looked around in wonder. Her thumb throbbed with pain but she willed herself to ignore it. Gabe evidently collected art as a hobby and modern art at that. Pictures, bold colorful pictures covered the walls. She thought one might be a Picasso. Art wasn't her main interest right now. Gabriel held full sway over every sensation in her now alert mind and body.

"I've must get you warm," Gabe said. "Let me run upstairs and get my bathrobe. Can you let me go of me for just a minute, Kate?"

She clutched him to her and shook her head. "No, no. Don't leave me alone, Gabe. "

He hesitated only a moment and then swept her up in his arms, carefully sheltering her injured hand as he carried her up the stairs.

"Did the ice help your hand, my dear? Should I get more?"

"Not really. I'm dripping cold water all over you as it is."

They'd reached the top of the stairs as she tried to speak to him, although her voice quavered. Her chattering teeth betrayed the shock still ruling her system and he looked at her with such concern she stretched her face up and kissed him in consolation.

Her action set a flame to a well-dried haystack.

He moved quickly, holding her face closely in his hands as he lowered his lips to hers.

Kate was lost in the sensations washing over her like waves of a raging sea. He wrapped his arms around her and held her as tightly as if she were his one hope of heaven. There was no doubt in her mind he loved her and she gladly gave herself to his devastating kisses. He could not kiss her with such marvelous passion if he thought of her only as a woman to be conquered and then tossed aside.

She leaned into his body, threw the cloths off her right hand and ran the fingers of her left through his hair.

"Please, Gabe. Please take me to your bed. I need you. I need you so much."

If only she hadn't said those last few words Gabe might have resisted. Or at least tried. He knew she did indeed need him, needed his body to erase all memory except for his heartfelt passion. Her body, pressed against his, still shivered even as she tried to get closer. If he showed her his love and his desire, it might help erase the terror of a degenerate scoundrel trying to force her to his will. He would not have her scarred by the memory of what had almost happened to her. He would not have nightmares haunting her as his haunted him.

Not if he could help it.

Did he really have no choice, or was he simply unable to resist the thought of holding Kate in his arms just once more?

It didn't matter. She wanted and needed him.

There could be no more powerful incentive for a man deeply in love to persuade him to give his woman pleasure.

# Chapter Thirteen

ﷺ

"Will you help me get my clothes off, Gabe?"

Kate was still shivering, not as much as before, but her hands were shaking. Her body no longer felt cold, but flushed with anticipation.

With a groan he sat her on the edge of his bed and with trembling yet careful hands began to undress her. It did not take him long to remove her outer garments and she was soon down to a shift clinging to her perfect body. He wasn't surprised she wore no corset. Her figure needed no help at all.

He knelt beside her, lifting the soft cloth of her shift over her head. He took his time, kissing and caressing her breasts and finally, her flat stomach.

Gabe carefully lowered her to the bed. He followed her down, lying beside her as he wrapped his arms around her and held her to him.

"I'm so afraid of hurting your hand, love. I want you as badly as any man has ever wanted a woman, but I'll not injure you further."

"Maybe I should wrap my hand up a little so I won't be tempted to use it? Otherwise I'll probably not be able to resist caressing your gorgeous body."

Kate smiled as she spoke. She was utterly appalled to see Gabe's face freeze into a caricature of his former loving expression.

"My body is anything but gorgeous, Kate," he ground out between his clenched teeth. "You'll never say so again if I let you see my scars. My loving you is probably not a good idea. My desire for you overwhelmed me for just a moment. I forgot what I am."

He sat on the side of the bed and started to rise, but Kate pulled at him with her good hand.

"Please, Gabe. Don't turn me away now."

Gabriel sat motionless, fighting his demons and knowing he was losing. Kate would never forgive him if he walked away from her now. She could never understand and would feel utterly rejected. He'd give her invisible scars to rival his. He simply could not do that to the girl he loved, the one who had just asked for his love, or at least his physical reassurance.

He unfolded his long body slowly, keeping his eyes fastened on hers as he rose. His gaze pierced her, as if he did not intend to miss a nuance of her response.

"I must tell you something before I go further. I was badly scarred during the war. I'm a hideous sight. No one except Raoul has ever seen what I'm about to show you. You'll be disgusted beyond measure, but I can't turn you away thinking I don't want you. Nothing could be further from the truth. But you will not want me after you see my ugly wounds."

Her enormous eyes fastened on his. Somehow she knew she dared not show a sign of pity. Had he then planned to make love to her partially clothed, as he'd done last time? Suddenly many times when he'd turned away from her became more clear.

"You will always be gorgeous to me," she said.

Gabriel's eyebrows raised in obvious disbelief as looked at her with despair in his cobalt eyes. Then he turned his back on her and proceeded to undress. His shirt came first and then his pants. Next he tackled his undergarments and shed them on the floor. Kate propped herself against the pillows and said not a word.

Sitting on the bed, his back to her, he took off his shoes and socks. She could hardly resist stroking his strong back. Or kissing the dimples below his waistline and then his muscled buttocks. She was mesmerized by the splendid strength of his masculine body.

Then he stood and slowly turned toward her. Below his waist he was a mass .of scars and welts, some red, some with the black marks of powder burns. It was as ugly a sight as he'd said. Welt seemed piled upon puckered welt. No wonder he'd not wanted to expose himself to the pity she knew instinctively she dare not show.

The welts came half-way down his muscled thighs. Then they stopped and the perfect body of Gabriel Jourdain again took over.

Her eyes filled at the thought of what he must have suffered. Obviously more than one welt had required stitches. Many stitches.

He stood as rigid as a statue, his eyes intent on her face.

Kate was silent for a long moment. She had no doubt at all what ever she said would determine their future relationship. Pray to the goddess she would choose the right words.

"Well," she said slowly. "That's truly impressive."

He started to turn away, despair on his handsome face. Her Druid sensitivity rushed to help, for she suddenly knew exactly what to say and do. She scooted toward him and patted his masculine member, just a few moments ago rampant with desire and now only partially erect.

She rubbed and caressed him, smiling up at him as his erection began to rapidly lengthen again.

"Aren't you lucky?" she asked. "If you'd had an erection like this when the shrapnel came through it might have shot right through this most interesting part of your body. Or even shot it off. I would count that a dreadful shame. "

She touched him again. "I'm so glad we've still got this impressive member of your body. I worship it, you know."

Gabe stared at her. He'd considered shock, even revulsion and of course pity, the ultimate insult. Never had he thought of a dispassionate comment on his good luck, for heaven's sake. And for such a reason.

She kept up her gentle stroking and he looked down to see himself as eager to make love as his wonderful Kate appeared to be. He was quite magnificently erect.

"Shall we go back to what we were about to do?" Kate leaned over and kissed his impressive arousal. "I find this much more interesting than a few scars."

He pushed her flat on the bed and stood over her, his eyes glowing with love and relief.

"Kate, Kate," he whispered. "Thank you, my dear one. Thank you."

His passionate hunger scented the room, an aroma of sexual desire mixed with his spicy aftershave. She gasped as she realized how much power she had over him and how much his desire matched, or even surpassed hers.

He grabbed his shirt and tried to carefully wrap it around her hand, but she shook her head.

"No, Gabe, I've changed my mind. I want my hands free to caress you. My thumb is a little sore, but I don't have to use it. I want to feel as much of you as I can. I love your powerful body."

"Even my welts and scars?" His voice was no longer bitter, but merely cautiously curious and Kate gave an inward sigh of relief.

"Of course your welts and scars. They are a part of you and reflect your honor in war and your suffering. The same way as does your beautiful hair. To me every part of you is precious."

He knelt on the bed quickly and then came over her. For a moment she felt his full weight, a delightful crushing emphasizing the strength she knew he'd never use against her. Then he raised himself on his elbows and smiled down at her.

"I'm a large man, I know, but I'll treat you as gently as I possibly can. I want this experience to be good for you, far better than the last time when I so foolishly rushed."

He gave her no time to protest his profession of guilt, but lowered his lips to hers and claimed them with a new intensity, a commitment his love ran deep and real. He rolled her to one side gently, carefully putting her wounded hand between their bodies. Then he began to worship her with his kisses and his clever, clever hands.

It seemed to Kate he touched her everywhere at once. He knew instinctively just where to put a little more pressure to possibly drive her mad. Not only his hands, but his lips and his tongue attacked her every sensibility.

She'd never dreamed of the sensations racing through her body. Up to now she'd been concentrating on getting Gabriel to acknowledge fully the powerful attraction between them. Now she'd achieved her objective, she was lost in a delicious swamp of sensation.

Lost to the thrill of being overwhelmed by Gabe and every appetizing particle of his luscious body. She could feel him hovering over her and then his hips lowering. Thoroughly aroused by his caresses, she surged her body against his. His quick intake of breath told her he welcomed her advance as he responded with ardor.

She could feel his male power, a power well able to demand and take what he wanted. She accepted his supremacy in this one area and gladly surrendered to the delight of his potency.

His groan rumbled deep in his chest as he caught her lower lip with his teeth, nipping her gently and then settling into a melting kiss. She involuntarily spread her legs a little and his hand quickly found her inner thigh, his fingers caressing her as they moved slowly upward. He took his time exploring her soft skin, caressing it with his lips as if he were tasting her essence.

Still he didn't turn into a conqueror she sensed he could be. He lured her with his caresses so she wanted him to beg him to continue. And perhaps even go faster. He paced his aggression to her surrender, so she never felt overwhelmed. Still there was no doubt in her mind he controlled every move. She thrilled to wonder what he'd next reveal to her.

His fingers moved upward until they settled on the little nubbin she'd hoped he'd find again and began a circular motion with his thumb on the core of her desire. She involuntarily tried to catch his hand, but he refused her silent request. Sensations started to spiral. She soon clutched him, her sore hand forgotten, as she wriggled to urge him to keep on with the sweet torture.

She started when he inserted a finger in her, but he kissed her into acceptance. When he inserted a second finger and used them to spread her a little, she began to writhe on the bed. He flexed his fingers, bending them and touching her inner passage so intimately she gave a small shriek. She ran her fingers through his lovely grey hair, to her the wonderful essence of Gabriel. His own special hallmark. His fingers opened her even more, the contact driving her wild.

"You feel so good to me. I can't tell you how I've longed for this moment." Gabriel's voice was low and husky, as he proceeded in his deliberate design to render her limp to his conquest.

She reached up and kissed his chest as he shuddered against her lips.

"I don't know what comes next, Gabriel. I only know I want it."

He placed his large member between her legs and kissing her breasts. silently urged her to open for him. She seemed to know instinctively what to do and she wrapped her legs around his waist. He still did not enter her, but kept caressing her with his thumb until she almost screamed again.

He was definitely trying to drive her insane.

"Gabriel, please," she gasped.

"Will you trust me, Kate? Will you let go when I ask you?"

"Anything, Gabe. Just do something."

He put his member warmly just inside her opening and then waited until she accepted his intrusion in her body.

"I'm not sure this is going to work," she gasped. He felt so large as to be impossible.

"It will , darling. Relax and trust me."

She writhed against him, but he held her hips still and then finally and slowly entered her fully. Giving her body a moment to adjust to him, he kissed her hair and then her lips. Then he surged forward.

She gave a small scream as she felt him immersed to the hilt. This was far different from the other time, as he immediately set up a rhythmic thrusting that had her clutching him wildly. She felt about to explode and although she tried to keep to the rhythm he'd set, she soon lost all consciousness of trying to please and simply felt the rapture he was giving her. She'd had no idea there was such pleasure available in this world.

Just when she thought she could stand no more of the wonderful suspense he'd induced, he gasped. "Let go, darling. Trust me and let go."

He gave one last thrust and her world flew apart into little starry pieces. Sparkling and glittering. Kate could see them floating in the air around her and felt light, fairy touches as she glided down to earth.

Gabe had fallen on his back beside her, breathing heavily. Still one hand crept over to caress her face and smooth back her hair.

"Dear goddess of us all," Kate breathed. "How miraculous."

Gabe gave her a reverent kiss and made a satisfied sound.

"It was all of that, Kate. I cannot thank you enough. Do you have any idea of the pleasure you gave me?"

"I think so, maestro," she smiled. "You orchestrated the measure very well."

He laughed and kissed her forehead. Suddenly he looked stricken. And he grabbed her hand.

"Your thumb. How is your poor thumb?"

She wiggled it a moment and then smiled. "Probably better for all the exercise. You truly are irresistible, you know. You're so big and strong and you make me feel protected and amorous at the same time. It's a good feeling for an independent girl like me. And I never thought I'd be so susceptible to the power of any male. You have me completely at your command."

He visibly preened and then lay back against the pillows.

"I suppose I should take you home. I'd love to keep you here all night and ravish your lovely body 'til dawn."

He leered at her and she laughed. She adjusted her body higher on her pillows.

"I like this part, too. This is so nice, lying here and talking as lovers. I suppose I should go home. I know you phoned my grandparents, but they'll still worry. Or maybe not. Mama V will be able to sense I'm fine. "

Gabriel shot her a dismayed look. "I keep forgetting your Druid powers. Tell me truly, Kate, have you ever used them on me?"

Kate shook her head. "No." She slowed her answer to be completely truthful. "I've been tempted to when I really wanted to know what you were thinking. But I knew unless you confided in me of your free will it would not profit me to probe your mind. The answer is 'no'. Nor will I unless you're in danger. Although I did send a warning to you just before I dropped to the floor tonight."

"And I knew exactly what you were planning. How amazing."

Kate shuddered as the thought of what might have been came over her and she buried her face in Gabe's shoulder. He felt so good and his skin smelled of soap and something spicy and his own musky-masculine-Gabriel scent. He put one big hand around her head and turned her face up to him for a long, drugging kiss.

"Castelet is gone from your life, sweetheart. You need never fear him again. If he recovers he'll either go to jail or a madhouse. I'll never let him near you."

She slung to him for a moment and then lay back with a smile.

"I love you, Gabe. You're everything in the world I want. I hope all our children look exactly like you. I could ask for nothing more."

To her astonishment Gabe made no answer at all. After a long pulsing moment he pushed her head from his shoulder, slipped out of her arms and to his feet.

"It's more than time for me to take you home. Get dressed, Kate. I'll be waiting for you downstairs."

Utterly dismayed, she watched as he almost threw on his clothes and stalked out of the room.

"Gabe?" she questioned.

"I'd appreciate it if you hurry, Kate."

His voice had been as cold as the ice he'd once gotten for her hand. And his face was just as frozen.

What in blazing fires had she said?

Had he resented her assuming they would marry? She could think of nothing else to account for his astonishing behavior. He'd given himself to her in the way she'd always dreamed he might and she'd been sure he felt great love for her. Could she be wrong? Somehow she didn't think it possible to fake the overwhelming emotion he'd shown.

Or was marriage to her such an unthinkable idea?

If taking her as his wife so disturbed him, then she'd lost her heart to a man who was either a deceiver or a fool.

Neither answer seemed possible to her.

That simply was not her Gabriel.

# Chapter Fourteen

ꟷ

Gabriel phoned for a taxi and they waited in a painful silence for its arrival. At one point Gabe started to say something and then turned and stalked out of the hall. Kate, even though wrapped in misery, began to suspect Gabe felt even more distressed than she did.

What was going on in the blasted man's mind? Her Druid instincts urged her to probe just a little, but she beat back the suggestion once again. She didn't want Gabe if she had to resort to forcing a confidence he determined to keep from her and that is what invading his mind really meant. The ride to her hotel seemed endless, as they each took a corner and kept their silence.

Gabe gravely handed her out of the taxi and took her arm as he escorted her through the hotel lobby and to the apartment where the Randalls waited.

Mama V immediately folded Kate in her arms and then set her from her for a searching look.

"Are you truly all right, love?"

Kate knew better than to try to hide her feelings from her Druid grandmother. She tried for a smile, which wobbled a little and then held out her hand.

"I think my thumb needs a little attention. Not much, but it hurts. And my cheek hurts just a little where that mongrel hit me. If you'll bring me an ointment, I think I'd like to go right to bed."

Her grandmother's look of alarm caused her to hastily add, "My thumb's just sprained, Mama V and Gabriel can tell Papa Devon all about the horrible evening that degenerate Adrien forced upon us. I'll fill you in too. Gabriel was wonderful and saved me from a horror I still can't comprehend. Adrien was really and truly evil and Gabe stopped him. Just like a hero should."

She started to walk away. "Come, I'll tell you what happened."

Gabe watched them leave the room, relieved and desolated at the same time. He'd experienced the most wonderful evening of his life, as well as the most devastating. Kate would want nothing to do with him now, nor should she.

He turned off his sorrow and proceeded to give Devon Randall an expurgated account of the evening's events. He mentioned the police would be there in the morning to question Kate and told them he'd go now to the station and try to answer as many of their questions as he could. There should be little need for Kate to do anything but verify the facts. Whether Castelet lived or died should make little difference to the law, since he was clearly the aggressor.

Naturally he made no mention of his passionate encounter with Mama V's granddaughter at his own apartment. He wondered briefly how much Kate would tell her grandmother. Very little, he guessed. Their lovemaking was too exceptional to be shared. He thought she'd gloss over the miracle of their passion, if she mentioned it at all.

Perhaps not, though. And if Kate did confide in her grandmother, it might be for the best. Maybe Mama V would be able to put her on the path of starting a new life without the odious Gabriel Jourdain.

Before he could make his escape, a good-looking man entered the room. Just a few years younger than himself, Gabriel estimated. A taller and younger replica of the impressive Devon Randall. Golden brown curls were clipped closely to his head, giving him a hint of an angelic look. Gabe had little doubt this was Devon's son Jamie who Kate often mentioned.

Jamie strode up to him and held out his hand.

"Monsieur Jourdain, I'm glad to meet you. Your exploits in the war are well-known. I am honored to shake your hand, sir."

Gabe colored as he took Jamie's hand.

"My experiences in the war have been exaggerated, I assure you. Are you in Paris, for long, M. Randall?"

Jamie laughed. "Not as long as I'd like. I'm waiting to see where I'll be deployed as a representative of her Majesty's medical corps. I decided I wanted to see a little of the world before I settled down to a practice. I'm hoping for Calcutta."

Gabe looked at the impressive young man with approval.

"You'll do well in whatever capacity you serve, I'm sure. I'm not surprised you chose medicine. I think the women in your family are all exceptional healers. Tell me, does Kate know you're here?"

Jamie shook his head. "My parents told me she was in some kind of trouble but you were taking care of it. They advised me to wait until morning until she had a little rest. Kate and her twin sister Vivie have brightened my life from the day they were born. I love them both dearly."

*Just the faintest warning in his last statement? Treat Kate well, or else?*

Gabe drew himself up to his impressive height. The light from the chandelier cast silver highlights on his thick grey hair. His face, planed and honed by battle and by suffering, clearly displayed his integrity and now, just a little of his battle with his feelings. To anyone with perception, he was an unhappy man.

"I hold Kate in the highest esteem," he said with the dignity so much a part of him. "I must say good night. I'm pleased to have met you, M. Randall. I think, however, I'd better check in at the police station before the gendarmes come after me."

He shook hands with both men, his grip firm and left.

Devon and Jamie Randall looked at each other.

"He's a most impressive man," Jamie said. "Whatever the trouble is between him and Kate, I'm sure it's nothing dishonorable. I hope they can work it out. He'd be a good addition to our rather exceptional family."

"You're right," said his father, laughing at his son's phrasing. "We can do little to help them, however and I treasure this time with you. Come have a brandy with me, Jamie."

* * * * *

Kate awoke the next morning, dazed and at first not realizing where she was. Then she remembered Mama V giving her herbal tea to help her sleep. She yawned and stretched. Evidently her grandmother gave her a more powerful potion than usual, as at first she couldn't think. Her mind was just a jumble.

Then it all came clear to her, as she sat up in bed and moaned. The terrible fate Adrien had planned for her. Dorie standing by with a knife, with sick gloating in her eyes. Gabe and Raoul bursting in and saving her. And finally, the wonderful experience of Gabriel making love to her.

And yet once again he'd turned away from her. Directly after making marvelous love, with what she would swear was his deepest sincerity. True, she was inexperienced, but still she didn't think she could mistake his feelings to this extent. How could he turn her aside yet again?

What on earth motivated Gabriel to reject what he clearly craved?

Were they then to go back to the barren relationship of maestro and student?

She wouldn't allow that. And yet what could she do? Break her own rules and her integrity in honoring others and probe his mind?

She pulled the covers closely around her shoulders and sat thinking. She knew Gabe was concealing a secret he felt so important it would wreck their love. She had few clues. She thought it had something to do with a child. Did he have an illegitimate child and feared she'd hold it against him? Did he not like children at all and didn't want to take the chance of having one? Neither reason sounded at all consistent with the Gabriel she loved.

She finally decided she would deal with it in her own way. She would not give up her steadfast beliefs and probe his mind without his permission. Nor did she intend to give him up. She would prove to him somehow, someway, her love would encompass and forgive what ever worried him so.

Now all she had to do was figure out a course of action.

Before she could settle anything in her mind, a knock sounded on her door and some one softly called her name. She knew the voice was familiar, although she didn't at first guess who it could be.

"Give me two minutes," she said, stepping out of bed and reaching for her house coat.

"Not one second more," the voice called, a little louder and Kate recognized him.

She ran to the door and threw it open, throwing herself into Jamie's arms. She'd always adored Devon's son by his first marriage, as had the whole family. Raised by Mama V since he was six, the whole clan counted him a true Dellafield.

She stepped back a little in his arms, admiring the handsome face so like his father's. He was stocky like Devon Randall, but taller. He didn't have a superfluous ounce on his body. Just as his body proclaimed his strength, his smiling face showed the sunny disposition making everyone love him on sight.

"You look wonderful, Jamie. When do we hear about a lucky girl that's caught your fickle interest? It's high time you married."

Jamie kissed her nose and chuckled.

"You women. You sound just like Mama V. Actually, until I meet someone as perfect as you Druid females I'm probably stuck in a bachelor rut. A comfortable bachelor rut."

He wiggled his eyebrows at her.

Kate laughed, took his hand and led him to a chaise in her room.

"Now. Tell me all. What are you doing here?"

His infectious grin grew wider. "I'm on my way to someplace with the British medical corps. I don't have a definite assignment yet so I thought I'd come here first and go back to Vivie's wedding with you. When I find out where I'm going, I think I'll try these new and audacious airplanes and see if I can fly part of the way. It will probably be India or Africa."

"Really, Jamie. Flying? Aren't you brave! How do you plan to go?"

"Probably I'll leave right after the wedding and fly back to Paris. Flights between London and Paris are established. Then I'll hire a private pilot as far as Rome. Some planes carrying commerce will take a few passengers. Then maybe conventional transportation. I'm working on the whole thing."

"So you think there's a future in air travel?"

"Of course. If Winston Churchill would just change his mind and give government support to private companies it would happen more quickly. But it will happen. Wait and see."

"Jamie, what fun. And how perfectly wonderful to have you at the wedding. Vivie will be so very pleased."

His expression grew more serious. "You know how much you twins mean to me. I helped you grow up and I want to be there when you're both married. You're truly my little sisters."

Kate looked down at her hands and then pulled at her left ear. Jamie stifled a grin. He knew that gesture well. His Kate was upset and trying not to show it.

"I don't think my wedding will be for a while."

Jamie did grin at that. Better not tell her he'd met Jourdain and admired him. The man had been consumed with worry for Kate.

"I'll let you get dressed. You had a terrible night last night and should be eating a big breakfast. Come join me, love, as soon as you can."

Jamie strolled out and Kate's smile vanished.

She wouldn't spoil this precious time with Jamie by telling him her problems, even though right now they seemed insurmountable. She'd put Gabriel out of her mind as much as she could and hope some solution would work its way through the foggy tissue of her distraught mind.

When she went downstairs she found Mama V waiting for her, her expression worried. Kate was so used to a smiling grandmother alarm bells immediately sounded.

"Mama V. What is it? Is it Gabe?"

She flushed as soon as she'd spoken, knowing her words would only confirm her grandmother's suspicion of how much Gabe meant to her.

"No, not directly, Kate. But an impressive policeman is here to speak to you. Gabriel told us last night one would come take your statement this morning, but I think he's here on a related matter. Do come in the parlor. I'll ring for coffee and rolls for all of us."

Kate hurried, stopping when she saw a middle-aged man instead of a young recruit as she'd expected. This man obviously was someone in authority. His very presence projected a confidence in his own ability as well as his senior standing.

He gravely rose to his feet when he saw Kate.

"I assume you're Mlle. Dellafield?"

Kate nodded as he continued.

"I am Inspecteur Général Marfont."

Kate's eyes widened. Inspecteur Général was a senior rank. This must indeed be important.

"Please sit down, Mlle. Dellafield. Matters took a serious twist during the night. In the first place, Adrien Castelet died without ever regaining consciousness."

Kate lowered her eyes for a moment and then raised them to look directly at the Inspecteur.

"I cannot pretend grief. He had lost his way and there was no path back for him."

The Inspecteur nodded again, as his eyes sharpened.

"Not the statement of a hysterical young lady," he said in a non-committal tone.

Kate kept her gaze fixed on him. "No, I am not hysterical. I am most interested in what this means to M. Jourdain, however."

"M. Jourdain is esteemed through all of France. He has given his sworn testimony and every indication verifies he speaks truthfully. He might have done better to let us talk to you last night, I think, but we appreciated his chivalry at the time."

Kate blushed. She thought probably she was red from her toes to the top of her head. If the police knew of their time together after the attack on her, what would they think? Probably, being French, they'd already assumed she'd spent the night in her champion's arms. What else?

She felt even hotter but said nothing more.

"And Dorie?" Kate asked. She hoped the red had left her cheeks, although she feared not. Still, this gentleman seemed sympathetic.

The Inspecteur had not shifted his gaze from her and now he gave a little nod.

"This is what we've come about. Mlle. Danton was taken to a hospital last night and a guard posted outside her room. She managed to escape."

Kate's gasp filled the room. "How can that be?"

Inspecteur Marfont looked even more grim. "She has the cleverness of a mad woman. We think now she heard the police talking outside her room. She heard Castelet had died. She waited a while, then pretended to be choking. When a nurse came to help she overpowered her, bound her with the sheets and exchanged clothing. The guard had been ordered not to leave his post, but that doesn't exclude his negligence. He claims he heard nothing after the pretended choking stopped. He let Mlle. Danton walk right past him in the nurse's uniform."

He shook his shaggy head as if he couldn't believe his own words.

"Dear goddess of us all," Kate murmured.

She put out her hand and Mama V took it, soothing it with her capable healer's fingers.

The Inspecteur looked his most severe as he stated. "She is determined to revenge herself on you, Mlle. Dellafield. She made it plain even when we interviewed her before sending her to a hospital. She will stop at nothing now M. Castelet is dead. She blames you for everything gone wrong in her life. Your 'witching powers must be halted', according to her."

Kate thought the miserable boils and how they'd magnified themselves ten-fold in Dorie's disturbed mind. Would she do it over again? Would she wish such an affliction on Dorie if she were faced with the same circumstances as her destroyed musical score? With a sigh, Kate realized she probably would. She'd not suspected Dorie was unbalanced. The girl herself was the outrageous one, not the minor retribution she'd brought on herself.

The Inspecteur seemed to know what she was thinking.

"Do not fret yourself, Mlle. Dellafield. Minds like hers give out sooner rather than later. She has a great deal of evil in her."

Jamie came to Kate and put a brotherly arm around her.

"I take it Miss Dellafield is in danger until this crazy woman is caught. A great many people, myself included, revere Miss Dellafield. How can we best protect her?"

The Inspecteur spoke up instantly.

"Do not let her alone any time at all, unless she is locked in her bedchamber. This *folle* will come after her, without a doubt. Vengeance is why she set herself to escape. She'd evidently tied her emotions into Castelet and when she found he was dead she seems to have lost all reason. Be very careful, all of you, until we again secure Miss Danton. She is dangerous in the extreme."

Kate sat back in her chair, her face white. How could she stand being cooped up night and day? What if they never caught Dorie and she remained out there hovering as a black mass of danger, threatening to smother the life out of her if she took a step toward the fresh air of freedom?

*Insupportable.* She couldn't live in such a furtive manner. All her future happiness depended upon her seeing Gabriel and somehow persuading him to confide why he still held himself aloof. Thoughts of their night together never left her mind. No two people could have shared more bliss than she and Gabe. Surely if she could talk to him she could get him to bare his secrets and then all would be well between them. Her goal was more important than cowardice.

She suddenly stood.

"I won't do it. I'll not live cowering in terror. I intend to live a normal life."

Jamie didn't seem surprised.

"We'll guard her as best we can, Inspecteur. Perhaps you could detail a man to help us?"

Kate looked about to explode and Mama V came closer and kissed her granddaughter's forehead.

"You'll never find the happiness you seek if you're not alive, my love. Be reasonable."

"I am not exaggerating the danger, Mam'selle," said the Inspecteur.

Kate's sigh was resigned. "I'll not go out alone. But I'll not stay cooped up, either."

Inspecteur Marfont nodded his head in resignation. "I'll have a man detailed to attending you as soon as I can get one here. In the meantime, I myself will stay with you. I'm very serious about this, Mlle. Dellafield. I do not want to disappoint one of France's most esteemed men. And I would wager an uninformed guess M. Jourdain thinks as highly of you as his country does of him."

This time Kate took the statement in her stride. In fact, she rejoiced to hear the Inspecteur speak so warmly of Gabe's feeling for her. The two men must have spent a lot of time together while Gabriel gave his testimony. She'd known Gabe would guard her but not that he would expose his feelings in any degree.

She turned to Jamie.

"Can we take just a little walk? I haven't left the hotel today and I need some fresh air. Can we just go around the block?"

Jamie turned to the Inspecteur.

"Is this a big danger, sir?"

The Inspecteur shook his head. "I'd rather you not. Mlle. Danton has no weapon that we know of, but she might have found one. And we have no idea where she is."

Kate snapped back.

"And the longer we wait the more chance she has of finding a weapon. Give me five minutes of fresh air and I'll go to my room for the rest of the day. I'm in the middle of a composition I'm anxious to complete. I just *have* to blow the cobwebs out of my musty brain."

"I know," said Jamie. "Let's race each other around the block. We'll get your brain pumping as well as your blood."

Kate grinned with delight. "Fantastic. Let's go, Jamie."

She headed out of the suite, racing toward the imposing lobby and then out the large double doors of the hotel. Jamie, looking surprised but also pleased, sprinted after her.

She flew out the door in a flash of her green skirt. Jamie was right behind her.

Mama V and the Inspecteur were close behind them both.

# Chapter Fifteen

ഇ

Just as Kate burst from the entrance to the Grand Hotel, Gabriel rounded the corner. He watched her come out the door and pause to look back and then he saw Jamie catching up to her. Neither one of them noticed Dorie, dressed in her stolen nurse's uniform, standing off to one side of the impressive entrance and talking to a bellboy.

The bellboy could have no idea of the true situation, as he answered her with grave courtesy. His voice carried clearly to Gabe as he came toward the hotel on the run.

"No, I haven't seen Mlle. Dellafield today. She's not come out of the hotel. Why don't you ask inside?"

It seemed to Gabe everything was happening in slow motion, although his brain knew it was really incredibly fast. He filled his lungs to shout a warning.

Kate stopped to look for Jamie, who was just coming through the door. Dorie turned and moved with an amazing speed, charging at Kate and slashing at Kate's face with a large broken piece of a china plate. Just before she struck, Gabe's roar alerted Kate and she stepped slightly aside to try to spot where he was. The sharp broken fragment caught her on her face, a little to the side of one eye. Without Gabe's shouted warning she might easily have lost the sight in that eye.

She stood motionless, not feeling the cut yet at all, but putting up one hand to touch the gash in her face.

Jamie reached Kate almost immediately and throwing his arms around her, put his body between hers and Dorie.

Dorie looked at the damage she'd done. Kate's face was slashed from the edge of one eye to the lobe of her ear. Blood poured from the cut as she now threw both her hands up to assess the damage.

Dorie screeched. "I meant to blind you, you Druid bitch. If you're not I'll be back and get you yet."

Gabe saw her start to run, but he was too far away to stop her.

The Inspecteur's voice rang out. "Stop, Dorie Danton, or I'll fire."

Dorie gave a shrieking, insane laugh and kept on running.

A single shot rang out.

The Inspecteur's aim was accurate and Dorie stumbled to the ground.

Then for Gabe everything seemed to relapse into normal seconds and minutes. The Inspecteur and Gabriel reached Dorie's body at the same time. As the Inspecteur knelt over her he felt the pulse in her neck.

"She's dead, Jourdain. I think I meant her to be. She was too dangerous alive."

Gabriel merely nodded and turned back to where Jamie held Kate while he futilely mopped at the stream of blood. Gabe tore his shirt off as he ran and when he reached Kate he handed the cloth to Mama V, who'd also gotten to the pair. He stood by, the dread in his heart showing plainly in his eyes, as Mama V wiped away the blood and then pressed the cloth against the long cut to try to staunch the flow.

"Let's get her inside and up to my room," she said. "This needs immediate attention."

Kate grabbed her grandmother's hand, now holding the material from Gabe's shirt tight against the cut, trying to staunch the flow.

"My fault," she whispered. "I'm so sorry, Mama V."

Mama V kissed Kate's forehead. "At least it's over. It could have been much worse. Will one of you gentleman carry her up to my room?"

Gabe reached over to take Kate from Jamie's arms, but Jamie glared at him and shook his head. Jamie swung her up and started inside the hotel. Guests and hotel personnel were gathered round the lobby in chattering groups, staring and elbowing each other to get closer to the excitement. They fell back as Jamie advanced. Jamie held Kate close to his chest. Gabe's shirt, bound around Kate's face, was soaked through with blood, as was Jamie's sleeve. Drops were falling on the lobby floor, as the small party advanced to the elevator.

Mama V walked beside her son and Gabe followed, feeling utterly useless as well as worried to the point of illness. His beautiful Kate, slashed by a demon with a miserable piece of china. He'd detested the sight and metallic smell of blood since the war, but that it was Kate's blood he saw and smelled nearly sent him to his knees.

He was not sorry Dorie was dead. He didn't regret his killing Adrien. He'd seen too many truly good men die in battle to regret the deaths of those two. He wished he'd taken the opportunity t o kill them both sooner.

Nothing existed but Kate's well-being. He knew well she might be scarred as the result of Dorie's vicious attack. The possibility mattered not the slightest. It was Kate, Kate the holder of his heart, who was of major concern. Not her outward appearance.

The little group made their way to Mama V's suite and Jamie, holding Kate gently in his arms, carried her in. The blood dripped slowly from Jamie's sleeve, but none of the ones who loved Kate noticed. Jamie tenderly carried her in and laid her on Mama V's bed.

Gabe immediately went to her bedside as Jamie stepped back to let him come close.

"Kate, my dearest love, I wish I could take your wound onto me. I cannot bear to see you suffer." He knelt by her bed, looking at her with terrified concern.

Kate reached out and put her hand on his shining hair.

"Gabe. I'm so glad you came. Do you think I'll be badly scarred?"

Gabriel briefly lowered his head beside hers on the pillow.

"Nothing in this world is less important than the amount of your scarring. Is there anything I can do to make you feel better?"

Kate turned her head aside on her pillow.

"I don't think so. Perhaps you'd better leave, Gabe. Mama V will doubtless set some stitches and I think I can bear it better if you're not here. I don't want you to see me like this. Please go."

Gabe started to protest and found an adamant Jamie beside him, urging him to leave.

"I'm sorry, Gabe. But if Kate wants you to leave, then you must. Mama V will take excellent care of her, you know."

Gabe's feelings were such a mixture he didn't know how to handle himself. He wanted desperately to stay and help Kate with whatever pain she must suffer during the stitching. Her not wanting him devastated him. He longed to hold her hand, kiss her dear face, be close to her in any way he possibly could. He definitely didn't want to leave. How could she not want him to stay?

Even as he turned away he knew he did not have the right to argue with her family. He'd rejected her once too often to have the privilege of being with her if she didn't want him. He could have claimed that right if he'd not turned her away so many times. He'd thrown away one of the most precious honors a man could have. The right to protect his loved one.

He was one of the world's biggest fools.

* * * * *

Mama V sponged away the blood from Vivie's face. The cut wandered down her cheek from the edge of her eye in a jagged line, but it had not shredded the skin. It was a cleaner cut than expected. It could be stitched without cutting any flaps of skin away once the wound was cleansed.

"Kate, my love, you know I'm going to have to hurt you. I want you to swallow a little wine with mandrake in it. It will take the edge off the pain. After the mandrake has a chance to work, I'll cleanse and stitch the wound. When that's over I'll give you a few drops of valerian. You've had enough pain for one day and I want you to sleep."

Kate's smile was a little twisted, but she did her best to reassure her grandmother.

"You know I'd rather have you take care of me than all the doctors in the world."

"Blessed be, my sweet girl," Mama V murmured as she set about getting her sharpest needle threaded with a special silk thread she spun herself. She gave Kate the sedative wine and set about securing Kate's abundant hair so it would not get in the way.

"My, but you've a lot of this stuff. You and Vivie both certainly inherited the color and texture of my hair. Makes me feel young again just to look at you."

She looked again at the length of the slash, hesitated and then opened a small bottle containing some ether. She dripped a little on her handkerchief and held it briefly to Kate's face. The ether worked quickly and Kate slumped against the pillows. Mama V rarely used the anesthetic, but she'd rather use a little now than have Kate suffer.

Mama V went on talking as she started to cleanse the nasty cut.

"You're lucky in one respect, love. Most of the cut comes close to your hair line. The scar will be as small as I can make it, I assure you. I can't promise no scar at all, but you'll be able to disguise some of it with your hair."

She went on talking as she worked, carefully setting the small stitches.

"Your red hair will grab the attention away from your scar. For some reason men love red hair. Ask my Devon."

Kate gave an approximation of a grin.

"You always said our hair wasn't red, but a deep auburn," she muttered.

The mandrake had now taken over and soothed the exhausted girl.

"Now Gabe and I are both scarred. I wonder if he'll mind mine any more than I mind his." Her words were slurred as she tried to hold still.

Mama V looked up sharply, but said nothing. She'd not given Kate enough anesthetic to eliminate the pain of the stitching, but enough to fully minimize it. Ether was so tricky and she feared using too much. She told her granddaughter sternly to be very still. Although Kate tried, she couldn't help a twitch or two and Mama V stopped once to give the girl time to force herself motionless again.

Finally the wound was closed, with tiny neat stitches that any surgeon would be proud to claim as his own. Kate took another swallow of mandrake and after a short time she muttered some words and then fell asleep. Jamie had been standing by, his face showing how he hated seeing his mother work on the girl he regarded as a beloved sister. Still he felt he must be there just in case he could help.

"Oh, do stop hovering, Jamie," his mother finally said. "Kate will sleep now. Through 'til tomorrow morning, I think."

She began to gather up the bloody cloths.

"Dear goddess of us all, I can't regret the death of that wicked Dorie. At least our girl is now safe from her. Will you go see if Gabriel is outside? I think he was devastated when Kate sent him away."

Gabe was in the hall, slumped in a chair, his head in his hands. He'd buttoned his coat as high as he could, but it was still apparent he was shirtless. He sprang to his feet when Jamie beckoned to him and hurried to the door.

"My mother says you can see her now, if you wish. She's asleep and the stitching went well."

"Of course I want to see her," Gabe answered.

He felt his bones creak as he levered himself to his impressive height. He'd forgotten how long he'd been sitting motionless. Never a good thing for him. He'd been thinking a great deal as he sat waiting. He didn't come out well in any of his thoughts. He'd decided he'd been a coward and an idiot to boot. Kate had shown him over and over that she loved him and he'd been afraid her love was not deep enough to weather disclosing his fears. How could she guarantee her love would stand the test of future trials? What person in this world could? Lasting love might be too much to expect, but he'd never given hers a chance.

He had no idea what she thought of his insensitivity. Even her angelic nature must rebel. Possibly it was her resentment coming to the surface when she suggested he leave her bedside.

He'd never discussed his doubts and his fears with her. She knew nothing of Amelie and her cruel rejection. He'd turned away from Kate without a word of explanation. He surely knew she was no Amelie. But he'd rejected her as if she were the same insensitive jilt.

That certainly made him a coward. The idiot part was a foregone conclusion.

He went silently with Jamie, following him with fear and regret in his heart. He stood silently, looking down at his sleeping love.

Tears filled his eyes as he saw her beautiful face, the cut closed but standing out in a bright red line against her pale skin. She was more beautiful to him than ever. Somehow her indomitable spirit shone even in her slumber.

"Thank you," he said to Mama V and Jamie.

He couldn't manage another word.

He turned and left the room, his eyes on the floor he could barely see.

* * * * *

Gabriel's castigation of himself seldom stopped. He could not believe he'd shut Kate out so completely. If ever a man regretted his pride, he was the man.

As soon as she was well enough to receive him, he'd go to her, his heart in his hand and convince her he wanted nothing in the world more than marrying her. If she'd have him. Her reaction when he admitted he could not have children would tell him if this lack would spoil her life. That he was obligated to confess was a foregone conclusion. He'd know a lot when he saw her reaction. If there was any hesitation on her part at all, then he'd disappear. Leaving all his hopes for the future, as well as his prayers for her happiness behind.

He felt he had no choice. Even without shutting his eyes he could see Dorie's vicious attack and the blood streaming down Kate's face. If there were any way in the world he could secure the right to protect her for the rest of their lives, he'd find it. She was his love. He wanted above all else the privilege of being her knight in shining armor. He wanted to be at her side through all the years to come, helping her and assuring her safety. The most precious privilege in the world.

If she would only have him once she knew the truth.

He started home to his apartment. Raoul would be pleased to know both Castelet and Dorie were dead.

Gabe himself must be patient until he could talk to Kate.

Or would plead be a better word?

# Chapter Sixteen

ꙮ

Kate called for a mirror as soon as she woke the next morning. Tears came to her eyes as they followed the long, jagged scar from the corner of her eye down her cheek. *At least anyone can now tell the difference between me and Vivie.* A shaky smile wavered at the weird thought and then she caught her breath to keep from sobbing.

Mama V assured her she'd only have one thin line when the wound healed. How much more had Gabriel had to endure all these years, feeling his hideous scars ripple and pull every time he moved his body. Deeply ashamed of the way his once-perfect body now looked. She'd heard a little of the gossip about a stupid girl who'd turned him away when he returned from war. Doubtless she'd contributed to his prideful retreat from close relationships.

She was now scarred also and she wouldn't let it affect her. She'd show Gabriel such things didn't matter. Scars were something she'd make him disregard, although she now understood more of his fears. In spite of her fortitude, she didn't really care to look in the mirror again. Not for a few days, at least.

Mama V entered the room, a tray bearing orange juice, *café au lait,* fresh rolls and butter in her hands. Her sharp eyes immediately noticed the tears about to fall and put the tray down quickly.

She dismissed the maid and going to the bed, cradled Kate's head against her body, carefully not touching the fresh wound.

"Come, Kate, have a little faith in me. You know I have ointments that will nearly demolish that scar."

"But not quite," whispered Kate.

"No, not quite, love, but truly almost. A little makeup will take care of what shows. I don't propose to let anything spoil your beauty."

"I didn't think I cared much about how I look, but I find I do." Kate sat musing, picking up the mirror again and finding herself more shocked than she could believe. "It's such a surprise. Vivie and I always were scornful of anyone overly appreciative of our looks. I suppose it's good for me. I've taken beauty for granted. I truly had no idea how distressing scars can be."

Mama V's glance was understanding. "You're thinking of Gabriel Jourdain, of course."

"Yes, but how did you know? His scars don't show."

She flushed red as she realized she'd admitted her knowledge of scars hidden under his clothing.

Mama V only grinned. "Child, I did something I've told you not to do. I invaded Gabriel's privacy to the extent that I know his scars are truly dreadful and he feels shame and horror for them. He doesn't quite believe they don't affect him as a man. I couldn't understand his reluctance to admit his attraction to you. Ever since I probed I've wanted to offer him some of my special ointment."

"Mama V, you're incorrigible. So am I! I'd like to not only take him the ointment but put it on him!"

Both women dissolved in laughter. Kate cherished a deep love for her grandmother with her acceptance of human frailties and wherever they might lead. She felt a moment of pity for Chantal, who'd never had such stable love when growing up. She'd grown up with only the dislike of her disapproving aunts, but had found her love in Sven. At least she now had Sven. They and their six future children could make their own stability.

"I do understand Gabe a little better," Kate said. "I still don't understand him completely."

"He has one more secret he must tell you himself," Mama V said. "I think he'll confide in you soon. The man is desperately in love with you."

Kate 's astonished look made Mama V laugh. "I know. I've always cautioned you to stay out of people's minds. I was so worried about you I broke my own rule and I'm glad I did."

"I suppose there's no use asking you what you found. No, I don't want you to tell me even if you would. I want to work things out so Gabriel and I have no secrets. He must do his share."

Mama V beamed at her. "You're right, love. Remember when you first met and Vivie and I advised you to treat him gently? It's even more important now. You now have so much power over him you must be more cautious than ever."

"His aura doesn't change much at all. I think he's a most guarded man. Of course the last I saw his beautiful blue aura the orange of anxiety laced through it. I'd never seen so much orange and I found it fascinating even as Jamie carried me to the room. The poor man was almost overcome."

"That's my sweet Druid, always thinking of others, even when you're dripping blood all over the hotel. No wonder Gabriel calls you a princess."

Kate laughed and lay back against her pillows. She'd wondered many times how to make Gabe confide in her. She thought he'd soon do so and she wanted to hurry him along. Whatever his secret was they could deal with it, but he had to come to her of his own free will.

Perhaps she'd present him with a mixture of detachment to worry him and loving kindness to soften him up.

She sat straight up in bed.

She knew just how to do it.

"Could you bring me some manuscript paper, Mama V? I've had an idea in my head for a long time. I think now's the time to write the song singing in my brain."

She settled down to work, a lovely smile curving her lips.

"Don't let *anyone* in until I tell you, Mama V. No one at all except you. I think I've just had a wonderful idea."

* * * * *

Everyone was turned away. Gabriel, Jamie, all the well-wishers from the Conservatoire who wanted to call when they heard how she'd been injured. Flowers soon filled her room, but she sent all of them to a children's hospital. All except Gabe's basket of lilacs. He must have spent hours finding so many and she couldn't have been more pleased. Their perfume filled the room and she inhaled the fragrance with pleasure. His bouquet told her he knew her preferred perfume and wanted to tell her how he longed to please her—with love in his heart, as his card stated.

She wrote her new song with perseverance. She worked night and day, serene in the certainty that the melody soared. Naturally she scored the music for her violin, but she thought Gabriel might someday add his version to hers and make a beautiful sonata. At least she hoped he would like her new composition as much as she did. She knew he came to the hotel twice a day, asking to see her. She'd directed that every caller be told the same thing, that she was writing a melody of great importance to her and she wanted no interruptions.

Mama V kept her informed of Gabe's reactions. At first he'd been worried, then indignant, then worried again.

The last time he came he almost exploded. He *demanded* to speak to her. He came close to blows with Jamie, who'd taken over the duty of turning him away.

"Please tell Miss Dellafield I'm amazed at her lack of courage. Surely she cannot be afraid to have me see her face, even if it's less than perfect. I'm disappointed in her. I truly thought she was above such superficiality."

Jamie restrained himself with effort. Of course Gabriel couldn't begin to know the hours she spent with her music, testing her song on her violin, day after day. Kate only wanted them to say she was composing.

"She said to tell you she'll see you very soon."

With that Jamie walked out of the room and left Gabe to see himself out.

Gabe fumed, about as thwarted as a man can be. He'd spent hours thinking of how best to tell Kate he would do anything to get her to marry him. But before that he'd have to tell her they couldn't have children. But if she wouldn't see him, how could he propose? He'd need to be holding her in his arms when he made his confession. He wanted to watch every nuance of changing facial expression. How she reacted would seal his happiness, or his unhappiness, for the rest of his life.

He was sure of only one thing. He must tell her his last secret and also how much he loved her.

He was one frustrated man. Even Raoul began to feel sorry for him, although he seldom missed a chance to inform Gabe he'd brought it on himself.

* * * * *

Gabe walked a lot, hour after hour.

After about a week of frustrating solitude, he let himself into his house after another long trek. The stars had come out above Paris before he returned, although he was too absorbed to notice the beauty of the night. The house seemed unnaturally quiet. He threw off his coat and started up the stairs to look for Raoul.

He'd just put his foot on the first step when a lovely melody floated down to him. He paused, spellbound with the beauty of the music. Then took the steps three at a time. He would recognize Kate's violin anywhere.

She stood in his bedroom, dressed in some slinky green gown clinging to her figure in all the right places. He caught his breath and came to a halt just inside the door, feasting his eyes on her beauty. He suddenly realized she was dressed as she'd been for their concert. His heart almost jolted out of his body as he folded his arms and leaned against the door jamb, reveling in the sight of his lovely Kate, her head bent over her violin, playing just for him.

She raised her head and smiled.

"Do I look much different to you?" she asked, a small anxious wrinkle showing on her forehead.

Gabe couldn't take his eyes from her. "What? No, do you mean your face? It's not even scarred, is it?'

Kate laughed. "Of course it is. Your eyes are definitely prejudiced. But if my disfigurement doesn't bother you that's all I want. "

He took a step toward her, but she held up her hand and he stood still.

"Don't ever use that word again. You're the loveliest girl I've ever seen. You'll always be beautiful to me. And it's not a disfigurement, it's a mark of courage. You could be covered with scars and you'd still be beautiful."

"Oh, Gabe."

She caught her breath, sighed and lifted her violin again to her shoulder.

He started toward her, but she held up her hand.

"You know I've been composing. I think it's the best piece I've written." She fixed her huge emerald eyes on him. "May I play it for you?"

Gabriel had no doubt in his mind this moment was of great importance to her and therefore to him. Looking at her, standing there gracefully in the gown she'd worn to their concert, he swallowed down the lump in his throat threatening to choke him. Something momentous was about to take place. He prayed he would not disappoint his Druid princess in whatever test she had in mind.

He leaned once more against the door jamb, folding his arms across his chest.

Kate looked at him, the picture of elegant masculinity. The light from the hall behind him shone on his hair, making him look to her like the archangel he was named for. He seemed to glow as he rested there, waiting for whatever she wanted him to do. No man could ever be more handsome. Or more appealing. She could feel his tension and see it in his aura, but his eyes were half-shuttered so that he appeared nonchalant and relaxed. Thank the goddess for her Druid powers. If she dwelt only on his appearance she'd be too nervous to play that first note.

This was as important to him as it was to her. She must not fail to get her message across.

She raised her violin and began to play. The music poured from her bow and her melodious violin. Her enforced spell of composing had given her thumb time to heal and she played as if her life depended on her conveying her emotion.

Which it did.

Would Gabriel understand what her music told him?

She played on, not looking at Gabe, but lowering her lids and looking inward at the passion she portrayed. The melody of her song filled the room and indeed, the entire house. Lilting and haunting, holding Gabriel completely enthralled.

The last plangent notes softened and then reverberated and she finally put down her violin. She knew without a doubt that she'd done her best.

There was a long silence, as they stared at each other.

Gabe finally moved away from the wall and came to her. He gently lifted the violin from her hands and put it on a nearby table.

"That's some of the most beautiful music I've ever heard."

His tone was awed, as he took her chin in his hands and forced her to look at him.

"But what did you make of it?" she asked. She was almost breathless with fear he would not understand the message of her music.

"Oh, your message came across," Gabe said. He moved with sudden speed, taking her gently in his arms. There was no sign of ardor. Only a reverence for her talent and for herself.

"But what did the music say to you?" she asked, burrowing her face in his coat.

He stroked her shining hair and then lifted her lips so he could reach them for a sweet kiss.

"You were very clear, Kate. You wrote a rhapsody to love. The music started with our regrettable meeting, although you kindly muted it a bit. A little discordance there I recognized and appreciated. I liked the way you changed keys to further delineate your mood. It's a work of art, Kate. It moved on to our slowly growing love and lingered there a while. The short expression of terror and horror at being captured by Castelet and Dorie were quite graphic. Your double stops were used with dramatic effect. And then you wrote of reunion and finally of a theme of gorgeous passion, underlined by a tranquility that promised love would last. Really, an astonishing musical feat. You told me plainly you love me, my dearest one, and that you want me in your life. You've written a love song, my princess. A love song to me."

He held her tightly and she clung to him but she didn't raise her head.

"Kate, please. Please tell me I've interpreted your music correctly. I'll die right here on the carpet if I'm wrong."

She lifted her face to him and stretched up to reach his lips. She seemed to Gabe to shine with happiness and her beauty awed him. This wonderful girl loved him and had told him so in terms the musician in him could not deny. Not a man on earth could turn away love so wonderfully expressed. Certainly not this man of music.

"That's exactly what I wanted to tell you, Gabe. If you hadn't understood I would have been devastated."

He claimed her in a blazing kiss that left her breathless.

"Dear god," he breathed. "Or goddess. I thought I'd never be allowed to kiss you again. How could you shut me out this last week, Kate, when I was trying to reach you to confess what an idiot I've been?"

She snuggled closer. "I was writing down my feelings for you. I found I *had* to set them on paper. It was vital that I be able to tell you how much I love you. But you can tell me now. Are you really an idiot?"

"Yes and you're a tease. Right now I don't want to talk anymore, you little minx. What did you do with Raoul, by the way?'

"I told him I'd booked a room for him at the Hotel Scribe. And that I didn't want to see him until tomorrow at noon. Does that give you enough time. maestro, to demonstrate you love me? After all, I've just told you musically I love you."

Gabriel looked into her glowing eyes and knew he had to tell her his last secret. He held her tightly for a moment and then set her body a little apart from his. He seemed to somehow fold into himself, although he stood as straight as the soldier he'd been and faced her. A stranger would have thought his face expressionless.

"Kate, I love you more than any other man has ever loved a woman. But I might not be what you want. You've seen my scars and my injuries. You know that area of my body was deeply injured. I must tell you I can never father a child. I know how important children are to you, you've revealed that to me time and again. I will not claim you as my own unless you fully understood what a terrible loss loving me will mean. We can never have children, lovely girls with your hair and your eyes, perhaps boys that resemble me. All that can never be. "

Kate was silent for a long moment.

"So that's what you've been keeping from me. Damn you, Gabriel. Blast and damn you! All these weeks of not being sure of your love. You've put me through more than you know, Gabriel Jourdain. I'd shake you 'til your bones rattled if you weren't so much bigger."

Gabe looked at his indignant love, bristling like a nesting bird about to fend off an invading fox. A wide smile spread on his face. She was not upset, except at him. She didn't turn and walk away from what he'd so dreaded telling her.

"Kate, please forgive me. I've been wrong about so many things. But my love for you is what's guided me through it all, even though I've so often been the idiot I mentioned. I truly wanted to insure your happiness. Please Kate, forgive me and let me kiss you."

Kate lifted her face and her hands stroked his shining hair.

"You're so handsome, Gabe. Every woman on earth must want you."

Gabe laughed as he nuzzled her nose.

"Hardly. What a delightfully prejudiced statement. Even if it were halfway true, I want only you. For all of time, Kate, I want *you.*"

She leaned back in his arms. "I see I have to indoctrinate you in Druid philosophy. Druids live each life, knowing that they never die. We're only sent to another life, to continue our journey toward perfection. How you live this life determines your next one. You, sir, are so gallant your next life will be even more wonderful."

His blazing gaze told her how tight a rein he'd clamped on his emotions.

"Then my next life will include you. I'm sure of that much. I cannot imagine another existence without you at my side."

He kissed her with all the passion in his grateful heart, letting his emotions loose as he never had before. The weeks without her had been impossibly miserable and he didn't intend to let her out of his arms until he'd proven with his body how much he loved her.

"We're in my bedroom, my love. Will you come to bed with me? Knowing how much I want to prove my love for you?"

He'd never envisioned as beautiful a sight as his Kate's face lit with joy and mischief.

"Of course, Gabe. Come show me how much you mean some of those extravagant statements you've been making."

With a growl, he lifted her in his arms. Then he stopped, although he didn't relax his grip.

"Your face. And your hand. Are they both completely well?"

"Don't worry. Just do your best, Gabriel Jourdain. I think I can match you."

He carried her over to his bed, thankful he'd always liked a big one to accommodate his tall frame. Still holding her tightly in his arms, he sank down on the mattress. She fell on top of him and as she wiggled to get free he found his stiff erection pushing at her and inadvertently helping her.

"Blessed Merlin," she gasped. "You've never been quite as big as this!"

He rolled them both over so he was on top.

"Of course not. Now I know you're mine I can let my emotions free. You'll never know the nights I've lain awake longing to have you just where you are. "

He leered at her and wiggled his eyebrows. "You're mine, my beautiful Druid. You'll be forever at my mercy."

He bent his head and kissed her sweetly. "You wrote a love song to me. To me! A beautiful love song. I'll never forget that, Kate. Not in this life or beyond. The strains will always sing in my heart. Thank you, my beautiful, beautiful Princess."

She saw the tears at the back of his eyes and kissed him with a passion that inflamed him.

He fumbled trying to find the fastening on her dress until Kate rolled over so he could see the hooks down her back. Very soon he had her dress undone, and raising her hips, she helped him raise it to her shoulders. She'd worn nothing underneath the slinky dress. Nothing at all.

He grinned and raised his eyebrows when he saw her nudity.

He watched her wriggle as he reverently took off her lovely dress. Her supple body and its graceful movements held him spellbound.

"No wonder the dress clung to you so delightfully," he murmured. "Were you by chance hoping to seduce me, you little wench? Don't bother to answer. I'll hope that was the reason. This is how I like you best, Kate. Without a stitch of clothing. "

He kissed her breasts with veneration and then began to caress their softness with his long, musician's fingers. Already aroused, she sighed into his mouth and responded so quickly he knew he'd have trouble keeping a leash on his emotions. In a way, this was their wedding night. He did not want to rush and claim her with the rapidity his body urged on him.

He concentrated on the lovely sensation of her naked body striving to get even closer to him. He parted her legs with one of his and kissing her breasts, began to work his magic fingers on the thatch of bright hair between her legs. Once again he found the spot that excited her so. It was too early to concentrate on it, so he started to move his hand away. She wriggled her body against his hand, telling him plainly she wanted more.

They both wanted more. Her persuasive ardor made it impossible for him to hold back. He caressed the now-distended nubbin until she begged him to hurry. She lifted her hips as he came over her and he found there was little chance of slowing down. He entered her with his fingers, moving them slowly into her passage and then curled his hand and let his knuckles caress her. She moaned with delight as, with a gentle thrust, he opened her wide and entered her. As she began to surge against him he gave up the battle to hold himself back. Only a few fiery strokes were needed before she screamed again and clung to him.

He reached his own climax with one more thrust and held her tightly as they both floated back to Earth.

Rolling over with her still in his arms, he kept her as close as possible until he could again speak. The loving might have been faster than he'd planned, but it surpassed anything he'd dreamed.

"Thank you, my princess."

Kate lay marveling that two people could be so closely one. Their bodies were still joined and she absorbed the incredible delight of his naked skin against hers. That two people could be connected so completely seemed a miracle beyond belief. This joining was superior to their others, enough to make her wonder. Evidently complete commitment helped in feeling the depth of rapture they'd experienced.

What a wonderful thought, that they had both given their hearts completely. Somehow she knew without asking Gabe to tell her.

Suddenly she jolted upright. "Gabe, I almost forgot. I brought you some of the ointment Mama V makes. That's what's helped my scar so much. I want you to use it too. Every day."

She started to scramble out of bed and he tried to hold her back. In a moment he rejoiced he hadn't succeeded. Her naked body, lit by the light from the hall, made him want to weep at his good fortune. She glided toward a big purse she'd left on the dresser and leaned over to open it. Gabe caught his breath. She looked like a goddess, her nude body gleaming, her beautiful hair falling around her face as she bent over to pick out the jar of ointment.

"You walk so beautifully," he said.

"Kate and I both learned to imitate Mama V. We practiced and practiced when we were growing up. Mama V once trained to be a Druid priestess and in learning to go quietly about her duties she developed this beautiful walk. We both loved it and copied her, although neither one of us ever managed to be quite as graceful. Oh, here's the ointment. She mixed it herself. She's a renowned healer, you know."

He took the jar from her. "I understand your mother and sister are also adept in Druid medicine. Are you, Kate?"

She laughed as she took the jar back, dipping her fingers in to scoop out a large chunk.

"No, not like the talented women in my family. They've all studied Druid medicine extensively. I know little compared to them."

She sat down on the edge of the bed. He lay on his back, his hands behind his head. She pulled back the light sheet drawn to his waist and began to massage the ointment into his welts. The bush of hair at his groin was the same dark color as his eyebrows. His hair must have once been the same color. No matter, she loved the steely grey.

At first he twitched a little, then settled down as her hands caressed him with every application of the ointment.

He gave a contented growl. "That feels wonderful. Do it some more, love."

Kate grinned and started on the welts a little lower. She was not surprised when his erection began to grow. And grow. She laughed as she continued rubbing the ointment onto the scars on the top parts of his legs, working the ointment in with circling motions that grew ever closer to his aroused manhood.

He finally grabbed her busy hands.

"Kate, you're a little devil. Put that jar down. I've changed my mind about needing the ointment. Come back to bed, love."

"Are you sure you want me to stop?" she asked, her face a picture of laughing innocence. "I think the ointment is doing you a lot of good."

"Little devil," he growled again.

He grabbed at her, pulling her into bed. He rolled her under him as he proceeded to show her just how much good the ointment was accomplishing. With a satisfied sigh, she gave herself over to the wonderful experience of being loved by Gabe.

The ointment would doubtless help him, probably more than he expected. Of course it would never erase his scars, but it should make them less taut and much more bearable. But for now she was content with the obvious results of her tender ministrations. Tending to his welts was a rewarding exercise.

His scars were going to need a lot of attention which she'd be happy to supply.

She'd take *very* good care of him.

# Chapter Seventeen

ജ

Hand in hand, they went to see the Randalls in the morning. Jamie grinned openly and winked at Kate. Mama V and Devon tried to be solemn, although their eyes were twinkling.

"Good morning to all of you. We've come to see about getting married," Gabriel said. "As soon as possible."

"Blessed Merlin, I hope so." Mama V kissed Gabe first and then her granddaughter. "You and Vivie both have given me so much trouble with your courtships," she remarked. A little laugh played around her mouth. "Nothing about either one of them was easy."

Gabriel merely smiled the smile of a happy man.

"Dear goddess," blurted Kate. "I've forgotten to talk to Vivie for ever so long."

"Just as well, Kate." Mama V was now openly grinning. "I think both of you are in the same realm where even sisterly confidences are not desirable. You both must know the other one is happy, though."

"Yes, I think we do, " Kate said in a wondering tone of voice.

"Do you have any definite plans?" asked Devon Randall. "Is there any way I can help?"

"We want to hold the civil marriage ceremony as soon as possible. That's the important one. The religious ceremony we haven't discussed. Whatever Kate wants is fine with me. Is there a Druid wedding ritual?"

Mama V shook her head. "The Druid union takes place in your hearts. I think you've already committed yourself to each other and so you are united in Druid terms."

Gabriel beamed. "I like that. I like that a lot."

Mama V kissed his cheek. "You're such a lovely man, Gabriel."

He grinned at her.

"But of course we need more in this day and age. I hope I have enough influence to hold the civil ceremony as soon as possible. Anything else Kate wants is up to her."

"I imagine the name of Gabriel Jourdain carries enough weight that everyone at the *Marie* will jump to oblige. But just in case that isn't enough, perhaps I can help."

Devon spoke as if he had no knowledge of his immense influence in government circles.

Kate laughed.

"The poor mayor. If you two descend on him he doesn't have a chance."

"You'll probably get the license this afternoon," Jamie quipped.

"I doubt that, but I hope to marry Kate tomorrow. Will you attend as our family? I have no one but Raoul and would be glad to be adopted into the Randall clan."

If anything were needed to make him dear to everyone's heart, Gabe had spoken the magic words. Mama V kissed him, Jamie and Devon shook his hand vigorously and Kate hugged them all.

The men went off to see what they could do.

Kate watched them go and then gasped. "Mon dieu, Mama V. We're talking about tomorrow! What will I wear?"

Mama V laughed. "The ages old grievance of women. How about the dress you'd planned to wear at Vivie's wedding? Since you're the bridesmaid and it's perfectly lovely, I think that should do."

They both stopped and stared at each other.

"You're thinking of the same idea, aren't you?" breathed Kate.

"That you make it a double wedding? Yes, indeed."

"I know Vivie would love it." Kate's beautiful smile showed how much she liked the idea. She and Vivie had done everything together since they were born. How wonderful if they could have their last act before marriage separated them by getting married in the same ceremony. Nothing, but nothing, could be better.

"Well, we've got some organizing to do. We're due to leave in three days. Now the question is, do we tell Vivie now or surprise her?"

"Oh, surprise her, definitely. This will teach her not to keep in touch with me. Although I know she's deeply in love with Alec. "

Mama V scribbled busily on a piece of paper and didn't answer. "I must of course phone the Duchess of Lambden. This will not necessitate a big change in her preparations, but she'll probably have to make a few arrangements. The main challenge will be a special British license for Kate and Gabriel and that won't be easy. Still, I think the Duke can take care of it. Lance and Morgan must know, of course. I'll talk to Morgan and answer all her questions about Gabriel."

Kate nodded. She'd talk to her mother, too, as soon as she could reach her mind.

"Give me time to talk to her first, Mama V," she said. "The news should come from me."

"Of course, love," Mama V agreed.

Kate turned away a little and a few minutes later her face lit up.

"Oh, there you are, mama," she said. "Wait 'til you hear what I have to tell you. Mama V will talk to you next, so stay with us."

Kate walked into the corner of the room and changed the conversation to a silent one, although Mama V could follow it through Kate's facial expressions. She hoped this was not the first Morgan had heard of Gabriel. Surely Kate would have mentioned him many times, as much in love as she'd been for weeks. Still Morgan might need convincing of Gabe's love, since the courtship had often been so difficult.

She smiled to herself. Gabe had one more surprise coming, but she'd let Kate tell him.

Kate finally came back to the center of the room.

"My mother is so wonderful. She's known for some time I'm irrevocably in love with Gabe. She thinks the double wedding is a great idea."

Mama V kissed her granddaughter's cheek. Kate possessed the beautiful complexion of all the Druid women and her skin was silky and smooth as cream.

"Now let's convince the men. Gabe is so much in love he'll give in eventually, but he's the one this is the hardest for. He's going to meet a great gaggle of your relatives, each of them formidable in himself. Thank the goddess he's so strong. He'll need to be to face down your parents and your grandparents."

Kate bristled. "They're the most wonderful people in the world!"

Mama V chuckled. "My dearest girl. Of course they are. Still, your father is one of the most eminent politicians in England. Your mother is an outstanding Druid. Your grandparents on your father's side are the Duke and Duchess of Lambden. Gabriel is an illustrious and well loved virtuoso in France. His reputation extends into England, but still… He'll need all his aplomb to face your formidable family. Let alone meeting your twin for the first time."

Kate sat down suddenly. She'd obviously been in such a daze of passion she'd seldom thought beyond the next time she could entice Gabe into making love to her. She'd not thought of his side of it at all.

"I'd better ask him," she said. "If he doesn't want to do it, I'll understand. At least I'd like him to go to the wedding with me. We'll be married in a French ceremony by then and I'll not let him know how much I'd like to be married with Vivie. I definitely need to consult him."

She wandered off into the next room. Her brain was in turmoil. Why did the simplest things get so complicated?

She giggled.

Marrying a prominent French musician when she'd told no one how much she loved him might give her family pause. She'd been too proud to confide in any one, particularly when she thought she had little chance of convincing Gabe they belonged together.

Pray the goddess Gabe wouldn't pay for her pride.

* * * * *

As soon as the jubilant men returned she knew they'd been successful.

"We'll be married day after tomorrow," Gabe told her. "We did our best, but couldn't make it sooner. This will do, though."

"I need to talk to you alone," she said, walking into the next room.

Gabe's heart plummeted. Not the joyful reception to his news he'd expected. He followed her with his long stride, his face sobering. She couldn't have changed her mind, could she? Was she then another Amelie, about to throw his love in his face?

The minute the thought surfaced he was ashamed. Kate was nothing like Amelie, nor would she ever be. He'd best find out what had her so upset and fix it.

Kate stood in the room, wringing her hands.

"I've been so unfair to you," she said. "Asking you to meet all my relatives at once and on our wedding day. I would have you joyous on that day, not worried about meeting my family. I'll go to Vivie's wedding alone if you want, Gabe. You can meet my family later."

He hoped the relief flooding his face didn't reveal his doubts and how much he'd like to take her up on her suggestion. He strode to her and took her in his arms.

"I think it will be easier to meet them all at once, Princess. Get it over with, so to speak. If you love them, then I'll learn to love them."

Her beautiful face cleared as she realized he meant to do whatever pleased her.

"Shall I come to you tonight? Will Raoul let me in?"

He kissed her sweetly.

"Raoul might let you in, but I won't. I've taken you too many times when I should not have. You're going to be my treasured wife and I can wait until we're married. It's only two days."

"That's the dumbest thing I ever heard," Kate said bluntly.

Gabriel laughed. "I adore your spirit, Kate. But somehow I think this is right. I can face your family knowing I showed at least some of the great respect I feel for you. Kiss me, love. Tell me you understand."

Kate pouted for just a moment. "I suppose I see your point of view. I don't have to like it, though."

"Nor do I," he muttered, folding her in his arms and kissing her until they were both breathless. When he got his breath he placed one last kiss on her forehead and turned to leave.

"I'd better go while I'm still the man I'd like to be. We'll go shopping together tomorrow and you can advise me on what to take to England. I suppose I'd better try to look smashing."

His grin made him even more handsome than usual. He seemed a different man now he'd secured the woman he loved.

Kate looked at him with so much adoration he almost turned back.

"You're always smashing, maestro. Just check with your bride-to-be."

He started toward her again and then turned and strode away, shaking his head.

He'd always suspected Kate could seduce a stone.

# Chapter Eighteen

ꟈ

Either Mama V knew what Gabe was thinking or had independently come to the same conclusion. In any case she decreed an early night for everyone so they would all be rested for the preparations and then the civil ceremony and the trip. Kate raised her eyebrows and smiled and then went demurely to her room. She'd prefer to go home with Gabe, but she was definitely outnumbered.

The civil ceremony was attended by all three Randalls and Raoul. A simple and lovely occasion, even though the mayor had obviously dressed for the marriage of one of France's favorite sons. Kate wore the lilac-colored dress she'd planned for Vivie's wedding. A very pale lavender, really just a blush of color that perfectly displayed the lilac bouquet Gabe somehow managed to produce. Not usually a color one would pick with auburn hair, but on Kate it was perfect. As Kate held the flowers, the pastel petals seemed to accent the creamy skin Gabe adored.

He wrapped his arms around her the minute the ceremony ended and kissed her with such passion even the mayor's eyebrows raised.

"Truly an *affaire de coeur,*" he murmured, before claiming the privilege of kissing both Kate's cheeks.

Mama V hugged her granddaughter and then Gabriel. "I knew you were a brilliant man. You've just proved my faith in you. Blessed be, my new grandson."

Gabriel kissed her cheeks. "You can't possibly be serious. You're far too young to be my grandmother. How about being my Mama V-in-law?"

Everyone laughed as if Gabe had uttered the most brilliant statement ever spoken.

Mama V patted his face. "You might not want to acknowledge me when I tell you what's on my mind. I think we should leave immediately for London. The weather in the Channel is frightening me and I don't want to miss this very special wedding."

Gabe's eyebrows quirked.

"I think you said immediately," Gabe commented dryly. "As in right away?"

"I did."

Viviane Randall was so serious no one could doubt her decision was based on something important to her, forcing her to what she knew was an unpopular decision. Devon Randal and Jamie shrugged in almost identical gestures.

Devon took Gabriel's hand and held it.

"I think you should know you're dealing with Viviane's Druid powers. Do not put them aside without thinking of anything but your natural desire to bed your lovely wife. She would not do this unless her reason was sound."

Gabriel thought of the other times his own Druid had demonstrated her abilities. He wasn't happy, but he recognized he had no choice but to go along with Mama V's decision. He sighed, a sigh that murmured softly throughout the room.

"When do we leave? " he asked.

"Immediately," said Viviane. Somehow she now seemed truly to be the High Priestess of the Druids she'd been trained to be.

She went to Gabriel and looked at him, her love and acceptance of him plain to see.

"I'm truly sorry, Gabe, but I think this is necessary. Kate would be devastated if she was not at Vivie's wedding, which we hope will also be her own. It's going to be a near thing, even if we rush. I'd not foreseen this at all."

Gabe turned to Raoul.

"Will you please bring everything I need to the Grand Hotel? I suppose we'll leave from there."

Gabe hesitated a moment and then strode over and vigorously shook Raoul's hand.

"Thank you for everything, my best of friends."

Kate also came over and took Raoul's hand in both of hers. "I trust you'll be with us and take care of Gabe forever, Raoul. I think you are very needful to him and therefore to me."

Raoul looked startled and then completely gratified.

"As long as Captain Gabe wants me I'll be here. May I say, my lady, you're marrying the best man in all of France. But I think he's lucky to have found you."

Kate's tears welled and threatened to spill down her cheeks. She'd been through so much in the last few weeks. Yet nothing affected her as much as her quiet acceptance by the man who revered Gabriel.

She went to Raoul and kissed his cheek.

"Please wait for us, Raoul. We'll be back as soon as we get married in England. That's important to me, but I won't keep Gabriel from France. We'll see you very soon. I hope you'll accept me as part of the household."

Gabe grinned at Raoul and then pulled Kate into his arms, not caring who saw or heard him.

"You're my wife. You're finally and really my wife. I'll go along with Mama V's plans only because I love you to distraction. Just know that. Anything that's important to you I'll go along with. But I don't like this, not one little bit. "

Tears brimmed again as Kate buried her head in his shoulder, burrowing into his body like a little puppy.

"I love you so much, Gabriel Jourdain. I'll make all of this up to you."

He grinned down at her, his eyes filled with tenderness mixed with a few devilish plans.

"I intend to see that you do," he whispered.

* * * * *

Gabriel changed his mind and went with Raoul to get what he needed for the wedding and the trip and the Randalls and Kate hurried to the Grand. Kate found Mama V had been busy and all she needed was neatly packed. Devon Randall arranged for a large limousine, a custom-made Renault with a chauffeur. In a surprisingly short time they'd picked up Gabriel and were on their way to the coast.

The automobile must have been built especially for the Grand Hotel. It carried six passengers and was certainly one of the largest autocars yet made. The men circled round it, admiring the impressive heaviness, although it's massive body looked stiff and unyielding.

"I hope you're all wearing heavy coats," Mama V admonished them all and then turned to the chauffeur, a sober man who obviously took his responsibilities to heart. Devon had checked him out and discovering he was almost an engineer when it came to cars, approved the choice.

"Do we have blankets, sir?"

"*Certainement, Madame,*" he said in his unsmiling way.

Mama V looked them all over and thought they'd do. They would be in the car for a long time and the weather looked more and more threatening. Devon and Jamie climbed in the front seat with the chauffeur, with Gabe and the two women in back. Gabriel immediately put one arm around Kate to shelter her as much as he could from the bumps.

They'd barely left the suburbs of Paris when rain came pelting down, growing steadily stronger until sheets of water beat against the car. Mama V sat in a corner, evidently communicating with herself. She had little to say to anyone. Gabriel and Kate held hands, as she gave up any pretense of not wanting to be in his arms and snuggled against him.

Lightning flashed in great jagged streaks and the crackling sky promised more to come. The distinctive smell of electricity permeated the air and the chauffeur fought to go as fast as was safely possible. Still the car slipped and slid and progress seemed almost non-existent.

"He's a good driver, isn't he?" murmured Kate.

"Thank heavens for that," Gabe said.

Mama V looked up and then sank back into her reverie.

By now the cold had begun to affect them all. Gabe took a lap rug from the pile on the floor and wrapped it around Kate. Mama V had one too and the men in front put one on their laps. The cold wind blew in every tiny crack it could find even in this luxurious car, surely the latest of engineering feats. Gabriel tried to concentrate on holding Kate as close to him as possible. He finally lifted her on his lap and wrapped the rug around both of them.

A little more warmth for them both, but the feel of her lithe body snuggling into his didn't help his repressed desires. He'd always thought his Kate had the roundest derriere he'd ever seen and now the feel of it nestling against his erection drove him mindless.

He tried to shut his mind to the fact this should have been an ecstatic wedding night and held her tightly. It was not her fault things had gone so awry.

The trip to Calais stretched out, long and miserable. At times it seemed as if the howling wind would force them off the road. Once a branch of a tree crashed behind the car, barely missing them. Dark shapes of twigs and uprooted debris flew past them, propelled by the ferocious wind. The towns and villages they passed seemed shuttered down against the storm, with almost no one on the streets. Conversation had almost effectively stopped in the car. No one could really tell where they were, but they were sure they hadn't gone nearly as far as desired. After they'd fought the elements for five hours, with diminishing progress, the chauffeur pulled off the road and stopped the car. He turned to Mama V.

"It's unsafe to go on, madame. I think we had best stay off the road for the rest of the night."

A little cry of dismay came from Kate. Gabe felt relieved. He didn't see how the driver had come this far, with so little visibility. While they'd all be utterly miserable, they would be safer off the road than on it.

"The rest of the night?" whispered Kate.

"I imagine so," answered Mama V. "I don't understand any of this, but I'll work on solving the problem while the rest of you sleep."

Kate sat upright on Gabe's lap.

"I'll have to step outside the car for a while if we're going to spend the night here. I hope I don't get blown away."

Her tone was facetious, but Gabe jerked up his head and pondered the problem. The men could easily relieve themselves so they could sleep comfortably. For the two women it would not be so simple. He didn't want Kate to go alone in the darkening day to find a secluded spot.

Mama V grinned at him.

"It's all right, Gabriel. We'll go together and hold hands. I'll not let her come to harm."

Kate kissed him and then left the car along with Mama V. They were not gone long and Kate returned and kissed him again.

"You're almost unbearably sweet, my husband," she murmured.

Gabriel left the car with the other men and returned to take Kate on his lap again.

"Don't say anything nice to me for a while," he murmured in her ear. "I'll not get any rest at all if you do."

She smiled, reached up and caressed his cheek, wiggled her bottom just once and then put her head on his shoulder to try to sleep.

Gabriel, feeling her rounded curves nestling against him, knew there would be little sleep for him. He fidgeted from side to side and tried to settle himself as comfortably as he could.

His last thought before he dozed a little was that this was definitely not the wedding night of his dreams.

* * * * *

The wind beat and howled around the car all night. In the morning, the weary party gathered themselves together as best they could. The chauffeur decided to proceed to Calais. There was really not much choice, as the roads were deserted. Calais was the nearest town with any kind of accommodations. At least they could get a hearty breakfast.

Calais proved to be another six hours away. A long, disturbing six hours, with Mama V communicating only with herself. They passed small inns where they could have stopped, but every one wanted to push on. Devon and Jamie Randall had long since run out of conversation and sat silently, each thinking his own private thoughts. Devon turned his head often to inspect his wife, a worried look on his face, but did not interrupt her meditation.

When they finally reached Calais their chauffer drove them to an attractive inn. They all unfolded themselves from the car, glad beyond reason to be able to move. All of them stood and stretched for a while to get the kinks out and then they gladly trooped in. All of them definitely needed a break in the journey.

Once again his thwarted desires pumped through his mind and his body. He'd been married for a whole day and had yet to pleasure his bride. Being with her every minute was delightful, but the most frustrating experience he could remember. Kate had slept, nestled against him for a good deal of the night. She was rested and cheerful. He felt grumpy, thinking mostly of when he might claim her lovely body once again. Perhaps they could take rooms for an hour or two.

He'd reckoned without the effects of the unusual storm.

Recognizing the importance of his visitors, the innkeeper was apologetic.

"I don't have a single room, M. Jourdain. I'd be so honored to have you stay with us, even for a short while, but it's impossible. *Je regrette beaucoup, monsieur.* I can keep others from the main salon and you can go there to rest, but that's the best I can do."

Gabriel spoke up, trying to assure his fellow countryman they realized he was doing his best. When they asked about a late lunch the innkeeper was delighted to do something to please his distinguished guests and led them with very French gesticulations into a small private parlor and then bustled out to take care of the feeding of them.

The lunch was magnificent and the men ate with gusto.

Gabe turned to Kate, who had filled her plate and then eaten little of it.

"Darling?"

Her smile was a little forced.

"Sorry, Gabriel. For some reason I'm not as hungry as I thought."

She looked rather puzzled as she pushed the pieces of ham around on her dish. "But don't worry. I'll make up for it in England. See, Mama V isn't eating much either."

As soon as the last bit had been consumed, Mama V was on her feet.

"I think we should go to the boat immediately," she said. "I'm still trying to get ahead of this miserable weather. If we delay it will only get worse."

Gabe froze his face. He was worried about Kate and thought resting in the salon would be good for her. Still, this didn't seem to be the time to question any arrangements Mama V called for. He knew nothing better to suggest than what she offered. As he held out his hand to help Kate back in the car, he looked at her closely. She was paler than he'd ever seen her. The drive had been brutal and surely everyone felt exhausted. No one said anything. No one but Mama V. She directed the driver to continue on to the docks. She seemed to know right where to go. To where a private yacht waited for them.

Gabe started when he saw the ship. Sleek and luxurious, but not as big as Gabe would have liked. It was pitching and heaving even before they'd finished boarding. The ship looked ridiculously inadequate to plough the cresting waves.

He turned to Mama V, the frown and his wrinkled forehead plainly showing his anxiety.

"You're sure of this, Madame? I wonder if it might not be better to miss the wedding than to capsize at sea."

Gabe was seriously concerned, but knew he'd alienate his bride and her whole family if he refused to board. So far he'd gone along. Now he had to speak.

Mama V was not offended. Rather she seemed to like his questioning her.

"I don't like this either, Gabe. But my visions show me all of us in London at the wedding with you and Kate standing beside Vivie and Alec. My visions are never wrong. I have to work something through, something's not yet right. I think I'm missing something here. Don't worry, just take care of your bride. We'll come to no lasting harm."

Gabe stopped short and looked at her, calling on all his intuition, trying to read her mind. Of course he couldn't do it. He doubted if anyone but another Druid could penetrate her sweet smile and discover her secret thoughts. She certainly believed what she said. He had no idea what she meant. He shrugged, a thoroughly Gallic shrug. There seemed nothing he could do but go to Kate.

He drew a deep breath and went to the stateroom. Something was wrong. Mama V had all but said so. But once again there was little he could do except walk away from the ship and he didn't intend to take such a drastic action.

He found Kate curled up on the bunk, holding her stomach and moaning.

"Oh, Princess," he sympathized. "You're seasick and we've got the whole Channel to cross."

"Get Mama V," she whispered, but before he could even rise from the bunk Mama V was there, tenderly lifting Kate so she could drink the potion Mama V'd prepared.

"I'm sorry again, Gabe. Dear goddess, I've spent the last two days apologizing to you. She'll sleep for quite a while. Hardly the wedding trip you envisioned."

Gabe's fleeting smile didn't even convince himself.

"Thanks at least for helping her sleep. I'd truly hate to see her suffer throughout the crossing."

"And you, Gabe? Do you need a potion?"

This time his smile reached his eyes. "I'm not at all affected by sea-motion. Unless you need me, I'll stay down here with Kate."

"What I need takes no help from any of us here. *I* need to figure out what to do. Get some sleep yourself, my dear boy. You are certainly not having the honeymoon you envisioned, but all will come right. You and Kate will come about."

Gabe made a very French moué and Mama V chuckled and stretched up to kiss his check.

"The goddess blessed our whole family when she gave you to Kate."

A rather thoughtful Gabe looked down at the girl he dearly loved. She lay perfectly still. Her face was turned to one side and the thin scar showed clearly. He'd once thought nothing could make his love any deeper, but her scar had somehow achieved the impossible. The covers were thrown back enough so he could see her perfect breasts stretching her blouse. She'd taken off the jacket to her dark green traveling suit and the white frilled blouse had come unbuttoned. Not that he needed any enticement. Just being in the room with her, smelling her lilac scent mixed with the aroma of her warm body caused him to wonder if he could stand sleeping next to her.

He needed the rest and there was nothing else to do.

With a sigh, he took off his coat and then curled up beside her under the covers and took her in his arms. She unconsciously moved closer to him and snuggled her bottom against him.

He held her closely, even though it made him still more aroused and uncomfortable. Not at all the wedding trip he'd envisioned. Still there were worse things than having Kate sleep in his arms.

With another sigh, a deeper one, he tried to exert his discipline to sleep.

If anything happened during the crossing, at least he'd be with Kate.

# Chapter Nineteen

ꙮ

The storm raged. Lightning and thunder erased all idea of sleep for everyone but the sedated Kate.

Gabriel finally got up to try to walk on deck. He wasn't sure he could keep on his feet with the ship pitching so, but he needed air. The cabin was stuffy and he had to get away from Kate's seductive body. As soon as he opened the cabin door he could smell the salty air and feel the wild blast of wind in his face. The sky loomed a dirty grey, much too grey for a morning sky. Flashes of heat and jagged light streaked in impossible patterns, like nothing he had ever seen.

Clinging to anything he could find, he groped his way to the upper deck. He could see Jamie and Devon standing huddled together in the distance. Their eyes were fixed on Mama V, standing in the middle of the deck. In a long white night robe, her magnificent hair hanging down her back, she rode the surging waves without a stagger. She seemed as steady as if she were standing in her own living room.

"Enough," she suddenly shouted. "I want no more of this nonsense from you two."

Gabe looked around. He could see no one else but Jamie and Devon. Surely she wasn't shouting at the men she loved!

"I knew you were heading for a battle and I tried to get to the Channel before you did. Now I'm seriously disturbed with you. You could have held off for a little while. I've always been respectful of your powers. I never called on you to help as some of the ancient priestesses did when they wanted the advantage in a battle. But now I'm angry. The people on this boat are dear to my heart. I ask you, no, I *demand* you take your forces to another place. Find another sea. Or a desert to roil around. I don't care where, but go! You simply must not disturb my loved ones so dreadfully."

An unexpected silence suddenly reigned. No gusts, no waves, no anything. Just silence. The winds quieted, the ship steadied. The water of the Channel steadied to a placid pond.

Gabriel stood still, hoping he'd not be noticed. He was too awestruck to move a muscle.

Mama V clapped her hands, a smile spreading over her face.

"I thank you sincerely," Mama V said. "I don't know why you're so angry with each other, but thank you for moving the battle. Maybe you should stop and think a little about if you really want to be tossing ships around like toys. It does have consequences, you know. Fine people have entrusted their lives to those boats. Take care. Your anger is not worth this destruction."

The silence and calm continued and Mama V stood erect, looking every inch the High Priestess she'd once trained to be.

None of the men moved and suddenly Mama V slumped to the deck.

Devon and Jamie both rushed to her and Devon picked her up.

"Darling, let me carry you. My god, how much energy did that take? Sweetheart, you're exhausted. Can you tell me now what this was about?"

Mama V's eyes were closing. "A fight between two powerful winds. My ancestors knew how to use them to advantage and possessed a certain amount of control. Sometimes the High Priestess would determine a victory for the Druids by calling on the winds to force back the enemy. My training never went so far. I'm afraid what little I learned about controlling nature I've almost forgotten. I should have called them to task sooner. It took me far too long to figure it out."

She brushed back her heavy hair from her face and leaned into Devon. "They've moved on now. We'll be fine."

Devon kissed her with a reverence Gabriel's heart echoed.

As her men bore her away, Gabriel stayed in the background. He waited until they were out of sight and then thoughtfully went back to his cabin.

He knew he'd have no trouble sleeping now. The Channel was calm and the ship was moving smoothly and fast. His last thought was one of respect for the former Druid priestess, Viviane Randall. Life held so much he'd never suspected. Kate had opened his eyes to so many wonders and he found himself astounded and grateful. His life would have been a paltry thing without these Druid women.

"Thank you, Mama V," he said and then fell into a deep sleep.

His last thought was how interesting the future surely would be.

* * * * *

They were greeted at Dover by the chauffeur the Duke of Lambden sent to convey his beloved granddaughter and her guests. The large Rolls Royce oozed luxury and comfort. The interior of the Rolls was fitted out like a drawing room, with the finest of tapestries on the seats and walls. Rare mahogany and burled woods added to the elegance. There was no doubt they'd be as comfortable as the Duke could make them.

Kate was still drowsy, but Gabe managed to get her dressed in the coat of her traveling outfit, then her long overcoat and her shoes. She revived a little as they entered a beautiful inn.

Breakfast at the Dover Arms was large and satisfying. Gabe had grown to like English breakfasts when he gave concerts in London. The sheer size intrigued him. These breakfasts were gargantuan as compared to the French croissants and coffee. He ate his share of the eggs and mixed fried foods, but after one sip of the coffee shuddered and asked for tea.

Kate laughed. She'd been in Paris long enough to agree with him, although she felt hungry enough to eat two breakfasts.

Feeling much more herself, she let Gabe hand her into the car.

"You're looking smug, sir. Will you tell me what you're thinking?"

Gabe grinned down at her.

"That this trip hasn't been bad in one respect. You let me take care of you more than you ever have. I love your independence but it's nice when you need me."

He carefully handed her into the car. Then he got in beside her, reaching out a long arm to draw her to him. After the big breakfast, Kate looked half-ready to go to sleep again. Visions floated in his mind of how to bring her completely awake and his arousal again stretched his trousers. In fact, he'd been in a state of semi-arousal for two days now.

He growled a little and Kate snuggled into him even more.

The trip to London was agony for Gabe and encouraged more restful sleep for Kate. He barely noticed the passing scenery, even though the Rolls whizzed through the countryside at almost thirty miles an hour. An amazing speed. Still it seemed to take too many hours to get to London. A rather grumpy Gabe stoically sat back in his corner as the car finally pulled up to the front of the ducal estate of Kate's grandparents.

He'd expected to be impressed and he was. As the car rolled down the long winding driveway, he viewed the extensive sweep of the lawns. The house was not elaborate in architecture, although certainly large and the grounds were extensive. Gabe knew that somewhere beyond the lawn and gardens was the small old chapel where he'd be married again. Fine with him. He'd claim Kate in as many ceremonies as she wanted. He looked out the window, aware of the life of old aristocratic London still lingering in ancient grounds such as these. Impressive, certainly. He'd called Kate "Princess" once with sarcasm and although this estate confirmed her lineage, now it was a name he used to designate her wonderful qualities.

He suddenly realized Kate was wide awake and looking at him very carefully.

"You've had a hell of trip, haven't you, love? I'm so very sorry."

Gabe jumped at such unaccustomed language from Kate. And then he had to laugh. She was always able to make him see an entirely different side of things.

"I agree. It's been a hell of a trip. I think there's been a lot going on here I don't quite understand. Evidently your grandmother's determination to have you married at the same time as your twin ran into a lot of trouble. She solved it, as you know. But I'd rather have stayed in Paris and had our honeymoon there." He shifted a little in his seat. "I find I dislike having to meet so many of your family all at once. There's only one of me."

Kate reached over, not worried that they were in the limousine surrounded by her family. She kissed him so passionately and for such a long time everyone else in the car started to grin.

"One of you is more than enough to outshine the King and the Queen. Not that they're attending our wedding, of course."

Gabe started to respond with his own passion and then heard someone clearing his throat, warning him they were not alone.

He raised his handsome head and snorted.

"Blast and damn," he said mildly. "I'm already fond of you all, but I wish you weren't here. Do you think you could kindly disappear?"

Everyone exploded with laughter and the limousine rolled smoothly down the flagstone drive.

* * * * *

When the car stopped, Gabriel knew immediately it was Vivie standing by the steps, anxiously waiting for them. Vivie, who'd he so often been told was identical to Kate. As he handed Kate out of the car he kept her hand tightly in his. He wondered if Vivie's reaction would break or seal his marriage. She was by far the most important person in Kate's life.

With a small shriek Vivie ran up to him. She was not identical to Kate. She was beautiful, but she wasn't Kate.

She tugged on Gabriel's sleeve. "You're my surprise, aren't you? Kate promised me a surprise. You're Gabriel!"

Gabriel's handsome face lit with pleasure. He no longer felt outnumbered. A feeling of being completely accepted swept through him. The sincerity of her reception seeped through his body. He'd not known he'd felt chilly, but Vivie was warmth and welcome. He felt as if he'd finally come home to the family he hadn't realized he needed.

He kissed Vivie on both cheeks, very much in the French manner, but with an enthusiasm not always present in the ritual greeting.

"I think I probably *am* your surprise. I'm Gabriel Jourdain, Kate's very new and delighted husband."

Vivie's shock was evident for just a moment. Then she grinned with approval as she looked Gabe up and down. Slowly, noticing his impressive figure, the attraction and authority fairly shining from him and also the loving and amused look he cast at Kate.

"Well. So you are. I think maybe we Dellafields can handle you as an addition to the family, Gabriel. I knew Kate had lost her heart to you. Welcome indeed."

Kate pushed Gabe aside and took her twin in her arms. "Isn't he marvelous? Oh, Vivie, I'm so happy to see you. You look absolutely smashing. Where's your handsome groom to be?"

Dr. Alec Stratton came up, shaking hands with Gabe and taking Kate into his arms for a sisterly kiss.

"Kate, I'm so glad you're here for our wedding. It would have been devastating if you hadn't come. We heard you had a little trouble crossing the Channel."

Kate looked at her Mama V with an appraising look. "Let's just say we made it. Mama V can be quite determined, you know."

She turned to her twin. "Vivie, I have an idea I'd like to propose."

Vivie gave a small shriek. "I know. I just had it too. You can repeat your vows and we'll be married together this very afternoon. Are you thinking this? Please tell me that's it, Kate. We've done everything together all our lives. How wonderful if you'd share our wedding with us. Nothing in the world could be more satisfying to me."

Kate swallowed the lump in her throat as she hugged her twin.

"This afternoon? But you're not supposed to see Alec before the ceremony! When I saw you together I thought you'd moved it to tomorrow."

"Oh, such nonsense. Why should we stay apart most of the day? The wedding isn't until four. Although if you hadn't appeared soon we'd have moved the ceremony to tomorrow."

"Too bad we didn't know that." Gabe's smile made the words almost harmless.

"We've all had too much delay. Certainly Gabe and I have." Kate's grin was delightfully wicked. "Let's find the rest of the family and get on with the wedding of the century."

* * * * *

It *was* the wedding of the century. At least to the main characters in the drama. Katherine, Duchess of Lambden, had insisted on perfection for the wedding of her beloved granddaughters. The Duke thoroughly agreed. In fact he'd tried to help so much that his loving wife called him a blasted nuisance. When he met them Gabriel was impressed with both their aristocratic appearance and their warmth. His new family would be easy to love.

The small chapel on the grounds of the estate was packed with all Kate and Vivie's relatives. The chapel had been built three hundred years before and the old stones showed their antiquity. The pews were small and fairly uncomfortable, but Vivie had wanted to be married here, at the heart of the ducal estate.

The three brothers, all handsome young men, looked Gabe up and down and evidently decided they'd accept him. Devon, Kate's oldest brother and two years younger than the twins, was the image of Lord Lance Dellafield. Gabe took one look at him and thought how the females were going to fall at his feet. Probably already had. The younger two were more an attractive mixture of Lance and Morgan and all three of them were very impressive.

Gabe need not have worried about meeting Kate's parents.

Morgan and Lord Lance greeted Gabriel with genuine affection.

"We know what you mean to our daughter, Gabriel," said Morgan Dellafield, an older edition of her twin daughters. Only her hair distinguished her difference. Her heavy tresses were a beautiful chestnut instead of the rich auburn of Kate and Vivie.

"I've talked to her enough through the months that although I don't know you as well as I hope to, I know you're the one she wants. To have captured her heart you must be everything we want in a son-in-law."

Lord Lance Dellafield shook Gabe's hand with enthusiasm. "I've admired your playing and your composing for years. We're delighted to have you in the family.

Gabe had nearly given way under such a genuine welcome. He thought Morgan lovely and Lord Lance the most impressive man he'd ever met.

"And I know what you both mean to Kate. She doesn't know it yet, but I can have three months every summer on leave from the Conservatoire. Sort of a composing sabbatical. I intend to claim that time and buy a small place near you and Vivie. We can both work and rest there. Do you think you can help us find the perfect spot?"

Morgan's delight again nearly did Gabe in, but after more hugs he got away without making an overwrought idiot of himself.

He felt almost swamped with emotion. He'd lived so long, he now realized, contained in a shell functioning as a shield. No one but Raoul had been allowed in his private enclave. A cold and empty enclave. He now belonged to a loving family whose big hearts welcomed him with genuine joy. And all this, plus much more, was due to his wonderful Kate.

He felt in a daze as he participated in the wedding ceremony. The chapel was aglow with candles and festooned with flowers. Before they'd left Paris he'd asked Mama V to make Kate's wedding bouquet of lilacs. Beautiful white lilacs spilled over her arm and added to the already perfumed room. Vivie carried white roses, adding their own fragrance. Both girls wore floor length gowns, flowing and gauzy and identical in cut. Kate's was the pale lilac gown he'd already seen and Vivie's was pale blue.

They were gorgeous women. Gabe thought Kate far lovelier, but then he was just sane enough to realize he should feel that way. He caught Alec flashing a smile at him and wondered if he felt the same about Vivie. Most probably.

Both grooms kissed their brides with such enthusiasm the audience, all relatives or very close friends, couldn't hold back. Little waves of chuckling swept through the chapel. When Gabe finally let Kate go he looked up, straight into the eyes of the Duke of Lambden. Who winked at him.

Gabe moved through the scrumptious wedding lunch in the main house like a smiling automaton. He knew he could grow to love his new family and was grateful in his heart for all having a family would mean to him. But he wanted Kate. He wanted to be alone with Kate. He wanted to talk to her, to tell her he loved her, to ease his body into hers and find the peace and rapture waiting for him.

Kate held his hand under the table. Once she turned to him and whispered, "Are you all right, Gabe? "

"Of course," he whispered back. "What could be better?"

She gave him a quizzical look and then lapsed into silence. Gabriel immediately wondered if she were talking in her mind to her sister or her mother. It was not like her to be silent at her own wedding.

He was glad the ceremony was over, but oh, how dearly he wished they could leave.

He'd just have to wait. He didn't know how long Kate would want to stay and she hadn't seen her family for quite a while. He could be patient.

At least he thought he could.

He pasted a smile on his face, stretched out his long legs and settled back in his chair.

# Chapter Twenty

ꟹ

He reckoned without his Kate.

She gave him a brilliant smile and rose to her feet. Raising her champagne glass she called out, her emerald eyes sparkling, her voice raised to capture attention. Everyone, her parents, her brothers, her grandparents, all her cousins, all her cousin's parents, everyone to a person hushed to listen to her.

"I love everyone here. Everyone of you. I'm so glad you all came to my wedding. Or I should our weddings, since both Vivie and I are sharing the wedding of any girl's dream. But maybe not all of you know Gabe and I were married in Paris in a civil ceremony three days ago. And we haven't done anything but travel, pretty rough traveling all the way. So now we're going off to find out why we got married in the first place."

The guests erupted in laughter, Viviane Randall most of all.

By this time Gabe was on his feet, laughing just a little, but mostly his eyes adoring his courageous wife. He hoped his face wasn't too red.

He turned and whispered to her, a stage whisper everyone could hear.

"I take it we're leaving?"

Again her brilliant smile, as she grabbed his hand and headed for the dining room door. She walked pretty rapidly but Lord Lance and Morgan met them there, both still laughing.

"I like a girl with courage," Lord Lance said, kissing his daughter. "Gabe, here's the key to your suite at the Savoy, Kate told me you usually stay there and we booked you in."

Vivie and Alec appeared and as Kate and Vivie hugged each other, Alec shook Gabe's hand vigorously. The two gorgeous men grinned. Alec, dark and elegant and Gabriel, distinctive as only a few men could be.

"Thank you, thank you, Gabe. We can go now too. I was afraid to make a move that might offend the family." Alec's face showed his relief and Gabe lost the last trace of his embarrassment.

"That's my Kate," he said.

Kate hugged her mother, swallowing the lump in her throat. "Please tell grandmama Katherine and my grandfather how much I love them and how much I thank them."

Her eyes were damp, but she smiled her gorgeous smile and took Gabriel's hand again.

She dragged him out of the house and they ran to the waiting car.

The Duke's chauffeur was waiting, holding open the car doors. Still holding hands and laughing, Gabe and Kate dashed to the car and scurried in. As soon as they got out of sight range of the waving family, Gabe grabbed her, lifted her onto his lap and kissed her with the most passionate kiss of their entire relationship. Then he took a deep breath and firmly set her in the corner.

"Wow." Kate said, her eyes shining. "I could grow to like this. When I get my wits back."

She started to scoot toward him and he stopped her.

"Don't touch me 'til we get to the hotel," he grated out. "Not even once. I'll go up in smoke if you do."

He folded his arms on his chest, looking as serious as Kate had seen him. He didn't meet her eyes again. In fact, he looked a little pained. Although Kate was tempted, she didn't move toward him. It might be quite interesting to see what going up in smoke involved, but she had a good idea it might be more than she could handle here and now. She'd better wait 'til they got to the Savoy.

When they got there Gabe seemed to find it painful to walk.

Kate looked at him and almost laughed.

"Don't you dare, you little wench." Gabe glared at her and she hushed.

Gabe handed the key to a bellboy. They knew the chauffeur would take care of their valises. They went straight to the elevator, still in silence and then to their room. Gabe generously tipped the bellboy who'd taken them to the suite and Gabe kicked shut the door.

"My God," he muttered. "I've never had such an erection. I won't make it to the bedroom, Kate."

She gave one look at his groin and began to step out of her drawers.

He certainly couldn't clutch her tighter if he were about to drown. The minute she had her drawers off he grabbed her and drew her legs around his waist. She tried to help by tightening her grip with her knees. This was her last coherent thought, as Gabe backed her against the wall and took possession of every particle in her body. Her mouth first, which he claimed in an erotic sweep of her senses. She was damp and ready for him, had been for two days, so now as he slammed into her wet body she knew nothing but a blazing ecstasy that soared before it slowly died down.

They clung to each other, not ready or even able to move and leaned against the wall with their bodies still joined.

"Blessed Merlin," Kate said, as she gradually regained her senses.

Gabe buried his face in her hair. "Did I hurt you, my dearest love? I didn't plan to attack you, you know. I meant to give you a long and careful loving you'd remember forever."

Kate laughed. "Hurt me? This was ecstasy of a different kind. I think I'm shameless. I seem to like everything you do to me."

She smoothed a thick lock of grey hair off his forehead.

"And I'll definitely remember."

"How can you possibly be so perfect?" Gabe asked. "Now let's go to bed."

He lifted her in his arms and started toward the bed. They passed through a large living room and into a huge bedroom.

Quite evidently the bridal suite and probably gorgeous. Neither one of them gave it a glance.

Gabe kept covering her face with little nips of kisses and she looked up at him with her most impish smile.

"Do you have any more surprises like that for me?"

He grinned a most devilish grin.

"I think I might, but we'll get undressed and go to bed so I can show you the rest."

He undressed her slowly, kissing every inch of skin as he exposed it. She tried to help but he wouldn't allow it, as he reverently worshipped each inch of her body he could reach.

When she was naked he picked her up again and laid her on the bed and quickly divested himself of his own clothing. She wanted to help, but he kissed her hands.

"Let me do it all this time. I want this to be for you."

His voice was deep and amorous, its very timbre suggesting erotic images. Definitely his most between-the-sheets voice.

He sat on the edge of the bed, as bare as she and he leaned over and kissed her with quickening passion.

"I want tonight to be good for you. I might even produce one of those surprises if you're a good girl."

The devilment was back on his face and she laughed.

"And I definitely have a surprise for you," she said, a little shyness he didn't understand crossing her face. He decided to ignore it and began to caress her breasts.

"I learned a lot when I went to war. The men talked pretty much incessantly about their wives and girl friends most of the time when we weren't under fire. I listened and found out there are some things about sexual intercourse I'd never known. We might just try them all tonight and see which ones you like."

The look of anticipation on his face struck Kate as humorous.

"Gabe, you aren't about to tell me you needed lessons? You, the most handsome male in France? I'll bet you've been beating off women since you were fourteen."

He looked so abashed she almost kissed him in a way to end the conversation.

"Kate, I don't know what to say. You didn't expect me to come to you as a virgin, did you?"

She tried to look severe. "Why not, sir? You expected me to be chaste, I'm sure."

Gabe looked so uncertain she took pity on him.

"I don't ever want to hear about your former affairs, Gabe. They don't matter, except they gave you the experience that drives me wild. Although other women better be a thing of the past. I will never share you."

Her serious eyes told him she meant every word.

"How can you doubt it, Princess? You're all in the world I'll ever want. In this life or any of the others we might be privileged to live."

Kate held him closely, loving the enveloping feel of his large warm body.

"One of the things I object to in this world is men have so much more freedom than women. They can do pretty much what they want. But I'll let you off the hook, my love. Your expertise is all to my benefit."

As he kissed her in gratitude for her understanding, he began his caresses again.

"You look just like a little boy about to have a dish of ice cream," she said as she giggled. She ruffled his hair, marveling again at its beauty and thick texture.

"Hmmm," he answered. "A little something one soldier recommended. Spreading ice cream with chocolate sauce on your lover and licking it off. I definitely want to try that."

The very thought set him hovering over her and licking her flat stomach with slow deliberate strokes of his wicked tongue, down to the fiery patch of hair at her groin. He settled in and she helplessly writhed as he brought her to climax with just his tongue. She screamed her pleasure, grasping him and collapsing against his hot body.

He barely paused. He held her tight for just a moment and then again began his expert caresses. She had no doubt where they were headed. Gabe intended to take them both into a world of pleasure, a large glorious world she was eager to explore.

He took his time, caressing her in spots she'd had no idea were so sensitive. Before long they embarked on what he wanted, a slower, more tantalizing, even more wonderful kind of love.

This time when they floated back to earth Kate looked at him in amazement. Stars of many colors drifted around them as they slowly came back to reality. Truly the most magnificent sight she'd ever seen. Gabe had given her all the pleasures she'd ever dreamed of, plus many she'd never imagined. He was her own private magician of love.

She kissed him all over his beloved face and then lay back against the pillows.

"Dear goddess, Gabe, what else do you have in mind? Surely you won't be able to attempt anything else tonight, but what else did those soldiers tell you?"

He lay back with her, his arms folded under his head. "Next time you're going to be on top. You'll be in complete control and knowing you, my independent witch, I think you'll like it. Give me just a little while and we'll try it."

She stared at him. "You're serious, aren't you? You really want to do it again?"

His big hand smoothed the hair from her eyes. His fingers touched her scar and he leaned and kissed it.

"I hope you don't mind your scar too much. Somehow it makes you even more a part of me. Something that binds us together."

"Then I'm glad I have it," she whispered.

They lay hand in hand, saying little of consequence, until Gabe suddenly remembered.

"You said you had a surprise for me too. What is it, my love?"

He quickly grew alarmed as she colored and wouldn't look at him. When she began playing with the hair on his chest and trying to twist it into knots, his alarm grew.

"Kate." Gabe's voice was serious. "Tell me, love. Whatever it is, we'll face it together."

Kate's strangled laugh wasn't assuring. Then she raised her head and looked at him, her face alight with joy and just the slightest apprehension.

"I might as well come out and say it. We're going to have a baby, Gabe. In eight months you'll be introduced to our daughter."

He stiffened and started to turn away.

"That's not funny, Kate."

"It's not meant to be, my love. This is truth. Mama V told me first and when I got so sick on the boat I knew she was right. Can we name her Morgan? We'll have the twin boys later, but this one is a girl."

Gabe stared, trying to stick to his disbelief, afraid to accept her words. He soon found it joyously impossible to do anything but believe in what her shining face told him. She and Mama V would know only the truth.

"But the doctors said…" He buried his face in his hands. When he finally looked up his eyes were bright with tears. "Thank god, Kate. Or should I say thanks to your goddess?"

"Thank anybody you want, my love. I've wanted to tell you ever since the Channel crossing but it never seemed the right time. So many people were always around. You can't know how I longed to let you know."

"Now's the perfect time," he said, nuzzling her hair. "Nothing can ever again be this perfect."

He held her silently for a while and then started up from his pillows. He leaned over and taking her face gently in his hands, kissed her with a new and devastating sweetness.

"I never imagined when you wrote me a long song, my Princess, how happy you would make me. Only one thing bothers me and I have to ask you. Is it all right to keep making love or will it hurt our baby?"

Kate's musical laugh rang out.

"Gabe, women have been having babies for quite a long time. They certainly don't stop making love for nine months. Making love won't hurt at all. I think this next time though I'm going to try being on top. I like the idea of controlling. I'm that kind of woman."

His startled look betrayed his thoughts had strayed.

"Kate," he whispered, "Did I hear you mention twin boys?"

"Twins run in our family, my love."

His eyes rounded and then smoldered as she reached down and stroked his burgeoning erection. When she leaned over and kissed where she'd stroked he gasped. A gasp wholly satisfactory to Kate. He pulled her body toward him, then lifted her over him, steadying her with his strong arms. His smile was one of both mischief and incipient passion.

He flung his arms out to his sides.

"Do what you want with me, Princess. I'm yours to command. We'd better do a lot of practicing so we'll be sure of those boys."

She leaned back against his bent knees and looked down on him. His long, strong body stretched out beneath her, willing for her to make whatever move she desired. The tension built as she savored his splendor. Her prince. Her wonderful Prince. His cobalt eyes blazed his love as he waited for her to make the first move. Motionless, vibrating with passion, but waiting.

Her sensuous smile betrayed her secret fantasies. Kate knew with a hot rush of pleasure she needed no instruction.

Neither one of them was disappointed with her instinctive handling of the situation.

# Kiss of a Druid Bard

ꙮ

## Dedication

ꕥ

*Dedicated to Helen, my clever and kind editor, who makes me laugh even as I'm learning so much from her. She's taught me the meaning of HEA, TSTL, and FLEs, among other POWs. My heartfelt thanks for her patience and her wisdom.*

*i.e. Happily Ever After, Too Stupid To Live, Final Line Edits and Pearls of Wisdom.*

## Trademarks Acknowledgement

ꕥ

The author acknowledges the trademarked status and trademark owners of the following wordmarks mentioned in this work of fiction:

Citroen: Société anonyme Immeuble Colisée III

Renault: s.a.s. société par actions simplifiée

# Chapter One

*Brittany, May, 1920*

ꟷ

Stephen sang his Druid lays of lost loves and fallen kings. His flute quiet in his hand, his dulcet singing reached out to everyone in the tavern. Touching their heart in the deep spot they'd tried to bury. His baritone voice, true and resonant, filled the room. In this small town in Brittany, still a land of the Druids, his audience sat spellbound, listening. And somehow they knew the imposing man before them had endured some of the sadness of which he sang.

When he stopped there was a moment of silence, surely the best tribute a musician can have. Stephen stood, put his flute in his pocket and accepted the proffered glass of wine.

He would be on his way tomorrow. This room, although full of kind strangers, was not where he belonged. Maybe the next town held some answers. After all, Brittany was filled with Druid tales and fascinating ruins for a wandering minstrel to explore.

He'd found interesting ruins and megaliths. He'd found friendly people and a surprising amount who averred to be Druids, or descended from Druids. He'd been treated well, beyond well, in fact.

He'd found no peace or happiness.

Stephen strode along, his red-gold hair glinting in the sunlight, his long legs eating up the miles. With skin bronzed deeply from months of walking in the sun, his blue eyes were a startling contrast under his bright hair. His handsome features and magnificent build proclaimed him a man to be remembered. The day grew warmer and he paused to remove his shirt and tie it around his shoulders.

Warm sun on warm skin, a feeling he relished.

He rounded the corner of the small town of Gouarec. Traffic was sparse and mixed. Some jangling horses with carriages and farmers' carts and a few automobiles. Two or three bicycles. The horses' hoof-clomping sounded louder to his sensitive Druid ears than the noisy engines of the few cars in this rural part of France. He noticed mostly Breton natives but also a sprinkling of sight-seeing foreigners. Brittany was a popular destination for tourists, with its interesting relics, marvelous weather and excellent beaches.

The streets of Gouarec weren't exactly thronged but it seemed like a busy and charming village. He paused, fascinated by the way the Nantes-Brest Canal and the river Blavet met in a swirl of water shooting off in various directions. A beautiful churning that he'd like to investigate. Tomorrow. He didn't choose to stop and pick which footpath to follow along the various waterways. He'd decide that later. Right now he wanted to stroll through the town.

He passed two attractive taverns. He'd decide on one for returning to for dinner. Singing his bardic lays would pass some time, as well as bring offers of food and drink. Nothing that would attach him but might give him some hours without having to lament. Or even feel.

Suddenly a puppy scampered across the road, a small Renault roared round the corner and a tiny girl ran after the puppy.

Stephen saw the drama converging, shouted a warning and started to sprint. *Damn fool must have been going fifteen miles an hour. In town too. Blessed Merlin, he couldn't reach the child in time to toss her out of the way.*

He reached the still little body first. A young woman was running up the side street but Stephen already had picked up the child and now sat at the side of the road, running his expert physician's hands over the tiny frame. *About four or five, I'd guess. A perfectly beautiful child.*

Before he could determine the full extent of the child's injuries he felt himself being thwacked hard with some heavy object and put up one arm to ward off the blows.

"Monster! Pervert! Take your bloody hands off Beth."

The young woman was beating him around the head and shoulders with her knapsack, her face wild and angry.

"Get away from her," the harpy screeched.

Stephen wrenched the punishing weapon from her and grabbed her hands.

"Are you crazy, woman? Your child is injured. You should thank your god I'm a doctor. *Now stand back and let me see to her.*"

She hesitated. Tears were streaming down her cheeks, flushed a beautiful rose with her anger. Blue-green eyes, startling in their ferocity, scorched him. He hesitated for just a moment, staring. A beautiful, floating pink fog seemed to hover around her, moving with her even as she moved. He shook his head. He must have been in the sun too long. He'd never seen anything before like this rosy cloud.

The woman was still spitting her words.

"You're no doctor, you're just a wanderer."

Her contemptuous tone didn't matter. He needed to check the child again.

"I trained at London General Hospital. Now let me see to the child, you ridiculous shrew. I'm Dr. Stephen Lovernios."

Skeptical eyes stared at him, animosity and contempt streaming from them. Stephen's air of authority must have finally reached her. She quieted, running one hand over the long, pale hair of the beautiful child.

"She's not dead, is she?" she hiccupped, her voice catching.

"No but she has a dislocated shoulder. I imagine the pain and the shock made her faint. I need to put the bone in place and I want to do it while she's unconscious. The pain is ferocious otherwise."

All the time he'd been talking he'd been feeling the tiny bones. Now he held the small body on his lap, face down and holding her steady with one hand used his other thumb to apply pressure. The click of the bone sliding into place could be easily heard by the hushed crowd gathered round. The young driver of the auto, shaking and pale, stood silently by, wringing his hands, his eyes fastened on the child.

Everyone waited, although Stephen kept checking vital signs. The woman knelt beside him, smoothing the white-blonde hair from the girl's face. After several minutes the baby, *for she's little more than that,* began to whimper.

"Someone find me a cloth to make a sling," Stephen called in a low voice. He certainly didn't want his deep voice to scare this darling infant.

A strip of what looked like a petticoat appeared and Stephen fashioned a sling, binding the tiny arm to her body. Just as he did so, big aquamarine eyes looked up at him. The same beautiful color as her mother's.

"I hurt," she whimpered.

The woman leaned over and kissed her child.

"Of course you do, darling. But this nice man has fixed you up. Oh, Beth, my love, you frightened me to death."

"But the puppy, Mairey. I had to save the puppy."

"The puppy's fine, darling. He dashed away a long time ago."

*Mairey. What a lovely Celtic name.* Stephen suddenly realized the females were speaking French and not the Breton most common in this area of Brittany. Theirs was a slightly accented French, so it was not their native language. He'd spent the last month studying the Breton language and although he was usually adept at picking up languages, found Breton strangely difficult. He was glad to speak French.

Stephen handed the child to Mairey and stood, shrugging into his shirt again.

"She needs a lot of rest and attention. She mustn't be too active for a while. You should keep the sling on for a week. She has no broken bones and you are both incredibly lucky, madam.

Now if you'll give her back to me I'll carry her and escort you to wherever you are staying."

He didn't even try to make his tone friendly. What the bloody hell was going through her mind, attacking him like a mad woman? Calling him a pervert and a monster? Was she dim-witted or just completely antagonistic to men? No matter, he'd see the child to their home and then find a tavern for the evening.

The Mairey woman handed Beth to him and walked beside him without any more outbursts. She gave him directions to a boarding house. So she was as transitory as he was. He looked back once to see a gendarme leading the young driver away. Doubtless he'd get little more than a horrific scolding since no real damage was done.

When they got to the doorstep the woman faced him squarely. Something flashed in her long-lashed eyes, a spark he could almost feel but couldn't read. Anger or fear, regret or gratitude? He couldn't tell. She put out her hand and touched his sleeve and then drew quickly back.

Stephen stared at her. Had she felt the frizzling reaction when she touched him? From her sudden flush, he thought so.

"I owe you an apology and my thanks. In my defense I'll say I know you earn your meals singing at taverns. Everyone around has heard of you. Beth means everything to me and I could not believe you're a doctor."

Stephen looked at her, trying to decide if this was an apology or not. It didn't much matter. He drew himself up to his full six foot three, not caring if his face showed some of his half-angry feeling toward this spitfire.

"I'll be around town for a few days. If you need me I imagine you can find me."

He strode off, not looking back. He didn't like bringing his medical skills to so much attention, although he'd never turn away anyone in need. The child was a beautiful darling and he was glad he'd been on the spot. The mother was another matter. Clearly well enough looking, although he'd only registered the rioting black hair and high cheekbones matching her Celtic name.

Oh yes and skin like ivory porcelain, rare and perfect. In another world, before he'd lost Vivie, he might have thought her beautiful.

Her eyes were unusual, showing every nuance of feeling as she shifted from emotion to emotion. Eyes betraying a wealth of inner passion. Passion for what? Her child, certainly but what else?

No matter, nothing he cared to explore.

Surely it was unseemly to dress as a man. He'd never cared for immodesty. Baggy trousers and heavy boots. Certainly nothing appealing about her attire but then no woman appealed to him since Vivie Dellafield told him she meant to marry his rival.

*A pervert! The loose-tongued wench actually called him a pervert. What in blazing hell did she mean?*

At a different time of his life he might have tried to find out why she'd been so unnaturally incensed. Now it wasn't worth the bother. Probably an unsettled mind. He'd never in his life been called a pervert. His sexual inclinations were well established. Underfed for some time but not at all in doubt.

He didn't like being named a pervert.

*Blazing fires.* He didn't like it one bit.

Even if she was just a wild-talking vixen, it somehow bothered him. He shrugged. He'd just forget such nonsense. Beautiful women were some kind of complication he could now do without. The surprising little frisson he'd felt meant nothing. Nothing at all.

*****

Stephen picked the most prosperous looking tavern and taking his flute, entered the barroom. He'd been in Brittany for some months now. Word of his melodic bardic tales of the early Celts, plus the evocative sound of his deep and resonating voice, spread throughout the provinces. In these small villages, history still lived, as well as the legends and tales of the Druids. A welcome awaited him wherever he chose to appear. Druids were still plentiful and well-accepted in Brittany.

The proprietor urged a drink on him but Stephen shook his head. He stood for a moment looking around the room. The usual natives, some of whom waved a greeting. Perhaps after he sung a little he'd be hungry. Now a new tune kept playing in his head and he wanted to try it out. He planned to weave the old tale of Merlin into this new lay, surely appropriate when so near the woods where Merlin was said to rest in centuries-old enchantment.

Lost hopes. Almost all his bardic songs referred to lost hopes. And lost loves. He was an expert on both. Merlin's tale would fit right in. Merlin, the Druid bard who'd counseled King Arthur and given him the idea for the Round Table. Certainly the most worthy of all lost hopes.

He began the opening notes on his flute, the melody carrying clear and true throughout the packed tavern. The tune was finished but he needed to settle on the perfect words. Still, he'd firmed a few of them and decided to start. He'd hum the rest for now.

Just before he lost himself in the melody, the door opened and three people entered, talking cheerfully. Three men. No, by the goddess, it was two men and that outrageous Mairey, dressed again without regard for convention. He stopped humming and automatically began playing his flute again, eyeing the group frankly as they took seats at a table close to him.

She wore a man's jacket over a long straight skirt reaching to her calves. A peculiar combination but on her it somehow looked enticing. If she thought a man's coat masked her figure she was mistaken. The jacket hung loosely but the limp lines followed her supple movements. She was no more than six or seven inches shorter than he. Tall for a woman. Slim ankles and legs promised an equally trim torso. Polished boots tonight, made of superior leather instead of the dirty wrecks she'd worn the other day. Did she know being different always raised question marks of one kind or another? If so and she was striving to look masculine, the frilly blouse she wore peeked out and spoiled the effect she might be seeking.

Did she resent being a woman, then?

Without the tears and terror, her face shone with a translucent complexion like none he could remember, as she laughed with her companions.

Stephen played on, gracefully thanking the audience for their applause with a low bow when he finished. Someone put a pint of ale in his hands and he got to his feet, stretching and flexing his strong shoulders. Carrying his mug, he went to the threesome.

Mairey—*what was her last name, anyway*?—looked at him with an expression telling him exactly nothing.

"I came to inquire about Beth. Is she doing well?"

Something lit Mairey's eyes but she tamped it down at once.

"The accident was two days ago. You might have asked sooner."

Her tone was mild and resentful at the same time.

"You might have sent word," he answered in a clipped voice.

As he turned to go away, the younger man in the group put out a hand to stop him.

"Bethan is fine, Doctor. Driving everyone crazy wanting to run around like a little demon when she knows she shouldn't."

Stephen smiled. "Perfectly normal. I'm glad to hear it."

*Another beautiful Celtic name. Bethan is one of my favorites.*

Clipped black curls, aquamarine eyes and something about the tilt of his mouth suggested this man was a sibling. The same chiseled features. Definitely not the husband of the beautiful shrew. He cast an admonishing glance at Mairey and turned to Stephen.

"I'm Philip Bronwyn. We came tonight especially to thank you. My sister and I both deeply appreciate your expertise the other day. I know enough medicine to realize Beth would have been in agony without your prompt assistance."

He put out his hand and Stephen was glad to shake it. He noticed Mairey's flush but said nothing. She did not extend her hand. Did she not agree, or was she unwilling to touch him?

The older man was also on his feet. "I'm Taliesin Bronwyn, the uncle of these two. It's a pleasure to shake your hand, Dr. Lovernios. You have my gratitude. Bethan is dear to us all."

Mairey hesitated, then raised her eyes squarely to his. "And I'm Mairey Bronwyn and I thank you too, most sincerely. My niece will be fine and I well realize it's thanks to you."

A real, true apology. And Bethan was not her daughter. Stephen murmured a few pleasantries and started to excuse himself.

He stopped and turned to Philip with a smile.

"How did you manage such a solid English name as Philip? The rest of your family has delightfully Welsh names. Taliesin of course was Wales' famous poet."

Philip grinned. "Something about the best friend of my father, I've heard."

"I'd better go." Stephen smiled back. "I'm expected to sing for my supper, as you know. I'm a Druid bard right now more often than I am a doctor." His even tone implied no resentment at the words she'd first used to him but her flush grew brighter. He'd never seen such gorgeous skin. Like the finest of parchment but with just a charming hint of warm peaches.

*What would it feel like to touch her incredible skin? Was it as smooth as the fresh cream it so resembled?*

Too bad she possessed such a difficult personality. And where were the child's mother and father? Were they traveling without their beautiful baby? Oh well, it was none of his business. And certainly none of his concern. Women, even intriguing women, were of no interest to him. It was doubtless just the inquisitive doctor in him that made him want to touch her cheek.

He went back to his music. The notes of his flute rang sweet and true, as Stephen played melodies to reach deep into the hearts of all those who had loved and lost. The customers in the tavern were temporarily silent, hearing his sweet notes and his true baritone touch their memories and their almost forgotten hopes.

He lost himself in his music, thinking of what might have been and playing from his heart the sounds expressing his regrets and his sorrow.

Stephen did not even notice when the three Bronwyns slipped out.

# Chapter Two

ꕥ

Mairey rose early, determined to walk off the disappointment lingering from the encounter in the tavern. What should it matter to her that Stephen Lovernios was irresponsible? Playing and singing for his food when he could easily set up an office and make a competent living. True, he possessed a lovely singing voice. An impressive speaking voice too, that seemed to reach down inside a person where all their emotions were hidden. He also seemed to project a rare empathy, which was probably why she felt so on edge around him. As if he could read her mind.

But what a waste of talent and training.

If one were highly trained, as he was, roaming around and singing for his supper was just plain regrettable.

And why did her wayward mind keep returning to him? True, he was gorgeous to look at. Tall and well-built, actually *extremely* well built, his golden hair with its reddish cast beckoned like a lantern. She'd never seen hair quite that glorious color. And a face most females would swoon over. When he'd been playing his face seemed all angles and planes but when he sang his features seemed softer under his glowing hair. His face changed as one watched, a face one definitely wanted to watch.

A more masculine man she'd seldom seen, in spite of his laziness and his haunting music. Power seemed inherent in his every motion.

Still, he was duplicitous. Pretending to be one thing when he was another. And negligent in his responsibilities. Surely anyone who traveled as a vagabond and yet hid the degree of a physician could not be reliable. Spending all those precious years getting a doctor's degree and then ignoring it must show a regrettable lack of dependability. Just as well she'd decided to put him out of her mind.

She dressed as usual, men's working trousers, heavy pullover and a farmer's straw hat tied under her chin. Beth wore duplicate clothes, only her little boy pants fit her much better. She was such an adorable mite of a child. Mairey finished dressing the child and gave her an extra hug.

"There, precious, we're ready. We'll have a good breakfast and then get to the site." Mairey patted her one last time.

"Do I have to still wear this sling, Mairey? I hate this sling." The delicate lips were pulled down in distress as Beth plucked at the linen strap Mairey was adjusting.

"Only one more day, sweetie. Surely you can stand one more day."

"But I can only dig with one hand, Mairey." The pout was so entrancing Mairey leaned over and kissed her darling niece.

"But you do so well with one hand. Look at the shard you found yesterday. Maybe there'll be more in the same spot." She patted the white-blonde head.

The child's face lit up. "Then I'm a good arc-e-lodge-ist?"

"The very best, sweetie. Let's have breakfast and then go to work."

She picked up her own kit of her professional tools and handed Beth her small box containing several dulled table knives, a long stick to poke with and some small brushes to brush dirt off whatever object she found. The child adored helping her. When they were both working they forgot the shadows of the past and concentrated on what to Beth was a wonderful game.

To Mairey it was much more. Her work and Beth were the fulfillment of her life. She needed nothing else.

She would never need anything or anyone else. Certainly not an irresponsible man. Just the fact her heart speeded up when he appeared only meant she'd been neglecting her social life. There were plenty of men eager to divert her if she cared to take the time away from her work. She'd have to remedy the situation when she had the time.

She at least was cognizant of the value of being a responsible person.

* * * * *

Stephen needed to make one last stop before he left Gouarec. He wanted to see the excavations taking place just west of town. This was the third year an archeological team had been digging and rumor spurred the report of marvelous discovered treasures. The site was reportedly well guarded, so he dropped in at the office of the *maire* to receive the required permission. No trouble at all, as a bored clerk hurriedly scribbled out a permit and settled back in his chair.

The dig was about four miles from the outskirts of town. Protection seemed to be well in place but then rumors of gold artifacts would demand extra precautions. High barbed wire fences secured the site and several guards were posted around the perimeter. He frowned in sudden thought. A pair of wire cutters would make mincemeat of the fence.

It suddenly worried him he'd received an entry permit by merely asking. Why did he receive a permit so quickly? Without even a question. A bit of laxity that should worry the head of the team if he realized.

Stephen walked about a quarter of a mile from the entrance before he came to the first excavation. Not as large as he'd expected, the pit was about three feet in depth. He stood at the edge of the pit, looking down and assessing the situation. Certainly a well financed and provisioned excavation, with all the necessary sifting screens and tools at hand. Off to one side was a small lean-to serving as a shelter for what seemed to be dolls and other toys.

There were only two people in the pit and one of them was very small. His eyes suddenly focused on the child. A beautiful little girl, with flyaway blonde hair peeking from under the wide brim of her hat. Wearing a sling. He shifted his eyes to the other figure. He was not surprised to see black curls escaping another broad brimmed farmer's hat. If she raised her head he'd doubtless see the lovely face of Mairey Bronwyn.

*Of course! The well-known Bronwyn family. Archeologists of renown. And the M. Bronwyn, PhD, in the credit lines of their erudite articles stood for Mairey. A young and beautiful Mairey who must have concentrated almost unnaturally on her education to have come so far, so fast.*

He stared at her, trying to assimilate this new information his lazy brain was finally giving him. As he stared, he saw Mairey suddenly surrounded by a rosy cloud, bigger than the one he thought he'd seen before. The same color and quite noticeable this time. Like nothing he'd ever seen. A warm pink cloud struck through occasionally with little darts of dark grey anxiety. It was definitely there, hovering around Dr. Mairey Bronwyn. An informative and alluring cloud.

An aura. It had to be an aura. His very first true aura. Stephen closed his eyes and thanked his goddess. He knew without a doubt his Druid heritage was finally helping him project power he'd always wanted but couldn't find until now.

How strange this difficult woman should be the one to inspire his latent talent. She was the last person in the world he'd think to associate with evoking such an ability in a Druid.

He stopped, completely stilled, taking in the wonder. All his life he'd felt inferior to Druids such as Vivie who counted auras as a common experience. Spellbound, he watched the colors swirl around Mairey's head. The rose color was lovely and seemed somehow to suit her. Why she was so anxious he didn't know but he suddenly realized he'd help her if he could. A long unused reaction for him. It had been a considerable time since he'd been concerned with another's inner problems.

Viviane Randall, Vivie's grandmother and the most powerful Druid alive, once hinted he possessed unused powers he should explore. How fascinating to think she might be right. Could he progress from this one small step? A giant step for him, although commonplace to Viviane and her family.

He also realized, somewhere in the back of his mind, that for the first time in many, many months he was also experiencing something beside despair. A wonderful feeling. Something very near elation.

The whole occurrence was quite amazing.

Jubilation flooded his mind and his countenance and he stood as if mesmerized. When Mairey looked up and saw him she wasn't sure he was the same man. This one's smile, though faint and turned inward to his private thoughts, transformed his face. She'd always thought him good-looking, even when she was thumping him with her backpack. He stood now with his hands clasped behind his back, which somehow emphasized his tall, muscular build. She was fairly tall for a woman but he must be at least three inches over six feet. Now, his unusual hair gleaming in the sun, his face transfigured with some private emotion, he looked too sinfully handsome to be mortal.

Like a Greek god of old.

She stood, lost in admiration for the most attractive man she'd ever seen.

She hesitated to break the spell. As long as he didn't notice her she could look at him forever. Just then Beth spotted him and ran toward him.

Stephen saw her coming, put one hand on the edge of the pit and vaulted in. He immediately stooped and scooped Beth up.

"Hello, chicken."

She reared back in his arms, her small face indignant.

"I'm no chicken. I'm a girl."

He ruffled her hair. "You scratch and dig in the dirt just like a chicken. I think I'll call you chickie."

He rubbed noses with her and then set her down.

"Could I feel one of your wings, chickie? Just to see if you can fly properly."

Beth giggled but stood still, as Stephen bent his long legs and squatted beside her.

"Yep," he said, tilting back her hat so her shining face beamed at him. "You're ready to fly. You can take the sling off anytime. I never saw a chicken with a sling, did you?"

She squealed with delight, hugged him and then ran to Mairey.

"Mairey, Mairey, did you hear him?"

Mairey helped the child take off the sling and stuck it in her own pocket. She couldn't help flashing a smile at Stephen.

"If it truly won't hurt her, I'm delighted to get rid of this blasted piece of cloth. Beth is ordinarily the sweetest child in the world but the sling irritated her beyond belief."

Stephen admired the first smile he'd seen on Mairey's face. Her whole being altered into a new one of a happy girl. Lighting up her whole face, the little laughter lines springing out in delicate curves at the side of her beguiling mouth. At one time in her life she must have laughed a lot. The smile revealed a come-to-me dimple in her right cheek. She looked like an entirely different person. In his life of seven months ago he might have considered asking her to be his friend and been delighted if she'd accepted.

He smiled slowly, glad he'd come to Brittany, even though he hadn't known he'd find Mairey and Bethan.

"Then I'm glad we can forget about it. I don't think you'll overdo, will you chickie? You're not going to use your arm to hang from trees like a monkey, are you? If you say 'yes' the sling goes right back on."

He frowned ferociously at her and Beth broke into laughter. Stephen listened, her joy clutching him in the heart he'd thought closed. She really was an adorable child.

He turned to Mairey to find her smiling even more broadly. That dimple was a killer.

"I'd like to know anything you can tell me about the excavation when you feel free and have time. I think everyone has a little bit of archaeologist in him. Uncovering long-ago civilizations, well, that *must* make every day exciting."

Mairey laughed. "Not really. You can go days without uncovering a thing. Most digs are uncomfortable. You're always stooping and the sun is generally beating down on your head. And you dig in mud or sand most of the time. You can get very, very dirty. Sometimes I think I'll never feel clean again."

Stephen nodded in understanding. "And that's why you wear men's trousers. And your big hats. As a doctor I highly approve of the hats. Your skin would turn to leather did you not."

He'd almost said "your beautiful skin" but stopped himself in time. Such a comment would probably be not only inappropriate but unwelcome. After all, the beautiful Dr. Mairey thought very little of Dr. Stephen.

Still, they seemed on better terms than they had been and he was full of questions.

"Have you found anything significant? I'm not asking for secrets, just a general impression of what you're discovering."

Stephen knew enough not to be more specific. On top of his other sins, he didn't want to be suspected of being a spy.

As it was Mairey took a while answering. "We've found quite a bit actually. I imagine you've heard the site is possibly an old trading center for the ancient Celts. The Blavet River was once probably more important than it is now. We've found quite a few artifacts already, swords, bronze cooking pots, many personal items. Not as rich a find as La Tene but close. We've even found a small replica of a two-wheeled burial chariot, just as at La Tene."

Mairey put one finger to her mouth, looking dismayed. "I'm sorry, I'm taking it for granted you know about La Tene."

Stephen's full grin flashed. "But I do indeed, any good Druid would. La Tene was the excavation in Switzerland establishing the Celts as worldwide traders. And it was certainly a Druid settlement. I've read everything I can find on it."

She lifted her eyes to his in relief at his understanding. It was so difficult to explain laboriously to persons with no background at all.

"These finds are so far not as important as La Tene. But they're impressive. We're all very pleased and feel it's been most worthwhile."

"And do they further the knowledge of Druidism as a remarkable culture?'

Something about the question, perhaps his lowered voice, perhaps the concentration of his gaze, told Mairey this was important to him. She liked him the better for it. He wasn't quite the uncaring troubadour she'd taken him to be. Still not a really responsible person, or one to trust with anything important but not as bad as she'd thought.

"Yes, of course they do. Some of the metal objects are truly beautiful. They show a highly advanced sense of the artistic, among other things."

Stephen didn't tell her rumors were flying around the town of fantastic objects wrought in gold. Surely she knew that. Doubtless one of the reasons for the guards.

"But there are more pits than this? Does your brother actually excavate like you do?"

Mairey flushed.

"I meant my comment in an admiring way, Dr. Bronwyn. I just wondered why you and Beth are alone."

Stephen's hurried explanation cleared the air, as Mairey briefly smiled again.

"I started this pit as an extra one just for us. Beth gets too excited if she's in the main pit too long. Too many people and too much stimulation for her. There are several other pits, some abandoned. But you must go see the key excavation. There's much more going on there but it's usually too frantically busy a place for a little girl to spend the day."

Stephen digested this and concluded Mairey seldom let Beth out of her sight. A little unusual, although Mairey might be overly-conscientious if she was not used to children and only been caring for Beth for a short time. Still, it was not his place to ask questions.

"Can you tell me why you picked this site to excavate? Druid settlements were usually close to a source of water, so the river qualifies, especially if it was a trading route. I know La Tene was between two lakes."

"Of course you're right, Dr. Lovernios. We knew water and trees were essentials to the early Druids. We picked this spot because we kept hearing stories of a large natural well which used to service the whole town. There are many local legends of the Druids who used to live here. I think you'll find legends guide a lot of archeologists to a new site. The well was used extensively, so the storytellers say and was more important to daily life than the Blavet River. We've found many traces of the well but not the main spring. Then some small objects kept working their way to the surface and we looked at all those the townspeople had saved. None of them truly important but indicative. It was enough to make us do a complete survey of the site."

"How very interesting. I think I will poke around a little. I'd like to say hello to your brother and uncle."

A shadow flitted over Mairey's expressive face.

"They'd enjoy seeing you. They both think it's wonderful you feel free to be a bard and wander the country. I think they envy you."

She didn't meet his eyes as she spoke.

He looked at her and half-raised his eyebrows, a small smile on his face.

"And you don't think it's wonderful and you're not at all envious."

His deep voice was soft, with no particular emphasis but Mairey flushed again.

"No," she said. "I don't and I'm not."

He looked smug, as if the answer was just what he'd expected.

"I won't be in the tavern tonight, so this is goodbye. I'm going to spend some time at the Forest of Broceliande."

"Merlin's magic forest," she murmured. "Although they call it the Forest of Paimpoint now in Brittany."

"Ah, you know about it. I can't resist visiting. I prefer the old Celtic name. I hear from everyone the feeling of mystery is quite strong as you walk under the trees. Amazing, if true."

He couldn't quite decipher the look she gave him. Some contempt, he was certain. Little of interest in the magical charm of the Forest. This girl would never be susceptible to magic, although he wished he had some at his disposal to try to shock her. It would be challenging to see if he could persuade this scientific and highly educated woman to believe in spells, auras and visions.

He wanted to know more about visions and spells himself. Now he was able to see auras he might experiment and see what else he could do.

The resolve settled in and lit his mind like a beacon.

Definitely he'd do just that. Life was again offering interesting possibilities.

# Chapter Three

ꟹ

Mairey watched Stephen give Beth a hug and then vault out of the pit as easily as when he'd levered his long body in. She wished he weren't quite so good-looking and physically appealing. He projected strength and power to a degree she found disturbing. She didn't approve of him and she didn't really like having him around. He disconcerted her.

But he possessed a marvelous way with children.

Unfortunately, his lambent eyes told her he had thoughts of other than children. When he was nearby she felt like a different person. Not at all the Mairey she was used to. She felt a stranger inhabited her normally comfortable skin. Being around him made her feel *itchy*.

Funny itchy and with a body that shivered when he looked at her.

If she could admire his character she'd feel better about him. Maybe she should concentrate on how well he got along with Bethan. As a doctor his easy humor doubtless served him well. This at least was admirable. Although on second thought maybe it was a feckless trait, being able to joke on a child's level. Not really so admirable after all.

She shrugged and gathered Beth to her for a quick hug. Then she sent the child back to where she'd been digging and turned to her own pile of dirt Finding buried civilizations didn't attract her right at this minute. This was the moment she had, however and she was darned lucky to have it. Few women possessed as much independence and the opportunity to explore her own intellectual worth.

Why then this feeling of discontent?

She stood musing for a moment, but finding no answer to her thoughts picked up her favorite tool, a spoon-shaped instrument and started digging.

To her dismay her thoughts slipped away from her again and back to the imposing Dr. Lovernios.

Would she ever see that blasted Druid again? Probably not. He was not one to return to a place he'd already visited. He had *wandering* engraved on some prominent site in his soul. He'd doubtless go on with his travels after he visited Broceliande.

She'd not be bothered by him again.

Stephen easily found the main excavation and the male Bronwyns appeared glad to see him. Mairey's brother Philip and her uncle Taliesin, both esteemed archeologists in their own right, were busily engaged when Stephen approached but dropped their work to come talk to him. Their pit was huge, with quite a few workers and a lot of equipment including large and small screens to sieve the dirt. Several buildings were nearby, the largest one as big as a warehouse. Since a guard stood by the door, Stephen assumed this housed the artifacts they'd already excavated.

He'd already noted the four strand barbed-wire fence surrounded the whole area, which was much larger than he'd expected. As far as he could tell, there was only one entrance and that was also guarded.

He talked for a short while with the Bronwyns.

"Can we do anything for you, Dr. Lovernios? Would you like me to take you in to see the acquisitions?" asked Philip. "They are all catalogued and of course registered with the French government and some of them are impressive."

Stephen looked around at the beehive of activity and didn't have the heart to accept, even though he longed to.

"Another day, perhaps. Somehow I think you're needed right where you are. May I come back another day, when I don't feel this sense of urgency hanging over you? I'd also like to see the grid maps you're using at another time."

Philip started and then smiled. "You're unusually perceptive. Yes, we all feel we're about to uncover something important. And yes, please come back. You're not a common man, Dr. Lovernios."

Taliesin Bronwyn came over with an equally pleasant greeting but Stephen sensed their minds were locked into whatever work was going on at the moment.

"I'll be back," he said. The three men shook hands and Stephen smiled as he turned and walked away. The intellects of the two Bronwyns had already moved into their own entrancing world.

He'd best start on his way to Broceliande.

The magic forest of Broceliande.

Haunted by the ghosts of Merlin, King Arthur and the Knights of the Round Table. Arthur, the fabled hero whose body Druid tales claim to have transported, sailed to the Island of Avalon. There he rests in peace, ready to return when the world most needs him.

He could hardly wait to be on his way. But why on earth had he told them he'd be back?

* * * * *

Stephen strode along, his brain occupied by the two females back digging in the first pit. Beth, a perfect doll of a child and her aunt Mairey. His newly developed abilities to see auras enchanted him and it seemed to be strongest when Mairey was near. He found it hard to believe an agnostic of Druid talents would be the one to inspire him. He'd noticed one surprising thing. The arrows of anxiety in Mairey's aura definitely darkened and multiplied whenever he approached Beth. What was the problem causing such over-concern? Surely it could not be normal.

He shrugged and walked on. Not his problem.

He'd sleep in Loudéac tonight and go on to the forest the next day. In fact, for the first time since coming to Brittany he felt like enjoying a luxurious meal and comfortable bed. No bardic singing tonight. He felt in the mood to soak up luxury. Laughing to himself, he thought of how surprised Mairey would be if she knew he could afford any extravagance he wished. She'd pegged him as a penniless itinerant and he'd done nothing to disabuse her of the notion.

He was almost to Loudéac when he saw a small motorcar parked by the side of the road. Not far off a woman leaned over a small boy, who was screaming with pain. As Stephen watched, the boy suddenly vomited and then fell to the ground gripping his stomach.

The doctor in him had him running to the child and pulling him away into a clean patch of grass.

"I'm a doctor," he explained hurriedly to the woman. No more misunderstandings if he could help it. "How long has he been like this?"

The anxious lines on her face relaxed as little as she accepted his competence.

"Not long. Max has been on the backseat playing with his toy soldiers. He's been unusually quiet for him, until he started groaning. I stopped the car at once and took him out."

Stephen stretched the boy out on the grass and began palpating his stomach. The child screeched with every touch. Stephen suddenly grinned, while the woman looked at him as if she was making a dreadful mistake, letting a madman touch her child. Stephen did not even have to close his eyes to see in his mind a large box of chocolates, now filled only with empty wrappers.

"He'll need to vomit some more of the chocolates, madam and then he'll be all right. With a sore stomach, to be sure and hopefully the knowledge one never eats a whole box at one time."

She started, stared at him as if he were insane and then ran to the car. Turning around, her red face showed she'd found confirmation of Stephen's strange diagnosis. Just then the boy leaned over and got rid of what Stephen hoped was the last of his forbidden meal. No wonder his stomach was so hard and distended. The little monster must have gobbled the chocolates as fast as he could swallow.

Stephen patted the child on the head. He looked to be about six and his eyes right now were filled with fear. Stephen went to the mother and stood between her and her child.

"Remember how anything forbidden was exactly what you simply had to have when you were a child? I hope you do. Your boy feels perfectly dreadful, both physically and mentally. He needs no punishment, madam."

She raised angry brown eyes to his blue ones. He held her gaze, facing her anger and willing it to dissolve. Finally he saw some of her ire fading.

"How did you know?" she asked. "We were taking a box of chocolates to his grandmother but you couldn't have known that. What kind of a doctor are you?"

She glanced over uncertainly at the boy, who was sitting now, his head in his hands.

Stephen laughed. Even as his laughter rang out he realized he could not remember when he'd last laughed with such sincerity. Certainly not with the pleasure he now felt when he considered his Druid powers seemed to be still developing. The box of chocolates, heart-shaped and bound with a red velvet ribbon, had appeared as clear as a photograph in his mind. How wonderful!

"Just an ordinary doctor, madam, who made a lucky guess. Good day to you. I hope you and your boy have an uneventful trip from now on."

He turned from her and walked past the car to the open road.

Filled with energy, he strode quickly along. He was looking forward to a steaming bath at a good hotel in Loudéac. He swallowed a chuckle. He'd definitely have to retrieve his credentials from his knapsack and have a little talk with the proprietor to get the kind of room he wanted. That and a large tip should do it.

But how wonderful his Druid powers were coming to fruition.

Totally unexpected and most thoroughly welcome.

# Chapter Four

ஐ

The sky was bright with spring's clearest blue as Stephen headed toward the forest. He came to the edge of the dense woods and paused. The sense of wonder so many reported reached out from the forest as if to beckon him in. The trees loomed huge and ancient, with hawthorn bushes nestling in between. The fragrant smell of so much greenery filled his senses. It was easy to imagine why mothers brought their children into the woods to be blessed by the fairies living here. Certainly it was an idyllic setting for magic and mystery.

He looked around him eagerly. He didn't really expect to see the white deer that reportedly appeared to travelers. Perhaps just as well, since legends told they were fairy women in disguise, capable of luring a hunter to his death. He smiled at the thought of himself as a hunter, either of women or deer. Still, the majesty of the forest enclosed him the instant he entered its dense dominion. The myriad trees hovering over him shaded his path but no gloom lingered under the ancient trees. He felt surrounded by mystery and peace.

Breathing deeply of the tree-scented air, Stephen stood still, filled with unexpected awe as he surveyed the vast woods that was the Forest of Broceliande. He definitely preferred to use the old Celtic name, for it was easy to see why this forest was still sacred to the Druids. Many oak trees, ancient and gnarled, dominated the groves before him. The oak, the most holy tree to a Druid, reigned in leafy splendor. Still there were many beeches, as well as areas of conifers. Mostly a forest of broad-leafed trees that loomed and darkened the forest, yet it still projected a sense of preternatural peace. He could hear a brook softly rippling nearby. He thought he heard another stream trilling a little farther away. No wonder the Druids through the ages loved these woods. It was easy to imagine this dense shadowy forest extending throughout much of the interior of Brittany as it had in the first centuries after Christ. No surprise the people referred to these lovely woods at the enchanted forest.

Being here in this lush and magical forest was exactly the place he wanted to be. He was sensitized to every leaf and blade of grass. The lower leaves of the trees were soft and untouched by the sun and the moss and matted grass under the trees were green and gave off their own scent. He could feel each tree reaching toward him and pulling him into a place where he dearly longed to be. Every step seemed to release the sweet smell of summer grass.

He felt enveloped by an atmosphere of mystery, not oppressive in any sense but definitely intriguing. He stopped to let the quiet of the forest invade his body and his mind. He felt as if he'd come home, home to the Druid instincts always lying just below the surface of his consciousness. Instincts that intrigued and beckoned but he'd never known how to tap. Instincts he would dearly love to turn into true Druid talent. Perhaps just being here would show him how.

He came into the middle of a beautiful glen, with another murmuring brook off to one side. Surely the goddess of the Druids had led him to this evocative place. Surrounded by a rich tapestry of green and a grandeur seeming to call to him, he felt like dropping to his knees in awe. His care and personal grief fell away as he surrendered to the sheer majesty of the woods. Nothing in his experience prepared him for the soul-shaking intensity of this experience.

He'd heard many times of the legend of Merlin, the bard and wizard of King Arthur. Supposedly Merlin was aware an enchantress would someday deceive him, putting a spell upon him that would ensnare him for all of time. Imprisoned by love. Viviane was the love of Merlin's later life and even though he knew she was the one who would someday enchain him, he could not resist her. He came back to her at the end of his earthly existence, here in this forest, knowing the danger he faced and willing to accept it. She imprisoned him in nine magical circles and joined him in the circles. Some legends call the circles as intangible as air, although other legends say it was a crystal prison. Now, according to the Bretons, they remain together for eternity, captive in the enchanted forest of Broceliande.

As Stephen walked along dreaming, he noticed a small clearing ahead off the path. The site, still called Merlin's Tomb was strewn with flowers and small gifts. Amazing that some people still worship there, believing either Merlin or his magic lies buried somewhere under the green grass.

The Welsh and British have similar tales of Merlin's enchantment, except they call the enchantress Morgan La Fay. Although both legends acknowledged the ensnared one was a Druid known as Merlin.

A charming, or a horrifying tale, depending on your point of view. Certainly you could not ignore it if you were a Druid bard trying to find your way back to peace in a world that had trapped you in misery. He turned his thoughts to the stories of Launcelot and Gawain, searching these same woods for some sign of the Holy Grail. Launcelot was supposedly born here where the Lady of the Lake had raised him. There were many stories of the vain quest for the Grail although there was a great variation in the different legends.

Truly a magical place.

Stephen breathed deeply and absorbed to his very bones the mystery and peace of the forest.

There was much hope here, as well as the sense of magic integral to the very air in the forest.

Every leaf, every tree, every breath he took encouraged his belief in himself as a Druid and as a man. His lost love had not wanted him but as he stood there in the forest he realized her decision was not due to any deficiency in him. Her fate had ordained her for another. Soothing comfort coursed through his mind and body, freeing him at last from useless regret. He was not lacking as he'd feared. Now it was up to him to find what wonders fate now held for him.

He had no idea at all of how to go about this private search. He was sure of only one thing. The recent proofs of his true Druid heritage were impossible to ignore. Somehow his Druid abilities would be important to his future. They had surfaced for a reason he had yet to learn.

A little frisson of excitement ran through him. How wonderful to feel positive emotions again.

Maybe he should do what he could to help fate along. There must be some small spells he could try. If he'd really come into his Druid heritage…he couldn't think of anything more exciting.

Hope and the future beckoned to him with the promise of deepening magic.

He stood still, alone in the forest, looked at the sky over his head and shouted with joy. Throwing up his arms, he exulted in his newfound Druid world.

* * * * *

Stephen sat on a mounded tuft, stretching his long legs in front of him and leaning back with his arms against the grass. He'd wandered around the forest for hours, feeling the peace and magic of the sacred forest seep into his soul.

He longed to try his hand at spells. He must be very careful not to breach the Druid dictum that magic should hurt no one, at least no one innocent. Looking around for inspiration, he focused on a small squirrel with an acorn in his paws. Closing his eyes he concentrated, putting all other thoughts out of his mind. When he opened his eyes, he saw the squirrel, looking down at the nut on the ground.

He'd done it. He'd made the squirrel's paws relax enough to drop the acorn. If he hadn't thought he could be imagining it, he'd swear the squirrel looked puzzled. Containing his laughter, he watched the squirrel pick up the nut again and scamper away on fast little legs.

Now what else could he try? Something just a little harder. His vision had always been superb and he noticed a crow heading for a thrush's nest in a nearby tree. Halting the marauder from his scavenging took much deeper and longer concentration, as the bird was a big one and farther away from his focus. He watched with satisfaction as the crow circled repeatedly and could not land on the nest. The intruder finally gave up with a series of loud caws echoing throughout the forest and Stephen's face crinkled with a grin of satisfaction. He'd done what he wanted, he could cast simple spells. And he'd not hurt anything in nature with his efforts.

*Blessed be*, he was a true Druid.

He suddenly realized he was very tired and yawned widely.

Evidently casting spells was exhausting but the exhaustion seemed unimportant beside the fact he could actually exert power. He'd only tried simple ones, true. Surely he could progress. He could really channel enchantment! He was a Druid with at least some of the mystical powers of a Druid.

With a delighted smile on his face, he leaned back on the hummock.

And immediately fell asleep.

* * * * *

Stephen awoke from a short nap, as refreshed as if he'd spent a night in a feather bed. Which he'd done last night but he'd never awakened to this sense of mixed exhilaration and contentment. During all of his long, hopeless courtship of Vivie Dellafield, now Mrs. Alec Stratton, he'd never felt contentment. He'd only known the underlying anxiety that nothing he could do would sway her from her deep commitment to Alec. Even though he'd worked side by side with her in her clinic, admiring her expertise and her compassion, he'd never felt relaxed and satisfied. He'd been striving so hard to win her approval he'd forgotten to replenish his own spirit.

Now the goddess of all Druids called him back to his roots. He would follow with joy in his heart. He could hardly wait to see what came next in this new and enthralling world.

Springing to his feet, he paused and mentally said goodbye to the spirits in the forest of Broceliande and their haunting mystery. It was time to join the outside world again and see what lay in store for him.

Definitely he needed to say a proper farewell to all the Bronwyns. All three of them were unusually interesting people and well worth knowing. He also wanted to make one last check on Bethan. A darling mite of a child. What had happened to her father and mother? Perhaps they were simply away on a long trip but somehow he didn't think so. The anxiety in Mairey's aura made no sense, if the answer were as simple as that.

He stayed at the same inn in Loudéac and enjoyed another night of luxury. For some reason he didn't try to analyze, he now wanted to present a different appearance to the world than the rootless itinerant. He stopped at a good men's shop before he went on his way again. He came out wearing well-cut trousers, expensive boots that would be excellent for hiking and a loose-fitting jacket. He flexed his large frame in satisfaction. Definitely he enjoyed good linen and fine leather again.

He'd been locked in misery and now he strode in the sunshine.

# Chapter Five

ꕥ

He set out on the road, suddenly eager to reach Gouarec. He went to the excavation immediately, first to see the male Bronwyns.

Both of them came up to shake his hand.

"It's good to see you again, Lovernios." Taliesin's hearty greeting carried only sincerity. "The last time you were here I believe we were much preoccupied."

Stephen grinned. "I had a definite feeling you were on the verge of digging up something special and were anxious to get on with it. Was I right?"

Both Bronwyns laughed. "Yes, you were right," Philip said. "We'd just uncovered the handle of what turned out to be a superb sword. A beautiful thing. Would you like to see it? I think the quality of the workmanship will surprise you."

Stephen started to answer yes, he'd love to and then something jiggled in his brain. An image flashed into his mind of someone falling, falling hard and fast. The picture flitted in and out but only enough to show him the figure had black hair. He tried to banish his concern as unreasonable but anxiety persisted and he finally surrendered to it.

"I think I'd like to see Dr. Mairey first. May I come back to you after I greet her? I wouldn't want her and Beth to feel neglected."

Both men laughed.

Philip humphed a little.

"Mairey's not the type to take offense but I agree little Bethan might. She talks about you all the time. Come back after you see them both. They visited us just before you got here and said were going to walk a little for exercise before going back to their private dig. You should catch them there."

Stephen looked around the whole area before he started out. He felt most uneasy and could see no reason for it. His palms were damp with apprehension and he couldn't understand why. The guards were still in place and the area seemed quiet except for the sounds to be expected at an archeological dig. Shovels, dirt being carefully moved, people consulting in low tones.

The sense of unease stayed with him as he walked rapidly toward Mairey and Beth's pit. Something was wrong. He conceded his Druid senses were telling him truly but he didn't know yet what was triggering this feeling of foreboding.

As he neared the smaller pit he heard a woman's scream and he broke into a rapid run.

He didn't know if he liked having prescience if his images came true. He hadn't counted on this aspect, not at all.

* * * * *

He sped to the pit and found Mairey crumpled at the bottom of the ladder and motionless. Beth must have run to her immediately and now pulled at her sweater.

"Mairey, Mairey, answer me. Are you all right?"

Stephen vaulted into the pit and knelt beside the prostrate girl. She was breathing, thank the goddess but her face was white and pale. Several charming freckles stood out on her alabaster skin. The fall knocked off her hat and her hair tumbled even more gloriously than he'd suspected. A veritable mane of dark curls descended to her shoulders. Even as he put his hand to the pulse in her neck she stirred and opened her eyes. Her beautiful eyes, unguarded now and soft as new velvet.

"Stephen." Her voice was surprised but not unwelcoming.

"Mairey, tell me what hurts the worst so I can fix it." Not quite the typical measured voice of a doctor but he didn't stop to think of that.

She looked puzzled and then straight at him, locking his gaze with hers. Her eyes were focused and he breathed another silent *blessed be.*

"My head," she said finally, her breath coming out in a sobbing sigh. "And my right ankle."

He gently cradled her head in his large hands, while he felt her scalp. As he'd suspected, there was a lump at the back where she'd hit the ground. Large and getting larger. He put her head down with care and then turned to her ankles. He had to slit her pant's leg to gain access. Pushing her ridiculous trousers up, he caught his breath. She possessed the most beautiful legs he'd ever seen. Legs to grace a dancer. Long, slim and shaped to invade a man's dreams.

Not really the proper professional thoughts.

Her right ankle was already swelling and he took a knife out of his pocket and quickly slashed the laces of her right boot. Even so it was not enough to let him slip the boot off her foot and he didn't want to pull. He carefully cut a slit down one side and lifted the foot out of its confining prison. The touch of his fingers, even though expert and gentle, made her wince and cry out.

After feeling her foot with his expert fingers, he gently lowered it back to the ground as he considered what to do.

"Nothing's broken, as far as I can tell. You definitely must treat it as cautiously as if you had broken some of the fragile foot bones, however. Too much weight could easily fracture an already weakened bone. I'll splint it for now and if necessary we'll make a cast. I think splinting will do, though but you aren't going to run any races for a good long while."

He'd meant to reassure her and was dismayed to see tears start to overflow her aquamarine eyes.

"I can't stay off my feet. I have to guard Beth."

Stephen could think of nothing to say to what he considered a most strange statement and he busied himself with looking around for material for the splint.

"Don't move, Mairey, until I get your foot immobilized. You'll be courting disaster if you do."

"I'd better go to the main site," he added. "They have lumber there I can use. Will you promise not to move 'til I get back?"

She reached out one hand to grasp Beth's. "Yes, of course. But you'd better vault out like you did last time. I broke the ladder when I fell."

Stephen looked at the ladder for the first time. The top rung had snapped in two. Surely a most unlikely happening, that a girl as slender as Mairey could crack through a solid wooden step. He went closer, mystified until he got there. Then he simply stopped and stared, anger coursing through his entire body. The broken rung had quite obviously been sawed through just enough to still hold its shape until someone stepped on it. Then it would splinter at the first application of weight.

Someone deliberately tried to seriously injure Mairey, if not to kill her. Probably just injure, as a three-foot fall was not likely to kill. Beth's small body would not have triggered the trap, in fact Beth was in the pit with them so she must have gone first. Someone who knew the habits of both of them well enough to bait the trap accordingly. He imagined if he scouted the perimeter of the site he would find some strands of barbed wire cut or else bent so a man could get through.

His silence reached Mairey.

"What is it? You've found something." Her voice reflected her fear and he hurried back to her.

"You and I will discuss this later. For now I must find the materials I need for your ankle."

"Stephen?" Her voice came out in a tremulous whisper. Damn women so intelligent they could almost read a man's mind.

"I'll be right back. Beth, tell your aunt a story so she doesn't move. Make up one about chickens and bears."

He was rewarded with two slight smiles. He ruffled Bethan's hair and vaulted out of the pit.

He hurried to the find the other Bronwyns.

He called to them as he strode up.

"I'm glad to find you together. I would speak with both of you. Privately."

Something about his tone made them both turn and give him their full attention. They walked a little away from another worker sifting the dirt with care.

"Mairey has taken a fall and I must hurry back to her but I wanted you to know the top rung of her ladder had been sawed so she would plunge when she set foot on it. If you have any idea who could be so vicious and underhanded, I'd like to know it. May I come and talk with you later? Now I need to fashion a splint for her ankle and carry her home. She won't be walking much for a while."

He turned aside and going to the area where artifacts were being encased for shipping, chose some pieces of wood and picked up a spindle of strong twine.

"This will do until I can get into town and find smoother material. I'll rip up my shirt for padding for now. Mairey doesn't need splinters on top of a painful ankle."

At the last minute he turned again to the silent men beside him.

"Why does Mairey feel she has to guard Beth every minute?"

Philip and Taliesin exchanged glances.

"You answer, Tally," Philip said.

They both looked grim but then Stephen knew the truth must be just as forbidding.

"It's not my story to tell, Dr. Lovernios. It involves Mairey's sister Alys who is now dead. She was Beth's mother. This much I'll say, Mairey worries about Alys' second husband. Her first husband, Beth's father, died from sheer carelessness and Alys remarried a poor choice of a man. I would guess he might be behind this accident."

Stephen snorted. "I wouldn't call it an accident. I'd call it attempted murder."

He noticed the two men looked stricken but not shocked.

Clutching the materials he'd gathered, he went on the run back to Beth and Mairey.

Mairey lay quietly, holding Beth's hand. Beth's tears left little rivulets down the dust on her cheeks and she put up a small fist to scrub under her eyes. Mairey's lips were compressed as if she struggled to keep from showing her pain. For the first time since he'd started his bardic journey, Stephen regretted he didn't have access to a clinic or hospital. If he only had medical supplies accessible, he'd see to it she did not suffer as she was suffering now.

He went over to her, smiling as best he could. Evidently it was enough, as she smiled back. Not enough to show her dimple but enough to show her resolution not to give in to her pain.

"Now I want to take you home, Mairey. I think I'd best carry you. I can cushion you from bumps better this way."

Mairey looked at him in surprised horror. "You can't possibly. It's over two miles. Way over."

"Well, we don't have a wheelbarrow so I'm the next best thing."

Drs. Taliesin and Philip jumped in the pit in time to hear the end of the conversation.

Dr. Tally laughed. "This accident has addled both your brains. What's wrong with a taxi? In fact, I'll go call one now."

He loped off. For a man in his sixties he appeared to be in excellent shape. Stephen watched him and ran a hand over his face.

"I wasn't thinking straight," he said, flushing and Mairey nodded and smiled.

"Nor was I."

*No wonder about me. Even with her injured and helpless my body jerks to attention when I'm forced to touch her so much.*

"I have another idea which might help in the future. Dr. Bronwyn, tomorrow can you have some of your crew make a ramp down the side of this pit? I noticed you have a large one in the other excavation. When Mairey gets a little better she can use crutches but she won't be climbing ladders for a while."

Mairey flashed him a grateful smile with a little of her dimple showing.

"What a fantastic idea. I dreaded not being able to come back for a long while."

"I'll do my best to make you a proper splint so you can come soon but you must stay off your foot for a day or two."

Stephen sat down on a big pile of dirt. Mairey lay motionless, with Beth curled up in the crook of her arm. Philip evidently didn't feel like talking either, although a peculiar half-smile seemed pasted on his face.

They didn't have too long to wait for the taxi. Directed by Dr. Taliesin, it drew up close to the pit and Stephen jumped up.

"I'll hand her up to you, Dr. Philip and then I'll come take her. I want to be sure she's correctly positioned in the taxi. In fact, I'll get in the taxi and you can hand her in. I can arrange the leg better this way. Why don't you come along and bring Beth in the front seat?"

As Philip handed her in, Stephen gathered Mairey into his arms, holding her carefully so his arms supported her legs without putting pressure on them.

She looked up at him and grinned. "I guess you're a pretty good doctor after all."

Stephen raised his expressive eyebrows. "Did you doubt it?"

Mairey's smile faded. "No, not really." She felt half groggy with pain. "Never your ability, just your lack of dedication."

Stephen looked down at her and his face turned to chiseled stone.

The rest of the ride was filled mostly with Beth's chatter.

# Chapter Six

ꟸ

Stephen carried Mairey into the boarding house and found himself surprised. The Bronwyns had taken over the whole house and rearranged rooms so each of the adults had their own small suite. It made sense when he thought about it. They were closer to the dig than they'd be in a hotel and the housekeeper and staff running the boarding house would serve them well. Certainly much better quarters for a long excavation.

He followed Philip and Beth to Mairey's rooms and carefully laid her on the bed. Then he excused himself to find a pharmacy handling the materials he needed for a proper splint. This took longer than he'd expected and when he returned he found Mairey asleep, with Bethan curled up beside her.

He stood looking down at them. They were each beautiful, in such different ways. Mairey's lashes looked ridiculously long and dark against her white cheeks. Her black hair fanned against the pillow in luxurious abandonment. Her lovely skin, although a little pale, still glowed. She was stunning. Any male in the world would echo his assessment. A fresh scent, something like a spring meadow of flowers, rose faintly as he leaned over her.

He didn't want to find her stunning and appealing.

He didn't want to think of her as a desirable female. An utterly desirable female. She didn't like him and although he knew he could change her mind if he told her more about himself he didn't choose to explain himself to anyone simply to enhance his own image. She could think of him as she pleased. His heart, long accustomed to yearning for Vivie, left room for no other woman to truly matter.

He needed to unwrap the makeshift bandage on her foot and knew she'd wakened at the first touch. She jerked as he'd expected and he put his finger to his lips and shushed her. Beth was still asleep and they both were grateful they must keep silent to avoid wakening the child. He brought her a glass of water and lifted her head so she could swallow a tablet to control the pain. He soon placed a proper splint on the food and straightened up. Then, without a word or a smile, he handed her the rest of the package of pills and silently left.

He couldn't know Mairey's eyes followed him as long as he was in sight.

Troubled eyes. And not just from the pain in her ankle.

* * * * *

The next two days were some of the most bothersome Mairey Bronwyn could remember. Stephen Lovernios attended her each day, flexing and exercising the muscles of her leg and finally, on the third day, bringing a pair of crutches and saying she could go back to work if she took special care not to fall. He was scrupulously polite, professionally adept and acted as if they'd never even been introduced.

She knew well she'd offended him with her remark about his lack of dedication. She'd commented on something definitely none of her business. She didn't really regret she'd spoken. He was sinfully handsome, his unusual hair flaring like a beacon when the sun shone on it. His tall, strong figure would impress a woman of ninety, let alone any girl who still had dreams of finding just the right man.

She wasn't that girl. She didn't want him. She wanted a man who had the character and power to devote himself to his chosen field. It didn't have to be *her* field but it must be one he would pursue with all his diligence. One he loved as she loved her work. Not a profession he would casually leave to go roaming.

How could a doctor walk away from needy patients?

She'd watch her sister marry a wastrel and only heartache followed. Certainly she'd never again suspect Stephen of improper longings, like her brother-in-law but she wanted a man of learning and commitment to his learning. One who believed in the value of hard work just as she did. How could he understand her and her dedicated love for her profession unless he felt the same?

Beth loved the man but then Beth knew only the laughing, teasing Stephen who could charm a frog into hopping out of his pond. Beth didn't recognize a grown woman needed a serious man. One who'd help her fight the other ones, the ones interested only in tramping on a woman's heart. As her sister Alys' heart had been trampled. Alys learned too late. Much too late.

She lay back against her pillows, thinking of Alys' first marriage and how happy she'd been when married to Beth's father. Her second husband, Walter Griffin, capitalized with expert skill on her loneliness and swept her into a marriage that proved a disaster from the beginning. Only Alys' death in a car wreck saved her from living a union of unhappiness and horror. Her husband turned out to be a pedophile who lusted for her small daughter and discovering his wicked carnality led to her death. For the thousandth time, she wondered if Alys hit that tree deliberately. Perhaps tears had blinded her sister. Mairey sincerely hoped it was the latter.

Who on earth decreed men were the dominant force in this world? Alys had been so much wiser and so much a better person than Walter. Why had he been able to impose his distasteful self and dominate a lovely lady like Alys? She'd been unable to stop him in his disgusting habits and unable to leave him without turmoil she found herself unwilling to endure.

At one time in the long-ago deities were goddesses who held the secrets of the universe. The secret of life rested in their hands and in their bodies. True, matriarchal societies were limited to the quite distant past. As so-called civilization took over the goddess traditions declined. Some research showed women still ruled the culture in isolated peoples but it was rare and fast fading. What happened that men were now so overriding, so belligerent and so dangerous?

She thought of Stephen. A dominant male if she'd ever seen one and one she couldn't quite respect. Still, she'd like to be his friend. She at last knew for certain he could never be a dangerous and threatening man.

She'd try to break through the barrier he'd erected before he left to wherever he roamed next.

When he next appeared she lifted her eyes to his and made the effort.

"Lovernios is a very old Celtic name. I know that much but can't remember exactly where I read it."

"It's a name of ancient Celtic kings. It means 'son of the fox'." His blue eyes met hers briefly, with no apparent feeling showing in his arresting gaze.

"Now I remember," she'd said, pushing herself to sit up in bed, her voice excited. He'd just finished checking her ankle and saying she could walk around using the crutches. "You inherited your beautiful hair color along with the name. Fox hair, it's called."

He'd briefly smiled. "You're right. If you see just this color it's doubtless a Lovernios or a descendant of one."

"But how amazing. I'd think you'd be very proud."

"I definitely am," he said dryly. "More than you know."

He moved a little away from the bed.

"Now you're well, or almost well, I'm leaving tomorrow. I want to explore the megaliths at Carnac while I'm this close to them."

Her heart plummeted to her shoes, which made no sense. She had no use for this man. She tried to smile sweetly.

"I understand they are magnificent. We all intend to explore them before we leave this area."

"Yes," he said simply. "Goodbye, Mairey. You may take off the splint in two weeks."

Without another word he turned to leave.

She'd watched his tall straight figure walk out of her life. If she could compromise her beliefs, she'd call him back. But she couldn't give up her essential values. No matter when she allowed herself to look into his eyes she fought the absurd impulse to move toward his arms and hope they would close tightly around her. Taking care of all her problems. He was a strong, charismatic man but one who was not for her.

A silly thought indeed. She was better off without someone so irresponsible.

Surely she knew that.

# Chapter Seven

Stephen enjoyed the long walk to the megaliths at Carnac. Summer had fully arrived and the weather was delightful. Wild daisies bloomed at the sides of the road and lazy clouds floated above his head. The scent of the tall grass that would soon be hay filled his nostrils as he passed. He couldn't help but remember the man he'd been just a few weeks before, when nothing interested him, even as he passed through some of the loveliest spots in Brittany.

He thought he might be a little overdressed for the part of a bard, since he'd bought a soft new shirt and wore the outfit he'd bought on the way back to the archeology dig and to Mairey. At least the excellent boots he'd bought were an advantage. They fit so well he felt he could stride along forever.

His mind suddenly jolted him. Had he actually thought the phrase "back to Mairey"?

Mairey, the beautiful girl he'd just left. The girl he kept trying to ignore. He couldn't deny she had a great deal to do with his current peace of mind. Certainly first seeing her aura shocked and delighted him. He could still envision plainly in his mind the lovely rosy color that was the essence of Mairey. He'd never truly solved the puzzle of the streaks of anxiety so prominent in his first vision of her aura. He suspected her bright exterior covered a secret worrying her nearly to distraction. Not just the care of Beth but something else, something she felt dangerous to Beth's very being.

What would it take to persuade her to confide in him?

He knew the answer. If she thought him the worthy man she didn't even realize she sought, she would be happy to confide in him and perhaps allow him to help her with her troubles. But doing so would involve him in her life, perhaps irretrievably. He didn't want to be committed to anyone. And if he did, it would be on his own terms. Didn't everyone want to be valued for himself?

He knew he could convince her of his worth and his underlying sincerity but wasn't sure he should even try. She didn't understand him at all. He was so used to being the laughing, carefree Stephen, the face he'd always presented to the world and one that served him well. Had this been wrong of him? If he'd let his sincere self show through sooner, would Vivie have taken him more seriously? Perhaps, although it would have been useless. He now knew in his Druid heart Vivie and her husband were destined to be together by the goddess of the Druids. Letting Vivie see his inner self sooner would not have mattered in the long run.

In this case everything truly had worked out for the best.

But should he show Mairey the real man? He'd like her to admire him just as she knew him, without explanations. He didn't want to feel it necessary to explain himself to anyone.

He put his introspections behind him and strode on.

The world teemed with so much to do and so much to see. A world turning miraculously beautiful once again.

He'd see and experience a lot before he even thought of any kind of commitment. He doubted he'd ever be ready for another serious involvement with any woman.

It seemed so much easier to drift along, alone and ready again to enjoy what came his way. Not a bad way to go, at all.

He walked on, just a little faster.

* * * * *

Stephen knew Carnac would be special but he was in no way prepared for the extent and magnificence of the megaliths. He'd bought a tourist book and done his homework but still he was astonished. Literally thousands of stones in three different sites running parallel to the nearby sea. Some in lines, some in circles known as cromlechs and many dolmens, or groups of standing stones with further stones laid across the top. These latter were assumed to be burial chambers as he already knew. He'd been prepared for the menhirs, the standing stones but not the sheer magnitude of them. Almost three thousand, again according to the guide book. Like no other place on Earth.

He suddenly remembered one of the tales of his heritage. Demonic beings were supposedly the builders of the menhirs. They'd buried fabulous treasure at Carnac and beneath one of the huge stones still lay the golden hoard. All the other stones were simply set up to better conceal the true hiding place. Another pagan tale insisted that one night each year all the stones walked down to the sea to dance and bathe. No one could confirm this of course, since any witnesses died quickly. Fanciful but intriguing, like so many of the early legends.

The megaliths were surely impressive enough in themselves to inspire extraordinary tales.

It would take days to track the various alignments and try to make sense of the whole display. Alleys of megaliths, with no definite explanation of why there were so many and why they were placed as they were. And then there was the nearby ocean and its beaches, a favorite vacation spot for all the French, not only the Bretons. The weather proved perfect and he loved to swim. He'd best find a friendly inn to house him comfortably, as well as welcome his flute and his bardic tales. He expected he'd be in this fascinating spot for days to come. Maybe weeks.

Stephen happily set off to explore the town of Carnac and find just the right inn. He felt confident his singing would make him more than welcome. A good thing since this was the first place in a long time where he'd want to stay a while.

While he stayed in the town he intended to try to find some books on archeology. He found he'd like to know more about the whole process.

Not for any special reason except it interested him.

* * * * *

He was having a marvelous time. He reminded himself of that rather often, as he walked around the huge expanse of the Carnac megaliths, or swam in the ocean, the gulls wheeling and calling over his head. He played his flute at night in the charming tavern he'd found. His Druid tales were so popular he was forced to laughingly beg for time to eat or sip his wine.

In the late afternoons he walked along the beaches, smelling the salty sea and watching the waves turn beautiful colors in the aftermath of the sunset. Rose, a bright true orange, deep reds and all shades in between. The ocean fascinated him. He loved to see the sun sink into the water and the sky gradually darken from the blazing sunset into a blue-green glow. Once he thought the evening waters bore some resemblance to Mairey's eyes. He shoved the thought away. For one thing, nothing could equal the intensity of the aquamarine of her eyes. For another, he didn't intend to think about her.

After the taverns closed he sometimes went back to the beaches on Quiberon Bay, enjoying the sights of the fishing boats and letting the waves lap at his feet. At night the breeze blew off the ocean, dispelling the heart of the day. Many of the boats sported the large bright lights necessary to entice the sardines to the fishermen's nets at night. The sounds of oars slapping the water on smaller boats floated clearly to where he stood. He loved the briny and fishy smells as he walked in the peace the ever-restless ocean brought. Though he often wondered why something so constantly moving brought him consolation and calm.

On the fifth night, he was playing in the tavern when he suddenly put down his flute and stared into space. As clearly as if he were standing beside her, he saw Mairey backed up against a wall in the pit, Beth clutched in her arms and sheer terror etched on her lovely face.

His audience, quieted, wondering why their new favorite stopped singing. The silence reached him and he started as if wakening from a trance.

"You've been the most marvelous audience in the world."

His deep warm voice conveyed his sincere gratitude for the appreciation the townspeople of Carnac had shown him.

"I will sing you one more song, this one the tale of Sir Galahad and how he came to Broceliande when King Arthur suggested he might find the Holy Grail in its magical woods. Then I'll ask to be excused."

At the cries of "No, no, don't stop" he merely smiled and raising his flute began the beginning notes. His audience quieted to hear him and his newly written lay, listening with utmost attention until he was done. When he finished they begged him to continue but still smiling, he waved to them all and vanished out the door.

It took only a few moments to pack his knapsack and pay his bill.

"I'm more than sorry to hear you're leaving, sir. You're the most popular singer we've ever had in town. You don't owe me a cent. You've more than paid your way with your entertaining."

Stephen shook his head. "My singing pleases me, also and I don't expect anything so kind. Thank you for the offer. You are most generous but I insist on paying my way."

He left a rather large sum of money on the counter and hurried out the door.

Mairey was in trouble and needed him. He'd just had his first vision and there no doubt at all existed in his mind. His first clear and true vision and a frightening one. What he'd seen was real. He'd walk as fast as he could to get back to her. He could only pray his vision would prove to be of something yet to come, not something that had already happened.

His long legs began to eat up the miles between Carnac and Mairey. He slept a few hours the first night under a tree with soft moss around its roots. His knapsack made an acceptable pillow. He'd left the road far enough to ensure he'd not be seen but he still slept with a dagger under his hand. An old Celtic dagger handed down through his family, which had well served each of the males who owned it. He was not especially worried, he felt only caution. He intended to be back at the Bronwyn archeology dig as soon as he possibly could.

Nothing or nobody could stop him.

# Chapter Eight

ഩ

He walked faster than when on his usual bardic stroll. Still it took him a day and a half to reach Gouarec. He'd slept but little and only for the short time in a small copse by the side of the road. He'd risen early and hurried on his way.

He headed immediately to the dig. The guard greeted him pleasantly, saying he hoped Stephen's journey had been a pleasant one. Stephen answered cordially but didn't stop to talk. Nor did he go to greet the male Bronwyns. He headed for Mairey's dig as fast as his muscled and honed legs could carry him.

As he came closer to the pit he could see Mairey, clasping Bethan tightly to her. Beth looked terrified as she desperately clutched Mairey's shoulders. Their pose was exactly the one he'd seen in his vision. Every nuance of both figures was the same. His vision was true, another gift from the goddess of us all.

He breathed a prayer of thanks to his goddess he'd come in time to have some influence on the coming action. Mairey looked straight ahead across the pit and never raised her eyes to see him coming. Her gaze seemed frozen in space, her expression one of horror. Her gorgeous skin had lost its creamy look and now shone pale and white. She seemed too terrified to move.

Stephen stopped as he tried to size up the situation. He stood close enough to see the whole area clearly but Mairey and the man facing her were too absorbed in their confrontation to notice anyone else. His Druid senses shuddered as the man's aura became plain. A nasty brownish color, with black streaks shooting through it. The whole aura loomed densely with no light glimmering through the dark mass. A malevolent, wicked man, without a doubt. If he had redeeming qualities they weren't evident in his aura.

Across from him, standing at the opposite side of the pit, the man with his hideous aura stood sneering at Mairey. His brown hair was curly and carefully tended. His small tight mouth, set in features too pretty to be handsome, repulsed Stephen. He leaned casually against the wall of the excavation, his hands in his pockets.

"Face reality, Mairey. I want Beth. I'm her legal father and have sued to have her returned to my custody. I want to take her with me now."

So. This was Walter Griffen, married to Mairey's deceased sister.

Beth turned and buried her head in Mairey's chest and Mairey flinched.

She patted Beth's head and whispered something to her.

Then she faced the man. "You'll never have her, Walter. Where did you file this ridiculous suit? In Wales? Not in Brittany, I'm certain. I would have been informed if you'd done so here."

Walter smirked. "It doesn't matter where. I'll soon be declared her legal father and I will have her."

Mairey threw up her head and snorted.

"You are only her stepfather and one of very short duration. Fortunately my sister wasn't married to you long before you drove her to her death. You have no grounds to prove you deserve Bethan."

A silence dragged out while a slow and purely evil smile spread over Walter's face. Stephen didn't move a muscle. He detested the other man on sight but didn't want to stop his boasting. It was far too informative. Walter might be good-looking at first glance, that he'd grant. His regular features could attract a female who couldn't read the lack of character in his shifting eyes. Those eyes never seemed to stay in one spot, raking over Mairey and especially Beth. Something about those moving eyes made Stephen long to abandon his inactivity and smash the grin from his smirking face.

Stephen flexed his fists but otherwise stood still. He hoped Walter would keep on talking before he flattened him.

Evidently Mairey's ankle was hurting, as she shifted her weight to one leg then put Beth on the ground and pushed the child behind her. She needed about two more days of wearing the splint on her ankle. He'd check and make sure her ankle was truly healed before he freed her to use her foot.

Walter kept scouring both females with his eyes, lingering on what he could see of Beth.

His voice was repellingly sweet and triumphant.

"I don't think you've thought this through, my dear Mairey. What if you were not in the picture *at all*? As her stepfather I would have precedence over an unmarried uncle who roams the world with his profession and has no credentials to being a good father. In fact, think of what would have happened if you'd been more seriously injured in your recent fall. What a dreadful shame it would be if you were no longer around to take care of Beth."

Mairey grew even paler as she absorbed the wicked implications of his words. Stephen's whole body flared with implosive anger. He'd had enough.

He strode to Walter, picked him up with one hand and held him about six inches off the ground and punched him hard with the other. Two punches, one in his gut and the other in his pretty face. Then he set him down.

"Would you like to go another round? I'd be delighted."

The growl in his voice would have made the bravest of the brave hesitate. Walter looked at his opponent, hatred marring his usually acceptable appearance.

He got out a handkerchief and wiped some of the blood from his nose. Both fear and anger streamed from him in an unattractive scent. Stephen sniffed in disgust and found a perfumey scent underneath the new odors of fear Walter couldn't control.

Walter pulled himself together and faced the man who stood there, his hands clenched and looking for a chance to do damage. Fear showed plainly on his face and so his refusal to give up and go away surprised Stephen.

"Who the hell are you and by what right do you come charging into a situation that can have nothing to do with you? I think the local authorities will be pleased to deal with you once I make a complaint. You can't go around assaulting people."

Stephen laughed. Not a pleasant laugh at all and Walter cringed.

"I think as Dr. Bronwyn's friend and protector I can launch a few complaints about you too. You have just threatened to kill her, as I will gladly testify if anything, anything at all, happens to her. You should hope she doesn't break even a fingernail. I think you should register what I'm saying and be very careful, very careful indeed, to make sure Dr. Bronwyn remains in good health. Besides testifying against you, I'm likely to take another injury to Dr. Bronwyn very personally."

Walter gasped. "I made no such threats. You're insane."

Stephen merely smiled. A smile guaranteed to scare off a much braver and more innocent man than Walter.

"I have an excellent memory. I can repeat word for word your incriminating statements about how much easier your life would be if Dr. Bronwyn ceased to exist."

Walter had recovered his normal color and some of his *savoir-faire*.

"You are utterly mistaken. But I do not choose to engage in arguments or fisticuffs with you. Although I'll lodge a complaint against you if you ever come near me again."

He gathered what little dignity he had and started to leave. Then he turned back and looked directly at Mairey.

"Be assured, however, I'll press my suit to be Bethan's legal guardian."

This time he walked away and Stephen rushed to Mairey.

She stood as motionless as a statue, her face frozen in horrified shock, her arms reaching behind her waist to hold tight to Beth's shoulders. As Stephen neared her face crumpled and she took one step forward and into his arms.

Stephen wrapped his arms around her and lowering his head, nuzzled her shining hair. Then he put out one arm and gathered Beth to his side, holding the shaking little body as close to him as he could. He was seized with an almost irresistible compulsion to raise Mairey's face and kiss her with an ardor he'd once thought he'd never feel again. He managed to resist the impulse, mainly because he knew it would not be welcome just now. The girl needed comfort, not passion.

Dear goddess, here he was doing it again! Whatever was wrong with him that he seemed to feel passion for women who didn't want him? Right now he knew he wanted to take Mairey closer in his arms and kiss her until she would submit to any one of the loving actions he quite suddenly longed to employ. A desire for possession he'd thought he would never again experience invaded his mind and body.

This was not the time or the place for his incipient emotions. Still, there was no longer a whispering in his mind saying Mairey was the wrong girl for him. Even though she disliked him, or at least his approach to life. He had a good deal of thinking to do once he soothed these two adorable females.

Keeping Mairey close, he reached down and drew Beth up to his shoulders and then wrapped his strong arms around them both.

"Here now. I don't have a third hand and you two are using the ones I've got. I can't reach for my handkerchief. Beth, there's a clean one in the pocket nearest your head. Be a good girl and get it out and dry your aunt's tears. That's my girl."

While still holding them both there was little he could do but beam at them as Beth mopped carefully at her aunt's face.

Then he smiled at Beth. "Now give Dr. Mairey the handkerchief so she can clean you up. You two are a real mess. I don't know that I should be hugging girls as disreputable as you two."

Mairey swatted him on his arm but there was little heat in the gesture.

"Knights errant are supposed to be overcome with gratitude they are allowed to rescue the fair maidens. One simply does not tease them about a dirty face." Her voice trembled a little but he could see and applaud that her fight for control was winning over her fear.

"Is she right, chickie?" Stephen rubbed noses with Beth and then moving slowly, disengaged his arms and set her down. "What should a true knight errant do? Tell me and I'll do it."

"Oh, Dr. Stephen, you should know. You kiss the ladies you rescued, of course."

"Of course," he agreed gravely. "I'm an unusually stupid knight errant." He kissed Beth on both cheeks. "You're a darling chickie," he whispered in her ear.

Then he turned to Mairey.

She stood and stared at him as if she'd never seen him. Standing very close to him, her beautiful eyes locked with his. Without otherwise touching her, he leaned over and kissed her lips with a lingering sweetness that had her clutching briefly at his shoulders. He put her gently aside. The raw desire riding him was not only inappropriate but unappeasable at this time. He took a very deep breath.

"Being a knight errant is a very fine thing," Stephen commented, his voice rumbling deep in his chest. "Especially when he's rescuing such gorgeous females in distress."

Beth hugged his legs tightly, as if she'd never let him leave her side again.

Mairey wheeled away and began to collect her tools and digging equipment.

"Come, Bethan, I think we should take the rest of the afternoon off."

She took Beth by the hand, not looking at Stephen, although the faint blush on her lovely face told him she was quite conscious of him. He stepped directly in front of them both, stopping her from any immediate departure. His gaze and his words were directed at Mairey, although he lifted Beth up for another protracted hug.

"I intend to be close at hand for a while. Be assured of that. I do not trust your enemy to give up and go away. I'd like to know a little more than I do of this matter so I can act intelligently. Do you think you could enlighten me just a little, Mairey? I won't go away, in any case but I'd appreciate whatever you can tell me to help me protect you and Beth."

Mairey still quivered inwardly with terror and the revulsion seeing Walter always produced. She looked down at the ground, not willing to face Stephen. He was asking so politely for something that surely he had the right to know. If he'd not appeared today Walter might easily have in some way knocked her out of commission and disappeared with Bethan. The guard might not have stopped him if he claimed to be Beth's father.

She needed Stephen. Her brother and uncle would of course help but Walter was smarmy enough to evade them or find a time when they were busy or didn't realize she and Beth were in trouble. As had happened just now. She couldn't ask them to be with her every minute. Nor would she ask such a commitment of Stephen. But having him alert and being an additional watchdog seemed by far the smartest thing for her to do.

A puzzling thought but he seemed to somehow have a prescient intimation of when she was in trouble. She didn't begin to understand it but he was there when she needed him. He was a wanderer, she knew that well. But she should not forgo the help he offered. He would not be available for long but certainly she should utilize his strength and concern while he remained with her.

The very thought of telling anyone about Walter and her sister made her shudder. Stephen obviously noticed, although he put out a hand and then withdrew it and waited for her decision.

Mairey squared her shoulders and looked into Stephen's riveting blue eyes. A true Celtic blue which seemed to emphasize the red-gold of his hair. No matter her private thoughts, he was a handsome man. An unusually handsome man. One irresistible to most females. He was so deliciously male, so strong and potentially overwhelming, doubtless most females fell at his feet. She didn't intend to. He knew that. She'd made her lack of interest in him plain. And still he stood ready to help her.

She needed to remind herself it would only be for as long as he wanted to stay around.

She drew on her innate resources and managed a smile.

"I agree you do indeed need to know a little more about Walter."

"I'll phone for a cab for you," Stephen said. "You shouldn't walk for many reasons right now, including the fact you're still shaking from head to toe. I'll come back after I call the cab and wait with you and then see you later tonight."

She nodded her thanks, too weary to speak. If he only were a truly reliable man, instead of being reliable in such unlikely patches.

Still he'd certainly helped her by being in the right spot today. She wondered what had brought him back. She hadn't really expected him to return after the trip to Carnac. It just proved nothing of importance interested him except his ever-changing whims.

When he returned they waited in silence for the cab.

He handed her into the cab and then lifted Beth onto her lap. Then he leaned over and kissed the lovely skin on both foreheads. Beth's skin was soft as is any young child's. Mairey's felt almost as soft, her own beautiful, almost translucent complexion enough to drive any man wild.

He solemnly shut the door to the cab and waved them on.

He'd see Mairey tonight. Hopefully he'd find answers to some of his questions. One question pretty sure to remain unanswered was one he couldn't ask her.

Why couldn't he walk off and leave her alone?

* * * * *

Stephen went to a small restaurant where he could be fairly sure he'd not be recognized and asked to sing. As he ate in solitude, he tried to assemble all the facts he already knew into one informative package. His deduction was one he didn't like at all. But as a doctor he'd witnessed almost every good or evil trait the world displayed and knew well the horrible sins humans committed on fellow humans.

His conclusion, although it did not surprise him, made him a little sick. Walter would do anything to gain control of Beth. His wicked plans extended to putting her aunt out of commission by any means whatsoever. Stephen reluctantly concluded it was not a normal desire for a child of his own. He wanted Beth, wanted her enough to attempt one murder and threaten another one. His interest was most probably the perverted one that made Mairey attack Stephen when she saw him running his hands over Beth to check her injuries.

He could see no other explanation.

Walter was a pedophile and of the worst kind. Beth was a true obsession.

He would use any means possible to possess the beautiful small child.

* * * * *

Stephen arrived early at the boarding house and waited patiently until Mairey appeared in the parlor.

"Shall we walk?" she asked simply. "Although I can't go far with this splint."

"Are you sure you feel up to it?" Stephen asked.

"I'd like to try. How I wish I could stride along like you do. This splint is driving me mad."

Tossing her head to push her hair back from her face, she led the way out the door. She reached up and retied the light scarf she wore over her flowing hair. A frilly blouse clung to her perfect breasts admirably. She'd changed from her digging pants to her tailored men's trousers, which Stephen was beginning to think had some advantages. They hugged her well-rounded *derriere* so nicely.

If she thought she downplayed her femininity in those sleek pants she was dead wrong. But he was not about to tell her and spoil the view.

The night surrounded them with the scents and sweet feel of balmy summer. They breathed it in and walked in silence for a little way.

"We don't want to put too much stress on your ankle," Stephen informed her. "I think we should stop and rest right here."

It seemed to him the stars were growing brighter and the air more fragrant. There was little sound. Just then he heard a night bird's dulcet call, with its tinge of eager rapture. Probably a nightingale. Right now Stephen thought they were beside someone's garden, a garden filled with lilies and roses.

He caught her arm to stop her.

"Do pause and take a few deep breaths. Nature is scenting the air for us."

Mairey paused and breathed deeply. "Glorious," she said in her softest voice. "Do you think nature is putting on such a show just for us?"

Stephen laughed, the deep laugh that sent sending shivers up her spine.

"Only if daylight reveals there are no roses and lilies blooming in the garden beside us. Then I'd think the goddess of us all somehow arranged such heavenly scents just for us."

It wasn't the words as much as the way he spoke them. He sounded so confident and at ease with himself. Mairey suddenly felt all things were possible if Stephen were at her side. Perhaps she should study Druid lore. When she found the time. Certainly she did not understand the big Druid walking next to her, slowing his long stride so she could be comfortable with her splinted foot.

She jerked her mind back to the present and found Stephen studying her face.

"Why don't we sit on the grass by the walk and you can tell me whatever you want. Surely we're in a blessed spot, which will make it easier for you to discuss what is doubtless a painful subject."

Again she fought off the spell of his voice and the strangely kind words he uttered. He was unlike any man she'd ever met. Irresponsible but interesting for all of that. Understanding and strong. Empathetic, in fact, almost too much so. She longed to pour out her problems and let his broad shoulders carry them for her. At least for the time he was with her.

He took his jacket off and folded it to make a cushion and then handed her down with his accustomed grace.

"Now," he said, his smile barely in evidence. "You may tell me anything you please. Don't worry about shocking me. I've seen almost every depravity sinful men have to offer. I think I know what Walter Griffen is like. The only thing I don't understand is why your sister married him."

Mairey swallowed a lump suddenly threatening to choke her.

"Alys made a dreadful mistake, of course. She'd lost her first husband Ronald six months before. Theirs had been a true love match and she was devastated. Walter played on her desperation."

"And she discovered too late he was a pedophile."

Stephen's voice was flat, with no question in its tone.

Mairey raised startled eyes and then lowered them again. Moonlight shone on their little spot of heaven, illuminating her features and her expressions.

It was evident continuing her story bothered her a great deal but she kept on.

"Yes, exactly. Alys found him fondling Bethan. She'd started out shopping and came back to the house almost right away because she'd forgotten her purse. Walter had Bethan undressed and was caressing her body. He hadn't progressed to any really damaging act and he swore he was doing nothing but admiring her. That he would never hurt her. I believe the first part, as Beth shows no signs of trauma."

Her voice began to quiver and Stephen suddenly lifted her on his lap. He held her loosely but his big solid body held a wealth of comfort.

"Go on," he urged gently. "I want the whole story."

Mairey sighed, leaned back and dropped her head on his shoulder.

"She dressed Bethan and left, bringing her to me. On the way home from my place Alys ran her little Renault into a tree. I'd begged her to stay the night but she felt determined to face Walter and kick him out of the house. It was her house, incidentally, as Walter moved in after their marriage. I'll never know if tears blinded her, or what happened but she died instantly."

Stephen tightened his arms around her. "And you haven't let Beth out of your sight since."

She nodded, swallowed hard and then continued in a shaky voice. "And Walter is still in my sister's house. I didn't stay to evict him. This dig was scheduled and I went with my brother and uncle as I'd planned. And thought I'd taken Beth out of his reach."

Her voice dropped to a whisper. "I can hardly talk about it."

Stephen stayed silent, although he began to stroke her hair where it hung down her back. She tried to ignore the comfort of his touch and he finally spoke.

"Did you think he'd give up?"

Mairey made a sound between a hiccup and a sigh. "I did. I thought he'd switch his attention once he'd been caught."

"You're a very intelligent woman and must have read about this problem. Now you know it's a true obsession and must be dealt with as such."

They both fell silent. Mairey made a movement as if she meant to move from his lap but he held her still, although he didn't say a word. She finally relaxed into his strength and sat quietly, relaxing against his broad chest. Like leaning against a huge tree. Just as solid. This peace, being held by a man who understood the horror she was fighting and one who would help her in her battle, felt strange and wonderful. She'd like to sit here forever, cradled in the strong arms now enfolding her.

The two other men in her family would fight for her too, she knew that perfectly well. But they had numerous obligations of their own. The government at Paris checked them closely to see no artifact went astray or unreported. A careful tally of each object unearthed was kept and the description, drawing and photograph recorded. All this besides overseeing the dig demanded a huge amount of work and her brother and uncle were in and out of pits and storage sheds constantly. If Walter got back inside the work area, one of them might or might not be handy.

She sighed deeply. She simply could not risk being injured again.

Stephen turned her face to his. "I'll be here, Mairey. I intend to learn how to be a good amateur archeologist so I can be with you every day. You'll have to teach me the rudiments so I can really help, as well as get your uncle's permission. But I intend to be here to guard you until we somehow dispose of Walter."

It was the "we" that undid her. When one of his big hands lifted her face to his she went still. She let him kiss her, his blazing lips hot on hers. No, she had to be honest. She *longed* for him to kiss her, holding her breath until his chiseled lips descended on hers. At first sweetly and then with increasing ardor. He pressed his tongue to her lips, asking for the entrance he sought and she let him in.

The kiss escalated rapidly, as his tongue delved into the corners of her mouth, tasting her like a dish of succulent fruit. Emotion swirled about and through her, making her put her arms around his neck and fully participate.

Just one devastating, demanding kiss and she turned into a piece of putty.

She'd never meant to respond so hotly. She'd never meant her pulse to accelerate so suddenly she could scarcely breathe. She held him to her as if she never wanted to let go, her hands roaming through his hair and then back to clutching him so she could move her body closer. She had no doubt he knew perfectly well she was willing to follow wherever he wanted this kiss to go. How could he help but know how he affected her when her heart pounded so madly? Molding her so closely to him, he couldn't miss the evidence.

She shuddered and dug her fingers into the back of his neck. There simply was no soft spot she could feel, even as she moved her hands greedily across his shoulders and tried to grab him closer. His skin smelled of musk and like the virile male he was, while the scent of his hair floated fresh and rain-water sweet. He exuded a raw sexuality such as she'd never encountered and had no idea how to handle. She kissed him back with all her enthusiasm, although she suspected she merely betrayed her lack of expertise.

His hands roamed over her body, feeling the curve of her hips and pressing her body closer against what she suspected was a large erection. She'd had little experience but the solidity of such an alien heaviness made her gasp. Still she clung, willing this kiss to go on forever. His burning lips felt like a fiery brand, marking her as a passionate woman she'd never suspected.

Just one kiss and the world and her heart turned over.

Suddenly he stopped and buried his head against her breasts. Then he picked her up and set her on his coat again.

"I have no right to kiss you at all, let alone in such a manner," he said stiffly. "Shall we blame the midsummer moon and forget I ever lost control like this? I will not do so again."

Mairey's stormy emotions kept her silent even as her blood raced to a faster tempo. She'd loved his kiss. She'd *wanted* him to keep on. Now she was the one who regretted a kiss that should never have happened. What had happened to her usual sensible self? Kissing a drifter of a man as if he meant everything in the world to her. When he meant nothing to her and never would.

But his mouth had been so warm and beguiling. She really hadn't known herself capable of the response she'd practically thrown at him. Grabbing him, her hands and her body begging for more. Letting her tongue mingle with his. Running her hands through his hair and loving the feel of that coarse silk.

She flushed with embarrassment, resenting the way he'd made her feel. And the worst of it was she suspected he might equally resent the way she'd made him momentarily lose control. If so, all the better. She wanted him to be as uncomfortable as she was.

She smothered her thoughts and smiled at him. Not a full smile but the most she could manage. At least he couldn't see her burning cheeks.

"Yes, of course. Let's call it a midsummer mistake. Just a kiss, after all." She swallowed hard before she went on. "I'll be glad to have you help at the dig and I'll tell Uncle Tally," she said. "I need all the backup I can to protect Beth."

She put one hand on the ground beside her and pushed herself to her feet while Stephen stepped away and didn't touch her. Then she began to walk as rapidly as she could manage to the boarding house.

Stephen easily kept up with her, catching her arm and forcing her to slow down. His mind and his body were still in a state of shock. He'd known he'd enjoy kissing her, as any male would but he wasn't prepared for the instant passion that almost overwhelmed him. She'd been so responsive and so much a female. He didn't understand at all why they'd both almost gone up in flames. So very quickly! He must try to think this out before he touched her again. Keeping his hands off her would be hard enough but he needed to figure out where they were going. Where he wanted to go.

He said nothing until they got to the door of the rooming house the Bronwyns had taken over as their own. Then he put one hand on her shoulder and stopped her before she could enter.

"Blessed be," he murmured. Turning her face up to him, he lightly kissed her cheek on the spot where her dimple fascinated him, then wheeled and left.

She stood in the doorway staring after him. What a damned shame he was so handsome and enthralling. When he'd held her, his chest so strong and steady, she'd felt every inch a woman when her breasts pressed against him. His kiss swirled her mind so she'd harbored no intention of breaking it off. She'd have clung to him forever. Thank heavens he possessed more sense than she. If she lost sight of her objective she might possibly fall under the spell of a charismatic man with no true goal in life.

He was honorable, she certainly knew that. A big plus after seeing her sister throw her life away for Walter and his completely dishonorable predilections. But Dr. Stephen Lovernios, honorable or no, offered no future except one of passion. Her big surprise was how easily she could melt into that passion. She'd never once suspected any man could make her dissolve like an icicle in the summer sun.

He was so very male. Muscles like rocks when he'd briefly held her to him. Nothing lackadaisical at all about his body.

She took a few deep breaths and walked slowly to her room, checking Beth first and finding her sound asleep. She stood for a moment looking down at the precious child. Her own desires meant nothing besides the necessity to keep this child safe. Perhaps she should have a guard stationed at night at the boarding house. If she knew her brother and uncle were to be away she'd do exactly that.

She knew she couldn't handle this situation with Walter on her own. Much as she hated depending on others, she could not ignore this one hard fact.

She needed help. In spite of her qualms she rejoiced that Stephen was the one who would help her.

And what kind of hypocrite did that make her?

She shook her head in puzzlement and disgust, glad no one could see her still fiery cheeks and unsteady hands.

# Chapter Nine

ꙮ

Stephen's step slowed into deliberation as he walked away from Mairey's boarding house. He must stay close to Mairey and Beth. He wasn't at all sure this would prove to be a good idea but he felt a deep obligation to do so. Although not completely ignorant of the science of archeology, he needed more knowledge to be truly useful at the Bronwyn site. The small amount of information he'd been able to find at Carnac helped him but a little.

Probably his best bet was to be completely frank with Mairey's family.

Late next morning he appeared at the excavation site, after learning what he could at the local library. The guard gave him no trouble as he wandered around the various pits and digs, nor did he see any of the Bronwyns at first. He learned enough about archeology to know the Bronwyns must have surveyed this site many times before deciding to dig here and their knowledge of what they might find had given them the perseverance to endure all the legal and paper work needed to convince the French government to allow them to proceed. He also learned the best surveys were done by walking the site over and over, covering every inch and then laying it all out in grids. A tremendous amount of labor went into preparation before digging the first spoonful of dirt.

He decided he could best help in the cataloguing of the finds. Even though this was often meticulous drudgery, he now knew he didn't have enough knowledge to even dig properly. The intriguing thought the Bronwyns might teach him new skills urged him on.

When he found them in their office both Bronwyns seemed pleased to see him. He told them a little about the marvels at Carnac and urged them not to miss seeing the wonders there.

"I'm sure we're here at Gouarec for some time," Dr. Philip said. "Certainly Carnac is one of the places we're determined to visit. Your recommendation makes it an imperative."

Stephen paused and then spoke. "I need to talk to you both seriously. Is this a good time?

Doctors Taliesin and Philip exchanged glances and then announced it a very good time. "We haven't really started the day's work, so let's go sit in the sketching shed. If we're lucky we might even commandeer a thermos of coffee."

A moment later Stephen found himself inside a shelter new to him. Several drawing tables, their boards tilted and filled with sketches, were ready for their artists to return and finish their work. Stephen would have loved to examine their efforts but kept his peace. Here was another place he might legitimately contribute to the dig. He'd always loved drawing and thought he could do a presentable job of sketching the artifacts. Another surprise, to find he could help in more than one way. Being cooped up in this shed, however, wasn't where he wanted to be. He needed to check constantly on Mairey, or else work beside her.

"Mairey is in danger," he told the men in her family. "I think it's pretty serious danger." He told them how Walter slyly threatened to put an end to her existence so he could have Beth. His audience reacted with the anger he'd expected.

"I always did want to go after the son of a bitch." Philip's voice was curt, his hand clenched into the fists he obviously longed to use on Walter. "Do you know where he's staying? I think I'd like a little talk with him."

Stephen shook his head. "I'd like to beat him to a pulp too but unless one of us kills him he'll just come back, more vindictive than ever and without warning. What I hope to do is catch him somehow so we can have him legally arrested."

"Do you have a plan?" Dr. Taliesin asked, his face as stony as his nephew's.

If Mairey had dropped by just then she'd find three men clenching and unclenching their fists.

Stephen ran one hand through his hair. "Not really. All I can think of is to be around as much as possible. I also think we should persuade Mairey and Beth to leave the isolation of their particular part of the dig. Somewhere they can be guarded more easily."

"I agree," Dr. Taliesin said. "Certainly Bethan's had time to adjust to the activity at the main dig. They must come over here. Mairey should really be more involved in the direction of the cataloguing. She's an expert at cataloguing and especially in identifying an object. She's wasted digging unless we reach something her fine hands are needed for. She has a good touch with delicate items, although so far we've found mostly quite durable relics."

Stephen inwardly breathed a sigh of relief. "I want to be involved also. I can sketch fairly well and I think I could help in cataloguing. I also could photograph the finds. I'd be willing to work anywhere you want to put me but I want to be on hand. Every day. You will probably think I'm insane but I think I have certain sensitivities as a Druid which might help."

Dr.Taliesin and Dr. Philip exchanged glances. They did not seem as dubious as Stephen had feared.

"We've been long enough in Brittany to have lost our skepticism about Druid abilities," Philip said wryly. "And we'll appreciate having you on the spot. Another place you might help is taking care of Beth sometimes and completely freeing Mairey to do the intricate work she's trained for. It's hurt me to see her digging day after day but she wanted Beth to be happy, even above her career."

Stephen liked these two men. Their rational approach to a problem, their obvious concern for Mairey and the child and their enthusiasm for their work were all appealing. They might even approve his feeling he would kill before he'd let Walter or anyone else spoil the beautiful innocence of Mairey. Although Mairey wouldn't agree she was innocent but she was. Innocent of evil, innocent of selfishness, innocent of knowing a man. He'd protect her from ever losing the innocence of the first two. Although he wouldn't promise himself he'd never teach her knowledge of this one man.

When Mairey and Beth appeared at the site, Mairey gave little resistance to the new plans. Stephen stood to the side but he easily spotted the flash of relief and pleasure passing over her mobile features. A brief revelation of how she longed to go back to the main area. Even though he knew the whole story of why she protected Beth, he marveled at the love and dedication leading her to sacrifice her true calling in archeology to what she considered best for her niece.

He wasn't at all sure he could be so noble.

It struck him like a thunderbolt striking between his ribs that in her different way, Mairey was every bit as loving, considerate and worthy a woman as Vivie. Vivie, who he hadn't actually mourned for some time. Vivie, who would applaud with sincere joy his interest in another superlative woman. He smiled with contentment. His urgings to take Mairey in his arms and kiss her witless suddenly made sense.

Fate had led him to a woman the equal of the one he'd lost.

He'd have to move very carefully with this one. But first he must decide if he really wanted to keep her forever. He must be very sure of his own emotions. He felt differently about her than any woman he'd known but he feared feeling too strongly about her and certainly hesitated to disclose his innermost self to her. She did not understand him at all and maybe she never would. She would have to come to this knowledge on her own. If not, they could have no future.

For now, all he could do nothing but guard her, guard Beth and keep a close watch on his battered heart. He would have to ignore the deep tug of desire he felt at just the thought of her lovely face.

He mentally shook himself and braced as if diving into waves of water breaking over his head. Still his heart sang with the peaceful joy of a long-lonely man whose life again teemed with wonder.

* * * * *

They all enjoyed a few peaceful days. Mairey was obviously pleased to be back with the hustle of the dig where she could use her expertise. Beth seemed equally happy. Mairey brought all the child's toys and their equipment from the smaller pit. She established a play area in her office as well as a cot. She brought a child-sized chair and table from the boarding house. After a hectic half-hour of running madly around the excavation, Beth settled down to getting acquainted with the workers she hadn't yet met and charmed them all. After the first day of wandering around talking to them Beth seemed to enjoy sitting down and playing beside her aunt. Sometimes she even climbed on the cot and fell asleep. The rest of the time she roamed around at will, not realizing several pairs of watchful eyes followed her every movement.

On the fourth day a young lady, a blonde-haired stunning young lady, tall and elegant in her government uniform, showed an official pass and asked to speak to Dr. Bronwyn. Of the three Dr. Bronwyns only Philip happened to be nearby, so he stepped forward with delight to present himself.

"I'm Dr. Philip Bronwyn. I see you're from the government and I imagine you want to inspect our acquisitions. I'll be glad to show them to you, Miss—"

He let the pause go on, wondering why this beautiful girl had come. They'd been visited just the last week, when Tally showed them the latest results of their excavations. Naturally everything was in order and it seemed a little soon for a new visit.

"I am Riva Broussard." Her tone didn't sound unfriendly but it certainly didn't drip with warmth. Definitely and deliberately neutral. "I'm deputy assistant in charge of antiquities in Brittany."

She held out her hand for a businesslike handshake. Still no smile, although Philip certainly smiled at her. She was the most luscious thing he'd seen in France. She looked at him with polite grey eyes while her creamy complexion and light eyebrows proclaimed her a natural blonde. Not that he'd expect anything except authenticity from a woman with the fortitude to obtain an education in a man's field. Just like Mairey, and he'd always admired his sister.

He wished he could convince her he was a friendly sort of man. Not much chance, just yet. First he must find out what brought the slight hostile cast to her lovely face.

"Perhaps you'd better tell me how I can help, Mlle. Broussard. I imagine you came from Rennes to visit us, am I right?"

She flushed a little, very faintly, her fair skin going momentarily rosy and then fading. She obviously didn't like him taking over the questioning.

"We've had a report filed on one of your recent workers that appeared serious enough I was sent to investigate." Her tone was still stiff, with little attempt to be more than decently courteous. So she'd been upset by the report, enough to come herself and check out whatever worried them at the Archaeology Department at Rennes. Certainly it seemed unusual for such a senior person to come herself.

"I cannot imagine who you mean. Suppose we go into the new discoveries shed where there are some chairs. I think I'd also like to have my uncle Dr. Taliesin Bronwyn hear what you have to say."

She nodded in acquiescence and Philip strode off. In a few minutes he was back with both his uncle and his sister. They'd left Beth playing happily in the sketching shed, at the feet of her new idol, Stephen Lovernios.

"Now," Dr. Taliesin said. "I understand you think we have a problem with one of our workers. I can't begin to think who. We've employed all of them a long time and they were thoroughly vetted."

Mlle. Broussard looked him in the eye, her gaze level and a little suspicious.

"But our information tells us this is not true. You have a new worker, one who came to Brittany a little over seven months ago. He claims to be a medical doctor but so far has done nothing but roam around the country, singing at various inns and taverns."

"You can't mean Dr. Lovernios?" Philip's tone was one of sheer incredulity. He'd never met a man he trusted more than he did Stephen. They'd certainly not asked him for credentials. It would have been an insult to a man of his stature.

"I believe that is the name he's going by," their beautiful inquisitor said. "An unusual name for an alias, so we researched the name itself. It's ancient Celtic, reserved for the most revered bards in the time of the Druids. It means 'son of the fox' and the old Druids who bore the name wore fox armbands to distinguish their high ranking. If this man knows Druid history, it might please him to take such a prestigious name. Although I understand he does sing old Celtic lays and has a beautiful baritone singing voice. All of which is a very good cover for a potential thief of Celtic antiquities."

All three of the Bronwyns stared at her. Mairey exploded first.

"Dr. Lovernios is an outstanding doctor and a good person. Who put such pernicious ideas about him into your head?'

She suddenly paled and sat down on the nearest chair. "Walter," Mairey whispered but Taliesin and Philip heard her.

"Of course!" Philip looked ready to explode. He forgot his admiration for the visitor's looks as his smile disappeared and a haughty look took over.

"You've been taken in by a scum of a man who has personal reasons for attacking Dr. Lovernios' character. Did you do even a rudimentary check on your informant? And how about Stephen Lovernios? Did you check out his credentials, including the fact he trained and practiced at London General Hospital? Surely the personal singularity of liking to vacation as the Druid bard he is has nothing to do with the Antiquities Division. I think I'm beginning to resent very much your coming here, Mlle. Broussard."

She did not back down, Philip had to give her credit. She held her head even higher, if possible. She looked around the group now united against her. They were an impressive bunch but so was she.

Her grey eyes flashed as she faced Mairey.

"We were also told you've recently unearthed a gold armband such as high-ranking Druids used to wear. Is this true?"

"Of course it is," Taliesin answered before Mairey could. "It's listed on our latest report to Antiquities. Someone came to see it a few days ago. I doubt if Dr. Lovernios even knows about it. We only found it last week while he was in Carnac."

The visitor looked satisfied. "Carnac. A long way from here, although it's a fine vacation spot. But he came back rather hurriedly, we are told. Could word of the armband have gotten back to him?"

Mairey spotted the problem immediately. She turned to the men, her face growing even paler as she thought of Walter and his wicked plans.

"We have an informer on our staff. If Walter reported the armband in an effort to implicate Stephen it means he knows much more than he should of what goes on inside the dig. Someone is leaking information to him."

She wheeled on Riva Broussard. "Your informant was doubtless Walter Griffen. Perhaps not the name he gave you but that's who he is. He has reason to hate Dr. Lovernios because Stephen flattened him when Walter tried to physically take my five-year-old niece from me. He's a wicked, vicious pervert and if you deal with him you deserve all the trouble you're likely to get. Now I'm going to fetch Stephen. I refuse to talk about him any more until he's here to defend himself."

Leaving the others Mairey marched off, indignation evident in every step. She returned fairly soon, with Stephen carrying Beth on his shoulders.

Mairey marched up to Mlle. Broussard. "Here is your culprit. You can explain to him why you're so mistakenly here. Come Beth, you and I will let Stephen convince this young lady he's a gentleman."

Beth however, didn't want to be taken from her favorite.

"No, no, I want to stay with Stevie. He plays nice games with me."

Stephen reached back and swung her to his chest. He put his face close to hers as he whispered to her. He didn't care if his deep voice made his whisper quite audible to everyone else.

"Now, chickie, you won't get the nice ear of dried corn I promised you if you don't mind your Aunt Mairey. I'd meant to let you sit on the ground and peck at it too."

Beth giggled. "I'm not a chicken, I keep telling you, Uncle Stevie. I'm a girl."

"You're my chickie," he murmured in her ear. "Run along and when I'm through here we'll think up a new game for just us chickens."

She planted a big, wet kiss on his cheek and slipping out of his arms, went off with Mairey.

"Not exactly the criminal type, is he?" commented Philip dryly.

Riva Broussard didn't say a word. The love evident between the big man and the little girl had shaken her but she'd experienced enough to know even the vilest of criminals can like children.

Stephen looked at them all for a long moment, while none of his friends wanted to speak up.

"Ah," he said. "My wandering ways are causing some concern? Is this the problem?"

"More than that," Philip bit off. "An informant has told Mlle. Broussard you are here to steal the solid gold armband we found last week."

"Really?" asked Stephen. "You haven't mentioned it. I'd love to see it. Is it the kind a Druid priest would wear?"

There was a small silence until Taliesin answered. "Yes, it's a beautiful thing. I'd be glad to show it to you, Stephen."

"My own ancestors wore armbands made of fur of the red fox. I don't think I've ever seen a solid gold one."

The silence began to stretch, until Stephen suddenly grinned. "I see now why I'm the likely suspect. Anybody who spends his time wandering and singing is undoubtedly a reprobate."

Philip laughed. "You've got it, old man. Added to that we've deduced Walter is the informant and has implicated you."

Stephen changed before their eyes. Gone was the insouciance, the lazy grin, the bright and joking eyes. He stood without moving, a large man who suddenly seemed much larger. And formidable, although he didn't say a word for a long moment.

"I wished I'd finished him off when I had the chance," he ground out. "Now he'll just keep making trouble. I can take it but if he turns on Mairey again I won't be responsible for any means I use to stop him."

Mlle. Broussard had been silent until now. "You've said enough to persuade me I don't have the whole story. I think I'll stay in town a few days. My report says nothing of a personal grudge. Dr. Lovernois, do you have credentials you can show me? I take it your friends here have never asked you but I'm asking you now."

The slow grin returned. "Of course I have credentials. Did you think I'd been gone from England this long carrying all the money I needed with me? I have official letters of credit, as well as introductory letters if I need them. I've not used the latter but am willing to show them to you."

Dr. Broussard had the grace to flush. "I'll rent a room in town and let you know where to bring your papers."

She turned to go but Philip stopped her.

"I'll go with you and make sure you're settled properly. I assume you drove from Rennes?"

At her nod, he smiled. "Good. In spite of the fact you've been badly misled, I'd like to know you better. Perhaps I can even persuade you of a few essential matters."

He took her arm and waved at Stephen and Taliesin. They went off, Philip talking earnestly and softly the whole time.

"She is quite lovely," Stephen said.

"And quite mistaken," Taliesin answered. "Would you like to see the armband now?"

Stephen's features were still stiff with resentment but he soon resumed his normal expression of watchful contentment as he started to walk off with Taliesen.

Stephen paused. "Of course I'd love to but I think I'll wait until you show it to Mlle. Broussard. I want to be able to tell her honestly it's my first glimpse of such a wonderful relic. Tell me of how you came to find it."

Still talking the two men walked off. Stephen thought furiously as he strode along, even though he carried on a normal conversation with Taliesin. Mairey seemed to ally herself on his side. Much more solidly than he'd expected.

Could she be beginning to think living the life of a Druid bard was not so reprehensible?

The welcome thought reverberated through his mind, bringing an extra spring to his step and a bigger smile than usual to his strikingly attractive face.

# Chapter Ten

ꟗ

Philip directed Riva Broussard to a comfortable boarding house not far from the one his family had taken over. Gouarec was a lovely town, situated by the Nantes-Brest Canal and filled with old schist houses, which were wonders in themselves. Where he'd suggested she stop was at a large mansion, steeped in the wonderful antiquity of the region and now run by two sisters who needed the income to keep up the money-gobbling old place.

"I think you'll like this better than the Hotel du Blavet, although the hotel is quite fine. Perhaps I'm wrong about you but I guess you prefer quieter surroundings. Although when we were reconnoitering the site for our dig, we stayed at neither of these but at the campsite called the Tost-Aven. A beautiful place, next to the canal. Spacious and with acres of grass and the canal waters rippling beside it. I think we all fell in love with the town right then."

"The town is completely charming, isn't it? I think I'm glad I must stay 'til tomorrow."

Her tone was reserved and Philip looked at her classic profile. A profile that might have been etched on any of the Greek coins he studied. He thought she could have posed for the head of Aphrodite. In his mind he envisioned with a visceral pleasure the statue coming to throbbing life in his arms. One thing he knew for sure. If she suspected he was interested in her at a sexual level, she'd run back to Rennes as fast as she could. She flashed too many signals of being tied up in knots about men and of course he wanted to know why.

He intended to learn. Already he knew his interest more serious than just sexual.

*Was this how love happened, then, this fast and so deeply? Like a bolt of lightning that changed the very particles in your body?*

He ignored his inner thought and turned to her with an easy, smooth charm.

"I'd like to take you to dinner, if I may, probably at the Hotel du Blavet. Their food is excellent. If I promise to be a very good boy and not mention anything of what brought you to Gouarec, would you honor me with your company? You have only to shake your head at me and I'll switch to another subject. I'm not interested in talking about our work in any case. I'd like to know you outside your professional capacity."

She hesitated for such a long while he thought he'd lost his one chance to know her. Then she turned a shining smile on him and took his hand as he came to open the car door for her.

"I'll be glad to relax. It's been an unusually hectic week. I'm happy to go to dinner with you if we talk about everything but archeology. Is it agreed?"

Philip would have agreed to standing on his head and waving his toes at her if that was the key to several hours of her company.

"Of course," he said. "The town is small and we can easily walk to the hotel. I'll come by at seven. And thank you."

Her eyes rounded. "But I should thank you." She smiled an impish and thoroughly enchanting smile. "At least I assume you're going to pay for dinner since *you* asked *me*."

Philip laughed, a genuine laugh ringing in the quiet air of the peaceful town.

"I think I might, provided you don't eat too much. We'll have to see, won't we?"

Her reluctant grin made him feel like a king.

"Is seven all right? And don't bother about not dressing up for the occasion. You didn't plan to stay and you already look wonderful to me. Just the way you are."

At her nod he gave her a little wave and walked down the street. He knew exactly what he wanted and where he was going. He must make no mistakes with this girl, already so special to him. He had no illusions she felt the same about him. She hadn't had time.

He had.

But he didn't mind granting her all the time she needed.

*****

Philip exerted all his considerable charm on the lovely lady named Riva. He insisted on first names almost with the appetizer and although she seemed reluctant, still she consented. She also tried her best to keep the conversation firmly focused on him and Philip let her draw him out for a while. No use scaring her away this early.

She proved expert at making other people talk. Before he knew it he'd told her all about his education and some of the places he'd been.

"We're all from Wales, you know and so we don't have quite the same accent as the British. I love Wales but I couldn't stand living there all the time. Fortunately, a good dig always appears just when I think I'll go crazy if I don't get away."

Riva sat upending her spoon, turning it slowly over and over.

"Your French also has a slightly different accent from the usual. I should have thought of the Welsh influence. Tell me about Egypt. I think you've been there, haven't you?"

Philip sat back and smiled at her. *Very clever, as well as very beautiful.*

"I don't think I will. Not unless we agree to trade confidences. I've talked for fifteen minutes straight and you've said nothing about yourself. I wouldn't deserve your company if I let you trick me with that."

Riva laughed. A hesitant laugh but still the first one he'd heard.

"I think I've met my match. I do so like to draw people out. I've done little traveling, so must do it vicariously. You've led a fascinating life."

He leered at her and waggled his eyebrows. "And I haven't even mentioned Mesopotamia. Will you concede now, my lovely, or must I resort to sterner tactics. I always keep thumbscrews in my right pocket, you know."

This time her laugh was genuine and unforced. Philip had a definite feeling she didn't often laugh with such real abandon. If she only knew, she'd soon laugh a lot, sincere laughter he wanted to hear through the years.

He couldn't believe his feelings had swamped him so rapidly and in such an overwhelming manner. Yesterday he didn't even know Riva existed and today he wanted only to avoid a mistake that would send her from him before he could plead his case.

No matter. He would make her his own, whatever the odds. She must have been treated poorly by some insensitive lout. The shadows under her eyes became more prominent when he pressed her for personal details. To him it seemed to suggest a past she'd prefer to forget. But until he could lure her into telling him her story he could only present himself as her most interested and assiduous champion.

She grinned at him in a way that set his pulse thudding once again. The woman had no idea of what she did to him. Just one look at her and his erection became serious enough to make him squirm in his chair. He'd not experienced such a spontaneous reaction since he'd been a randy teenager.

What the hell had happened to him?

He was thirty-three years old and certainly hadn't abstained from relations with women. Women of all types and variations. He loved women, their feminine smell, their yielding bones, their soft hands and skin. He demanded only they be willing and also someone he truly liked. Now he knew, knew in his heart Riva was meant to be his. Not just a passing and passionate bedmate. But the one destined to be his own. He felt fairly sure she had no idea of the ardor banked within her slim body. Something about her repressed stance, the almost hidden look deep in her eyes, the way she stiffened when he touched her assured him he was not mistaken in her reluctance. It would be his pleasure to unveil her depth of feeling to her and soon.

He shook his head. This was ridiculous, in a way but he couldn't deny the certainty of his feelings.

His inner self grinned. His thoughts were beginning to resemble the Druids he studied. One who believed fate proclaimed only one path for an individual. He hoped he could achieve his sudden and irreversible desire. Riva was his one path to a delightful future.

Philip picked up the hand resting lightly on the table.

"And now you're going to tell me about you. Anything, any little detail. Where were you during the Great War? You already know I served as a lieutenant in the British Air Force. Where were you?"

To his surprise she looked down at their joined hands and blushed. She tried to pull her hand out of his but he wouldn't allow her.

"I was a little young to be of much help. I went to school in the daytime and manned a telephone exchange for the army at night."

Philip stared. "In other words you held down two jobs. Which means, as I see it, you were brilliant in school or you wouldn't have your present position after working only two years. Or is it one year? When did you obtain your degree?"

Riva's blush seemed to spread. Philip could hardly keep his eyes away from the swift rush of rose to her neckline of her blouse.

"I graduated the spring before the armistice was signed. The government liked my work on the exchange so they hired me immediately to work in Antiquities where I'd asked to be assigned."

Philip was still staring. "So you're even smarter than I thought. Definitely a young genius, to have held down two jobs and graduate with honors, which I'll wager you did. Aha, your lovely color gives you away. Why are you hesitant about owning up to such a sterling record?"

Riva lowered her eyes and refused to look at him. Philip scooted his chair closer to hers and using both hands, raised her face so her grey eyes, still lovely but now not at all calm, looked directly into his. She tried to wriggle away but he held her firmly.

She finally tossed her head in defiance and almost spit the words out.

"Men don't like women to be too intelligent," she said. "A fact I've learned well."

Philip humphed. "You're mistaken. This man does."

He leaned over and sweetly kissed her trembling lips, a kiss filled with respect and admiration and only a touch of the passion he felt for her. Even so, they were both breathless as he raised his head and repeated on a sigh. "This man definitely does."

He dropped his hands and she looked down at her plate during a long pause. Philip could see his attentions made her uncomfortable and he pushed his chair back.

"I know Dr. Lovernios will want to call on you tonight. He'll probably bring you his credentials. Would you like me to be there?"

She bristled at the suggestion she'd need any help from a male.

"Not at all but I thank you. It's almost too late for him to bring me his data but if he's not available don't concern yourself. If he's the man you think he is, he'll bring them tomorrow."

Philip placed a light kiss on her nose and rose to help her to her feet.

"Come. I'll see you to your room and then tell Stephen where you are. He'll probably come by tonight but if not first thing tomorrow. You're going to end up liking him, you know."

Riva stiffened and then smiled. "Certainly he has strong advocates in all of you Bronwyns. A partiality I cannot ignore. But one that will not sway me until I can assess all the data."

Philip merely smiled at her and then offered her his hand to raise her from the table. Lord, she smelled so sweet. Like a garden filled with jasmine. As she place her hand in his he couldn't resist and raising it to his lips kissed each finger in slow progression.

"I hope I can sway you a little on more personal matters," he murmured. "I warn you I'm going to try."

She froze.

"Good night, Dr. Bronwyn. I'll see you tomorrow, I'm sure. And thank you for dinner."

The last remark seemed an aftermath, a stiff response courtesy demanded she voice. He walked her to the boarding house, speaking seldom and of inconsequential matters. She spoke not at all.

He'd rushed her. He must learn to take it slow and easily. The lady could not be pushed. He smiled at Riva, lifted both her hands and kissed them lightly and then walked away.

She just needed a little time to acknowledge what he already knew. He'd have to learn to be patient.

He frowned for just a moment and then relaxed. There'd really been little concrete she said to make him think she'd been hurt by someone to a point which would make his courting difficult. He was probably imagining difficulties which weren't even there.

At least he hoped that was so.

# Chapter Eleven

ჱ

Philip presented himself at what he thought was the proper time to escort his lady to the Bronwyn excavations and found she'd already breakfasted and gone for a walk before heading to work.

"Sure and she's a fine young lady, Dr. Bronwyn," the landlady told him. "Considerate and quiet. You can bring any guests like her to me as often as you wish."

Philip agreed, his pleasure at her praise of Riva overshadowed by the knowledge he'd have to wait to see her at the site. Still he'd learned one more fact about her, she was not a lag-a-bed. Not that he'd ever expected her to be anything but dedicated to her work.

When he got to the site he found Riva, Stephen and the other members of his family gathered in Taliesin's office. Naturally, since he commandeered the bigger office. Philip's was smaller but adequate for his needs and Mairey's barely so. They'd all learned to do their best with any temporary buildings where they found themselves.

Stephen and Mairey greeted him with nods, while Riva smiled. *A faint smile but still better than a frown.* Beth ran up to him and held her arms to be picked up, which he gladly did, nuzzling her fairy-blonde hair as he hugged her. Philip started to hand her to Mairey but Stephen reached out and took her, settling her on his lap with some whispered words that made her giggle and then settle quietly.

"Morning, Philip," his uncle said. "We're about to go to the acquisitions building and show both Mlle. Broussard and Stephen what we've accomplished so far. I assume you'll want to come along."

A knowing grin made Philip suspect his discerning uncle already knew of his incipient interest in Riva. No matter, they'd all know soon enough. He intended to lay siege to the lady's heart in a concentrated and blatant manner.

He gave his hand to raise Riva from her chair, then walked beside her to the acquisitions building, the biggest in the encampment.

"Since this is your first visit here, I hope you're not disappointed. While we've uncovered some beautiful things, we haven't unearthed the quantity we hoped for. It's early days, though. We're only about one-third through the grids we paid out. But then you know that."

Riva walked along, looking at the ground. "Yes, I know to the item what you've unearthed. So far, while the results haven't been as momentous as La Tene, they're still respectable. I'm sure I'll find them beautiful and I'm anxious to see the torque and the armband."

"No doubt of their loveliness," he said softly, laying a gentle finger on her shoulder.

She reacted as if he'd brushed her with fire, moving away and walking by Mairey.

Philip now found himself walking by Stephen, with Beth perched on his shoulders as usual. The fact she held on by clutching his hair seemed to bother him not at all.

"The lady is uncommonly skittish," Stephen said in a low dry tone.

"You're right," mused Philip. "I think I'd best find out why."

"Women are wonderfully weird," said Stephen as he and Philip exchanged amused glances.

The guard unlocked the door for them and then opened it. As they all filed in, it took a moment to adjust their eyes. The building was well-lit but the change from the bright sunlight required a moment's adjustment.

Stephen's nostrils flared as he registered the sandy smell of some objects still not completely cleaned, as well as the expected musty odor of long-buried treasures. He loved the odor, one he always associated with old museums and long-closed attics full of surprises.

"We haven't properly cleaned all the lesser objects," Taliesin said. "We're behind but new tasks keep calling us. The gold armband is on this next table, where we have the true treasures. All of them are completely cleansed, as you can see."

The table he pointed out was covered with beautiful riches from long ago. Swords with carved bronze hilts, axes, silver bowls, bronze vases and a magnificent golden torque. Doubtless the prize so far, although a small replica of a two-wheeled cart driven by a goddess came close. Stephen's Druid blood surged with delight. Another proof of how advanced the Celtic culture had been, the interpretation of these objects would keep scholars busy for years. He'd never seen the La Tene artifacts so he couldn't compare but he thought these simply splendid.

He was about to ask Taliesin where the small cart had been found. Before he could say a word, he noticed the deadly quiet in the room. He glanced at Mairey and found her coloring and not meeting his eyes. It only took him a moment to catch on.

"The gold band isn't here," he stated.

Taliesin rubbed a hand over his eyes. "No. I saw it on this table last week. I haven't been in since then, as nothing worth bringing in has been catalogued and ready to be moved here."

He turned to Riva. "I do not understand any of this. I will call all the guards together and see how such a theft is even possible. I know one thing. Dr. Lovernios has never been in this building before."

She looked up, fixing grave eyes on his distressed face.

"I think you should add, Dr. Bronwyn, as far as you know."

Philip was silent with shock and Mairey looked distressed beyond bearing but still she spoke up.

"Aren't we all jumping to conclusions? The report Dr. Lovernios stole the missing object was made by a known villain. I think his poor character also has considerable bearing on the matter."

Stephen handed Beth to her and then stood silently for a long moment, his gaze blank. His eyes were half closed and he seemed gone into another world. Everyone watched him, a sense of eeriness invading the room, as Stephen took a journey in his mind into a realm none of them knew or understood. Then, with a sudden smile, he came back to them.

"I realize I'm tying a knot around my own neck. But I just saw the gold armband. I can tell you where it is."

His voice was quiet and steady. He flashed a brief look at Mairey and then seemed to settle into himself to wait for reaction to his astonishing statement.

Dr. Taliesin came up to him and looked closely in his face.

"You'll have to explain, Stephen. I still see the person I trust but I don't understand you right now."

Stephen seemed calm and strangely happy. "You'll have to accept I'm telling you what just happened to me. Since coming to Brittany my powers as a Druid have been expanding. I can't tell you what a delight this is to me. Just now I saw the golden band. It's indeed beautiful and it's pushed up high on a tapered leg of a small stand. The stand has a fluted trimming around the edge hiding the band. I don't know where this stand is, although it's old and rather scarred. I hope one of you knows. I feel somehow that it's quite near."

There was complete silence. Even Beth seemed in awe of the gravity of the situation. No one said anything for a moment. Then Mairey spoke.

"I have a stand like that in my office. Stephen has never been in my office, nor could he know about the stand."

Stephen flashed her a grateful look.

"The fact that you and I know I've never been in your office is known to us. But not to Mlle. Broussard. Let us go see if my vision is accurate. Although I have no doubt it is. I'm not often blessed with visions but so far they've been exact. Let's go see this table, Mairey. I'm as curious as anybody here."

A rather shocked group followed Stephen as he stalked out. His head held high, the joy in him sending waves to all around him of his delight to be fulfilling his Druid heritage. No doubt existed in anyone's mind Stephen felt only an intense pleasure in these developments. His face glowed with a blissful satisfaction. There was no trace of guilt to be found, even by the beautiful inspector from the Bureau of Antiquities at Rennes who was scrutinizing every aspect of his face and bearing.

His glowing face left all those near him staring with perplexity. His was definitely not the countenance of a guilty thief.

Except for Beth. Beth was not confused. She ran to him and when he picked her up she gave him one of her smacking kisses.

"You're happy, Stevie. Then I am too."

"Bless you, chickie. Now lead us all to your Aunt Mairey's office and find the missing golden band."

They all set off. Stephen and the beautiful child hand in hand, leading the way. She skipped along beside him, her pale hair floating around her shoulders.

Everyone was thoughtful and bewildered. Except for Beth and Stephen, who walked with certainty and joy.

No one expressed surprise to find the golden band, gleaming in the light from the window as Philip up-ended the table. He drew the band off the table leg into full sight and then laid it on the table.

Stephen leaned over it and stroked the smooth lustrous surface.

"What a beautiful thing," he murmured. "I wish I knew if one of my ancestors once wore this. Although their everyday insignia was the fox band, this might have been worn on more formal occasions."

He straightened and looked at all of them. "I'm most proud of my Druid heritage and that it allowed me to show you all the hiding place of this gorgeous band. I hope by doing so we've thrown an unwelcome surprise in the plans of this would-be thief. He could not have expected we'd find this at all, let alone so quickly."

Even Riva Broussard was impressed by Stephen's elation in his discovery. She could see no reason why he would lead them directly to a hiding place not liable to be discovered for months, if ever. The band was completely hidden by the edging on the table. A more secure place to hide an object would be hard to imagine. The perplexity illuminating each face showed everyone with the same thought. If Stephen were the thief, why did he then disclose the secret and do so with such unmistakable joy?

Riva needed time to think. Although she prized herself on her intellect, all of this ranged beyond ready comprehension. Stephen himself seemed to still glow with euphoria. None of this made any sense to a girl who was proud of her ability to think clearly and reach the heart of any problem.

She looked around at the group. Both the Bronwyn men seemed stunned, whether by the discovery or Stephen's revealing the hiding place she couldn't know. Mairey stood still, her lovely face showing her bewilderment as she fastened her gaze on Stephen. Beth, still the only one reacting as expected, ran to Stephen.

She clung to his leg. He seemed still mesmerized by the band, his eyes locked on it.

"Stevie, Stevie, can I have it? It would make a boo-ful crown for one of my dolls."

Stephen swung her up in the air and whirled her around his head. She screamed with delight, her white-gold hair flying behind her. He gently lowered her to the ground.

"Chickie, you're a marvel. If it were mine I'd give it to you. But it's nobody's to give away right now. I think Mlle. Broussard should take charge of it. We definitely must not put it back in the Acquisition Building so the thief is alerted to our discovery."

He handed the stunning gold band to Riva. His normal pleasant expression was back on his smiling face. Gone was the mystical Druid and instead there stood before them only a bronzed, handsome man, red-gold hair as gleaming as the armband Riva now held. Smiling at them all but most particularly at Mairey. Each one fixed the other with questioning glances, no less potent because they were unspoken.

Riva turned to Dr. Taliesin.

"I don't pretend to understand any of this. Why Dr. Lovernios would act to lead us to the band if he were the thief is not at all plain. Still, he knew where the armband was hidden. He's shown me his references and they are impeccable. I would not charge him at this time with any unsubstantiated crime. He has the backing of people too prominent in England for my government to welcome a mistake on my part. However, I would ask him to stay in town and in touch. I intend to stay in this area until I find some answers to some of my many questions."

Philip moved forward. "Let me help you find a working space in the compound where you can have your own desk and organize what you need to do."

His idea obviously pleased Riva and she nodded to them all and then moved away with Philip. She slipped the armband into her leather purse so it no longer shone so obviously. They could all hear her asking him if he could send someone to Rennes for her papers and some clothing.

Taliesin looked at Beth clinging to Stephen's pants leg and then at his niece.

"Why don't I entertain Bethan for a while? Will you come with me, sweetheart? I can show you a new silver cauldron we dug up this week?"

Beth immediately ran to him and placed her small hand in his.

"Silver, Uncle Tally? Do you mean it's shiny? Like the band?"

"It's still a little dirty to be properly shiny. Maybe you and I should see about cleaning it up."

As they walked, Beth dancing three steps to each of his long ones, Mairey and Stephen looked at each other.

"I'm grateful to him," Stephen said. "We need to talk."

His sensuous smile did nothing to reassure Mairey. Butterflies kept flipping their wings someplace deep inside her stomach whenever she thought of being alone with Stephen. He was a most disturbing man. And now he claimed even more Druid powers.

Mairey nodded her head, her eyes going directly to his for a moment and then dropping.

"Yes, let's stay here in my office. It's as private as any spot in this bustling place. I have so many questions I don't know where to start."

"I expected you would." Stephen's smile faded to blazing intent as he suddenly clasped her hand and swung her into his arms.

"Mairey, Mairey, do you have any idea what this means to me?"

Still filled with the elation they'd all noticed in him, Stephen raised her face to his and lowered his lips. Once again he kissed her, this time a bruising burst of power that claimed her as his conquest. His first kiss had swept away any denial of his appeal to her. This second one left no doubt in her mind he could kiss her at any time he wanted, in any place and she would welcome his ardent and demanding lips.

She wound her fingers through his beautiful hair, luxuriating in the blaze of sensation he'd let loose in her.

*Another amazing kiss. His lips have only to touch mine and I'm ready to do anything this incredible man wants. I don't understand him but I don't have one bone stiff enough to push him away.*

She couldn't draw breath to resist him, even if she desired such a stupid thing. His strong body, honed solid by months of walking, made her feel more feminine and fragile than she could ever remember. Instead of infuriating her with a sense of helplessness before his strength, she melted against him with liquid pleasure.

Stephen groaned deep in his throat as his tongue swept into her mouth and explored her every crevice. This time her tongue mated with his and he rumbled another deep moan and molded her body to his. His hands swept over her, caressing the sides of her breasts and finally settling on her hips, as he clutched her body to him.

"Dear goddess but I wish we were someplace where I weren't afraid of somebody walking in on us at any moment."

He nuzzled her hair, breathing in the fragrance of the lilac water she used as a rinse.

"You smell almost as good as you look. You're beautiful, Mairey but then dozens of men you have known must have told you so."

To his surprise she reacted as if he'd dealt her an insult, glaring at him and trying to break away although he wouldn't let her.

"Of course they haven't," she snapped. "I haven't known dozens of men. And I think it's a good thing we don't have more privacy than we do. I don't like the way you make me act, or make me feel. I don't understand any of this."

Stephen knew his face must have mirrored his astonishment. "For Merlin's sake, I didn't mean 'know' in the Biblical sense. I think you're beautiful enough for any man who meets you at least to want to tell you so."

Mairey tossed her head. "I'm perfectly ordinary and I don't understand you at all. Why I let you kiss me so, so…*warmly* I can't begin to comprehend."

Stephen tried to control his merriment but didn't quite succeed and Mairey glared as he chuckled.

"My dear girl, there's a chemistry between us you can't deny. If you try you'll just mislead yourself. The first sight of you elicited my very first vision of an aura. The first in my entire life. Do you have any idea at all what that means to me? Yours is a beautiful rose color and at first I didn't even recognize if for my very own miracle. You're responsible for the steady development of my Druid powers and such a wonder can't be an accident. You and I are destined to find some future together."

He tried to draw her closer in his arms, until he saw she appeared to be not only angry but frightened. She shook from some emotion he could not understand. Stephen dropped his arms, setting her free, although he did not step back. Mairey whirled away the moment she could.

"Nonsense. All of your Druid allegations are nonsense."

Stephen's face again mirrored his surprise.

"Including the fact I came back in time to help when the ladder broke? And the vision that led me to be there when Walter came after Beth? Do you think it all coincidence then?"

She slowly shook her head. "No, I can't think that. There is so much I don't understand. I don't really know anything for sure except you're not a thief. You may be many things I don't comprehend but you're not a thief."

Stephen moved close enough to lean over and kiss her, a brief, sweet kiss of benediction and thanks. He made no attempt to take her in his arms again and Mairey stood perfectly still, mesmerized once again by his warm and firm lips.

Then she almost ran out the door.

Stephen looked after her, puzzled but not discouraged. He knew in his Druid heart matters would eventually be resolved, although he didn't even try to think of the next step. Since the moment he'd seen Mairey and her rosy halo, his world had changed. Up to now he'd lived his life in a rather carefree manner, although the setback of losing Vivie had crushed him. He'd never truly hoped to win Vivie and while her rejection devastated him, he'd not been shocked or surprised. Still it changed him and he'd lost the confidence that had always before been naturally his. From his first sight of Mairey, even as she beat on his shoulders with a knapsack, his view of the world began to take on the hue of her aura. Somehow he *knew* she was his touchstone to happiness, although he hadn't the slightest idea what would happen next.

Certainly a future with her in it was appealing. From the moment of meeting Mairey, the goddess had favored him. She'd just have to help him work some of the wrinkles out of the complicated road ahead.

One fact he knew for sure.

Mairey wasn't about to fall into his arms. She'd have to be courted carefully.

# Chapter Twelve

ജ

Mairey decided not to collect Beth from Taliesin and seize some much-needed time to think. She couldn't leave the compound and be too far away from Bethan but she craved solitude. Stephen was in her usual refuge, her office and the acquisitions building was too big to be conducive to thought. She needed a secluded spot with the certainty she'd not be interrupted.

Surprisingly, there were not many such sites in this large excavation compound.

She decided to go back to the smaller pit where she and Beth used to spend their time. She walked down the ramp to the bottom of the pit and headed for the little shelter where Beth had napped and played. Sitting on the ground, she folded her legs into the pose of a reflective Buddha and then withdrew into herself. It had been far too long since she'd taken time to really analyze her thoughts. Beth, dear as she was, took all her spare time and energy. Now she seethed, her mind roiling with an urgency to examine her feelings for the confusing Druid who dominated her dreams. He offered her a future of rare sexual pleasure. That conviction was a certain one, at least. Her emotions boiled over anytime she let down her shield.

Where were they going and what did she really feel about any kind of a future with Stephen? The first was easy enough to answer. They'd head straight into a steamy love affair if she let him keep kissing her. She couldn't understand her boneless and mindless response to his kisses. She felt like a pool of warm liquid butter when he wrapped his strong arms around her and took her lips with his. The flame melting the butter swept over her, weakening her knees so she clung to him and his big solid frame. His handsome face smiled down at her, his eyes ardent and sweet all at once. In order to keep from falling into his appealing arms like a malleable lump of clay she'd better strengthen her determination.

She shut off thoughts of Stephen and deliberately brought up memories of Edward Stanley. She didn't want to repeat the disaster of when she'd loved Edward. She'd not seen him for two years but he'd left his mark. Edward had wooed her with determination, lauding her beauty and her accomplishments. Her days began with thoughts of him and seeing him was her hoped-for highlight. Her disillusionment when she discovered his perfidy cut deeper than she could have dreamed.

One night they'd gone together to a pub in Cardiff and she'd excused herself to find the ladies' room. While still in one of the closed compartments she'd heard the door open and after a short pause two female voices sounded plainly through the room.

"Don't know why you're fixing your lipstick, Essie. Looks like your boyfriend's caught his latest pigeon and is going to stick to her. He's with stodgy *Doctor* Bronwyn again, has been all night. Disgusting the way she hangs on his every word."

The other voice, low and with a vicious note, sniffed. Doubtless this was Essie's, since Mairey hadn't heard more than two set of heels.

"He tells me he might even have to marry the bitch. He won't stay with her of course, at least not after he takes over her job. He'll be in solid with the other Bronwyns then. Eddie's smart. He has long-range plans and they don't include her for very long. He'll leave all the Bronwyns behind."

"I don't know when you see him. He's with her most of the time."

"Don't worry about that." Essie's sneering voice was triumphant. "He comes straight to me from her. He's so starved for sex I can tell she's not giving out any. I make sure to give him all he wants and let me tell you he's a greedy one."

Both females laughed, knowing laughs that made Mairey cringe. She hastily drew her feet up out of sight. She hadn't been spotted yet and now she definitely didn't want to be.

Voice one spoke after a malicious laugh. "She deserves to be put down. Fancy a woman getting a degree in archeology. That's a man's field and always has been. I hate women who put on such airs."

"That's just what Eddie says. She has no business taking work away from a good man like him. But he'll worm his way into the business, show everyone how smart he is and then manage to convince everyone she's making all kinds of mistakes at work. He's clever, Eddie is. He'll see she's at fault when they break up. Not that he intends to be faithful to her for much longer than the honeymoon. Wait and see. I'll win out in the end. That overeducated bitch can't beat me. She doesn't know how to bind a man to her like I do. "

"Then you're actually planning to take him back? I'm not sure..."

The voices and their sneering laughter died away. Mairey remained shivering in the stall, shaking and cold with tattered nerves and disillusionment. Completely disgusted with herself as well as Edward. Afraid to come out and needing time to face the world.

Edward had raved about her beauty again and again. He'd been loving and assiduous in his courting. To think she'd actually felt fortunate to have attracted a man of equal learning so they could easily converse.

She'd gathered herself together, walked out of the stall and out of his life. She'd passed him at their table and sailed right by to a taxi.

It had been two years since she eliminated him from her life, refusing to ever see or speak to him again. Even now she cringed at the thought of her stupidity. Philip tried to console her, saying he and Taliesin were taken in too. She heard this for brotherly solace and never quite believed him. She was the stupid one. *Really* stupid.

*But what to do about Stephen? A man who melted her defenses with shocking rapidity. Was she willing to be hurt so badly once again, just because his kiss gave her delirious delight? Much more powerful and seductive than Edward's had ever been. Certainly no one in this world could kiss like Stephen.*

She rose to her feet with no decision made except to be cautious. On her guard whenever she came near the blasted beautiful man.

But she wasn't sure if Stephen reached for her again she'd even remember her resolve.

* * * * *

Stephen and Philip walked the entire perimeter of the large compound forming the dig at Gouarec. They could find no break in the barbed wire.

"I can't believe this barbed wire fence would stop a determined thief in any case," Stephen mused. "Just the fact we haven't found a break yet doesn't mean it would deter future robberies."

Philip sighed. "It's such a big area. Barbed wire was all we had the funds for to do the job."

Stephen snorted. "Anyone can cut one of the lower wires and scramble through on their stomach. Your fence would certainly deter casual and curious visitors but not determined thieves."

Philip chewed on his lower lip, his pleasant face shadowed by the thought he and his uncle might have been negligent.

"The French government sponsored this excavation. Perhaps we should have pressed them harder for more funds for security but since they have first rights to anything we excavate, we tended to go along with their recommendations. Now we all might be sorry."

Stephen was striding up and down, thinking on his feet as he pondered the problem.

"Even so, getting into the compound is not the real problem. Getting into the acquisitions building is the crux."

Philip walked along with Stephen, matching Stephen's long strides as best he could.

"The armband was stolen and then hidden to implicate you. That smacks of a personal vendetta and of Walter. The thief could have walked away with this tremendously valuable object. He'd have little trouble selling it. There are many collectors who'd pay the price just to gloat privately and keep it in their secret hoard."

Stephen stopped abruptly. Philip nearly ran into him but stopped in time.

"Call your shots, man. I'd be bowled over if I ran into your big frame."

Stephen grinned and clapped Philip on the back.

"I think you should talk this over with your new love. You've said something beginning to make sense of this muddle. How active are smugglers along the coast? They'd be the ones to pay the most for the golden band. Carnac is likely the closest port to this dig that's easy to lurk in. I found the waves especially gentle in the fishing waters of Quiberon Bay. The long arm of the Presqu'ile provides excellent shelter. A lovely spot for fishing boats. This gives me all kind of interesting thoughts. Is our thief an agent sent by Walter to ruin me, or was his main aim putting the band aside to be picked up along with a future haul?"

Philip stopped short in his tracks and Stephen sidestepped to avoid running him down.

He laughed his deep, genuine laugh, charming any listener.

"Now you're the one who should call his shots, Philip. *I* nearly barreled into *you* this time. Let's step aside and sit on this unattractive log. Not the most comfortable seat in the world but the best around."

Stephen flashed his smile of trust and generosity, which would surely convince any opponent and perched on the log. He crossed his long legs and flexed the muscles in his back, wriggling a little as he tried to find a comfortable position. He stretched out, leaning backward and bracing his arms on the grass.

"We need to attack this from a logical angle. Walter undoubtedly wants to eradicate me as a champion of Mairey and Bethan. I think it's possible he's also tied up with some kind of smuggling. I know I'm taking a leap of imagination but somehow a theory I feel we must consider."

Philip started. "You're not serious, are you? Walter is a bastard of a person but smuggling?"

Stephen did not back down. His demeanor became even more somber as he rose and began to pace back and forth in a crisscrossing pattern. His hands were clasped behind his back as he thought on his feet.

"You have many items here a reclusive millionaire would pay almost any price to secure for his private collection. Never to be viewed by anyone but himself. There *are* such stratospheric millionaires, you know. The band would be used first to intrigue them and convince them of riches to come. It also implies whoever is responsible for all this will be back for more."

Philip was beginning to follow Stephen's reasoning.

"And you think your vision of the hiding place of the golden band upset the time table. Hmmm. An interesting theory and I suppose possible but still far-fetched to my way of thinking. Why do you think Walter is involved?"

"Because Riva was put to investigating me. That could be no one else but Walter. Ergo, whatever is going on involves Walter."

"Damn, I hate all this." Philip jumped to his feet and also began to pace. "I just want to do the job I'm trained for. Now you're talking about spies and smugglers and god knows what all. And I've met a girl I'd like to know better and all this *merde* is going to get in the way."

Stephen laughed with genuine amusement.

"Go fetch her then, Philip. I have nothing to hide. Let's find her and see if she can add anything to our deductions. A novel courtship perhaps, to ask the investigator to help the accused. I'm willing to include her if you are."

Philip's face lit. "Yes, let's involve Riva. It's a good idea for more than one reason. If smuggling is involved, she'd know the likely villains. I imagine the Bureau of Antiquities keeps track of known smugglers."

He bounded off, his face mirroring his happiness at the thought of seeing Riva.

* * * * *

Stephen continued his pacing. He deeply disliked not understanding a situation and this one baffled him. "Wheels within wheels" as his grandmother used to say. One thing he knew for certain. Walter was capable of any villainous trick and Stephen knew one danger for a certainty. Beth was definitely in peril.

If Walter was actively trying to discredit Stephen he hoped to force him out of the way before his own next dangerous move. Therefore, Stephen must make progress in the investigation as soon as possible and turn the tables on Walter.

And then there was Mairey. As alluring a girl as he'd ever seen. Her appearance, while startlingly beautiful, was just one desirable facet of her personality. More important to him were her outstanding traits of character. Her transparent honesty, her admirable love for Beth, her loyalty to those she'd accepted into her heart's almost closed circle. He'd made entry to her circle as a friend. He wanted more, much more.

Certainly the physical attraction between them was a rare blazing force. He'd desired Vivie, of course but even reaching deep into his memories the intensity of his feeling now and then didn't compare. His love for Vivie had been almost a reverence. He'd not felt this overwhelming and undeniable urge to make her his. With Mairey he wanted to grab her and kiss her senseless the instant he saw her. He guessed their passion puzzled her too. When they were together he half expected the room to start sending up smoke.

A vivid and exceptional attraction existed between them.

Their bodies recognized each other. Could he make her mind and her heart do the same?

Stephen looked up to see Philip approaching with Riva. Not much doubt Philip had been smitten at first sight. He was grinning like a child just given a promised treat.

"Riva is baffled, Stephen but she admits you're probably not the culprit in our little drama."

Riva cast a reproachful look at Philip. "I said 'probably', Philip. I admit I can't see any reason at all for Dr. Lovernios to expose the hiding place of the golden band if he wants to steal it. Also your credentials are impeccable, Dr. Lovernois. My staff in Rennes has been checking and you are undoubtedly a gifted physician and surgeon. Why you choose to spend uncomfortable months as a wanderer I don't know but that is definitely your business. Not mine."

Stephen laughed, a contagious laugh that made the others smile automatically.

"You keep forgetting I'm a Druid and a bard. Think of how Merlin wandered through Brittany and England, most often as a bard, when he wanted to go unnoticed for a while. The past few months of my life have let me travel in disguise, as it were, while I thought some issues through."

Riva surveyed him, taking her time and scrutinizing his pleasant face.

"I don't think anyone as presentable as you can stay long in disguise, nor do I understand why you left a well-paid and flourishing practice of medicine."

Stephen just grinned. "You'd better check a little harder, Mlle. Broussard. I left a clinic where most of the patients could pay our fees because they were modest. Certainly one of the definitive experiences of my life but not one I embraced for money. I'm not particularly interested in wealth for wealth's sake."

Riva shook her head. "You confuse me, Dr. Lovernios. But I'll admit my department is concerned about smugglers. They seem to operate from a fishing boat moored in Quiberon Bay. We think they've already taken some artifacts from the Carnac area."

Stephen nodded. "Thank you for telling me, Dr. Broussard. Now I'm going to go find Mairey and see if she'd like to walk the barbed wire fence with me. If there's been a break-through I want to know it. She will too."

He strode off, leaving Riva baffled and Philip pleased to be alone with the girl who so enthralled him.

* * * * *

Stephen finally found Mairey in her little shelter and his blood froze just before it nearly boiled over. He couldn't believe she'd gone alone to an isolated place where Walter or one of his minions could easily find her. It was too damn dangerous and he thought she'd understood. He paced up to her, his angry stride eating up the yards between them.

Before he knew it he'd grabbed her shoulders and hauled her to her feet, shaking her 'til her hat fell to her back, held only by the ties.

"You little fool! You must not be alone in an exposed place like this until we catch Walter. Haven't I made it plain you're in danger?"

Mairey looked at him with wide, frightened eyes. This Stephen was one she didn't know, not when he could be so angry at her. Her own Welsh temper flared as she tried to shake loose.

She tossed her head in automatic defiance. She succeeded in further loosening her black curls, already tumbling from their pins. As her hair fell about her shoulders Stephen's anger evaporated.

"I'll go where I please, Dr. Lovernios. You do not rule me."

Frustrated, Stephen did what he wanted to do anyway. He tightened his grip and kissed her once again. What started out as a punishing kiss of frustration soon changed as she first resisted and then softened in his arms and kissed him in return. In fact she grabbed his hair to pull him still closer. For a brief moment he let his hands stroke her on any spot he could reach, her arms, her back, her sides where the beautiful swell of her breasts demanded much more than soft touches.

*Blessed Merlin, this girl will be the ruination of me. If this keeps up I'm likely to try to seduce her in broad daylight with her whole family looking on.*

He deliberately gentled his kiss and then, clutching a mass of dark hair, pressed his lips to it while he regained control. He held her loosely, letting the passion between them ebb so they could breathe again.

"I never dreamed kisses were such dangerous things," he murmured. "I'm already a suspicious character and if I did what I wanted right now I'd be kicked off the entire excavation."

Delighted to see her breathing as labored as his, he dropped his arms and stepped away from her.

After a minute or two he smiled wryly.

"Believe it or not I came for a legitimate reason. I'm going to walk the perimeter of the fence and look for signs of a breakthrough. If I promise to try to behave will you walk with me?"

Her eyes were enormous, puzzled and half-angry as she gazed up at him.

"Why do you keep kissing me when I told you I don't like the way it makes me feel?"

She pushed a black strand of curls from her face, looking like an indignant child being punished unfairly.

Stephen merely smiled and did not attempt to answer. She definitely was not ready to hear the true answer to her question.

"I would like very much to have you along. If I find anything suspicious, it will be better for me to have a witness. You'll be doing me a huge favor."

"Will you promise—" she started and he put one big finger on her lips.

"No. I can't, Mairey. But please come anyway."

Mairey looked at him as carefully as if he were a stranger she'd just met. She shuddered to think of her first assessment of him as a pedophile. He'd never mentioned her assault on him, gentleman that he was. Now she saw the strength of character behind the humorous front he showed the world. He was basically a good man. True he liked to wander, something she detested. She repeated to her racing heart her mantra that people with the superior abilities and education should dedicate their lives to their profession, not to drifting around the world. *Still, he was an honorable man.*

It was not his fault she behaved so wantonly when he kissed her. Doubtless she'd become a frustrated spinster and she should read up on how to handle her surprising temptations. She didn't need to succumb to him so easily if she accepted him as a special friend and made it plain only friendship was involved.

One thing became clear to her while she'd sat thinking. She wanted him as a close and reliable friend.

She also wanted to be with him. She turned to him as she held out her hand and he smiled his sweet smile and led her out of the excavation pit.

By unspoken consent they both chatted about inconsequential subjects as they headed toward the barbed wire fence and began to walk its perimeter. Stephen was more than content to have some moments of relaxation with Mairey. It seemed so much of their time together was stressful and he found small talk definitely palatable right now.

She told him she was beginning to teach Bethan her letters. Stephen mentioned he was considering a new rooming house where he might have larger quarters. Since he intended to stay at Gouarec for a while he wished to be more comfortable. Although this raised questions in Mairey's mind, she kept her peace. She put it away in her memory, however, that he was not strapped for funds. Interesting. As interesting as the other contradictions he posed.

How long did he plan to stay?

They were walking slowly, each of them enjoying their time together in amity. Suddenly Stephen stopped.

"I'm doubly glad you came. Look right there. The lower strand of wire is clipped on one end. Our intruder didn't even try to tack it back up. A man could easily crawl under the second wire."

Mairey wasn't too surprised. Stephen seemed in the habit of making accurate predictions.

She walked over to the fence. "Look, the ground is scuffed all around here. Our villain probably scooted through on his stomach."

Stephen's grin was not his usual pleasant one. "And you can bear me out we found the wire already cut. Although Mlle. Broussard will doubtless reason I could have cut it during the night. Thank you for coming, Mairey."

"But I'd never doubt you if you came back saying you'd found such an opening."

"Our lady from the Antiquities Bureau is bound to believe only facts. Your testimony makes this a fact. Let's go tell her."

He looked around carefully and saw the break almost exactly in line with the building holding the Acquisitions. Not surprising but worth noting. He took Mairey's hand in his and held it on the way back, caressing her palm with this thumb. She didn't protest, although she quivered once from head to foot.

They walked together with their hands joined to report to the others.

* * * * *

Riva and Philip were deep in conversation and both stopped and looked guilty when Mairey and Stephen approached. Definitely they were not talking about the possible thefts.

Stephen wore his solemn look, the one seldom seen but nonetheless impressive.

"We've found a break and definite signs someone has used it as an entry. Would you like me to take you to inspect the break, Mlle. Broussard?"

Riva shook her head. "Not necessary. If you both say so, then you've had an intruder. Can you tell me approximately where it is?"

"It lines up directly with the Acquisitions building. A likely spot to have a break, of course." Mairey spoke in unmistakable confirmation.

Stephen gave Mairey a warm and grateful look. He was glad for more than one reason she'd come along. That she'd wanted to come along especially pleased him.

"I haven't been in the building for a while," Mairey said. "Not since we went to check on the golden band. Have you been in today, Philip?"

Philip looked startled. "No, I haven't. Suppose we go check now."

They started toward the Acquisitions Building and its place in the middle of the long ellipse forming the encampment, the four of them chatting easily.

As they approached each one noticed the guard sitting in a slumped position on the chair by the door.

"I don't like this at all," murmured Philip. "Although the guard doesn't have to stand his whole shift, he should have seen or heard us coming and sprung to his feet."

"I'll wager none of us is going to like this," added Stephen. All vestige of pleasantry seemed wiped from his face. Instead, Mairey thought he projected an air of deep foreboding and she shivered. She might not completely believe in his powers and certainly not that anyone could have frequent prescient visions. Mostly she shut off her mind when she tried to yet figure out how he knew where the band was hidden. She understood so little about him. Still she trusted his ability to see matters more clearly than most. She didn't doubt his powers of perception. Not at all.

Philip motioned the ladies back and he and Stephen approached closer to the guard, who still didn't move a muscle.

"Let me go first, please," said Stephen. "Just enough to make sure there is no unknown danger."

"That's hardly likely." Riva's small chin set with stubbornness. "And it's my job to check everything that might have any bearing on my assignment. I'm the one to go first."

She forged ahead past Stephen who hesitated to physically restrain her. And so she was the one who stopped short and gave a small scream.

"My god, he's dead."

Stephen and Mairey rushed to her side and joined Riva and Philip in staring down at the guard's body. He was most definitely dead. His throat had been slashed and the ground about him was soaked with blood.

Riva stood shivering with shock and Philip put his arm around her and bound her to his side while he commented in a low voice.

"He took the midnight to noon shift. From the amount of blood and its dried state I'd say this happened some hours ago. Look, someone tied him in position so he wouldn't fall out of the chair. The rope runs under his coat."

"Which also means no one has had reason to approach the building until now. Taliesin's with Bethan and we've not thought of coming here."

This from Mairey, who stood still and staring. Stephen could smell the distinctive metallic smell of blood, as well as a definite smell of fear. Did the guard see his attacker then but trusted him till the last moment? He'd certainly allowed death to come quite close to him.

Philip spoke in a hushed monotone. "And we finished cleaning nothing new yesterday, so no one would be bringing anything in."

Mairey seemed mesmerized by the sight of the dead man, her eyes unnaturally large and her lovely complexion a drained white. She didn't seem able to move and Stephen went up to her and put his arm around her.

"Come, my dear. We need you. We must check to see if anything is missing from the building and then call in the gendarmes. Only you and Philip can tell us if this is involved with a theft or not."

Philip nodded in agreement and took his sister's hand. As they started into the building he turned back.

"Aren't you coming, Stephen?"

"The rest of you go. I think someone should stay with the body to make sure no one touches it. Perhaps Mlle. Broussard should stay with me also."

He didn't need to add he wanted a reliable witness but Riva understood and nodded to him.

"He's right, you know and prudent as well. Go ahead, Philip. I'll wait with Dr. Lovernios."

Neither Stephen nor Riva attempted conversation during the long wait for the others to check the inventory in the Acquisitions Bldg. Riva stood for a while, then fidgeted and finally sat down in the dirt and bowed her blonde head on her upraised knees. She avoided looking at the corpse and Stephen didn't blame her.

The body strained at the rope binding it and Stephen knelt down to look at the face of the corpse. The features showed an awareness of the death about to overtake him. He'd probably recognized his murderer or murderers. There was no surprise on his features, only horror. Stephen straightened and leaned against the side of the building, lost in thought.

The others were gone a long while. Both Stephen and Riva knew as soon as Mairey and Philip appeared something else was missing. Their countenances were a mixture of regret, indignation and apprehension.

"We knew right away what had been taken but we needed to check carefully to see if anything else was gone. The most valuable article we've found so far is stolen but nothing else." Philip's face had paled too, as he spoke with reluctance.

"It's the torque," Mairey added. "The solid gold torque. It once graced a Celtic nobleman of long ago. Now it's gone. Nothing could be more disastrous."

"I saw it and know its loveliness. Thank the goddess you have multiple sketches and photos." Stephen went up to her and took both her icy hands in his, chaffing them softly as he spoke.

Mairey nodded. "Oh, the sketches didn't do it justice. Of course it's the usual shape of a torque, a large ring open at the front but its measurements show it bigger than usual. It was made to fit around a rather large neck. The finials of wild boars showed it to be the necklace of a prince because of the amount of gold and an exceptional fighter because of the boars. Only the very highest Celts could afford such a lovely thing. It was so very beautiful, as you know." Her voice broke but she kept on. "You could hardly keep from stroking it."

"That it was a royal warrior is certain," mused Stephen. "But it could have been a princess. Boadicea wore a golden torque into battle against Caesar's army, you know."

Mairey looked surprised. "You're right, of course and I'd thought of that. But you didn't lift it. This torque is quite thick and heavy, the heaviest I've ever felt. A prince, I think. One would need a strong neck to wear it, although I grant you Celtic women were tall and powerful."

She flashed a genuine smile at him that surprised and pleased Stephen.

"I think we can assume the theft and the murder took place in the dark of night. A golden torque of such weight and size isn't easy to conceal." Riva spoke slowly and moved closer to Philip.

"Nor is murder," Philip said, taking her hand and holding it. "I agree it took place in the dark of the night."

"Then it's indeed a shame we didn't check sooner." Riva's sigh swooshed out in the sudden silence.

She turned to Stephen. "I want to say I privately absolve you of all guilt in these latest calamities, Dr. Lovernios. You are just what you say you are. I've come to know you enough to be sure you are not a thief or a murderer."

Stephen strode over and took her hand. "Thank you, Mlle. Broussard. Your faith in me is most appreciated."

As he bowed over her hand to kiss it, two other sets of eyes looked on, ambivalent about what they saw.

Philip moved in and took Riva's other hand in his, lacing his fingers through hers.

"I'm glad we all agree Stephen is innocent. We must inform Taliesin and the French police. I'll go to Taliesin and you inform the police, Riva. I'm sure you must also report to your superiors. Oh lord, what a mess."

He walked away, head down, to find his uncle. Riva looked at him as he left and then set off briskly to find the nearest phone.

Stephen saw Mairey glancing at the dead man. Her expression was one of revulsion and fear. He enveloped and folded her in his arms.

"Come away, love. Things will play out as they are meant to be. You and I will have each other to see us through."

Mairey raised startled eyes to Stephen's smoldering ones and then relaxed into his embrace.

He held her in his arms for a long loving time, not moving to demand her lips or her body but willing his strength to be taken into hers.

He no longer had any doubts.

He knew she had many.

Which he would deal with, one by one, as they surfaced and he could conquer them all.

# Chapter Thirteen

ꟃ

The next few days were a horror, gendarmes tramping over the site interviewing them all and taking copious notes. Stephen felt he was not the primary suspect but still one to be regarded warily as a possible one. He began to feel grateful Riva had concluded her preliminary investigations and in her mind, at least, cleared him. Her neutral opinion of him kept him from being the concentration of the police efforts. It was always easier to blame the latest arrival and one who had no real connection with the excavation or a valid explanation for being there.

An inspector of police came from Rennes and methodically began collecting information on all of them and on the murdered guard. Of course he already had the guard's resumé and application information and he set about finding more data from the locals.

Mairey went silently about her duties, her face lighting only when with Beth. She avoided Stephen, a situation he didn't intend to allow to continue.

He was determined to marry her. He didn't know what he felt for her was love but he certainly lusted for her. He didn't expect or believe in lasting love. It didn't matter, he felt more than enough. He'd been lonely too long and he wanted someone to sleep with at night. And someone to share the everyday joys and sorrows. Beyond the delights of the marriage bed he wanted a lifelong companion. They were suited in every respect. He would make her his, one way or another. They were well-matched for a lifetime together.

She was bright, beautiful and honorable to a fault and he couldn't keep his hands off her.

He thought of invading her mind, as he could do now as a capable Druid. He wouldn't resort to such spying with a loved one, although he longed to know what she truly thought of him. He knew well he attracted her physically. The way she melted against him when he took her in his arms told him all he needed to know on that score. He also knew she'd resist him. She thought him irresponsible and carefree. He'd once thought her mistaken feeling a hindrance to their attraction for each other but now it didn't matter. He wanted her even if circumstances made him seduce her and force her hand.

He'd marry her and then tell her he possessed wealth enough to see them through life without his ever working again. His parents died early from a vicious plague and left him more money than he needed. It was immaterial since idleness was not his aim or his pleasure. Still, she deserved to know all about him. Being interested and productive definitely was what he wanted. He had not yet worked out exactly what to do with his life but he knew the lodestar of his life was Mairey.

Pondering his goals was one reason for his bardic wanderings. Until he'd first seen her and her astonishing aura he'd had no clue to his future. Now he knew.

He wanted to marry her and overwhelm her with the delights he knew they could find together. He planned to bed her so thoroughly they could then talk rationally about the problem of what to do with the rest of his life. Mostly he wanted to bed her. Right now she was prejudiced against his idle wandering, not realizing that for him it had been a way of seeking and recuperating his spirit.

He'd found his spirit. His now wonderfully Druid spirit. He possessed so much now he knew himself to be a true Druid.

They'd discuss their future after he took her to his bed and completely compromised her. He didn't think he could talk her into marrying him unless he overwhelmed her with the passion she didn't even know she possessed.

He came to a decision that made him smile.

He would seduce her as soon as possible.

* * * * *

The next day the world tilted on its axis.

Stephen looked up from the sketch he was making of a small bronze cauldron. The handles were intricately twined in a way he'd not seen and he'd determined to draw the pattern accurately. He'd felt Mairey's presence the moment she arrived at the door of the sketching room. When she was near all his senses went on alert. She had the wonderful and maddening ability to make his whole body come to attention in a startling manner such as he'd never known. Definitely embarrassing. He didn't want anyone but Mairey seeing him with a large erection straining his trousers. Even she would be discomfited if she recognized his often rigid state.

He saw her look around the room and then relax. Her gaze went to his face but slid away from meeting his eyes.

"You're alone. I'm glad. I want to ask you something." Her voice cracked on the last word and Stephen's warning signals told him this would not be an ordinary request.

"You must know I'll help you in any way I can, Mairey." He made his voice deliberately soothing but his blue, blue eyes never left her face.

"I want you to marry me," she blurted out. Then she gulped.

The thought of marrying her brought immediate visions of a Mairey naked in rumpled sheets and his body grew even harder.

"But of course," he managed to reply.

"No, no, you can't accept without understanding. I'll let you go after Walter is captured. I know you think he's tied into the guard's murder and the theft of the torque. If he is, French law will be after him. If he isn't, he's still a danger to Beth. If you could just stay married to me until Walter is gone from my life I promise to divorce you anytime after that you want. Divorce is a disgrace but that's a problem I'll face. I promise to let you go free."

The thought of marrying the girl he so passionately desired and then letting her go made a small smile come to Stephen's carefully controlled face. He put down his sketching pencil and steepled his hands.

"We can discuss my wanting a divorce later. Now tell me, please, why you've come to this decision."

Mairey wrung her fingers and watched their twining for a moment. Then she looked up at him, her blue-green eyes shadowed. Her fingers showed her distress but she couldn't seem to stop their frantic movement.

"Yes, you have a right to know my thoughts. First I'd best explain the sleeping arrangements at our boarding house. I have a large bedroom, with a half flight of stairs leading to a smaller room I use as an office. A very desirable arrangement for a person who doesn't like to be surrounded by clutter. Beth is next door to me. That is no longer safe enough. Anyone can crawl through her window and so I've moved her into the small office up the stairs. Now Walter will have to first dispose of me."

Her belligerent tone amused him, although he carefully didn't smile.

"A smart move on your part, Mairey. And you want reinforcements."

He congratulated himself on speaking so calmly.

Her rosy blush was so charming Stephen could barely stop from grabbing her then and there, shouting "yes, I'll marry you this minute" and kissing her senseless.

"Yes," she said. "I want you to move in my bedroom." She raised embarrassed and courageous eyes to his. "I know whatever is between us is stronger than I am and I won't be able to keep you out of my bed if you're in the house with me. I propose a marriage until Walter is gone from our lives. It takes ten days to get an approval of a French civil marriage, I believe and you can stay in Beth's old room in the meantime."

Stephen smiled his charming, carefree smile bringing laugh lines to his bronzed face and accentuating his chiseled features. He picked up both her hands and held them to his lips, holding them tightly when she tried to withdraw from his grasp.

"It will be my distinct pleasure to move into your house, Mairey. But I will not stay in Beth's old room. I not only want to be with you, I think it essential for your safety. I insist on one thing, however. We fill out the necessary papers for a French civil wedding and do it today. I believe in some rural areas that's enough excuse for living together. I'll inform Philip and Dr. Taliesin and then I'll move in tonight. I intend to sleep in your bed from now on."

Mairey looked so startled Stephen almost laughed. Did she think she could hold him off for ten days? While he lay in the room next to hers, picturing how irresistible she'd look in her nightgown?

"I don't think my brother will allow that, Stephen."

He smiled with quite startling confidence. "It's up to me to ensure he does. Let me talk to him and we'll see. We'll go to town within the hour, as I have several other items to clear up requiring a solicitor."

He smiled at her but his face showed such determination she couldn't seem to smile back. This was a Stephen who would not be deterred.

She almost backed out the door, her beautiful face clouded. He hoped it was with doubt and not regret. His body smoldering at the thought of being in Mairey's bed at last, he set out to find Philip. He knew this was exactly what he wanted to do. His lovely and astonishing wife-to-be just moved the timetable up a notch.

Not that he was about to complain.

With his widest smile illuminating his glowing face, he went to find Philip.

* * * * *

Philip laughed when he first heard Stephen's proposition.

"I can't believe I'm not trying to punch out your lights for suggesting sleeping with my sister on the basis of an application for marriage. But you're a hell of a lot bigger than I am, for one thing. For another, I know the application can be considered as binding as the actual civil marriage. Still I can't quite like it."

Stephen relaxed just a little. "I have more to tell you. Some people might consider me wealthy. I inherited a great deal. I propose to see a solicitor today and settle everything irrevocably on Mairey. Whether the actual marriage takes place or not, Mairey will be my heir. If Walter succeeds in eradicating me she'll be a rich woman."

Philip's silence filled the room.

"Well, I'm impressed by your forethought. I'm not too surprised you have money. Your taste in boots gives you away."

"I intend to execute this will leaving everything to Mairey regardless of your approval and I also intend to move in with her with or without your approval. I'm only informing you of this so you won't worry I'm taking advantage of her. I'd like you to go to the solicitor's with me this afternoon. To help me with the formalities and to convince you this will be in every respect a valid marriage."

Another long silence while Philip studied his fingernails. "Does Mairey know any of this?" he finally asked.

"No, nor will I tell her just yet. At present she thinks I'll be complaisant about a divorce as soon as Walter is out of the picture. Not so. I intend to protect her and Bethan in every way I can for the rest of my life. If Walter succeeds in eliminating me, which I'm convinced he'll try, Mairey will have the funds to hire an army of bodyguards."

"Whew." Philip regarded the man in front of him with wonder. "I liked you from the beginning, Stephen but I didn't appreciate your depth of character 'til now."

Stephen grinned, a more devilish one than usual. "I have to teach my bride many things, it seems. Some of them will take time, some will not. May I move into your house tonight, Philip?"

"Yes."

The simple, quiet answer brought Stephen to his feet and hurrying over to shake Philip's hand.

"I'll fetch Mairey and we'll all go start the marriage process. Will you ask Dr. Taliesin to come too? He can bring Mairey and Beth back here, while you and I visit a solicitor."

"Yes," said Philip again, grinning up at the large handsome man who'd taken over his family's life and their problems. Stephen was only about four inches taller but somehow he seemed bigger. Philip had no doubts of Stephen's Druid abilities. He thought those unusual skills might be badly needed in the skirmish with Walter lying just ahead. How it would all play out he didn't know but he couldn't think of a better man for his sister. Still grinning, he went off to find his uncle. This time at the thought of some of the things Stephen would be delighted to teach Mairey.

* * * * *

A thoughtful Dr. Taliesin, a nervous Mairey, an amused Philip and an elated Stephen set out for town in Taliesin's motorcar. An exuberant Beth went along, overjoyed to be going anyplace with her loved ones and her uncle Stevie. The knowledge he would soon be legally her uncle meant little to her. He already held a prime place in her heart. She only realized she'd be seeing more of him than usual.

Stephen concentrated on not thinking about the coming night. The instant he did his arousal hardened to an embarrassing degree. As a result, he treated Mairey with a polite detachment, bringing anxious confusion to her lovely features. He noticed—*how could he not*—but he had no choice. He didn't want to spend the entire day with an erection straining his trousers which would mortify them all.

He'd make it up to her in the night. Again he was obliged to switch off his thoughts. Philip stood by smiling a smile so knowing Stephen longed to plow down his future brother-in-law. Cooling thoughts were hard to come by, as Mairey stood by him and they signed the necessary papers. Now began the ten-day wait for a formal civil ceremony, which Stephen regarded as a mere formality. Mairey was his wife, now and forever.

With an inward sigh of relief he watched Mairey, Beth and Dr. Taliesin go back to the excavation. Dr. Taliesin remained a little stiff but raised no overt objection. Philip had evidently done enough persuading to manage the matter.

Dr. Tally took Stephen aside for only one comment. "I think you mean well or I wouldn't let this go ahead. But if you hurt Mairey I'll make you very sorry."

Stephen nodded solemnly. "I mean to make her happy, Dr. Taliesin. It will be the main purpose of my life."

Taliesin turned away, although Stephen thought his countenance a little lighter.

The meeting with the solicitor Philip recommended took a very long time. Fortunately Philip possessed the reputation and presence to persuade the man Stephen was legitimately Dr. Lovernios. The same Dr. Lovernios with the impressive credentials from some leading British politicians, including Lord Laniston Dellafield and the Duke of Lambden. Once Stephen produced his letters of credit the lawyer became quietly respectful. Before they left Stephen signed papers stating Mairey Bronwyn, soon to be Mrs. Lovernios, inherited everything he owned in the event of his death. Even if the final marriage did not take place Mairey Bronwyn inherited.

Stephen insisted on the documents being drawn up on the spot and finally got his way. He signed, with Philip as a witness.

Philip's face was solemn when they left the lawyer's. His new brother-in-law was proving to be a dark horse indeed. Stephen's manner was the triumphant one of a man who'd achieved exactly what he wanted. He thought he'd win the coming battle with Walter but at least he'd seen to Mairey's protection if he were wrong.

As they stepped down from the doorway, Stephen suddenly halted. He stopped still on the stoop, his mind listening in amazement. A voice clearly sounded in his head. "Well done, Stephen, well done. Call on me when the time comes you need me. I'll be with you."

Philip stared at Stephen in puzzlement as an ecstatic expression took over the quiet elation on his face.

"What is it, Stephen? What happened to you just then?"

"An old and revered friend just spoke to me in my mind. Madame Viviane Randall, the most powerful Druid I've ever met. I've been blessed."

Philip shook his head. "I definitely don't understand you, Stephen but I can tell you're beyond happy. Will you come to dinner with us tonight? It's so late you might as well go pack your things and bring them on over."

Stephen laughed aloud, his joy ringing over the quiet street.

"Yes, of course. I'll be there in about an hour. I own little in the way of material objects." He added as almost an afterthought, "At least here in France. It won't take me long to pack my knapsack."

* * * * *

A burnished Stephen appeared at the door of the rooming house the Bronwyns rented. Somehow he'd found a shop open, or bribed a shop to open and he was immaculately attired in tailored trousers and a fine linen shirt with its open neck showing his bronzed chest crested with golden hairs. He'd also purchased a twill jacket. It might have been tailored for him, its closely fitting cut emphasizing his broad shoulders and magnificent physique. His excellent boots were polished and his hair freshly washed. Its beautiful golden-red color served as a beacon, drawing everyone's glance. He was breathtaking in his handsome manhood and the sight of him thoroughly flustered Mairey.

He was the most appealing man she'd ever seen. He'd doubtless had women chasing him for years and had become well versed in seduction. He might expect some actions from her she didn't even begin to comprehend. She stared at him silently as he came in the room and directly to her side.

"My lovely wife-to- be," he murmured. He kissed her lightly on her lips and then he turned to the others in the room, flashing his most persuasive smile.

"Are we drinking toasts tonight? I'd like to propose one to our long and happily married life. I'm sure Mairey will join me in this propitious wish."

Mairey was too stunned to do anything but stare at him and so he placed her glass in her hand and slowly wrapped her fingers around the stem just before a servant scurried around filling every glass to the brim. Stephen's eyes fastened on hers in an ardent challenge.

"Let's drink to our long and happy future, my dearest Mairey."

She felt a flash of fury at him for putting her in such a predicament. She'd told him plainly this would be a temporary arrangement. He must have gotten her brother's and uncle's consent by promising eternal love. She didn't believe him for a moment. The realization had been slowly growing on her that Stephen Lovernios was the answer to any woman's dream of a virile lover. Well, she'd determined to accept this aspect of him. A frisson ran from her toes to the top of her head at just the thought. She'd asked for his protection and if learning about lust was part of it, she'd meet him more than halfway. She could also jostle him a little.

She rose to her feet.

"To our mutual love, my dearest Stephen."

She watched his eyes narrow and then the familiar laughter creep back.

He raised his glass in a salute to her and then, tilting his glass, drank the wine with one long draught.

Mairey returned the gesture with a flip of her hand and drank hers down as well.

She smiled at him in a challenge he could not mistake.

* * * * *

Mairey excused herself soon after dinner. She murmured something about checking on Beth but Stephen wondered if she was as nervous as she suddenly appeared to be. Or would he find the siren waiting for him, the one who'd proposed the toast and goaded him with her glance?

He waited what he hoped was a decent interval of time and then said good night to the other two men. Philip looked amused and Taliesin resigned.

"I'm not tired," Philip said. "I think I'll take a little walk."

No one doubted Philip's stroll would take him in the direction of Mlle. Riva, in hopes of finding her still awake and willing to walk with him.

"Blessed be," murmured Stephen as he watched Philip eagerly set off. "Blessed be to you both."

He himself planned a definite assignation and a most pleasant one. He turned and hastened his pace.

He could hardly wait.

# Chapter Fourteen

Stephen found Mairey curled up in a big chair in her bedroom, a book open on her lap.

He stood in the doorway, exulting in the sight of her. Just looking at her hardened him to an unbelievable degree. She would soon be forever his. In this life and the next. He'd make sure before the night was over she understood this one simple fact. Understood it so thoroughly she'd never resist him again.

Right now the siren had disappeared and his bride looked frightened. Her lovely eyes met his squarely but he saw the tremor in her hands. His wife was no coward but then he knew that. Still the flicker of genuine fear he saw in her huge aquamarine eyes troubled him.

He hurried to her and picked her up in his arms. To his amusement, he found her dressed in a flannel gown covered with a heavy bathrobe.

"It's a warm night, love, you must be sweltering."

He sat down with her in his lap and tackled the bathrobe, slipping both her arms out easily.

She jumped from his lap and stood facing him, her face rosier than he'd ever seen it.

"How stupid, simply stupid of me. However I'm dressed I know you'll take everything off. I didn't mean to act so silly."

He lounged in the chair, appreciating her beauty and her spirit.

"Don't fret, Mairey. Your fears tell me one thing I appreciate knowing. You're inexperienced in the art of love."

He hadn't thought her charming blush could grow deeper but it did. Completely enchanted, he held out his hand.

"Come love, sit on my lap for a while. Let's finish taking off your robe but not your gown. Just come relax."

She looked at him as if he'd made the most ridiculous suggestion she'd ever heard but she slowly paced back and perched gingerly on his knees.

With a joyous chuckle he wrapped his arms around her and held her against him, her body half-prone and nearly rigid.

Hoping his huge erection pushing against her wasn't frightening her, he held her a little away from his body and tilted his head over hers, taking her mouth. He made no move to caress her, as he gradually deepened the kiss and then, just as he felt her responding, moved to little nipping kisses all over her face, concentrating longest on the dimple he loved. To his delight she wriggled around to find his lips with hers and reaching them, kissed him with an innocent ardor that nearly broke his control.

She might be inexperienced but she was filled with passion. He allowed part of his deep feeling for her to surge into his next kiss as he invaded the sweetness of her mouth and tasted every crevice. His tongue swept through her mouth with a joyous certitude of being right where he belonged. Although she started at first, she soon joined him as their tongues mated and swirled.

The rational part of Stephen cautioned him to slow down. His glands were telling him something very different. He'd not been with a woman since he first went to London more than two years ago. After he met Vivie, no other appealed to him. Now, thanks to his goddess showing him Mairey was destined for him, he held his beloved woman in his arms. His long-throttled desire almost swamped him. The rosy glow of her aura warmed his heart even as he told himself he would frighten her if he didn't make his possession of her long, slow and pleasurable to them both.

He rose to his feet, holding her carefully in his arms.

"I'm taking you to bed, love. Don't worry about your night-robe. I mean to take it from you, admiring you inch by inch. You are so very beautiful, Mairy."

To his surprise she stiffened and glared at him.

"Men just admire women when they want their way. I'm nothing out of the ordinary, as you very well know. You don't have to say such things. I've already given you the right to take me."

Warning signals were clanging in his head and he knew whatever words he now spoke might determine their future relationship. He must treat this seriously, although he found it hard to believe her words.

"Mairey, to me you are the most beautiful woman I've ever seen. You not only have beauty, you possess every other quality I've always wanted in a wife. Your beauty is important but it's not the primary appeal. You offer me so much more. Everything about you is enticing."

She lay rigid in his arms for a moment and then suddenly softened and reached up to stroke his face.

"For tonight, I'll believe you. My gorgeous, wandering bard."

He lowered his lips to hers. She was all he'd ever desired. More than just intelligent, dedicated to her own principles and to her loved ones. She was perfection.

He rose, holding her in his arms like the precious package she was and walked to the bed. He tried not to race. He didn't want to frighten her more than she already was. He would woo her slowly and sweetly.

"Mairey, I want to see all of you. Let me take off your gown."

She quivered and then looked at him and nodded, her glorious eyes alight with a charming desire to learn all he could teach her.

She flexed her body as he lay her down on the bed, raising her hips so he could strip the gown from her.

A groan came from deep in his throat as he uncovered a body Venus herself would have envied. Slender hips, long, long legs, delectable curves in all the right places. And the loveliest breasts he'd ever imagined. Her black hair streamed around her, adding to a beauty so perfect it nearly stopped his speech.

"Mairey, my dear wife, why can't you believe that to me you are perfection?"

He moved over her, even as she stared doubtfully. Then she slightly swayed her hips and he made a sound that was half chagrin and half desperation.

"I can't wait any longer, love. I've wanted you for so long."

He'd meant to take his time, stoking her passion as expertly as he could. Instead, he found himself parting her legs and positioning his body over hers to take her immediately. At the last second, he realized he couldn't do that without damaging their relationship. He lifted himself on his arms and with a shudder stilled himself. With a determined effort that shook him to his soul he smiled as best he could.

"I think you'll need some convincing I truly want to be your husband. Are you ready for me, my love?"

Mairey lay under his beautiful body, thinking she'd never imagined just looking at a nude male could be so thrilling. He was perfectly formed, his large frame flawlessly proportioned and his jutting male member astonished her. She'd read all about the reproductive process but none of the pictures she'd seen began to approach the magnificence of Stephen's phallus, throbbing and eager. Still he held back. His self-discipline astonished her. Perhaps he truly cared for her, just a little. Surely he would not restrain himself unless he was also considering her pleasure.

She felt a mixture of primal admiration and thankful appreciation for this man. He held his body by his elbows above hers, shaking with what she was sure was desire. Desire for her. Her own passion increased as he guided his penis to stroke her mound, stimulating her to an extent she could hardly believe.

"Yes," she said. "Oh yes."

With a moan of relief he plunged into her. She felt only a twinge of pain as he broke her barrier and went deeper. Still he didn't ravage her but excited her with steady long strokes hinting of a burning summit of delirious fulfillment. She clung to him, matching his rhythm as well as she could with her lunging hips and let him carry her toward a bliss she'd never imagined.

He never let her find the bliss. Instead he paused once more, their bodies united, resting his forehead on hers and taking a deep breath.

"Stephen?"

"I don't want to rush you, love." His voice sounded low, tortured and almost unrecognizable. "I'm going too fast."

"But I want you, Stephen. I want you now."

He plunged immediately, back to the thrusting she knew would carry her someplace wonderful. The knowledge he'd actually consider her at such a time touched her with gratitude he was such a caring lover. He hadn't really needed to pause. She could hardly wait to find the fulfillment his body promised.

He discovered every secret spot on her body stimulating her passion and then ruthlessly exploited his knowledge. His hands were clever, so very clever and relentless. He drove her up to the crest at his will and his will now was to love her quickly and well. She ran her greedy hands over his slick skin, feeling each inch she could reach of his strong body and heard a groan that seemed to come from the depths of his soul. He quickened his thrusts, plunging into her vibrating body as he frantically caressed a sensitive spot he'd found in thick curls at her mound.

She was not a passive lover. She might be inexperienced but she found following Stephen's lead was something like following a partner in a dance. A vigorous and amazing dance almost too quickly taking her to the peak. Her heart beat so loudly she wondered it didn't alarm them both. But it seemed definitely immaterial as she clung to him. If she died now she'd die in ecstasy. He continued his expert caressing and sent her over the mountain peak, marveling such wonder existed in the world. Then she lost all thought, as she fell in unison with him.

They clung together, gradually floating down to reality. Stephen rolled off her but kept their bodies joined, cradling her as if she were his most precious possession. It took a while before their breathing calmed and he spoke.

"Mairey, you can't begin to know the joy you've given me. Thank you, my dearest love."

His voice was humble and she couldn't resist reaching up and kissing his warm lips.

"I enjoyed it too, you know. Will you want to do this often, Stephen? I found it most pleasurable."

She let her fingers wander through the crisp hairs on his chest as he lay there his breathing almost quieted. A most solid chest, covered with beautiful red-gold curls. She would never be tired of looking at his magnificent body and the feel of his hard muscles moving under her hands. With a witchy smile she let her hands wander just a little lower.

She watched the delighted grin spread over his face. A slightly devilish grin

"What do you mean by *often,* I wonder. A word with many meanings."

He set his knowledgeable hands to caressing the sides of her breasts, then moving in circles toward her relaxed nipples until they again began to stiffen into peaks.

She gasped as she felt a new surge of emotion gathering in her belly and several interesting spots below.

"Well, I just thought I'd ask. Maybe once or twice a week, or something like that? This must be very weakening for you, expending so much energy. But I'd like to do it again. Sometime soon?"

She squirmed to inch closer to his hand as he began playing with her lower curls again, his fingers expertly telling her without words she didn't have long to wait.

"Mairey, you are such a delight. I will want you quite often, if you will have me. I regard us as truly married and as your husband I intend to pleasure you and let you pleasure me much through many hours of many nights."

As he found the amazing spot between her legs he'd caressed before and began to rub it with his thumb, she turned to him with a gasp.

He never stopped his sweet torture but he looked down on her, his hot eyes asking her a question.

"Now?" She wriggled against him. "So soon? Oh yes, Stephen. Yes."

* * * * *

The next morning Stephen found an ironmaker and commissioned bars to be put on Beth's windows. He didn't tell Mairey he paid double the price so the work would be done at once.

The murder investigation almost stopped work at the excavation. The guard's background checkup showed he'd been an exemplary employee on all his jobs. Which meant either he'd been overpowered, or succumbed to a large bribe and helped his murderer into the compound. Considering the affair of the armband occurred two days before the murder, it seemed likely the guard knew theft was involved and went along with hiding the golden band for the promise of greater riches to come. Probably everything collected would be delivered to a smuggler. Also there was not much chance he'd been unaware of the first theft and the clever disposition of the shiny golden band.

If Walter was behind this hiding of the band with some idea of using it to implicate Stephen, he must be furious his plans had so misfired.

Philip took Riva to dinner every night and each night returned to the house later than the night before. He felt he was making progress. He knew he must persuade her to share the past that so affected their present. He'd finally found the right time and the courage to ask her why she distrusted men to such a degree.

"I can't help but wonder why you don't trust me more than you seem to do. I know you've been pursued for your beauty and brains but surely you've found a way to deal with being so lovely. Have the men you've known been too aggressive, Riva?"

At first she stiffened into her usual rejection of any personal conversation.

They were seated at a table at the Hotel Blauvet and long ago finished their coffee and dessert. He held her hand in his, gently caressing her fingers.

"My interest in you is sincere, Riva. With you, I'm positive I'm with the woman I've been looking for. I'm not asking idle questions. I want to know you, your thoughts, your dreams. Your inner self as well as your beauty enthralls me."

She remained stiff but left her hand in his.

*Progress. Now if I can only make her confide in me.*

He sat patiently, willing himself to silence while she struggled to speak.

She raised anguished eyes to his and then lowered them to the table where all but their demitasse cups had been cleared away.

"Maybe I should try to tell you. If I can."

She moved restlessly but did not shift away. Philip watched her expressive face as she slowly began to confide in him. He knew this was important to their relationship and didn't move a muscle except to clutch her fingers a little tighter.

"I seldom mention this but let me tell you about growing up in a man's world, a girl valued by her parents and most of her friends only for her looks. Fortunately two outstanding teachers, one in lower school and one in Polytechnic, became interested in my mind. They gave me the encouragement I needed to pursue an education not normal to women. Maybe in the future women will have an easier time but now, even in this year of 1920, women are regarded as unacceptably odd if they have a brain. You're expected to hide it, not use it."

The bitterness fleeting over her face told him she was sincere. He moved a little closer and took her other hand. She smelled like a garden of spring flowers blooming just for him. Her hair shone as she turned her head and the light from the many candles lit a blonde tress falling across her forehead. His jubilant heart told him he'd struck the heart of her rejection of men. This was what he needed to know to forge past her automatic barriers. She'd shut him out for too long. He held his breath, willing her to continue.

She lowered her head so he couldn't see her eyes as her abundant hair fell like a silken veil over the side of her cheek.

"When I first started working I found myself blocked at almost every step by men who thought I was trying to take a job from them." Her deep sigh told him how hard she found it to continue. "When I progressed anyway, some of them suggested in a roundabout way I help them. Even the men I went out with. They hinted I could help with the papers they were writing, in classes they were teaching, there was always a situation where they would benefit from my learning. At first I was eager to help, thinking it a compliment. After a while I realized they were interested only in exploiting me and I refused to help. Then they regarded me as ungrateful for being allowed so close to a real man's world. Sometimes a remark told me plainly I was a misfit who should be home raising offspring. I found most men think women are only good for children and cooking. And going to bed with, of course."

Philip sat in silence. This hurt went very deep with her. He'd given little thought to what a bright woman must do to break out of the mold. Teaching and nursing were acceptable but a higher vocation was seldom approachable. The Great War had opened factory jobs, although most of those were now reclaimed by returning soldiers. No challenge for her in those, anyway.

He thought he'd have been sympathetic to the young and ambitious Riva. At least he surely hoped so. Certainly, if he were fortunate enough to ever have daughters, he'd encourage their intellectual bents and smooth their way.

Daughters as beautiful and bright as Riva would suit him just fine.

She'd picked up her coffee spoon and was tracing patterns on the tablecloth.

"It still goes on, you know. I wonder if the resentment will ever stop. Men treat me awkwardly at first, which turns into an attitude of 'can I use her someway and then take over her job' or they'd plot behind my back to bring me down. They considered their conduct excusable on the grounds I'm uppity for rising above a woman's lot. It's now beginning to succeed at my office. I think if I don't do well on this job I'll be in trouble with the powers in my profession."

Philip sat too stunned to say anything for a long moment.

"You don't believe how bad it is, do you? I'm convinced you're a decent man and would not act this way. You're unusual, Philip."

"Blazing hell," he said quietly. "I find all this disgusting. I don't know if you've had bad luck in your acquaintances, or if I'm just unaware. Our family always encouraged Mairey and was proud of her."

"She was luckier than she knows, then." Riva put down her spoon. "Shall we go?"

She started to rise and Philip pulled her back. "In a moment, my love. You are my love, you know and are becoming daily more precious to me. I value your brains and applaud your talents. I'm shocked at your story but I believe it is every bit as bad as you say. Listen to me, Riva. I think anyone who does not value you must feel a definite inferiority to you. If a man behaves in such a despicable manner there's no doubt he truly is."

Her enormous grey eyes filmed over with tears. "Philip, you are such a special man."

"Ah," he murmured in her ear, smelling her singular fragrance and tasting her soft skin with his lips. "We make progress."

He nipped the lobe of her ear lightly, delighted when she started to move away and then settled back in her chair. He massaged between her shoulder blades with long, slow strokes.

"I don't blame any man for thinking what beautiful babies you'd make. But when and with whom should be of your choosing, not at the whim of some clod who pushes you around."

Philip rose and took both her hands in his.

"Come," he said. "Let us walk the long way home."

It was a warm summer's night and he planned to walk slowly. He knew just where to stop at the doorway of a building which always seemed dark and uninhabited. Time his lady learned a little of just how sincere his feelings for her were.

* * * * *

His lady didn't seem inclined to cooperate to the extent he craved. Although she held his hand as they strolled along, she stiffened when they came to the doorway he remembered and tried to pull her into his arms. She let him kiss her, at first responding with some ardor but then her reluctance surfaced and she tried to pull away. He held her a little away from him, not wanting to completely let her go but puzzled.

"I thought you were learning to trust me a little," he murmured in her ear.

Her long shudder alarmed him.

"I'm trying. Philip. I'm really trying."

For a moment he said nothing at all. Trying was not exactly the word he wanted to hear. True, better than not trying but it implied he was far from the success he hungered for.

"What can I do to convince you I'm not like those other thick-headed louts? I want very much to have your trust and affection." *It's too soon to broach the word love.*

She buried her head against his shoulder but said not a word.

"Let's walk on," he sighed. Right now he didn't know what else to say.

He swung her hand as they strolled toward her rooming house. What could he do to convince Riva they belonged together?

Well, he'd certainly never backed down from a challenge before. She was just the most important he'd ever encountered.

* * * * *

The inspector who'd taken charge of the murder case talked very little to any of them. He'd asked them to go over the whole story at least six times but he scarcely spoke. Nevertheless Stephen decided he was a shrewd man and that it would be a serious mistake to take him for a slowtop. The inspector cruised around a great deal, checking on what each person in the compound was doing. He didn't seem to favor one over another of the main parties involved and pretty much kept his own counsel.

On the third day Stephen decided he wanted to know what transpired in the inspector's mind. His nights with Mairey were ecstatic but he saw the circles under her eyes grow larger day by day. He knew she slept little. While they made love he could distract her, totally and completely but he often woke during the night and found her staring sleeplessly into the dark.

He invariably turned to her and claimed her body, now his for the asking. Sometimes she even turned to him. There was no doubt she relished their mating, responding to him with fervor and enthusiasm. Each time his love grew stronger and his concern deepened.

They all waited for Walter's next move and they were all on edge. Stephen's knowledge strengthened that the bastard lurked out there someplace.

Stephen went to the office set aside for Inspector Chantilly. Not that his name gave any softness to the man.

"I would like to know any results you can tell me of your investigation."

He stood towering over the inspector who was seated at his desk.

"Do sit down, Dr. Lovernios. It stretches my neck to keep looking up at you."

Stephen wasn't sure if the inspector were being humorous or not but he gave a brief smile and sat in the proffered chair.

"I am particularly interested if there is word of any smuggling going on in the area. As I've told you, that's my guess of the cause for these criminal actions. I also feel Walter Griffin is mixed up in the affair. He would not scruple to make money by ruining me and my wife Mairey."

The inspector didn't comment on the word "wife". Many peasants counted the petition for marriage to be the same as marriage. Evidently this very learned and sophisticated doctor felt the same.

Chantilly stilled his hands and looked at the imposing man before him.

"You are a puzzle, Dr. Lovernios. Why a man as wealthy as you would spend six months or more wandering around Brittany, sleeping anywhere he could and singing for food and tips is beyond me. You puzzle me but I do not think you are a murderer."

Stephen flashed his attractive grin.

"Bless Merlin for your faith," he said. "Yet I would like very much to know if my theory of possible smuggling is correct. To me it's the only thing making sense of the guard's murder. The torque is gone but we can't know whether to an ultimate owner or only a recipient who will pass it on. If that recipient is Walter Griffin he will be lurking around the area, wanting to receive his reward but also wanting to get his hands on my soon-to-be daughter. Mairey and I intend to formally adopt Bethan."

Chantilly's face was devoid of expression, although his eyes were locked on Stephen's.

"We are investigating Griffin and I can't like what I hear of him. However, we have no reason to think he's in the neighborhood or has any connection to this crime. He's unsavory I'll grant you but I can't arrest a man on that basis and with no evidence."

"I feel we'll soon be able to give you evidence," Stephen said. "My Druid intuitions tell me he is nearby and readying himself to act."

The inspector only raised his eyebrows at the last statement and then with a nod, went back to his work. Stephen left, knowing his instincts were correct but not knowing what to do about them. Walter was skulking nearby.

Plotting and waiting.

* * * * *

Philip also wanted to know more of what was going on in the inspector's mind. He found the door open one day and asked to come in. At the inspector's brief nod he took the only other chair in the room.

"Can you tell me anything at all?"

"Only this, we do find some strong signs of smuggling in the area. I'm surprised. I thought Mlle. Broussard was seeing ghosts where none existed at first but my own investigation shows the same thing."

"You didn't trust her judgment?" Philip asked softly.

The inspector leaned back. "I've seen too many hysterical females in my time to take one seriously."

Philip rose to his feet and leaned over the desk.

"You're saying Mlle. Broussard is a hysterical female?" His voice was dangerously soft.

The inspector missed the anger and heard only words of confirmation.

"Well, aren't most of them? Not that she isn't smart, in her own way."

The condescension in his voice barely reached Philip through the red haze in his mind. This then and snide remarks like it, were what Riva endured time and again. Nothing most people would even notice, unless you were a woman or a newly sensitized man.

"You are a regrettable bigot, Inspector. You probably don't even know it."

He wanted to say much more but even in his rage he knew Riva would be the one to suffer if he did. He wheeled and left the office, to find a white-faced Riva outside the door.

"I was coming to see him. I didn't mean to listen," she said before she turned and fled.

Philip ran after her and caught her easily. He used his arms and caged her against the wall.

"My god, Riva, I had no idea of how prejudiced men are. Even after you told me, I didn't truly know."

He leaned over, wrapped her in his arms and kissed her with all his stored ardor. To his delight she locked her hands in his hair and kissed him back.

Philip felt his heart literally turn over as he settled down, there in the hall, to show her what a pleasure kissing should be.

* * * * *

That night when he, Mairey and Beth went home Stephen performed his routine check of the house and the garden. His excellent vision alerted him to saw marks on one of the grills at Beth's window.

Walter was getting ready to make his move.

He went slowly back into the house. Should he tell Mairey? Mairey was already worn by anxiety and she could do little about the situation. Still he thought he should alert her. Walter could assail them suddenly, hoping to catch her off guard. Much as he hated to do so, he decided he must tell her.

He couldn't bring himself to the point, although she kept glancing at him with a question in her eyes. She was so blasted intelligent. He grinned at how hopeless it was to try to delude her about his feelings. He had no choice but to talk to her about this latest development.

He waited until Mairey put Beth to bed and they were alone. Even then, when she turned to him with a questioning look, he seized and kissed her wildly. As usual, she melted in his embrace, going gladly with him into the special realm they'd found.

Mairey knew his passion pulsed with a different urgency. Something had upset him and she meant to find out what it was. Still, she was glad to have the respite of this time together. Every night forged their passion higher. She'd grown to love every inch of his big body. Exploring him with her hands and her tongue brought her a truly astonishing pleasure. She couldn't resist the appeal in his eyes and his fingers as he began to show her the bliss she'd come to crave.

She felt his body tremble as he held her closely, using his magic hands in the most improbable places. He'd found sensitive spots she'd never imagined. One at the base of her spine, which his clever touch could always find and send her soaring. Her breasts, of course, which seemed to delight him as he sucked and fondled them. She even shuddered when he licked and kissed her dimple. And then there was her mound, which she alternately wished he'd go to and then wished he'd not. She smoldered and then went up in flames when he finally concentrated on the sensitive button of flesh he could always discover, powerless to do anything but writhe beneath him and wish she could never leave his arms.

Tonight he caressed her at length, over all the sensitive spots of her body, making her lunge against him and beg him to hurry. He slowed his hands so they moved over her almost leisurely, as if he was enjoying exploring her secrets and driving her crazy. He didn't even have to hurry. She was ready to crest at any moment he gave her leave.

He plunged his tongue into her mouth again, urging her to join him in a mock-mating dance to further incite her. She joined him gladly with her now intelligent tongue and tried to reach for his member but he gently held her hands away.

"There's no hurry, my love. I want to enjoy you tonight at leisure."

She couldn't manage to rush him, although he set her hands free and let her caress the rest of his body. He was slick and muscular and powerful as a god. He looked a god to her as he rose above her, thrusting, then almost withdrawing again and again and then thrusting deeper. A bright shining god of commanding beauty.

His mouth came back to hers as he paused and kissed her more deeply than ever, with greed and a kind of desperation. The muscles in his back trembled under her hands but he still refused to take them both to culmination.

She was finally sobbing and damning his self-control before he moved deeper and slowly, much too slowly, began to surge again. She raised her hips and thrust against him, forcing the full contact she needed and craved. From then on he seemed to lose his ridiculous restraint, as he immersed himself to the hilt and pounded into her, taking her to the heaven she now knew awaited them whenever they both desired. Even though she'd come to expect the ecstasy of release, the rapture this night seemed extraordinary.

She lay on her side, clutching him as they both drifted back down to earth, their bodies still joined. Exulting in the feel of his hard and contoured body as she played with the crisp hairs on his chest, thinking life could not possibly offer more than this man.

When she could finally speak she asked him, "Am I wrong, or was this a special time for us? The pleasure we find sometimes frightens me, Stephen."

Stephen gripped her in his arms and nuzzled her hair.

"Blessed Merlin, Mairey. When you move to take me further into your body the pleasure also frightens me. You bring me such rapture. I have never known, nor did I ever expect anything half so wonderful. If you disappeared from my life I don't know what I'd do."

He buried his face in her neck with the near-desperation she'd already suspected and kissed her soft and fragrant skin.

She swallowed the lump in her throat. This was the closest he'd come to words of love. Words of passion, plenty of those, whispered hotly and often in the night. But none of lasting love.

She understood all too well she'd lost her heart to him. He was a wanderer and when he roamed away from her she mustn't complain. She'd known exactly what he was. An incredible man, a stunning and gifted man, who could have any woman in the world if he beckoned to her. Why on this Earth would he settle down to one woman?

She'd been incredibly stupid to fall in love with him. The last thing in the world she'd meant to do.

"I don't intend to disappear," she murmured. "I like it right where I am."

She sighed and squirmed her face into his masculine shoulder. He smelled sweaty and erotic at the same time. And with it all was the indescribable scent that meant Stephen. His very own distinctive scent. She'd know him from across any room by his masculine and pleasing aroma. A touch of bay rum in it, she sometimes thought.

They lay limp for a while in each other's arms, until Stephen half-raised himself and leaning over her broke the silence.

"I feel I must tell you something."

Something about his voice alerted her instantly.

"Walter," she stated.

"I'm afraid so. When I made my usual inspection of the premises tonight I found saw marks on the bars of one of the grilles I had installed at Beth's windows. Undoubtedly he is around. I know you are always careful but don't take any chances at all. See someone is with you and Beth at all times. I'll try to be but if I'm not promise me you'll not stay alone. Go immediately to Philip or Dr. Taliesin."

She tried not to but a little sob crept out.

"I hate this, Stephen. I've come to think we'd have a chance at happiness if Walter would disappear from our lives."

He took her face in his big hands and kissed her sweetly. She opened her lips and turned it into a long drugging kiss, frantically clutching him as she tried to incite their mutual passion and shut out the frightening reality.

It was not too hard to do. They had only to touch each other and the whole world seemed to ignite. She almost expected to see them surrounded by a ring of fire. Dear heaven, how could she endure losing this pleasure when he inevitably left her?

He rose over her again and for a long lovely time they succeeded in forgetting the world and all their problems.

# Chapter Fifteen

ꝏ

Stephen found he was interrupted more and more at the excavation. The guard would send a message someone was at the gate asking for him. He asked to have a medical shack erected near the gate, a simple lean-to with a table and three chairs. Stephen wanted to help the people who came to him in a way that wouldn't compromise the excavation. He'd also learned early in his medical life it was never wise to interview a new patient without a witness.

Word had gotten around the small town a skilled physician was working in the compound. People from all classes came to see him. Mostly the poor ones who could not afford the usual fees of a doctor but often those who'd lost faith in the medical profession and wished to give him a chance to change their mind.

He saw them, one and all. No one left disillusioned and the word kept spreading. The basic medical supplies kept at the dig soon ran out and Stephen found he must replenish them fairly often, which he insisted on doing out of his own pocket.

Most of the cases involved quite minor problems. A child falling from a tree and breaking his arm, a pregnant wife worried about how to avert a second miscarriage, an assortment of bumps and scrapes among the younger set. All ages and both sexes seemed to trust him and want his advice, even if he dispensed little medicine. When someone appeared at the gate asking for him, he always responded. Immediately and with a smile. He refused payment but asked the patient to contribute to whatever religion or charity appealed to him.

He confused Mairey. A good doctor and a good man and the most wonderful lover in the world. Still she wondered about his apparent lack of any goal. She knew she'd fallen deeply in love with him. How could she not when he had only to touch her and she vibrated like a plucked string on a harp? She couldn't see a future with him and yet her soul withered at the thought of one without him. She kept her silence as she watched him honor his physician's oath to render assistance, helping anyone and everyone who came and asked. She couldn't reconcile his dedicated attitude with her impression of him.

Beth was ecstatic her uncle Stevie was now so accessible. His living in the same house meant she could see him often. She climbed up his legs as if he were a ladder, throwing herself at him as he wrapped her in his arms and hugged her. There was no doubt to anyone who saw them that the love between the two was both genuine and extraordinary.

Stephen watched and waited. His Druid senses told him Walter was lurking nearby. He tried to conceal his apprehension from Mairey but doubted if he was succeeding. His wife was perspicacious as well as beautiful. He smiled at the thought. If he tried to add up all Mairey's good qualities he'd run out of the goddess's own time.

All he could do was enjoy her in this blessed interval of peace and try to show her his complete dedication. She was not fully committed to him, he well knew. She'd come to relish their passionate nights, that he realized with great satisfaction. He was determined to be a faithful husband, even if it turned out only lust bound her to him. But how could something so wonderful be anything but right? Surely love for him must grow from their impassioned nights of pleasure.

Mairey watched him and tried not to think of how she would feel if he decided to go on one of his bardic journeys. He could easily become tired of her and leave her at any time. They had no binding commitment. It would break her heart she well knew but how could she resist giving that heart to a man so caring of others, so impressively beautiful and such a marvelous lover.

They were both working in her office one day when a guard appeared and reported another patient was asking for Dr. Stephen. This time it was a girl of about thirteen, holding her bent arm close to her body and complaining of extreme pain every time she moved it.

Stephen examined the arm and could find nothing wrong but the girl insisted she was in great pain. Stephen had been stooping over her and now he rocked back on his heels. The girl did not seem to be exaggerating and tears came to her eyes when he moved her arm. Still there was a wariness about her putting Stephen on the alert. She was far too frightened of what he might say.

"Can you tell me a little about when this pain started?" Stephen watched both mother and daughter closely as he waited for an answer.

The mother seemed puzzled and half angry.

"Sally complained when I asked her to do some bit of work around the house. I think it was washing the dinner dishes. She never likes to do the chores but now she says she's in too much pain to do them. I hope she's not just trying to avoid her responsibilities. Seems to me she hurts more when there's something to do but I didn't want to take a chance. Goodness knows I did a lot more to help out when I was a girl. If she's making this all up she'll be one sorry young lady."

She sniffed and glared at her daughter.

The girl looked down quickly and said nothing.

"Can you tell me more, Sally?"

Sally shook her cast-down head.

Stephen decided this was a time to call on his Druid powers. The girl's aura was cloudy and shot through with spikes of some strong emotion he couldn't decipher. Resentment? But resentment of what. Jealousy? Of whom?

He reluctantly decided to probe her mind. He was not going to get much information from her.

The Druid ability to enter another's mind carried with it the prohibition never to be intrusive and never to cause harm. He probed seldom and then reluctantly. He'd never use it on anyone he loved without permission, although he often longed to know what Mairey truly thought of him.

He studied the girl through half closed eyelids, mentally assessing her as she bristled, glared at him and hugged her arm even closer to her body.

What he found in her mind didn't surprise him. She might not be in bodily pain but certainly her emotional pain was great. There was a sister involved, a much younger sister who'd been born five years after Sally and who'd immediately become the focus of all attention in the household. Sally tried being the best girl in the world but when that didn't work decided to be as bad as possible.

She was too nice a girl to be as wicked as she wanted but if she didn't get some attention from her parents, attention of the favorable sort, she might turn out badly indeed. Still, an outright battle between her and her mother would rip them both apart. He could sense a great deal of unexpressed love around them both.

Stephen decided to try shock tactics.

"I think Sally needs to go to a hospital immediately. In fact I suggest one I know in Wales, which specializes in these hard-to-treat cases. I'll make arrangements immediately for her to be admitted."

It was not easy to tell who was more shocked, Sally or her mother.

They spoke almost simultaneously.

"I don't want her to leave and go that far," blurted the mother. "Sally means too much to us to let her go so far away."

And from Sally, "No, no, I don't want to go so far away."

Stephen let the silence drag out a little.

"Really?" His voice was dry and almost disinterested. "Why are you both objecting? You, madam, spend most of your time and thought on your younger daughter. You, Sally, are unhappy at being passed over again and again for your sister. Don't you think the whole family would benefit if you rid yourself of Sally? Think how it would simplify both your lives."

The silence dragged out while mother and daughter stared at each other and tears came into Sally's eyes and then rolled down her cheeks.

"I didn't mean to cause this much trouble," she sobbed.

Her mother, her face a picture of utter shock, went to Sally and folded her in her arms, hugging her girl for a long moment.

"Let's go home, Sally. We can work this out together."

Stephen noticed with amusement and some satisfaction Sally was hugging her mother with both arms.

The mother looked over the shoulder of the sobbing girl in her arms.

"Thank you, Dr. Lovernios," she said with a wry half-smile. "We heard you were an unusual doctor. Now I know you're a perceptive one as well."

Stephen watched them leave with a pleased smile on his face and then wandered off in search of Mairey. He was more and more enchanted with the possibilities of using Druid powers. Certainly if directed properly they could lead to great good. Perhaps the time was here to talk to Mairey about this aspect of his heritage. Although he didn't know how much she believed in his Druid abilities.

Thoughtful now, he walked on, his long steps seemingly easy, yet covering an amazing amount of ground. He needed to refresh his spirit, get away from medical problems and see his darling girl.

* * * * *

The strain of waiting began to tell on them all and on Mairey in particular. She knew in her heart Walter skulked someplace near, waiting his chance to snatch Beth. She could feel his evil presence hovering about her night and day. It created a kind of miasma in her mind clouding all her thinking.

She'd started Beth on lessons in reading and writing and spent an hour each morning and evening on teaching her the rudiments. Beth lapped them up and begged for more lessons but Mairey decided two hours was enough for such a young child. Still, she'd already laboriously learned to print out *Bethan* in large block letters.

Still Mairey worried about her lack of companionship with children near her own age. Since Mairey had taken over the girl's care they'd been mostly at the dig. Beth didn't seem to mind but it was an additional item of concern to her anxious aunt. She wanted the child to have everything her mother, Mairey's beloved sister, would have wanted her to have. And had been cheated out of giving her. Anything and everything good in the world must be secured for Beth.

Mairey was well aware the love she felt for Beth ought to be controlled or it would turn into an obsession. Stephen helped a great deal, as he laughed and joked with her when she became too serious or overly anxious about the little girl. His straightforward attitude and his joyful outlook on life meant a great deal to her. If she'd not fallen so much in love with him sexually she would still think him a fine influence on everyone he met. He smiled and joked with seeming ease but she could see the seriousness behind his actions. He was not a clown. He was a sensitive man trying to smooth the path of life for others.

He also was a very clever man. One day she was walking near the entrance when she saw Stephen approaching the entrance and the medical lean-to. She stood still, watching and loving his long stride. He handled his big body so effortlessly.

She looked up to see who'd called him to the gate this time and saw two young girls, their hair cut short in the newest style Paris decreed was the mark of a free-thinking woman. The "flapper cut", she thought it was called. Both wore so much lipstick as to look almost grotesque, plus kohl underlining their eyes. Mairey mentally raised her eyebrows. Their parents must be having a time with those two.

This was going to be interesting. What excuse would they have for asking to meet with Dr. Lovernios?

Stephen checked his stride just a second and then walked out the gate and greeted them pleasantly.

"What can I do for you ladies?" His tone was impeccably polite but Mairey sensed he was on guard.

The girls smirked at each other and then the dark-haired girl spoke up.

"I'm having terrible pains in my stomach, doctor. Low down and in the middle."

Stephen sighed. "How often does the pain attack you?'

"Oh, often. Not this minute but I know it will come back. The pains are really horrible."

The redhead chimed in. "Don't you think you should examine her, Doctor? Surely you have a more private place we could go to."

They both smiled at him with what they doubtless thought were siren's smiles. Actually, with their painted faces they looked more like clowns.

Mairey grinned. Poor Stephen, these two were so obvious as to be ridiculous. They were both batting their darkened eyelashes at him.

"How old are both of you?" he asked.

"I'm fourteen and Claire is fifteen."

Claire was the one with the horrible pains.

There was a long silence. Evidently Stephen was deciding how to handle this pair. What did they intend to do in a private surrounding? Pull down his pants, probably, the minute they got him alone. For the first time Mairey thought of doctoring from the standpoint of a virile man, one more handsome than they'd probably ever seen. Or would ever see again.

Smiling to herself, she kept perfectly quiet.

Stephen finally spoke. "Oh, I don't think we need to find a private spot. I probably won't have to operate but we'll be able to tell once I admit you to the hospital."

Both of them blanched.

"Hospital? What do you think I have?" squeaked Claire.

"Jillyitis," Stephen pronounced in a dire voice. "A bad case of Jillyitis."

Both girls stared at him and then started to walk rapidly away. After a few yards they broke into a run and Stephen watched them go, shaking his head. Where were their parents to let them out of the house looking like young whores?

Mairey stayed silent, marveling at the man. She'd always been convinced it possible for one significant act to delineate a person's basic character. She'd seen Stephen commit many considerate deeds but this one revealed the essential goodness of his unselfish soul. Kindness, tact, a knowledge that led him to turn the girls away without revealing to anyone except themselves how foolish they were.

As he walked back through the gate Mairey's admiration gave way to giggles. She broke into helpless laughter while Stephen joined her. No matter that the guard could hear every word and see them plainly, Stephen grabbed and kissed her once, hard.

"You miserable woman, how long have you been here?"

"Long enough. Would you like to examine me, Doctor? Oooooh, I think I have a bad case of Jillyitis."

Stephen looked at her with amusement.

"May the goddess help the parents of those two. Although I've seen the reverse situation, where a rogue doctor takes advantage of a sexually frustrated housewife. That's even worse."

Her eyes rounded as she pondered his last statement. Something else she'd never considered. Just as she'd not expected to see Stephen illustrating so perfectly her conviction of one illuminating act. She'd been so blind. Not one but every act of Stephen's showed his extraordinary compassion.

"A clever name for the girl's disease. Did you make it up on the spot?"

For some reason, Stephen took his time answering. "No, I overheard a friend of mine use it once. A Dr. Stratton." *The man he'd resented for so long for marrying Viivie. But both Stratton and Vivie were his friends, a truth he now knew. The realization warmed him.*

In the past he'd tried in vain to put bitter thoughts of Alec Stratton out of his mind and now the bitterness didn't even exist.

Hand in hand Stephen and Mairey walked back toward the main dig.

His Druid empathies seemed to add important dimensions to his healing. He was definitely a superb doctor, as well as an unusual one. As she watched and studied him, he shook many of her taken-for-granted beliefs. He was in so many ways a magnificent man.

One day a small screaming boy was carried to the gate and Stephen as usual rushed out to see if he could help.

The father and mother stood by, as Stephen performed a quick examination.

"He's broken his arm," he said. "A simple fracture. It will be easy to set, if you'll let me carry him in to table where I can fix it and apply a temporary splint. You'll then have to take him to the hospital to acquire a proper cast."

The child never stopped screaming and Stephen knew he must calm him down. He had ether in his supplies but the child was making himself more frantic with every scream.

"There's nothing to fear," Stephen said to the little boy. "I promise you you'll feel nothing when I fix your arm. You want it fixed, don't you?"

The boy raised huge frightened eyes but kept screaming. Stephen felt forced to probe the child's mind. Something was very wrong.

*Blessed Merlin, he's terrified of his parents. He thinks they'll beat him again for being so much trouble to them.*

Stephen remembered cases like this from the clinic. Fortunately not too many but enough to turn his stomach at the thought of beating a small child to the point of breaking his arm.

"On second thought," he said smoothly to the parents, "I want you to leave him with me. Tomorrow I might have him well enough to discuss his case. I'm sure you don't want anyone to think he hasn't been cared for properly."

He took the boy in his arms and walked back in the compound, motioning to the guard to shut the gate. As the boy saw the gate close behind the astounded parents, his screams stopped. No matter his father was shaking his fist and shouting to the guard to open the gate. Stephen stalked away as fast as he could stalk, which was very fast indeed.

After the ether sent the child into a light sleep, Stephen quickly set the arm and turned to Mairey.

"Easy to fix a bone. What to do now with the child is not. I need help from Dr. Taliesin, I think. He'll know the proper authorities to find a foster home while his parents are investigated. I have no doubt they'll find he's beaten quite often. Look at the bruises on his little body. Some of those greenish ones are quite old."

Mairey blanched as she inspected the child. "Dear heaven, he's not much older than Beth. I'll find Uncle Tally and I think, Riva. She knows the local situation here better than we do."

The horror of everyone on learning the true situation proved to Stephen they knew little of such situations.

*I'd be just as appalled if I hadn't seen such cases before. Even so, it's* always *dreadful.*

"Well, we need two things. A place for him tonight and then to start procedures for protecting him from his parents."

Riva raised stricken eyes from the child's damaged body. "I think I possess enough authority to take care of this. The rest of you might land in trouble if you tried. Bretons don't much like foreigners mixing in their affairs. Let me take him home with me tonight and tomorrow I'll find what to do to locate a place where he can heal safely."

Philip's eyes shown with admiration. "You're a wonderful girl, Riva. I'll check into your boarding house so I'll be there to help you. He's going to need care during tonight and I can lift him around for you."

There was a good deal of adoration in the glance she sent him.

"Thank you, Philip. I'm grateful."

"Now we better go to a clinic and let me put on the cast." Stephen looked at them both with approval. "Once I have the supplies I can do it quickly. Then you two can take him."

"Perhaps I'd better go with them too." Dr. Taliesin looked doubtfully at Stephen. "Anyone who beats a child is evil. The parents might try force to snatch their son back before he implicates them with the authorities. You said they seemed quite wild after you shut them out, didn't you?"

"Good point," Stephen agreed. "Child abusers often will do almost anything to cover up what they must know in their hearts is a sin. They probably thought bringing him to me was safer than to a local doctor."

Even as he spoke he realized this new complication meant he and Mairey would be alone this night. He accepted the thought with fatalism, knowing this was the way it should be. He and Mairey were supposed to fight this out on their own.

The visions he'd seen the last two nights showed Walter on a boat, with Mairey holding a sleeping, or unconscious Beth. If this vision was a true one, the other members of her family were not involved. So far all his visions had proved true and he did not doubt this one. He would be there, he knew, no matter what happened. He'd not let Mairey out of his arms tonight.

From the worried looks not a one of them but understood the implications. Still, an injured child must be sheltered.

Philip carefully picked up the small boy and with Taliesin and Riva flanking him, started out. Stephen followed, his eyes on the ground. He turned to Mairey.

"This will not take long. Don't leave the compound 'til I come back."

Mairey nodded and stared after him. No genial Stephen this time. His face was as serious as she'd ever seen it.

The air was thick with the knowledge that not only would Stephen and Mairey be alone but the ten days of waiting were over and they could have the civil ceremony of marriage the next day if they so desired.

Blessed Merlin but Stephen hoped they would all be there for a ceremony tomorrow to celebrate his and Mairey's formal union.

Stephen alone was certain the night would bring the crisis. He knew in his Druid heart he was intended to meet the emergency on his own. Fate was again showing her preordained face.

He said nothing at all except to speed the little group on their way with the boy.

# Chapter Sixteen

ജ

Stephen suggested an early bedtime and Mairey agreed. Beth was already asleep and they'd been sitting pretending to read.

Stephen folded his love in his arms as soon as she appeared fresh from her bath and dressed in a long flannel nightgown. She'd put it on at Stephen's request, although his suggestion baffled her. In summer? But something about Stephen tonight made her want to go along with whatever he decreed. It was as if he were a sage of old, knowing exactly what he was doing and compelling others to follow his path. A mystical aura hung about him like a cloak. She wondered if Merlin's enchantress felt this way when she went into Merlin's arms. Did she know disaster loomed for them both?

As soon as she came onto the bed Stephen folded her in a tight embrace, kissing her with near desperation. He didn't wait to take off her gown, merely lifted it high around her waist and began to make impassioned love to her.

He started with her breasts, kissing and caressing them and finally suckling her until she almost screamed. He seemed almost frantic and she felt him watching her reactions as he played upon her senses as if she were a violin and he the maestro. She was helpless before his assault, as he passionately aroused her and expertly took her to the peak. They both fell over the crest together and she landed back in the realm of the ordinary world after a prolonged period when time did not exist. At least for her. When her breath calmed, she opened her still dazed eyed to find him holding her tightly, his own eyes clear and full of anxiety.

"I want you all the time, my love. Every minute of my days and nights. So badly I could not keep from taking you now, even though my Druid instincts tell me trouble might come later tonight. Walter is not yet here. I would have you sleep a while and I'll keep watch."

She jerked out of his arms and sat up in the bed. "You expect Walter tonight?"

"I do," he said. "But not for a while. I would never have indulged in my passion for you were I not positive of the timing."

Something about his resigned tone made Mairey think back over their coupling. She realized Stephen had expertly led her to ecstasy but never lost control of his own senses. In fact, he'd seen to it they crested together in the quickest loving they'd ever experienced. His haste had been deliberate. He was clearing the decks for action, first taking and giving her what he feared might be their last pleasure. Yet if Walter had tried to enter any time during their loving Stephen would have come fully alert and stopped him.

The thought frightened her, as did his unbearably sweet control.

"Then I'll not sleep tonight. I'll remain alert with you."

He kissed her with love and not passion.

"I might be wrong, you know. Nothing at all might occur tonight, I'd rather you rested. My Druid sensitivities don't tell me everything. I'll certainly wake you if I think anything at all is happening, or about to happen."

He kissed her and pressed her back against the pillows, running his hands over her body for a few blissful moments before he pushed her away.

"Sleep, my dearest one."

She sniffed but turned on her side. As the hours went by she gradually relaxed into a light slumber. Stephen, lying tensely by her side, remained starkly awake.

Toward morning, Stephen thought he heard a scratching at the window. He gently eased his arm from around Mairey and rose to investigate. The minute he got to his feet, he felt a crashing blow on his head and he pitched to the floor.

* * * * *

He came to his senses when the sun was just rising into an already brilliant blue sky.

Groaning and pushing himself to his knees and then slowly to his feet, his heart sank in despair. He knew without looking Mairey and Beth were gone but he checked anyway. There was no sign of a struggle in Beth's room. Doubtless Walter or his minions drugged her before carrying her off. A scuffle had taken place near their bed but of course his Mairey would have put up a fight. An aroma of ether still hung around the room.

He examined his mind and found it clear of all but pain. They hadn't found it necessary to use the ether on him. He'd been put out of the action with very little effort. They'd kicked him in the ribs just for good measure but he hardly felt that in his anxiety. They must surely have underestimated his powers of recuperation.

He staggered to a chair and sat, examining his body and collecting his thoughts. He felt the hard lump on his head. A large club, he thought, or some kind of post. His brain was still reeling. He put his head in his hands, leaning over as far as he could to force some blood back to his brain. Still, it was some moments before he could force himself to think with rationality.

Walter has been lurking and waiting. When he'd seen the other Bronwyns leave for Riva's, he'd been ready. His thugs moved in. They needed to do little more than put Stephen out of commission and then drug and carry off Mairey and Beth.

He'd allowed his enemy to outmaneuver him, even though he knew the enemy was coming at him. His pounding head in his hands, he groaned deep and low. He doubted if he'd ever forgive himself.

For a few moments he sat there, still trying to gather himself together. His mouth felt as if it were coated with dried mud. He made to the bathroom, slapped cold water on his face and rinsed his mouth until it felt cleaner. He must go after his enemy as soon as possible. His main advantage was that Walter would think no one knew where he'd gone. Stephen knew very well.

Walter, Mairey and Beth were on a boat in nearby quiet waters and quiet waters meant the calm seas of Quiberon Bay.

The beautiful town of Quiberon was located on the narrow penninsula of Presqu'ile de Quiberon. The sandy spit provided protection from the Atlantic Ocean. A favorite of professional fishing boats and a marvelous safe spot to anchor for smugglers who needed to linger. They were in the location Riva once identified as the smugglers' likely haven.

Stephen mentally reviewed what he knew of the town which he'd visited when he'd walked to Carnac. The beaches there were sandy and beautiful. The bay provided livelihood for a large number of fishermen, catching huge quantities of sardines, oysters and other fish. A lingering fishing boat would not be thought unusual. The town of Quiberon was near the tip of the peninsular arm and was crowded with fishermen during the fishing season. Many of their wives worked in the canning factories, so the town would be crowded. All the easier for strangers to remain unnoticed.

Walter could have no idea Stephen was coming after him. This would be Stephen's trump card and he knew he needed to plan carefully to take advantage of it. The plan just beginning to take shape in his mind meant he must find a helper. He hurried out to tell Philip that Mairey and Beth were gone. He had no doubt at all Philip would want to go with him. It was what he wanted also. He could desire no better helper than Philip.

# Chapter Seventeen

ꕤ

He woke all his friends at the boarding house and told them what had happened. He didn't give them much time to respond but said he was leaving immediately and wanted help in finding the fastest autocar in Gouarec.

"That's probably mine," said Philip. "Since of course I'm coming with you you've already got the car. I'll do the driving. You need to rest. Where are we going, by the way?"

"To the Bay of Quiberon," Stephen looked straight at Riva as he spoke. "Where the smugglers are."

"Are you sure?" asked Doctor Taliesin.

"Yes, as sure as I can be. I've seen strong visions of Mairey and Beth on a fishing boat in calm water. This is our best chance."

Philip went to Riva and turning her face up to his, kissed her gently.

"Stay close to Dr. Tally until you place the child safely in a hospital or some other place of your choosing. Take care, my dear."

She unexpectedly threw her arms around him and held him close. "You're going into danger. I just know it."

Philip kissed her nose. "Probably," he said with a grin. "But I'll come back to you, Riva. Nothing in this world can keep me away from you."

The two had as good as made a public declaration of love and both knew it.

The men turned to go and Riva suddenly gasped. "Give me one minute. I have an idea that might help."

She ran from the room and came back holding her purse and rummaging through it.

"Here." She handed a paper and a badge to Philip. "Here are my credentials. If you're questioned and it can help you, say you're investigating on my behalf. I also remembered there's an honest man at the very first dock as you come into Quiberon. He'll rent you a trustworthy boat."

Stephen leaned over and kissed her forehead. "Blessed be," he murmured.

He and Philip strode out. Riva's wistful eyes followed them as long as they were in sight.

She'd made her choice and for that she rejoiced. She'd chosen well. This man was admiring and supportive of her talents. He valued her for much more than her appearance. He was the man she'd hoped and waited for all her life.

Now all she could do was pray her man returned.

* * * * *

Stephen tried to figure out in his agonized mind how much time had lapsed when he'd been unconscious. If he'd been out of commission too long, even the fastest car in the world wouldn't make up the difference in lost time. He knew he'd been awake long into the night and early morning, so it possibly wasn't too long.

Philip's car was a snappy Citroen roadster with big wheels and large chrome headlights. Any bachelor would adore it and its speed was fast enough to give Stephen hope.

He tried to cast his mind into the future, praying for another vision. He found only hazy images. He thought he saw Mairey and Beth speeding in a small boat. Not the large fishing boat he'd seen before. Walter was not in this image, which might be promising. Try as he might, he couldn't make the picture come clear. His head throbbed so badly he finally shut his eyes and leaned back, trusting Philip to do his best. He knew no Druid could force a vision.

Certainly Walter and his minions would have been afraid to go this fast. If Walter was stopped and the police found two unconscious females, he'd be in serious and time-consuming trouble trying to explain. Walter would stay under the speed limit. He'd probably be using a slower moving sedan since he'd want his henchmen along to drive or help if needed. Altogether, he should be forced to drive much slower.

Philip paid no attention to anything but racing to their destination as fast as they could. They sped along at nearly forty miles per hour and surely they gained on Walter with every minute.

The speedy car did give them an advantage, Stephen tried to work out just how much but gave up. He couldn't even begin without knowing how long he'd been unconscious.

They were not stopped. How different this road seemed when whizzing along at such an unnatural rate from when he'd walked to Carnac and back. Walking was hot, dusty work, as was the dust thrown in their faces by their fast rate of speed. While the summer's dust still worked its way into their hair and lungs, the wind caused by their racing rapidity refreshed them both.

The roads were good until they reached Baud. Then they were forced to slow down and Stephen fretted about losing their advantage.

"They'll have to slow down too, you know," Philip said dryly.

"But the difference in our speeds is now lesser," Stephen almost snapped.

At Auray they could again go faster and they sped on, slowing down again to drive through Carnac and onto the Presqu'ile de Quiberon.

They drove over the sandy spit, with the ocean on both sides of them. The water stretched away on the north, with cresting waves and limitless water to the horizon. To the south, the waters of the Bay of Quiberon extended in the calm waters for which it was famous.

Fully alert now, Stephen spotted the small boatyard Riva had mentioned and Philip slowed the car and drove in. The boatyard manager came out of a shack quickly and looked over the Citroen with admiration.

"How fast can it go?" he asked without bothering to greet them.

"We just come from Gouarec and kept her above forty most of the time. A little slower between Baud and Auray, of course."

"Forty, eh? *Pas mal du tout.* Why do you want to drive so fast?" The typical cautious suspicion of a Frenchman showed in his face and voice.

Philip extended his hand with Riva's badge and the paper listing her job and title.

The Frenchman looked it over for some little time. Stephen was about to take action when the man spoke up.

"I know this department. Some of their men have been around asking a lot of questions."

"You were highly recommended by Mlle. Broussard as someone who can help. We need the fastest motorboat you have."

"We also need to be able to row it at times," Stephen added.

The man now thoroughly inspected them. "I think I've got what you want. I hope I'm not making a mistake. Don't bring it back with a lot of bullet holes in it. And I want to write down the number on the badge you just showed me."

"We'll do better than that," Philip said. "We'll leave the badge and the papers with you."

Stephen grinned. A small grin but still the first in many hours. Philip did not want Riva's name known to the enemy in case they lost the coming battle. *Smart man.*

Philip held out a sizeable deposit and followed their guide to the boat dock.

The motorboat was exactly what they wanted. Sleek looking and undoubtedly fast.

As they climbed in Philip turned to Stephen. "Just by the way, my friend, where are we going?"

"To the outer ridge of the fishing boats. The smugglers will not want to raise suspicion if they come in close but don't fish. Or don't fish much. Walter might be clever enough to have a crew who fishes some of the time. The boat has several quite large lights to attract the sardine schools at night and I imagine truly is a fishing boat. The smugglers will use it to stash their booty until a bigger and faster boat comes to collect it."

"Amazing," Philip said, his eyes beginning to sparkle. Almost against his will, Philip began to anticipate whatever was coming. He wanted to go back to Riva alive and in one piece but he couldn't help but admire Stephen and his grim determination. Walter might have a whole crew at his disposal but he'd still bet on Stephen. He was glad to be along on this adventure. A ruthless look passed over his face. He wouldn't mind at all if he were forced to kill a pedophile like Walter.

Stephen ran his hands through his thick hair and grimaced when he hit the sore bump.

"I think we have a chance of being right behind them. If their auto could only go twenty to twenty-five miles an hour we're not far behind."

* * * * *

Mairey felt consciousness returning and was careful not to blink. She was on the floor of a large sedan, with what felt like two boots on her stomach. The briny smell of the ocean was strong and she could tell by the scrunching noise the car was passing over a long strip of sand. She couldn't hear any sound that might be coming from Beth, so if the child was here she was doubtless still drugged. Walter's voice was saying something from the front seat.

A strange, rough voice answered in the accent of the Parisian gutters. A hired thug, probably.

"I can't go no faster, m'sieu, so stop asking me. You told me you didn't want to be stopped by the gendarmes. So do we keep to the speed limits or don't we?"

The sarcasm was almost scorn. Was he speaking this way to Walter? She wasn't surprised, Walter never learned how to keep from sounding superior and offending subordinates.

She lay without moving, hoping to escape notice for as long as possible. She hadn't learned much so far. She could feel only two feet atop her, so there was evidently only the one thug back with her and the driver with Walter. And where was Beth? She stilled her panic. In a moment the driver's voice sounded again.

"You sure seem to think a lot of your daughter there. Holding her as if she were a piece of glass. How come you knocked her out with ether if she's your daughter? Don't make sense to me."

"Her mother and the mother's sister have poisoned her against me. When she sees how much I love her it will all be different."

Walter's voice sounded reluctant to explain to an underling. An underling he doubtless needed enough to force him to be halfway polite.

Mairey could imagine the gloating look on his face. Was he stroking the child's body even now, the touch of his hands a desecration? Maybe not, since he could be observed. Still, she couldn't repress a shudder the thug noticed.

He immediately leaned over her. "Ha, you're coming to life, aren't you missy."

He shook her shoulders so she was no longer able to keep up the pretense. Her head fell back and she glared at him in disgust.

"Hey, Mack," he shouted. "Our prize package just woke up. Makes it nicer for us, doesn't it?"

The driver chortled and half-turned around. "Haven't rammed a good looker like her for some time. When we get to the boat we'll throw dice to see who has her first."

The thug's grin was so lewd she briefly shut her eyes. Then opened them and glared. She'd not show fear to these despicable types.

Her defiant look evidently amused her captor. He leaned over and pinched her breast with strong, cruel fingers. "We'll show you a good time, girlie. Hey, Mack, she don't seem to much like being touched."

They both erupted into lascivious laughter and Mairey shuddered again.

The car stopped and she was pushed out on the sand. Hot sand, smooth and stretching to the blue almost motionless water. Thanks be she'd automatically put her feet in her slippers when she got out of bed to investigate the thud of Stephen's fall. She'd hate to walk on this scorching sand in her bare feet.

Rigid from so many hours in one position, she fell on her knees, which the men thought funny.

Walter came and stood over her, grinning and holding Beth in his arms. He leaned over and slapped her hard on her face.

"You can't imagine the pleasure I derive from seeing you on your knees to me. I'll enjoy it even more watching when Mack and Pierre take turns with you. They're both virile men and will doubtless put your precious Stephen to shame."

His grotesque laugh sounded as he walked off. "Bring her along. Drag her if she can't walk. We need to get to the fishing boat."

He headed toward a motorboat which was drawn up and waiting on the beach.

Mairey nearly panicked. She looked frantically around for help. She was a speedy runner. Could she run fast and fast enough to get away? Probably not but maybe she could force them to shoot her to make her stop. If she could be sure a shot would kill her it was worth the chance. Better than submitting to the gross ruffians called Mack and Pierre. Both of them were unshaven, dirty, foul-smelling denizens of the Parisian gutters. Disgusting and lewd, just looking at them made her skin crawl.

Her eyes followed Walter, heading to the boat with Bethan. Of course she couldn't even try to escape. If Beth was being carried to the boat and she must go along. No matter the personal cost.

She shuddered and swallowed a sob.

She'd do what she could to fend the gutter-types off but had no idea as yet how to overpower them. Certainly her brother taught her how to knee a man where he'd fall to his knees but there were two of them, plus Walter. She couldn't hope to put them all on the ground. Still she'd fight as much as she could. She knew well she might lose. Would Stephen ever want to even touch her after she'd been defiled by Mack and Pierre? He was a magnanimous man but how could any man forgive such degradation?

Probably not. Nor would she permit him to ruin his life by marrying a sullied woman, even if he could bring himself to forgive her. His pristine character could not be ruined by such soiled goods. Her insides clenched as she was overwhelmed with the knowledge he was the purest soul she'd ever met. His high sense of honor might force him to forgive her but he should never stoop to recognize her after she came out of this debacle. *If* she came out of it. There was a good chance Mack and Pierre would use her and then casually throw her overboard.

His handsome face, his impressive build and figure, his beautiful red-gold hair suddenly came as clearly into her mind as if he were standing beside her. His blue eyes smiling with what she now knew was love.

She'd held in her hands everything any woman could want and stupidly never told him she loved him and bound him to her. She'd never spoken a word. Too late, she realized her dislike of his wandering ways meant nothing compared to his superlative character. She'd been so unbelievably stupid. Why hadn't she told him long ago she valued him for himself alone? He could leave her for his bardic journeys anytime he pleased, as long as he came back to her.

Her heart keened at what might have been as she stared at the sand she could scarcely see. Then she straightened her shoulders and held her head high. And headed toward the large motorized skiff.

Bethan would soon be on the fishing boat. With a drooling pervert cradling her in his arms.

She had no choice at all but be there with her.

# Chapter Eighteen

ꟹ

Mack piloted the boat. Mairey and Pierre sat on the bench behind, Mairey trying not to cringe when his stocky legs in dirty trousers nudged her with Pierre openly leering. He did not touch her with his hands, however. Thinking it over, it was not surprising. Evidently Pierre and Mack had some sort of agreement to leave her alone 'til they all boarded the fishing boat and they could both attack her.

The boat was fairly large and looked like held a crew of ten or twelve. Whether any of those would be actual fishermen she didn't know. Probably so, as the smugglers would have to keep up some kind of show to avoid suspicion as they loitered in these waters.

Mairey turned around and looked carefully at Beth, still held tightly in Walter's possessive arms. She stretched forward and felt the child's forehead. Beth was completely limp, her fairy-like hair hanging over Walter's arm. At the cold feel on her skin Mairey exploded.

"How much ether did you use, you wicked fool? She shouldn't be this comatose this long. I want to examine her once we're on deck."

Walter reached out one hand as if to strike her but then settled again.

"I gave you both second whiffs when we were on the road. Couldn't have either of you waking up too soon, you know." His voice was reluctant but just a little fearful.

"You idiot," Mairey cried out. "She's so tiny too much ether is extremely dangerous. If you used the proper amount she'd be stirring by now. I insist on trying to rouse her when we're on board."

Both Mack and Pierre protested. "You said we could have the *putain* when we reached the big boat. We done everything you said and we want her now."

Walter's face darkened. "You'll have her but after she cares for the little girl. Nothing is as important as knowing the child is well."

"You're an idiot." Mack turned away in disgust. "Having us kill the guard just because he was blubbering about not knowing where the gold band was. We should have forced him to tell us more before we killed him."

"You're the idiot," Walter snapped back. "He'd let us in the building twice. We couldn't afford to leave him around after we took the torque. He was trying to double-cross us. No matter. The bitch gets to examine the girl when we board the boat."

The men were silent, while Mairey realized the full extent of their guilt and how merciless the men were who were holding her. Murderers, all of them. Mairey was almost sorry she'd spoken, She'd only waken Bethan to a horrible world she could not endure. Yet she was worried to perdition about the child. She didn't like the way she looked and felt. She was forced to try to help her recover, even if it was to face a miserable future. She didn't have it in her to do anything else but love and help Bethan.

She prayed someone would soon rescue Beth just as Stephen had saved the abused child. What had Riva and Philip done with the boy? Could they find him a decent home?

She swallowed a sob as she saw the fishing boat looming near them. A rather large boat, it featured the huge lights to be expected to attract the shoals of sardines that swarmed in the Bay of Quiberon at night. The bay was a fisherman's paradise, protected from the more violent waves by the large land arms reaching out into the ocean. Many boats were anchored in the waters, although the *Marie* was the furthest one from shore.

She had no doubt she was about to board a smuggler's boat. The *Marie* could easily rendezvous with a larger vessel, pass over the smuggling loot and continue posing as a legitimate fisher while gathering stolen artifacts.

It seemed but a minute to Mairey before they were alongside the boat. The lower end of the *Marie* displayed a small rope ladder, hanging over the side and easy for anyone to climb.

"I won't move until I'm sure Beth is safe on board."

"You're sure a stubborn bitch." Walter glowered at her and stepped to the front of the skiff to board the ship.

As he realized he couldn't negotiate the ladder holding Beth, he glared in fury at them all.

"I'll go first," he snapped out. "Pierre, hand the child up to me when I'm on board."

Mairey held her breath as Walter handed Beth to Pierre and then climbed the ladder to the boat, The *Marie* rode quietly in the sea and the ladder was placed where the distance between the water and deck was the lowest. In spite of her apprehensions, when she climbed it was an easy ascent.

How thankful she was Stephen had insisted she wear her heaviest nightgown. It fell like a tent around her and even though she knew it wouldn't deter the two lascivious men eager to have her, she was glad she wasn't exposed to their lecherous regard.

How much had her Druid foreseen of this disastrous night?

Once again the thought of his prescience astounded her. Probably more of his Druid power, which she could no longer discount. His powers were as potent as he claimed.

As soon as she reached the deck, Mack grabbed for her. Two voices protested loudly.

"Hey, I'm first," Pierre shouted.

"Leave her alone 'til she sees to the child," Walter shouted. He reached in his pocket and drew out a small gun. "Do as I say, you scum. I'll tell you when you can share her."

Mairey blanched. What a horrible predicament. She knew she must work on reviving Beth but the instant she succeeded she'd be thrown to the two wolves eyeing her.

They turned to bickering between themselves as to who got her first.

"Do you suppose there's any chance she's a virgin?" Mack asked. "I don't like virgins. They scream too much. Makes a man's dick downright limp, it does."

Pierre forgot his anger and chuckled. "Not much chance, *cretin*. We found the whore in his bed, didn't we? I like virgins. Nice and tight. She'll probably fight us anyway if she's only had one man."

Mack looked doubtful. "Okay, you take her first. I like to watch. You can loosen her up for me."

Shuddering in every bone in her body, Mairey shut her eyes. She'd had a faint hope the two would turn on each other and at least postpone the rapes. Not to be and she exerted all her willpower to force her thoughts back to Beth. She clasped the little girl as Walter handed her and went to sit with her on a length of rope coiled on the deck. She felt Bethan's pulse and found it alarmingly weak.

"Dear heaven," she murmured. "You've nearly killed her."

"I only wanted to take care of her," Walter blubbered. "Do something, Mairey. Do something."

"So you can ravish her sooner?" Mairey asked bitterly, chafing Beth's arms and shoulders. She had the mad impulse to strip off her gown and swaddle the child. Not a good idea. The two ruffians would rage out of control and nothing would be accomplished.

"Bring me some blankets and some water."

Walter glared at Mack and he grumbled and then went below.

"I don't know why I'm bothering," Mairey said bitterly. "You'll surely kill her if you force yourself on this mite of a child. I think on the whole it would be better to let her sleep quietly on."

The shock on Walter's face astonished Mairey.

"No, no," he screeched. "You're all wrong. I only mean to take loving care of her for a while. I wouldn't dream of making her my bride until she's at least nine or ten."

Even Pierre looked horrified.

"You're a bloody pervert," he whispered. "I'd never have helped you snatch her if I'd known."

Walter looked offended and turned on his man. "Don't call me such filthy names. I can kill you this minute if I want to."

Mairey shut her eyes for a second to shut out the sight of the two men glaring and shouting at each other. As she opened them briefly she slapped her palms over her mouth as she nearly cried out.

Stephen's shock of hair had suddenly popped up behind the side of the far deck. Wet and slicked darkly to his head, still that golden shock was unmistakable. She had only a glimpse but she could plainly see his blue eyes looking at her, signaling love and encouragement. It was only for an instant and she saw nothing below his chin but she didn't need to. By some miracle, her Druid had found her. She lowered her head and examined Beth with almost sightless eyes. Her mind seethed with a mixture of gratefulness, hope Stephen could somehow set things right and desperate fear for him.

Was there a true chance of rescue? Where were Mack and the rest of the ship's crew? What could she do to help?

She looked around frantically for a weapon. There was none. The ship was immaculately neat, even if it was a decoy. She was afraid to look up for fear someone would glimpse the sudden hope in her eyes.

She closed them while she sought to figure out this amazing development.

She could find only one explanation. Stephen had somehow used his Druid abilities to do the impossible and find her. His powers were real. She would never doubt him again. Never again.

He was truly gifted and like the wonderful man he was, used those gifts only for the good of others.

She breathed a prayer for him, as well as herself and Beth. Surely Stephen's goddess was with him for him to have been able to come this far and find them.

She kept searching the deck, trying not to be conspicuous. She finally spotted a small coil of rope. Perhaps she could wind it around her hand and use it as a weapon. Not much of a weapon but better than nothing. She memorized the angle of the location so she could grab the rope without signaling her interest by keeping her eyes on it.

For the first time in hours she took a free, unrestricted breath.

Stephen was here.

* * * * *

When action erupted, it flared like an explosion.

Stephen hoisted himself over the edge of the boat and vaulted in, landing precisely behind Pierre. Exactly where he wanted to be, as he felled him with a blow of his gun on the back of his head.

Walter, leaning over Beth, heard the loud grunt as Pierre went down. He wheeled, grabbed his own gun from his pocket. Mairey, who'd been waiting, grabbed the coil of rope and threw it in his face. His shot went wild and Stephen immediately grabbed Walter as a shield, just as Mack came charging on deck.

"Don't move an inch," he commanded. "I'm not fond of your employer anyway and would gladly eliminate him and take on you. I've got a gun and a knife, so I can kill both of you quite easily. The knife's against this one's back and my gun's pointed at you. Now move back."

His voice left no doubt he'd have no qualms about carrying out his threat.

Mairey longed to go to him but was afraid to distract him.

She stood up with Beth in her arms.

"What do you want me to do, Stephen?"

He never took his eyes from Mack or the knife point from Walter, who was now shaking and almost blubbering.

"They're both all right, Lovernios. Take them and go. Don't cut me up, please. I couldn't stand to be cut up."

Stephen ignored the whimpering specimen he'd be glad to erase from the earth if he had the slightest provocation. He pricked Walter's back, who gasped and then held perfectly still.

"Philip is right below, Mairey. Throw Beth down to him and then climb down yourself."

She opened her mouth to speak but then closed it. Going to the rail she spotted Philip, standing in a motorboat and holding up his arms. Why hadn't she heard the motor? Then she spotted the oars and realized they'd rowed the last part of the way.

She leaned over as far as she could and dropped the blankets, then tossed Beth over, almost shrieking as Philip nearly lost his balance reaching for the child. Then he caught the child and righted himself.

She heaved a sigh of relief and scurried down the ladder into Philip's embrace.

They could hear but not see what was happening on board the ship. To her astonishment Philip began to start the motor. She grabbed his arm and shrieked at him.

"Have you lost your mind? Stephen's still on board."

"Stephen's orders," he said. "He wants us out of the range of gunfire before he jumps. Let's hope he's as good a swimmer as he says."

They heard two thumps which Mairey hoped were hard gun blows on Walter and Pierre's heads and then a shout from Stephen to get moving. Wanting to scream at the thought of leaving Stephen behind, she swallowed her protest and buried her face for a moment in Beth's silky tresses. She was almost afraid to look up as Philip raced the boat to a distance he considered safe and then idled the engine.

"Oh blast," she said. "I should have helped him disarm them before I left."

"Too risky," Philip said. "Let's have a little faith in Stephen. He's the most remarkable man we'll ever meet."

She'd heard the phrase "heart was in your mouth" and now she knew exactly what it meant. She could hardly breathe as Stephen executed a beautiful dive from the ladder and surfaced about seven yards from the boat. He started toward them, his powerful strokes slicing the water in perfect rhythm as he rapidly drew away from the *Marie*.

Even so, it was not enough. Two figures appeared at the edge of the boat, both of them firing at Stephen. He dove underwater at once and surfaced much nearer to her, as she watched in agonizing suspense. Had a shot hit him? He'd visibly lost his striding stroke just before he went under. He was struggling when they next saw his head and his speed had slowed. Blood stained the water amid jubilant shouts that came from the boat.

The next shots from the firing guns fell short and Mairey took the helm while Philip hauled Stephen into the boat. Blood streamed from his shoulder and Mairey immediately rushed to pull off his wet shirt and inspect the injury. The bullet had scoured through the upper part of his arm and the wound was producing an amazing amount of blood.

"Stephen," she whispered, her voice filled with the love she now knew she felt for him.

He looked at her, his blue eyes glowing in the summer sun and drew her lips to his for a brief and fierce kiss.

"I love you, Mairey."

"I hope so. I love you too." She smiled for the first time since she'd been abducted. "Let's go, Philip. Take us out of here."

Stephen gave a shout of joy. "What a time to tell me, Mairey. When I can't do a thing about it."

Mairey blushed and inspected the wound. Relief flooded through her when she found the blood beginning to slow.

"Philip, give me your shirt, please. It's certainly cleaner than this grungy nightgown."

As Philip stripped off his shirt he sent Stephen an admiring glance.

"Glad to be of a little help, at least. Stephen deserves all the credit so far. Now let's make waves."

Stephen directed Mairey how to apply the bandage, watching her as if he'd never let her out of his sight again. She fidgeted under his intense gaze even as she gloried in the fact he was alive and with her. Philip restarted the motor and they headed toward shore.

Stephen lifted Bethan onto his lap and looked her over carefully, feeling her pulse and listening to her heartbeat. His face was sober when he lifted it.

"She should be all right but I hope she'll wake up soon. The longer she stays asleep the more her system slows down. I'll work on her when we reach shore. A bouncing boat is not the best place to do any doctoring."

Their motorboat was running at full speed and the distance between them and the fishing boat increased. Stephen had placed Beth on blankets on the bottom of the boat and leaned back with his good arm around Mairey. How very wonderful to feel his large warm body close to hers once again. She nearly sobbed her relief and then stopped herself in consternation. She was not that weak a woman. She'd do nothing but glory in Stephen and the rescue.

She closed her eyes and thanked all the gods of every religion. Surely Stephen's goddess had helped them this day.

They were safe. After all, what could happen now they were successfully in full flight?

# Chapter Nineteen

ꕥ

Suddenly Stephen sat up straight.

"Blessed Merlin," he murmured. "They're lowering a motor boat from the *Marie*. I think it's larger than ours. They're coming after us."

Fast as they were going, Stephen seemed to have no difficulty in standing in the boat. Although they were far out in the bay, the smooth water spread around them like a slightly unsettled pond. His eyesight, almost supernaturally keen, now served them well. Every sense was alert as he peered at the boat heading toward them.

"They're still a long way off. There are three men in the boat. I think it's Walter and his two henchmen."

Philip looked up at him calmly. "Do you think there's a chance they might catch up with us before we reach shore, Stephen?"

No one had to mention the obvious fact that if the violent and vindictive men in the second boat could reach them none of them could count on surviving. Not even Beth if irrational anger took over.

"I'll have to observe for a while. I can't tell yet. I think it's possible they're gaining, however."

Stephen's voice was as calm as if he were describing a beautiful sunset.

No one spoke. Philip applied himself to forcing the most speed possible out of their boat and Stephen remained on lookout. Mairey sat staring at Stephen. A commanding figure, he looked to her like a god of old, one whose grim determination and amazing abilities would surely prevail. Surely they could not come this far only to be murdered, or worse yet, tortured, by the vengeful men speeding toward them.

After a few minutes he said quietly, "They're gaining."

"Will we make it to shore?" Philip asked.

Stephen shook his head. "I'm trying to do a little mental arithmetic."

After a minute or two he turned around and came to sit beside Mairey. She was holding Beth and he took them both in his arms.

"I love you more than I love life itself," he said. "If possible I'll kill them all. If not, know I'll be with you in our next life."

He took her face in both his hands, ignoring his wounded shoulder. As he held her tightly the desperation in his kiss told her he had little hope.

Mairey returned his kiss with all the passion in her heart. "Stephen, my dearest love."

He held her with his good arm and she concentrated on his beloved features. If they could only be together on the next world as he believed, she could stand whatever horrors faced them.

With her gaze fixed on his dear face she saw his expression change. A look of hope swept over it, lighting his eyes and bringing him to his feet.

"What did you just think of, Stephen? Something good, I know."

He turned to her, his smile now full-blown. "I forgot all about calling on Viviane Randall. I'm too new at this kind of communicating but she just spoke to me. She's going to help us. I'll do whatever she says. Now I'm going to shut out any voice but hers, my love and I hope to be back in your arms quite soon."

He got to his feet and faced the boat coming toward them. It was now noticeably larger. There was no doubt it had a more powerful engine. Even though it was still a distance away, the enemy was gaining.

*Well, Stephen,* a familiar voice spoke in Stephen's head. *You've waited almost too long to hear my voice. We can conquer them, you know. Your powers have increased impressively and my daughter*

*Morgan is linked with us. The three of us must be potent enough to do what I want you to do.*

Stephen stood straight in the boat, his feet braced apart and his face reflecting his sudden joy and hope. To Mairey and Philip he looked like a beautiful avenging god, his tall frame steady in spite of the speed of the boat. He threw back his head, his hair ablaze in the sunlight, and faced the sky.

"Madame Randall, I can't tell you how glad I am you're here. I can't feel the boat in my mind yet, though, if you want me to try to stop it. All I can feel is the water."

A pleased chuckle made him grin.

*Exactly what I want. You're going to raise a wall of water between you and the other boat. It will frighten them half to death when they see it in a bay usually so calm. I want you to raise it about six feet high.*

Stephen's grin disappeared. "I've never even dreamed of doing anything so forceful. Are you sure we can?"

Viviane's voice grew sharper. *Not unless you believe we can. I always said you have more power than you think. Morgan and I will do our best, which I assure you is a very great deal. Now concentrate on the water, Stephen. Think of nothing else but the water. Remember I want a wall at least six feet high.*

Stephen turned his mind completely to his one task. It didn't truly surprise him when the water rose gradually, then seemed to gather strength and size. A huge body of water many feet thick. A dense blue-green, it hung ominously and incredibly as a solid barrier between the two boats. Concentrating completely, he saw the wall of water lift from the ocean bay until it was easily six feet high. Or higher. He tried to subdue his awed elation, keeping his mind solely on the task Viviane had set him.

As the water rose and rose, he disappeared into the spell he was helping to cast. He didn't hear the gasps behind him, or the frenzied cries sounding from the oncoming boat. He only heard Viviane's voice, talking to him with triumph.

*You've done it. Now, Stephen. Now. Take your power away all at once. Let the wall of water crash.*

He did as she said. Following her instructions proved surprisingly easy. His Druid heritage came to the fore, overshadowing all his doubts and proving him a true child of his Druid ancestors.

The huge barricade crashed all at once, with a resounding blast. For a moment nothing could be heard but the roar of the plummeting waters. Those in the boat watched spellbound as the waters quickly spread. The bay lay not quite yet quiet but filled with soft waves not present before.

The small boat, bearing three evil men, had disappeared completely. From their sight and from their lives. No one in the boat spoke.

Stephen lifted his face again to the sky, a shining sky not as blue as his joyous eyes.

"Thank you, Viviane Randall. And you too, Morgan Dellafield. You have saved my loved ones and I owe you much. I'll try to live up to your expectations."

He heard two soft laughs and then two soft voices. *You already have, Stephen. You already have. Blessed be.*

He sat down, his limbs shaking and his skin showing white under its bronze. He didn't have the energy to even smile.

Mairey reached over and took his hands.

"Stephen, my dear one. I don't know what to say."

"I think we're both speechless," Philip said quietly.

A new, small voice spoke up. "Uncle Stevie, did you see all that water?" Beth asked, sounding as awed as they all felt.

As Mairey buried her face in his good shoulder and started to cry, Stephen reached over to pat the little girl. Tears on his own cheeks, he answered softly.

"Indeed I did, chickie. Indeed I did. Come now to your aunt Mairey."

* * * * *

When Philip drew the boat up on the sandy shore, they were immediately surrounded by excited and nearly incoherent swimmers and fishermen.

"Did you see the wall of water?"

"How close to it were you?"

"What on earth happened out there?"

"I've never seen anything like that in this bay. Or any bay."

"It seemed to come so fast and then go just as fast."

Philip carrying Beth in his arms, turned and smiled at the crowd. "Perfectly amazing, wasn't it? Something you can all tell your grandchildren and see if they believe you."

Several of them chuckled and didn't realize Philip had turned the conversation away from the questions. A few of them opened their mouths to ask more but Philip stopped them. He handed Beth to Mairey and went to aid Stephen. White and exhausted to a point nearly beyond his control, Stephen attempted a step and then slumped to the ground.

Mairey didn't miss a beat. She turned to the crowd. "Can someone please help my brother carry my husband? He's an awfully big man."

She spoke as calmly as if a large man dropping to the sand was an everyday event.

Immediately several men stepped up to help.

"Is he sick, or what?" "Did he have a seizure?" "Looks bad to me," were some of the comments swirling around her head. The remark frightening her most was when she heard someone say, "Do you suppose this has anything to do with that wall of water?"

"Does he need a doctor?" asked the man who'd reached Stephen and Philip first and now grasped Stephen around his shoulders. "I see he has a bandaged shoulder."

"Just an old wound," Mairey said. "Nothing to worry about."

Actually she was praying his wound didn't open from the pressure of being half-carried. She'd never dreamed she could lie so glibly. No point in telling them anything, including the fact Stephen himself was a doctor. She wanted to take him away from this beautiful place where they'd all nearly been killed. She wanted him home where she could take care of him.

"Nothing wrong at all." She told another fib without a qualm. "He's just had too much sun. It's happened before."

She spoke in a nonchalant manner as if nothing at all were out of the ordinary.

Philip grinned at her and followed her lead, nodding in solemn agreement. "We just need to take him home where he can rest. He'll be fine. He's had too much sun several times before. His fair complexion, you know."

Another big man stepped up. "You lead the way, sir. I'm glad to help."

Under Philip's direction the two brawny men half-carried Stephen to where the car was waiting.

"Can one of you take the boat back to the boat dock?" Philip asked and when a young man agreed, thanked him and slipped him some money.

Amid complimenting comments on the Citroen, Philip directed the helpers to put Stephen in first, so Stephen could hold Mairey and Mairey could hold Bethan. Not the most comfortable arrangement for any of them but their only choice. Stephen never moved from where they put him, his head lying back against the seat and his eyes closed.

Philip started the engine amidst more approving murmurs of the dashing roadster.

"Goodbye, everyone," he called out. "Thank you for all your help. We'll certainly never forget the Bay of Quiberon and our time here."

*The understatement of my life. Wait 'til I tell Riva.*

He looked at his precious passengers as he started the powerful motor. Everyone he held dear was either with him, or would be delighted when they came home.

With a singing and reverent heart he headed the car for Gouarec.

He didn't even know how he'd describe what had happened to Tally and Riva. It was so improbable and yet he'd witnessed it all. He'd always thought Stephen to be special but he'd never realized how extraordinary he truly was.

Thanks to him they'd made it safely through a confrontation none of them could ever forget. Not ever, no matter how long they lived.

Stephen's goddess and his own goodness had seen them through.

* * * * *

Stephen fell into a deep sleep as soon as the car left the beach. Mairey, almost afraid to wiggle for fear of disturbing him, talked softly now and then to the still drowsy Bethan.

Once, right before she dozed again, Beth swiveled her body and looked at her aunt. "I guess we're being quiet so Uncle Stevie can sleep."

Mairey squeezed the little girl. "Yes, darling. He's worked hard to come find us and bring us home. He needs to sleep."

"I love Uncle Stevie," Beth whispered.

"I do too. We all do," replied Mairey. "I think everyone who meets him does."

Philip gave her a smiling glance. "True, Mairey. I'm glad you finally understand how wonderful he is."

She smiled over the tears which unaccountably sprang easily to her eyes. Funny, during her ordeal she must have been too angry to waste time weeping. She looked out at the landscape she'd not seen on her way to the Quiberon. *Not much to see if you're on the floor, after all.* One couldn't really take in much of the scenery with a villain holding you down with two large boots.

She shivered and turned her thoughts away from the conquered terror and to Stephen.

She rejoiced in the certain knowledge Stephen was a superior man. Superior in every respect. So unusually gifted she didn't really believe he'd want to marry her now. She'd been nothing but trouble. He was wounded and ill because of her. She'd told him she'd set him free once Walter was out of their lives. He'd done everything he'd promised and more. No other man could possibly equal his gallantry and unselfish devotion in saving herself and Bethan.

Worst of all, she'd refused to completely believe in his Druid abilities until shown proof not a person on god's Earth could ignore. Her lack of trust was inexcusable. She'd almost *sneered* at him. She'd certainly never given him sufficient credit for the many times she should have been on her knees thanking him.

Their nights of mock-marriage had been ecstatic. She could not imagine ever, *ever,* going to bed with another man. If they'd only had one more day together he might have married her. Although she'd promised to offer him a divorce once they were wed, he didn't need anything to release him now. He could just walk away. If they'd actually married it might have kept him close to her while they worked things out.

*If, if, if.*

How would she bear the nights without luxuriating in the knowledge his big body was beside hers, keeping her safe while he taught her delights she'd never dreamed existed? At least she had memories no one could ever duplicate. Reminiscing might be her only alternative. A bittersweet one indeed.

Tears started again in her eyes but she shook her head to clear them. She simply would not weep when they were all alive. She stared out the window, not really seeing much of anything, as Beth dozed in her arms.

Still, she must honor her word and offer to set him free.

* * * * *

Stephen slept a sleep of deep exhaustion permeating both mind and body. He did not stir until the Citroen drove up to the boarding house where Riva and Taliesin awaited them. Riva immediately threw herself at Philip as if she'd never let him go. Taliesin took Beth in his arms and helped Mairey rise from Stephen's lap.

He cast an inquiring look at Stephen, who was just beginning to stir a little. He'd regained most of his color and when he opened his eyes and saw where they were, joy lit his face. Moving a little slowly and wincing, he unfolded his long length from the car.

"Blazing fires of Beltane, Philip. That's a fast car but a damned small one. Next time we go to rescue two fair maidens let's take a bigger one."

Riva straightened from Philip's embrace and glared at them all.

"*Tiens!* No more rescues. No more danger of any kind. Do you all hear me?"

She bristled like a fierce mama cat defending her young. They all laughed the laugh of near hysteria which often surfaces after release from an almost unbearable ordeal.

Philip tweaked her nose and then dropped a kiss on it.

"Yes, mam'selle. We're only too happy to obey, mam'selle."

Entering the boarding house, Stephen's steps began to regain their spring. He entered into the conversation but little, although he looked embarrassed as Mairey and Philip heaped praise on him. Both Riva and Taliesin showed their astonishment at the tale of the wall of water but could not doubt such impeccable witnesses as Mairey and Philip.

"I didn't do much of the actual raising of the water," Stephen said. "I merely channeled energy from a power normally beyond my reach. We were fortunate indeed the source was open to us."

They were finishing the meal of cheese, bread and wine Riva's landlady had supplied as soon as they all came in. All of them felt much better as they lounged in their chairs and relaxed, tired but knowing for a certainty the danger was at long last over.

Walter was gone.

"You do realize the torque is still out of reach? I'm sure the fishing boat left immediately after they saw their motorboat disappear." Philip posed the question, looking at Riva to see how important this was to her.

"I'm certain too it's gone from us." Stephen's voice was still not quite his own. Fatigue laced every syllable. "I saw the *Marie* growing smaller as she turned and ran. I would guess the smugglers have left this area."

Tally smiled a grim little smile. "I've already put private investigators onto watching the illegal sources known to deal in stolen antiquities. We might never see the torque but then again we might. It's going to be a little harder to sell than the smugglers thought."

Riva looked pleased but then spoke quietly, her voice laced with regret she tried to hide. She, of them all, had not succeeded at her task.

"I'm to report to my superiors tomorrow," she said. "I don't think I'll tell them the whole story, just that you all were in terrible danger and escaped. There's no need to go into excessive explanations."

Philip looked at her, his face solemn as he realized what this all meant to her. And they'd left all her papers behind in the custody of the boat lender.

"And you'll be demoted, won't you?" Philip asked in a subdued tone.

Riva threw back her head, looking as proud as if she'd received a promotion.

"More than that, I'll probably lose my job. I think they'd been waiting for a good excuse," she said. "But all of you are safe. I ask nothing else." She beamed at them all, reveling in the safety of her man and his beloveds.

Philip took her hand and got to his feet.

"Now I have something to ask you, Riva. I meant to do this privately but I can't wait. Will you marry me?"

It was simply said but no one could mistake his heartfelt love. Riva couldn't find her voice. It was lodged in some inaccessible part of her body, so she nodded "yes". She kept on nodding until Philip swept her in his arms and kissed her with the profound love he felt.

As they all laughed, Taliesin stood and raised his glass. "To the new member of the Bronwyn family. I always did want an acquisitions expert on our team. Congratulations, Philip. You've found a wonderful woman."

The lines on Stephen's face grew ever more deeply etched, even though he laughed and congratulated the couple. Then he stood, wavering just a little.

"I think I'll make my goodnights," he said. "With my deepest thanks to everyone. Everyone here is an integral part of our success. But I think I'll see if the landlady can rent me a room for the night and retire."

A profound silence fell over the room. Mairey hadn't shed a tear during her ordeal, she'd been far too angry. Now to her dismay her eyes suddenly filled to overflowing, which Stephen, toasting Philip, did not see.

She did not reach for a napkin to mop her tears. She simply sat there, letting them run down her face. She would not make a scene, even though Stephen was rejecting her. Perhaps he wouldn't notice if she kept quiet. She didn't want to call attention to her distress. He didn't deserve any praise.

He'd said he wanted a room for overnight. He planned to leave in the morning. She sat motionless, her head high, until finally the silence reached Stephen and he looked up to see three shocked faces and one weeping one. The weeping face was staring at the opposite wall, refusing to look at him. Only Beth, sitting on Tally's lap, looked happy.

He crossed to Mairey immediately and seized her hands,

"What's wrong, love? Did those bastards hurt you and you didn't tell me?"

She shook her head, refusing to look at him. She started to rise to leave but he held her by one hand as he cast a bewildered look around the room. No one said a word but everyone glared at him. Exhausted as he was, it took him a moment. It must have been something he said, since he was obviously the culprit. He finally caught on and grabbed Mairey in a tight embrace.

"Blessed Merlin. I'm an idiot. It's only this one night, my love. I refuse to sleep with you again until we're legally married. My belated idea of honor. If you'll have me, we'll be married tomorrow."

The tears still running down her cheeks, Mairey huffed.

"You miserable man. You might have said so."

He hurried to her and folded her tightly in his arms.

"Never, ever doubt my love for you," he whispered in her ear. "I want you to get some rest too. You'll definitely need it."

Turning to the others he flashed his glorious Druid smile.

"What a day today turned out to be. And tomorrow will be even better. I'll drink to that in my mind, even though I don't have the strength to raise a glass."

As he turned and weaved out, they all, without any planning, raised their glasses to his departing back.

# Chapter Twenty

ꝏ

Mairey slept a dreamless sleep, contrary to her apprehensions. She'd feared the nightmares of the day would haunt her but she fell asleep easily. She woke to find Stephen sitting on the bed watching her.

He was magnificent. Rested, dressed immaculately and as shining as the sun in a blazing sky.

"You look wonderful," she murmured, as she reached up and drew his face down to hers.

"I bought this outfit last week," he confessed. "Just in case I could persuade you to go through with the marriage ceremony."

She broke into laughter. "And I did the same thing. We'll be a gorgeous pair."

They clung to each other, kissing wildly until Stephen drew away. "I'll take you this minute, you little siren, unless we get you dressed. Of course I'll have every stitch off you the minute I can but you'd better not go naked to the mayor's office."

"Just think of the time we could save. I wonder if I should rethink this whole thing. Marrying a man who wants me clothed so much of the time when I'd rather stay just as I am."

"You're a regrettable tease, my love. Now get up and get your clothes on, vixen."

She started to rise but he held her down for one last wicked kiss. She thought of taking her nightgown off on the spot but decided it was too dangerous. If they once started to make love they'd never make it to the marriage ceremony.

He groaned and settled into an armchair, sitting with crossed legs while she dressed.

They *were* a gorgeous pair. Stephen in dark trousers and coat. The white shirt with ruffles at the front accentuated his bronzed skin and his cobalt eyes. Mairey wore her newly purchased dress, a full skirted yellow chiffon floating around her long legs and emphasizing her small waist and pointed breasts. Her high-heeled shoes were held on by a tiny strap across the arch of her very feminine feet. Her dark hair skimmed loose to her shoulders and her aquamarine eyes were so happy Stephen grinned.

He moaned audibly when she stood in front of him and then rose and kissed her nose.

"Goddess of us all but you're beautiful. You're simply gorgeous. I'll never complain about your trousers again. In a dress like that you're a danger to mankind. I think even your boots are a good idea. You'd try the virtue of the most righteous saint of the Celtics. Let's hope the mayor doesn't take long with the ceremony."

She grinned at him. "Maybe it's a good thing we aren't in Wales. I wear dresses most of the time there."

"And I'd delight in taking all of them off." His grin was as sinful as hers.

He nuzzled her neck and then set her aside with a guttural sigh. "I can hardly wait to strip your gorgeous dress from you."

He'd just discovered another fascinating aspect of his Mairey. When she was happy and unworried she was a decided tease.

She grinned and reached for him but he batted her hands away. He kissed her forehead while he held her hands still. She let her forehead drop against his chest for a moment and laughing together, they set out for the mayor's office.

Philip and Riva were waiting for them at the *maire*. They'd already taken out their own wedding license and stood hand in hand as the mayor conducted the brief service for Stephen and Mairey. Taliesin and Bethan were there, of course, Beth still a little pale but deliriously happy to know her Uncle Stevie was now hers for life.

Mairey looked at her husband with surprise when he merely pecked at her lips at the end of the ceremony. This was definitely not the kiss she expected. Stephen simply didn't kiss like that. A little disturbed, she turned to Beth.

"Lovey, you look bright and happy. Are you truly feeling so well?"

"Oh yes, Mama Mairey. I can call you that now, can't I, now you're married and have made a papa for me?"

Mairey refused to feel anything but joy on this most wonderful day. She gulped down the large lump in her throat.

"Of course, darling."

"Uncle Taliesin says I can't go home with you just yet but I can soon."

"Very soon."

It was Stephen's deep voice. He'd had come up as they talked and now lifted the child and swung her around in a large circle.

"Very soon indeed, chickie."

He hugged her, gave her to Taliesin and took Mairey's hand.

His smile spread over his whole face. Even his body seemed to be smiling.

"Come, wife. We have some things to—er—discuss."

To the accompaniment of laughter they ran hand in hand from the confining office.

* * * * *

To her surprise he took her to the boarding house where he'd spent the night. He smiled at her questioning look.

"I want to take you to bed right now. I don't intend to wait 'til tonight, which we'd have to do if we went to the Bronwyn house. Anybody could come home there at any time. I wouldn't be surprised if Philip and Riva headed straight for his room, hoping for the privacy. I want to guarantee ours. I arranged with the landlady to keep the room another night."

He saw the little shadow disappear from her lovely face.

"My dearest one, will you never fully trust my love for you?"

"I do, Stephen, I truly do. You're the most honorable man I've ever known. I just wanted a warmer kiss at the mayor's office."

They'd stopped right inside the front door and Stephen immediately wrapped his arms around her and kissed her with the passion she'd missed at the civil ceremony.

She felt a little shamed she'd doubted him even slightly. It just seemed impossible this wonderful man was hers. Now she felt filled with joy as she realized he thought the same and they both were in awe of their incredible good fortune.

"Your kiss was so, so *neutral* after the ceremony."

A faint rose underlay the faultless skin Stephen adored. He'd never seen another person with quite that alabaster color in dramatic contrast to her black hair and blue-green eyes. He laughed his low laugh. Partly at her innocent concern and mostly as the realization swamped him he'd actually married her.

"You little goose." His tone was affectionate, although just a little breathless.

"Don't you know the effect you have on me? The kiss I wanted to give you would have caused me to have an instant erection. I'm not presentable in company even when I barely touch you."

She buried her flaming face in his good shoulder. He still wore a bandage which she could see through his linen shirt and she carefully avoided pressing him there.

"I never thought of that," she muttered.

"You're my delight," he chuckled. "Now let's go to bed."

"But your shoulder?"

"Is fine. Now what else is wrong?"

"It's daylight."

"Of course it is and I'm thankful. I can see every inch of your beautiful body. Any other fears or objections?"

She raised her head and looked at him, her eyes shining with anticipation.

"Not a one, my wonderful Druid."

He caught his breath and swept her up in his arms despite her mumbling about his shoulder. His powerful large frame and strong legs made short work of the stairs. Turning the handle with one hand and kicking open the door, he strode to the bed and deposited her on it with rare gentleness.

"You're mine," he said in deep husky tones. "You're really mine. Forever and ever, in this life and beyond."

His clever hands stripped her dress from her quickly. When she was down to her underthings, he stopped her hands.

"Just for a minute I want to look at you. Do you have any idea what an alluring body you have? Every curve you've got is exactly in the right place. The way your hips flare from your waist, the arch in your back, your tight little behind. You take away my breath, my love. "

"Then let's play fair, husband. You take some clothes off too. Or better yet, let me undress you."

"I don't know if that's a good idea," he muttered. He stripped off his coat and his shirt as fast as he could. When he started to unbutton his trousers she moved to stay his hands, holding them away and kissing his fingers.

"My job," Mairey said, with a sultry smile. "Definitely my job."

She strove for self-control. Her instinct was to grab him and wrap her legs around him there where he stood, guiding his huge erection into her. She'd never heard if people mated standing up but right now it seemed the quickest way and a very good idea. She put her thought aside, although she didn't try to control the sultry glance she sent to him at just the thought. Then she concentrated on what she knew how to do. She slowly slid his trousers from his hips. He was swollen and ready, as was she.

She ran her hands slowly over his bare chest, stopping to kiss each nipple and moved down to tug on his underpants.

Stephen came undone.

"You're killing me, Mairey. I can't stand any more."

He pushed her down on the bed, tearing off her step-ins with one large hand as he rose over her and plunged into her.

She was warm and wet and he slid into her easily and took her with long, fierce strokes. She thought he'd taught her about loving but this madness was like nothing she'd experienced. Desire and excitement flooded her body, more intense than she'd ever known before. Passion such as she'd never imagined shot through her system, as she met every advance of his with almost frantic caresses of her own. She touched every inch of him she could reach, hot hands roaming over hot flesh. It was a primeval mating, as he pounded into her and she urged him on with her lunging hips. Both were consumed with a desperate need, as they clutched each other and tumbled madly over the sheets.

There was nothing in the world but the feel of their slick bodies, clinging together and demanding more and yet more. She dived at him and pressed her open mouth to his chest, while he caressed the hidden core of her desire with frenzied fingers. She convulsed against him at once, urging him on with the gyrations of her hips. He brought her almost again to the crest of desire, as his clever fingers seemed to attack her everyplace at once.

They climaxed together more quickly than they ever had before and lay panting for long minutes, still joined and wrapped in each other's arms.

He stroked her gleaming hair and looked a little abashed. Leaning over to give her a sweet kiss, he sighed.

"Mairey, I was determined to give you a long slow loving to prove how much you mean to me. You completely turned my plans on their head."

She wriggled against him once as she felt him withdrawing from her body.

"I can't say I'm sorry. I couldn't wait to feel you inside me. I think I'm a wanton, Stephen, I've never been so frenzied before."

Her voice sounded so puzzled he rolled on his back and took her on top of him, laughing up at her.

"I've always heard danger increases your sexual appetite. We'll go slower the next time." He grinned. "And the time after that."

He began to caress her breasts but then stopped.

"I want to talk just a little bit before the next time we again taste our own slice of heaven. I've made some decisions I hope you'll approve."

He flipped her onto her side and lay facing her.

"Did I ever tell you how much I love your hair?" he asked, taking a thick strand and bringing it to his lips.

"And that's the decision you made?" Her eyes showed how she loved teasing him. A thoroughly enchanting facet of her personality.

"Little imp. Just listen."

She assumed such a mock-serious face he gave her a quick kiss.

"No, really listen. I'm well aware at the beginning you thought me an irresponsible man with little purpose in life. I deliberately allowed you to think so."

She started to protest but he put a finger on her lips. "Just listen, Mairey. I need to know how you feel about some things that might be news to you. In the first place, I have plenty of money. I'd never have to work again."

Her dark lashes suddenly shielded her expressive eyes and he knew she was thinking of how she'd misjudged him. Maybe a little anger mixed in he hadn't told her before.

She looked at him with a little reproach. "I don't mind you having money but I do mind your not telling me sooner. Surely you could have told me when you first took me to your bed."

"Yes, of course you're right. I was so intent on making you love me for myself alone, I didn't think of anything else. I'm sorry, love, I'll never keep anything from you again."

He turned and lay on his back, keeping her close to his side and stroking her hair until he felt her completely relax.

"I want to consult you about something else. I don't want to work again in a regular hospital atmosphere. It's too regulated for me. I thought perhaps of setting up a clinic wherever your work carries you. Whatever country we're in. I know most digs last three or four years. The way people seek me out here makes me think that in other parts of the world a doctor's care might be quite welcome. If I do that, I'd put aside their fees, which would be minimum in any case, to create a fund to keep the clinic going after we leave."

Tears sprang to her eyes as she whispered, "What a wonderful idea, Stephen. Just like the man I've come to love so much."

"I've just had another idea." He almost sat up in excitement. "Your home and base is Cardiff, isn't it?"

At her nod he continued.

"I imagine everyplace on earth needs more medical attention. We can start a clinic there and hire someone to train with me to keep it open when we're gone. I'm sure there are long stretches while you plan and organize another dig. I'd forgotten about those stretches of time."

He kissed her sweetly. "Mainly, I want to be wherever you are. That you might travel around a great deal pleases me. It will help me keep in touch with the bard in my nature. And luckily for me I have the skills to help others wherever we go."

She opened her eyes and stared at him. "I never expected anything like this Stephen. You've certainly proven yourself responsible many times over but this— I'm overcome with the amount of thought you've put into our future."

"Someone had to." he grinned at her. "You'd almost decided we had no future. Outside the bedroom, that is."

She sat bolt upright in bed. "Stephen, can you read my mind?" Her eyes were so alarmed he laughed with delight and pushed her flat again.

"I'll answer you as honestly as I can. When you're in danger knowing what you're thinking and feeling is almost automatic. It's something that's just there. Otherwise, although I probably could invade your mind, I'd never do so without your permission. And a lot of the time, my dearest love, it's not necessary. Your expressive face gives you away."

She whacked him with a pillow and then lay on her side and began to stroke him slowly.

His beautiful body, showing an amazing amount of bronze when he was nude, made her catch her breath with the wonder that such a magnificent man was hers. His masculine aroma, tinged with the sexy scent accompanying such a tumultuous loving, filled her nostrils. She always loved the way he smelled. Before, during and after their mating. She sniffed his skin and licked and kissed his neck.

Not really surprised when his erection began to swell, she leaned over and kissed that too.

"Merciful Merlin," he gasped. "The effect you have on me still astonishes me."

"Good," she said. "I love your being such a wonderful bard but I don't want you to ever roam again. Not unless you take me with you."

He flipped her on her back and came over her, supported by his elbows as he locked her gaze with his. His eyes changed from passion to a riveting intensity.

"I know now my travels were always a search to find myself. I only roamed on this last journey because I was lost. Now I've found myself in you. I have no more need to wander."

*The perfect answer from the perfect man. The only man in the world for her.*

Mairey smiled up at him with love and joined him in the rapture of the long slow loving he'd promised.

* * * * *

A considerable time later and after they'd napped a little, Mairey woke to find Stephen leaning over her and suckling her breasts, holding them in his large hands and moving his lips from one to the other.

"Great heavens." She came awake with a start.

His grin was wicked as he paused. "I've been awake for some time admiring my beautiful wife."

She stroked his shining hair. "But you are the beautiful one. Your kindness and goodness illuminate your face. Which is already far too handsome. Sinfully so."

She let her hands play through his hair and then wander lower. She kissed his chest and giggled. "To say nothing of other intriguing parts of your body that nobody but me had better ever see."

He lifted his head and put her hand on his erection.

"You surely don't mean this, do you?" She'd never seen such a wicked, laughing grin.

She took him in her hand even as his fingers roamed in tormenting circles over her breasts.

"I feel quite wanton, husband. Do you mind?"

He drew a deep and pleasured breath and half-rising, leaned over her.

"I've always adored wanton sirens."

He began to play with the long strands of black curls lying on her breasts, as his expression grew thoughtful and just a little mischievous.

"Maybe it's time to start making my newest vision come true."

She jolted up but he pushed her flat with a demanding kiss that melted her bones.

"You've had a vision?" Mairey asked. "A real one?"

"A very real one. A lovely one requiring complete cooperation on your part."

"Stephen, stop teasing me. Was it a good vision?"

"Oh, a fine vision. Very fine."

His voice deepened as all joking disappeared from his face.

"You were surrounded by our children, Mairey. One girl had your gorgeous coloring and one had hair just like mine."

"One?" she squeaked. "How many do you see?"

"The vision didn't last long enough for me to count. At least three. Maybe four?"

She stared into his brilliant blue eyes and realized he meant what he said.

"You're serious, aren't you?"

"I don't think there were more than four."

His face and voice softened even further. "I'm serious, darling. My visions come to me seldom but they're always been true. I hope you won't mind being saddled with an indefinite parcel of children."

"Merciful Merlin," she breathed. That newly discovered teasing smile was back in her eyes. "Then we'd better get to work so we can find out how many there will be. You don't really seem to know."

With a shout of joy, he grabbed her in his arms. She believed in him and his powers completely and she'd just told him so.

He rolled her on top of him, love radiating from every inch of his body as he kissed her deeply, clasping her to him and luxuriating in the feel of her supple body dissolving into his. He knew in his Druid soul this joining would be their most meaningful act of love.

Definitely an endeavor requiring his whole-hearted cooperation. Worthy of any man, let alone a Druid passionately in love with his wife.

He kissed her lips and applied himself enthusiastically to his task.

## Also by Jean Hart Stewart



## About the Author

Jean feels she's very much a Californian although she was born in Ohio. California has been home for a good many years. Life changed drastically for her when she was six and her father died incredibly from an errant golf ball. A dishonest insurance agent forced her sheltered mother to seek work, and she became a teacher. Her hours required Jean to be alone in the house in the afternoon, and since she was forbidden to leave till her mother got home, she became an avid reader. The local library supplied most of the books and she early focused on her two main interests, Jane Austen and King Arthur.

Reading is still one of Jean's favorite activities, although she sometimes has to push it aside to make room for her enduring love of writing. Her journalism degree was used infrequently until recently. Marriage and raising two children pleasantly got in the way. After twenty years of being a real estate broker and with the kids raised, she finally could devote her time to writing, her first love.

Few things in her life have been so satisfying, especially when all her books have a happy ending. Wonderful to make happen. It only gets more interesting when a secondary character demands his very own book. Who would want to deny him? Not Jean!

Jean welcomes comments from readers. You can find her website and email address on her author bio page at www.cerridwenpress.com.

## *Tell Us What You Think*

We appreciate hearing reader opinions about our books. You can email us at Comments@EllorasCave.com.

# Why an electronic book?

We live in the Information Age—an exciting time in the history of human civilization, in which technology rules supreme and continues to progress in leaps and bounds every minute of every day. For a multitude of reasons, more and more avid literary fans are opting to purchase e-books instead of paper books. The question from those not yet initiated into the world of electronic reading is simply: *Why?*

1. ***Price.*** An electronic title at Ellora's Cave Publishing and Cerridwen Press runs anywhere from 40% to 75% less than the cover price of the exact same title in paperback format. Why? Basic mathematics and cost. It is less expensive to publish an e-book (no paper and printing, no warehousing and shipping) than it is to publish a paperback, so the savings are passed along to the consumer.
2. ***Space.*** Running out of room in your house for your books? That is one worry you will never have with electronic books. For a low one-time cost, you can purchase a handheld device specifically designed for e-reading. Many e-readers have large, convenient screens for viewing. Better yet, hundreds of titles can be stored within your new library—on a single microchip. There are a variety of e-readers from different manufacturers. You can also read e-books on your PC or laptop computer. (Please note that

Ellora's Cave does not endorse any specific brands. You can check our websites at www.ellorascave.com or www.cerridwenpress.com for information we make available to new consumers.)

3. ***Mobility***. Because your new e-library consists of only a microchip within a small, easily transportable e-reader, your entire cache of books can be taken with you wherever you go.
4. ***Personal Viewing Preferences.*** Are the words you are currently reading too small? Too large? Too... ANNOYING? Paperback books cannot be modified according to personal preferences, but e-books can.
5. ***Instant Gratification.*** Is it the middle of the night and all the bookstores near you are closed? Are you tired of waiting days, sometimes weeks, for bookstores to ship the novels you bought? Ellora's Cave Publishing sells instantaneous downloads twenty-four hours a day, seven days a week, every day of the year. Our webstore is never closed. Our e-book delivery system is 100% automated, meaning your order is filled as soon as you pay for it.

Those are a few of the top reasons why electronic books are replacing paperbacks for many avid readers.

As always, Ellora's Cave and Cerridwen Press welcome your questions and comments. We invite you to email us at Comments@ellorascave.com or write to us directly at Ellora's Cave Publishing Inc., 1056 Home Avenue, Akron, OH 44310-3502.

Cerridwen, the Celtic Goddess of wisdom, was the muse who brought inspiration to storytellers and those in the creative arts. Cerridwen Press encompasses the best and most innovative stories in all genres of today's fiction. Visit our site and discover the newest titles by talented authors who still get inspired - much like the ancient storytellers did, once upon a time.

Cerridwen Press

www.cerridwenpress.com

# Cerridwen Press

*Cerridwen, the Celtic goddess of wisdom, was the muse who brought inspiration to storytellers and those in the creative arts.*

*Cerridwen Press encompasses the best and most innovative stories in all genres of today's fiction.*

*Visit our website and discover the newest titles by talented authors who still get inspired—much like the ancient storytellers did...*

*once upon a time.*

www.cerridwenpress.com